Praise for the Irish Country series

"Patrick Taylor has become probably the most popular Irish-Canadian writer of all time."   —*The Globe and Mail*

"What Herriot did for Yorkshire, Taylor does for Northern Ireland . . . minus the animals, of course, but with all the good sentiments."   —*Kirkus Reviews*

"The author laces his heartwarming moments with liberal doses of whiskey and colorful Ulster invectives."   —*Chicago Sun-Times*

"Wraps you in the sensations of a vanished time and place."   —*The Vancouver Sun*

"Taylor is a bang-up storyteller who captivates and entertains from the first word."   —*Publishers Weekly*

"Taylor masterfully charts the small victories and defeats of Irish village life."   —*Irish America*

"Both hilarious and heartwarming."   —*The Roanoke Times*

By Patrick Taylor

Only Wounded
Pray for Us Sinners
Now and in the Hour of Our Death

An Irish Country Doctor
An Irish Country Village
An Irish Country Christmas
An Irish Country Girl
An Irish Country Courtship
A Dublin Student Doctor
An Irish Country Wedding
Fingal O'Reilly, Irish Doctor
The Wily O'Reilly
An Irish Doctor in Peace and at War
An Irish Doctor in Love and at Sea

Home Is the Sailor (e-original)

An Irish Doctor in Peace and at War

PATRICK TAYLOR

A Tom Doherty Associates Book
New York

AN IRISH DOCTOR IN PEACE AND AT WAR

Copyright © 2014 by Ballybucklebo Stories Corp.

All rights reserved.

Maps by Elizabeth Danforth and Jennifer Hanover
Map of Alexandria Harbour based on research by Dorothy Tinman.

A Forge Book
Published by Tom Doherty Associates, LLC
175 Fifth Avenue
New York, NY 10010

www.tor-forge.com

Forge® is a registered trademark of Tom Doherty Associates, LLC.

The Library of Congress has cataloged the hardcover edition as follows:

Taylor, Patrick, 1941–
    An Irish doctor in peace and at war : an Irish country novel / Patrick Taylor. — First edition.
        p. cm.—(Irish Country books ; 9)
    ISBN 978-0-7653-3837-2 (trade paperback)
    ISBN 978-1-4668-3888-8 (e-book)
    1. O'Reilly, Fingal Flahertie (Fictitious character)—Fiction.   2. Physicians (General practice)—Fiction.   3. World War, 1939–1945—Northern Ireland—Fiction.   I. Title.
    PR9199.3.T36 I765 2015
    813'.54—dc23

                                                            2015003925

ISBN 978-0-7653-3837-2 (trade paperback)

Forge books may be purchased for educational, business, or promotional use. For information on bulk purchases, please contact the Macmillan Corporate and Premium Sales Department at 1-800-221-7945, extension 5442, or write to specialmarkets@macmillan.com.

First Edition: October 2014
First Trade Paperback Edition: September 2015

Printed in the United States of America

0   9   8   7   6   5   4   3   2   1

To Dorothy

Acknowledgments

The Irish Country series would not have been written and published without the unstinting assistance of a large number of people, most of whom have been with me, guiding and supporting from the very start. They are:

In North America

Simon Hally, Carolyn Bateman, Tom Doherty, Paul Stevens, Irene Gallo, Gregory Manchess, Patty Garcia, Alexis Saarela, and Christina Macdonald, all of whom have contributed enormously to the literary and technical aspects of bringing the work from rough draft to bookshelf.

Natalia Aponte, my agent.

Don Klancha, Joe Meir, and Mike Tadman, who keep me right in contractual matters. Without the help of the University of British Columbia Medical Library staff, much of the technical details of medicine in the thirties and forties would have been inaccurate.

In the Republic of Ireland and the United Kingdom

Rosie and Jessica Buckman, my foreign rights agents.

The Librarians of the Royal College of Physicians of Ireland, the

Royal College of Surgeons in Ireland, and The Rotunda Hospital Dublin and her staff.

For This Work Only

My friends and colleagues who contributed special expertise in the writing of this work are highlighted in my author's note.

To you all, Surgeon Commander Fingal O'Reilly MB., DSC., and I tender our most heartfelt gratitude and thanks.

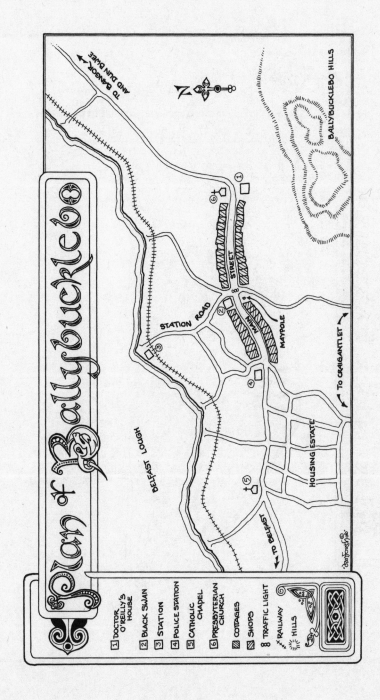

Plan of Ballybucklebo

TO BANGOR AND DUN DIVEE

BALLYBUCKLEBO HILLS

STREET

STATION ROAD

MAIN

MAYPOLE

To CRAIGANTLET

BELFAST LOUGH

HOUSING ESTATE

TO BELFAST

1. DOCTOR O'REILLY'S HOUSE
2. BLACK SWAN
3. STATION
4. POLICE STATION
5. CATHOLIC CHAPEL
6. PRESBYTERIAN CHURCH
   COTTAGES
   SHOPS
8. TRAFFIC LIGHT
   RAILWAY
   HILLS

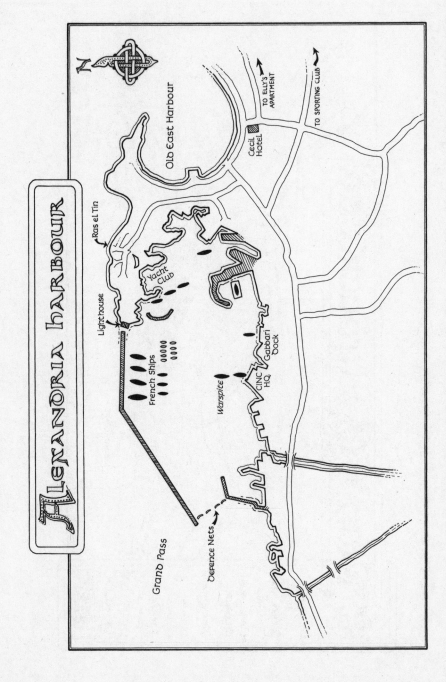

An Irish Doctor in Peace and at War

1

A Rose by Any Other Name

Someone was ringing the front doorbell of Number One, Main Street, and insistently at that. Doctor Fingal Flaherty O'Reilly was eating a solitary lunch of cold roast ham, hard-boiled eggs, and salad while his partner, Doctor Barry Laverty, was out on an emergency home visit. "Coming," O'Reilly roared, put down his knife and fork and, grabbing his sports jacket from the back of a chair, headed for the front hall. His housekeeper, Kinky Kincaid, usually answered the door but today she was preparing for her wedding the following day.

The noon sun brightened the afternoon, but even its late-April radiance could add little lustre to the full vestments of Mister Robinson, the Presbyterian minister, who stood at the doorway wringing his hands. His rusty black robes, O'Reilly thought, made the man look like a dishevelled crow. "Yes, Your Reverence? What's up?"

"Doctor, can you come across to the church at once? Please?"

"Somebody sick?" O'Reilly asked, shrugging into his jacket. "I'll get my bag." He turned, but was forestalled by the minister grabbing an arm.

"Nobody's sick, but the war of the roses is breaking out in my church. There's a row and a ructions, and I don't know what to do. Please come. If anybody in Ballybucklebo can stop it, it's you." He turned, trotted down the short gravelled drive, and was forced by a lorry heading from Bangor to Belfast to wait for O'Reilly to catch up. As soon as there was a gap in the traffic, the minister hurried across the road to the church with O'Reilly trailing behind.

"What row?" O'Reilly asked, catching his breath as they passed under the lych-gate.

"Maggie Houston and Flo Bishop."

"Who? Maggie and Flo?" O'Reilly frowned as they passed into the shadow of the old yews in the graveyard. "But they're old friends, for G—" Better not say "God's sake." His frown deepened. "I think," he said, stopping in his tracks, "you'd better explain before we go in."

Mister Robinson sighed. "The ladies of the Women's Guild take it in turns on a weekly rota to look after decorating the church for services and ceremonies. Maggie Houston's on the duty this week. Because we all know Kinky's fondness for wildflowers, Maggie's got them by the great gross—"

"For the wedding tomorrow."

"Correct, but Flo Bishop, being matron of honour, even though it's not her turn to do the flowers, has assumed responsibility for decorating the church with hothouse roses because she says Kinky deserves the very best. She's formed a subcommittee with Aggie Arbuthnot and Cissie Sloan. Maggie whipped up support from Jeannie Jingles and Alice Moloney and . . ."

"And you have two regiments going at it hammer and tongs? The wildflower fusiliers and the red-rose rifles, right?"

"Right. Mrs. Bishop and her gang have commandeered the communion table and choir area and Maggie and their friends have placed themselves strategically—"

"Say no more." O'Reilly, while being sympathetic to the minister's dilemma, was having great difficulty controlling an enormous grin. "Lead on, Macduff," he said. "This is something I've got to see."

"Thank you, Doctor. They won't listen to me. But you'll make them see sense."

O'Reilly followed the minister until they reached the nave, where the perfume of flowers was overpowering even the dust of two hundred years that usually haunted the old building.

On Maggie's side, heaps of freshly plucked wildflowers were piled on the front pew. Roses on the opposite side of the aisle formed Flo Bishop's ammunition dump.

The two groups, led by their respective champions, stood facing each other at the top of the nave.

"You'll do no such thing, Maggie MacCorkle—"

"It's Mrs. Houston to you, Mrs. Bishop."

Both women stood facing each other, arms akimbo, eyes afire, leaning forward, chins jutting. Flo's teeth were clenched and there she had Maggie Houston née MacCorkle at a disadvantage. The older woman wasn't wearing her false ones, and clenched gums were less than threatening.

Lord, O'Reilly thought, harking back to his boxing days, *And in the blue corner at one hundred and eighty pounds* . . . "Ladies," he said. "Ladies, whatever seems to be the trouble?"

He could make no sense of all the women's voices speaking at once, but made a shrewd guess about what was being said.

"All right, all right," he said, "now settle down. *Settle down.*" He waited as Flo smoothed her dress as a just-pecked mallard duck would waggle her tail feathers.

Maggie adjusted her hat. It had a single wilted bluebell in its brim.

"Can we not sort this out like the civilised people we are?" he said.

Flo glowered at Maggie. Maggie folded her arms across her chest. Their supporters closed ranks behind their principals.

"All right," said O'Reilly, "let me see if I can get this straight. Maggie. *Maggie?*"

"Yes, Doctor O'Reilly."

"You and your friends love Kinky and you want her day to be perfect, don't you?"

"We do, so we do, *but*," Maggie turned her frowning face sideways to Flo Bishop, "thon Flo—"

O'Reilly cut her off. "Flo, you and Aggie and Cissie feel the same way but think you know a better way to make Kinky's wedding day shine?"

Flo glowered and said, "Me and the ladies do love Kinky and she told me that on the night Archie proposed he give her red roses and *that's* why—"

O'Reilly cut her off too. He wanted no more petrol poured on the flames. "Whoa," he said, "whoa, calm down and pay attention, the lot of you." It wouldn't hurt to throw his weight around just a little bit at the beginning. Take control. "Now listen. I think I know Kinky Kincaid better than anyone in the village and townland. Wouldn't you all agree?"

Subdued murmuring of assent.

"Good. And just so we're all clear, can we agree again that we love Kinky?"

Flo scowled at Maggie, who scowled right back.

"Ladies?" O'Reilly put an edge of steel in his voice. "Are we all agreed?"

"I am," Cissie Sloan said. "I mind the day she first come til the village, so I do. No harm til you, Doctor dear, but it was way before your time, sir. It was a Wednesday—no, I tell a lie it was a Friday, and she—"

First defection on Flo's side, O'Reilly thought, but let's not have Cissie ramble on too much.

"Houl your wheest, Cissie Sloan," Jeannie Jingles said, but with a smile. "We all remember her coming and it doesn't matter a jot or tittle exactly when. What Doctor O'Reilly says is true. There's not a woman in the whole townland more widely respected."

A breakaway from solidarity with Maggie. "And what," said O'Reilly, "if the respected Kinky was a fly on the wall here today. What do you reckon she'd be thinking about all these silly selfish schoolgirl shenanigans?"

He waited, quite prepared to re-ask the question, but Cissie had started the rent in the fabric of Flo's group.

"I think," said Aggie Arbuthnot, tearing it further, "she'd be sad to see her friends falling out over nothing, and," her voice cracked, "I'd not want for Kinky to be unhappy about nothing on her wedding day." She sighed. "It would be a right shame if she was, so it would."

"You're dead on, Aggie." Jeannie Jingles spoke for the opposition. "You just said a mouthful." She smiled.

"I'll give you my twopenny's worth," said Alice Moloney. "I don't agree, and please let's not anybody get upset about that, but Kinky's a very sensible woman. I don't think she'd be sad at all. I think she'd be laughing like a drain at the lot of us going at it like a bull in a china shop—and all because we want the very best for her. We're all daft." She turned to O'Reilly. "We're like a bunch of kiddies. Thank you, Doctor, for helping us to see that."

O'Reilly inclined his head.

"Buck eejits," said Maggie very quietly, "the whole lot of us, and I'm sorry to have been so thran, so I am."

A lovely Ulster word for "bloody-minded," O'Reilly thought.

Mister Robinson, who for the duration of the recent discussion had wisely, O'Reilly thought, until now distanced himself from taking part, said, "'Blessèd are the peacemakers,' Matthew five and nine."

"May I make a suggestion?" O'Reilly said.

Maggie and Flo's "Please do, sir" was as one.

"Kinky's a country girl from County Cork. She's loved wildflowers all her life. I'm sure she'd be delighted to have them at her wedding."

From the tail of his eye he saw Maggie's grin start, so quickly added, "But Flo has a point too. I remember well the night Archie asked me for Kinky's hand and the beautiful red roses he brought with the ring that evening. I think they'd add a really romantic touch." Flo's smile kept Maggie's company. He waited.

"So why," said Maggie, "don't we do both? If that's all right with you, Flo?"

"Aye," said Flo, "it is, Maggie, dear. We should have thought of that before, so we should." She turned to Mister Robinson. "I'm sorry about all the fuss over nothing, sir."

"It's perfectly all right, now you've kissed and made up," he said.

"And," said Maggie, "once we're done, I think the six of us and," she hesitated then said, "Mister Robinson and Doctor O'Reilly if they'd like, should all go home to my house for a wee cup of tea in our hands and," her toothless grin was enormous, "none of youse'll go hungry. I just baked two plum cakes today, so I did."

"That would be lovely," Flo said, "wouldn't it, ladies?"

The other four women nodded in agreement.

O'Reilly caught the minister's eye. He'd seen the same glazed look on the face of a rabbit cornered by a fox. Clearly Mister Robinson had experienced Maggie's stewed tea and cement-like fruitcake before and was searching desperately for an excuse so he could decline. O'Reilly himself had no such hesitation. "I'd love to come, Maggie. I haven't seen your cat, General Sir Bernard Law Montgomery, nor Sonny's dogs for ages, but you'll understand a doctor's day is not his own?" She and the others would at least think they did, and any doctor could claim being needed by the calls of his profession. "But nothing, not a team of wild horses, will keep me from the wedding tomorrow."

2

If You Have Tears, Prepare to Shed Them Now

Fingal O'Reilly patted the pocket of his sports jacket for the dozenth time that day. The little velvet-covered, dome-lidded box was still there. He looked over at the petite, fair-haired woman beside him. He and Deirdre Mawhinney had been keeping company for two years, since the summer of 1937 when he'd been working as a trainee obstetrician in Dublin's Rotunda Maternity Hospital and she'd been a student midwife.

He reached out his hand, she clasped it, and together they strolled toward the seafront along the winding mossy path of Strickland's Glen, the secluded little valley that lay off the road between the seaside towns of Bangor and Ballybucklebo. He was planning to produce the box at just the right moment today, but when was that right moment going to be?

He'd never thought he'd get over his first love, Kitty O'Hallorhan, but as the months had passed, Deirdre, the lively twenty-two-year-old from Clough Mills, County Antrim, had surprised him. And so had the depth of his feelings for her.

She continued to surprise him and it was one of the things he loved about her. He'd collected her this morning from the nurses' home of the Ulster Hospital in Belfast's Mount Pottinger Road. His second-hand 1928 Hillman 14 had rattled and banged, but it had got them safely to the Crawfordsburn Inn for a lunch of roast beef and Yorkshire pudding followed by sherry trifle. The chilled bottle of white Burgundy that Fingal hoped might give him the extra bit of Dutch courage had put them in a relaxed mood after a hectic week. He knew he was going to need it once he'd got her to a secluded, romantic spot.

He skipped for a couple of steps and heard her contralto chuckle. He inhaled the almond perfume of whins mixed with the piney smells of the Douglas firs that towered overhead. It was Saturday, the first of July, and gloriously warm, so hot he would have taken off his sports jacket if he'd been inclined to free his hand from Deirdre's firm grasp. But he wasn't.

"It was a lovely lunch, Fingal, thank you," she said, "and it's a beautiful afternoon. Look at the way the sunbeams are coming through the trees."

Deirdre's ability to take a childlike pleasure in the simplest things, sometimes even clapping her hands with unrestrained joy at a new song, or a scene she'd never seen before, delighted O'Reilly.

"Aren't they—aren't they—like fairies' lights?" she said, gazing up.

If there were such things as fairies, the Little People, he could not imagine a more perfect home than Strickland's Glen. By God, but he was happy to be here. Happy to be walking this ivy-tangled lane with this woman. Happy to be working in Ballybucklebo. And overjoyed that now Deirdre was a qualified midwife she'd left the Rotunda and taken a post in Belfast in April this year to be near him. Political changes in Southern Ireland had made his prospects in Dublin bleak, and he'd had to come north last year. He loved her very much and, hard as it was for him to believe, she loved him.

He glanced up to follow her gaze. Rays of bright light danced as a light breeze sent the branches swaying and trembling. He was close to trembling himself as he looked round. Nobody. They had just come round a sharp corner and the path turned left round laurels about twenty yards ahead. This was the perfect place, a private dell sheltered by the laurels. Now, he told himself, get on with it, you eejit. She won't say no. Dear God, don't let her say no. He stopped, forcing her to do so too. He looked down into a pair of smiling blue eyes separated by a tip-tilted snub nose. Her eyes were wide and inquiring under the fringe of her fashionable hairdo, its fair back and sides in reverse rolls tucked into diamond-mesh netting studded with tiny jet beads.

"Deirdre," he said, "I want to ask you—"

"Come back here." A man wearing dungarees and a duncher was racing after a young Irish terrier. Now, where the hell had they come from? Fingal's grip on the box slackened and it fell into the bottom of the pocket. The tan puppy had the square muzzle, beetling eyebrows, and goatee beard of its breed and was in sore want of training. It bounded over to Fingal and put two outsized paws up on his clean flannels.

"Get down, you buck eejit," the stranger said, tugging at the beast's collar. He touched the peak of his duncher. "Sorry about that, sir. He's only young, so he is. He just run off, like."

Fingal forced a smile. "Don't worry about it." Bloody dog. The moment was ruined. He started walking, all the while groping for the little box in his pocket.

Deirdre, soft-hearted as ever, bent and patted the puppy's head, and it waggled its stiff tail so hard its backside swung from side to side. She looked up at the owner. "What's his name?"

O'Reilly, who had stopped, immediately thought, Who gives a damn, but seeing Deirdre's gentle enthusiasm he could only smile.

"O'Reilly," the man said solemnly.

The dog wagged even more ferociously at hearing his name.

O'*what*? Fingal thought. It can't be.

Deirdre's laughter tinkled through the glen and she clapped her hands. Then, controlling her features, she said, "That's a lovely name."

"Thank you, miss." The man touched his cap's peak. "Come on, O'Reilly." Together they left, the terrier frisking and frolicking.

Deirdre trotted over to O'Reilly, chuckled, took his hand, and said, "Come on, O'Reilly," and immediately burst into peals of laughter.

And although O'Reilly could not control his own mirth, inside he hated to have lost the moment.

Deirdre seemed to have got her giggles under control. "What was it you wanted to ask me, Fingal?" she said, cocking her head, still smiling.

He couldn't ask now. Not now, with the man and his pup still in view and two blasted schoolboys, Bangor Grammar lads judging by their yellow-and-royal-blue-ringed school caps, charging up the path. One chased the other, pointing his right hand with the thumb cocked up and the first two fingers extended and yelling, "Dar, dar. Got ye. You're dead, Al Capone, so you are."

"I saw it in the paper," said Fingal to cover his confusion. "About Al Capone. D-did you know that he's going to be released from Alcatraz in a few months?"

"You, missed me, G-man," shouted the other boy. "You can't shoot for toffee." He stopped, held both arms as if firing a Tommy gun, made a rat-tat-tatting noise, then ran on.

"No," she said, rolling her eyes at the boy and laughing. "I didn't. And what's that got to do with the price of corn anyway?"

"Nothing," he said, and now that the hound of the Baskervilles and public enemy number one were round the far corner and no one else was in sight he quickly kissed her and said, "I love you, Deirdre. I really do."

"And I love you too, Fingal Flahertie O'Reilly, you great, shy, tongue-tied bear. I know what you were going to say." She pursed her lips, cocked her head to one side again and, raising one eyebrow, stretched up and kissed him hard. Then she hitched up her grey mid-calf-length skirt and, looking down at her shoes, said, "I've got my walking shoes on today, Fingal, so if you can't beat me to the shore, I'll tell you what it was." She took off like a fawn.

Fingal chased her. He might not be able to catch her—after all, she'd played hockey for Ulster, and he knew she was fleet of foot.

Two girls . . . both beautiful, one a gazelle.

You got that right, Willy Butler Yeats, Fingal thought, as his brown boots pounded on the springy moss underfoot. He grinned. At fourteen stone he was more like—he struggled for an analogy— more like a Canadian moose, built for endurance, not for speed. Beside him, the stream that since the last ice age had receded and gradually eroded the valley gurgled and chuckled. They ran out from under the trees, Deirdre ahead of him, and crossed the short stretch of coarse marram grass hillocks that lay between the glen and the shingly shore. Deirdre stood grinning, her skirt already returned to its proper length. She was patting her hair back into place and her breathing was slow and regular, but there was an attractive flush on her cheeks.

Behind her, yachts made valiant endeavours to race across the waters of Belfast Lough on what was probably the only day of the year when they were so smooth they could reflect in mirror image the hulls and flapping snowy sails. On the far shore, even the usually brooding Carrickfergus Castle seemed to be a lighter shade of grey and much less menacing, and above the blue of the Antrim Hills melded gently as their colours softened into the cerulean of the sky.

"All right," he said. "You win." For a moment the place was deserted, so he picked her up and kissed her before setting her back on her feet.

"I love you, Fingal," she said, "and I know you were going to—"

He laid a finger across her warm lips, fished out the little box, and flipped open the lid to reveal a simple gold band with a small solitaire diamond. "Deirdre, I love you. I always will." He still couldn't quite come to the point and instead said, "You know old Doctor Flanagan's offered me a partnership?"

"I do, Fingal," she said.

"And you know he's going to give me a raise next January?"

"I do, Fingal," she repeated, quietly.

"Then, will you marry me?" And bugger the stupid man and his Irish terrier emerging from the glen.

"I will, Fingal," she said, levelly. No screams of delight. No simpering. No histrionics. Deirdre Mawhinney wasn't that kind of girl when it came to serious matters. "Yes, I will, Fingal. Gladly." She held out her hand. "Please put it on for me."

He did, feeling the warmth of her hand and, glory be, it fit.

He heard her deep indrawing of breath over the susurration of wavelets on the shingle and the piping cries of a small flock of oyster-catchers flying along the tide line, skimming the washed-up brown sea wrack that in its dying gave the sea air its salty tang.

"It's beautiful," she whispered. "Thank you, darling." She kissed the little stone and looked into his eyes. He saw hers sparkle and fill until a single tear, bright as the gem on her finger, trickled down her cheek. "I'm so happy," she said.

And Fingal Flahertie O'Reilly, champion boxer, international rugby football player, tough as old boots, looked at this petite soft woman—and felt his own tears start and his heart swell.

3

In Holy Wedlock

No teams of wild horses had appeared and O'Reilly, Kitty, and Barry Laverty sat in the second pew of the bride's side of the peacefully flower-bedecked little church. Today, Tuesday, the 26th of April, was the occasion of the nuptials of O'Reilly's housekeeper of twenty years, the long-widowed Mrs. Maureen "Kinky" Kincaid née O'Hanlon, to the widower milkman Mister Archie Auchinleck.

"I now pronounce you man and wife," said Mister Robinson, with that lightness of voice common to all clergymen who are coming to the end of a wedding ceremony that has gone off without any calamities. No one had, for example, pulled a stunt like one a month ago. When a local lad had repeated, "With my worldly goods I thee endow," someone yelled, "There goes his bicycle and that's all she's getting, for your man hasn't a pot to piss in." The story had gone round the village in record time.

But today's ceremony had contained no such outburst. "What God hath joined together let no man put asunder. You may kiss the bride." Kinky, her silver chignon shining in the sunlight filtering through a window high in the nave, beamed at Archie Auchinleck. He, resplendent in a rented morning suit, his hair shiny with Brilliantine and precisely parted in the centre, bent, lifted the veil from his new bride's face, and planted a resounding smacker.

Sergeant Rory Auchinleck, who was best man, had love in his eyes as he watched his father and Kinky embrace. Archie himself had been a colour sergeant in the same regiment and was so proud of his son's recent promotion. And Flo Bishop, the matron of honour, wearing a hat large enough to shelter half the wedding party should it come on to rain as they left the church, was grinning broadly and making little subdued clapping motions with her gloved hands. She jigged from foot to foot as if the tiles of the floor were red-hot.

Although no one would dare interrupt a Presbyterian service with anything as irreverent as cheers or real applause, a subtle murmuring of approval filled the air. It might be a cliché, thought O'Reilly, but the bride did look radiant. The pale green silk of her outfit glowed, her agate eyes sparkled, and her cheek-dimpling smile was vast. O'Reilly today, at Kinky and Archie's request, had given the bride away and he had had, he thought, almost as much pleasure from doing so as it clearly had given Archie Auchinleck to take Kinky as his lawful wedded wife. O'Reilly stole a glance at Kitty, his own bride of ten months, and was rewarded with a saucy wink. Their marriage had been the keynote event of the year 1965 in Ballybucklebo.

Mister Robinson was in the middle of preaching what he had promised O'Reilly would be a very short homily. ". . . And now these three remain: faith, hope, and love. And the greatest of these is love."

The greatest of these is love. The words echoed through the old stone church and O'Reilly took Kitty's hand and looked at her again while she looked back. In her eyes was the love that had begun more than thirty years ago. Bless you, girl. When you came back into my life in 1964 you helped me move on. Until then it had become a complacent round of work and village life and he could still not believe that he, a confirmed widower of twenty years, could once again have found happiness with a woman. He knew that Archie and Kinky had contentment too. He grinned. And now that their ceremony was nearly done, O'Reilly could, like the "ranks of Tuscany" in Macaulay's epic poem *Horatius*, "scarce forbear to cheer." Well done, Kinky Kincaid. More power to your wheel. He knew that the entire congregation shared his sentiments, so important was she in the life of the village.

He glanced around. The church was ablaze with the harmoniously arranged flowers which the competing groups—after yesterday's nudge from O'Reilly—had happily arranged. White wood anemones, bluebells in profusion from the bluebell wood near Sonny and Maggie Houston's home, yellow celandine, pale blue forget-me-nots and violets, and yellow coltsfoot—all the April-blooming wildflowers were Maggie Houston and her group's contributions. Flo Bishop and her ladies were responsible for the red roses that O'Reilly discovered had been bought from a florist's in Belfast. There was no such facility in Ballybucklebo.

A half turn to the left let him survey Kinky's family members sitting in front. Her two married sisters, Sinead and Fidelma, and their husbands Malachy and Eamon and their tribes, as well as her bachelor brother Tiernan, had all come up from County Cork, a drive of more than three hundred miles. Given the state of the Irish roads, this was no small undertaking. They all had the rosy cheeks of Irish farming families. He overheard Sinead, who Kinky had, in a moment of weakness this past week, admitted could be a touch bossy, whispering to Fidelma. "Your Eamon will do no such thing. It's Malachy's turn to—"

O'Reilly thought it charitable to look away and he missed Sinead's pronouncement. To the right, Fingal saw Archie's eighty-seven-year-old mother, who'd come from Greenisland on the other side of Belfast Lough. There was an elder brother, Neill from Liverpool, whom no one in Ballybucklebo had even been aware existed. He was a shorter, older version of Archie and ran a public house, an occupation not necessarily smiled upon by the more devout Ulster Presbyterians.

In the body of the kirk, the villagers were out in force. Donal and Julie Donnelly and their ten-month-old daughter Victoria Margaret, known as Tori, sat behind O'Reilly. She let go with a roar of "Da-da, mu-mu, ga-ga-ga, ba-ba-ba," followed by a piercing shriek that echoed from the barrelled vaults above. Julie cuddled her daughter, who subsided into a series of giggles followed by a happy but emphatic, "Goo-goo." Mister Robinson gave the Donnelly family his "suffer the little children" look and gamely carried on.

Aggie Arbuthnot was sitting beside Helen Hewitt, who would be taking the second part of her first-year medical school exams in June. And behind them, Sonny Houston sat straight and tall, back as rigid as the monolithic Stone of Destiny in County Meath. Beside him Maggie Houston smiled from under a straw boater with primroses in the hatband. Somehow she'd made the toes of her black Wellington boots shiny for the big day.

The Browns were here, Lenny and Connie and their son Colin. O'Reilly had heard that Colin had threatened to mitch school if he was not permitted to attend the wedding, and the Browns, easygoing parents that they were, knew well enough that when Colin's mind was made up even mules looked tractable. The boy kept footering in the pocket of his school blazer. O'Reilly frowned and, looking more closely, saw a pointed nose, whiffling whiskers, and darting black eyes before the head disappeared back under the flap. The child was mad about animals and was always acquiring new pets.

"Kitty," he whispered, "I think Colin Brown's brought a mouse in his pocket."

"I hope he keeps the crayture there," she whispered back, chuckled, then said, "but you never can tell with Colin. I'll keep my fingers crossed."

O'Reilly accepted a friendly nod and smile from Lord John Mac-Neill, Twenty-seventh Marquis of Ballybucklebo, and smiled back. His lordship and his sister Myrna sat in the third row. It was a singular mark of his regard for Kinky that a peer of the realm would accept an invitation from a housekeeper, but then as O'Reilly well knew, John MacNeill was a perfect gentleman who could "walk with Kings—nor lose the common touch." Rudyard Kipling would have approved.

Councillor Bertie Bishop sat near the front as befitted his station both as councillor and as husband of the matron of honour.

"If you will follow me?" Mister Robinson was heading toward the vestry for the registry signing, pursued by the bride and groom, best man, and the matron of honour.

Cissie Sloan fired up the ancient harmonium. The sounds of Debussy's "Clair de Lune" filled the little church, but in a version that owed more to the great Canadian jazz pianist Oscar Peterson than to Vladimir Horowitz. O'Reilly found his foot tapping.

"Cissie's getting into her stride, rightly," O'Reilly's immediate neighbour announced, sotto voce.

O'Reilly turned to the speaker, Doctor Barry Laverty, glad of the young man's company after a six-month absence. "I think Mister Robinson's got a lot less restrictive about wedding music since he let Kitty walk down the aisle to the theme from *The Big Country*."

"Trust you, Fingal," Barry said. "You'd liven up a requiem mass if you thought you could get away with it."

"I've never been enthusiastic about gloom and despondency. I like things to be cheerful." O'Reilly chuckled. "Pity your Sue couldn't come to the service." He thought of the copper-haired young teacher who had, with remarkable ease, filled the void in Barry's life left by a certain Patricia Spence.

Kitty leant over. "It's a school day, silly."

"I see that didn't stop Colin Brown. Then again, he's not on the payroll," Barry said with a smile. "But Sue will be at the Crawfords-burn Inn for the reception."

"Grand," said O'Reilly. "And seeing nuptials are in the air, if you don't mind me asking, you said before Christmas last year you were saving your pennies and hoped to—"

"Pop the question?" Barry sighed. "I—I've been busy. I know that sounds feeble, but it's true."

"It does. Just don't leave it too long, son," O'Reilly said, and glanced at Kitty.

"Fingal's right, Barry," she said, a little furrow appearing between her finely shaped eyebrows. "Don't leave it too long."

"I won't," Barry said.

The Debussy stopped and the bridal party reappeared. The harmonium wheezed in anticipation as Cissie prepared to play the recessional, but then the instrument emitted a series of banshee-like howls and discords. Cissie was standing on her seat yelling, "A mouse. I saw a mouse."

O'Reilly looked to where Colin Brown had been sitting. The lad had vanished.

"It's all right, Julie." Donal's voice rang out as his wife, clutching Tori, leapt up onto the pew.

"Mice? Where? Where?" A woman's voice. "That's desperate. I'm scared skinny of mice, so I am."

"If he's a church mouse he'll be poor." Was that Gerry Shanks's voice?

A groan. "Away off and feel your head. That one has whiskers, Gerry."

"So has that bloody—sorry, Your Reverence—mouse. There he goes."

O'Reilly had difficulty keeping a straight face as the rodent's progress was marked by people squealing and leaping up on pews. Judging by the direction of those standing, the animal was heading straight for the wedding party.

With the fluid grace of a ballerina reaching for her toes *en pointe*, Kinky bent and stretched out her arm. When she stood up she cradled a white mouse in her right hand. "The poor wee mite's all atremble, so." And he wondered, was it chance that had led it her way or had the little animal somehow known that no one in trouble would ever be turned away by Kinky Kincaid—no, Auchinleck now.

Kinky said, "Don't be afeared, *a cuishle.* Wheest now."

"Translation, please, Fingal," said Barry.

"*A cuishle*? It means 'pulse of my heart.' "

Barry laughed. "That's Kinky for you. A soft touch for all of God's creatures."

Colin Brown, who must have been crawling along under the pews, stood up in front of Kinky.

She cocked her head and shook it. "And I don't suppose you can cast any light on this matter, Master Brown?"

People were stepping back down to the floor; dresses and skirts were being rearranged and smoothed down. There was muttering, but a fair bit of laughter too. O'Reilly was pleased that some folks could see the funny side. He and Barry and Kitty were chuckling.

Colin sniffed. "His name's Snowball, Mrs. Kincaid. I'm awful sorry, so I am."

She tousled the boy's hair. "And my name's Mrs. Auchinleck now, Colin, bye." She looked fondly at Archie. "Isn't it, *muirnín*?"

"Darling," O'Reilly said, translating for Barry, and wasn't the Irish language grand with musical-sounding endearments?

"I'm sorry. Honest to God." Colin stretched out his hand. "Please can I have Snowball?"

"Here." She gently passed the little animal back to its owner.

A woman's voice O'Reilly could not identify, soft at first and then with more intensity as the church became quiet, said, "Well, I think it's a disgrace, so it is. That wee lad should have til go til bed without his supper."

At least it was a less violent punishment than getting his arse tanned, O'Reilly thought.

A man replied, "It's all that there television, so it is. Them Yankee children calling their mammies and their daddies by their Christian names. No respect. You mark my words. The young generation? See them? Crowd of skivers and wasters. Now in *my* day—"

Kinky's voice rose over that of the complainer. "Saving your presence, Mister Robinson, can we all try to understand that to err is human, so, and although I am far from divine—"

"But you look it today, Kinky," the marquis said.

She blushed scarlet and dropped a small curtsey. "Thank you, my lord, but what I want to say is, please don't be too hard on wee Colin. He's only a little boy and it was only a very shmall little mouse, so."

"You are a fine example of Christian charity," Mister Robinson remarked, "and I for one concur."

The noises of assent gladdened O'Reilly.

"Very well then. Miss Sloan, please proceed," Mister Robinson said, and Cissie Sloan took her seat again, warmed up the harmonium, and set off on a very syncopated rendition of Mendelssohn's "Wedding March" from *A Midsummer Night's Dream*.

The recessional re-formed and O'Reilly fell in with Kitty on his arm behind the bridal party. "I reckon," he said, "Archie and Kinky'll remember today . . ."

"Like I remember ours, pet." Kitty squeezed O'Reilly's arm. "But they'll also have the mousecapade to chuckle over."

"You mean," O'Reilly misquoted, "when they are old and grey . . . and nodding by the fire?"

"William Butler Yeats," Barry said. And as he spoke they followed the bridal party into the good air where the salty tang of the nearby lough mixed in a subtle blend with the piney scent of the ancient yews in the churchyard. From the branches came the low-pitched melodious warble of a blackbird.

The April sun beamed down. A crowd of villagers was waiting. They all couldn't possibly have been invited to the church and reception, the budget would only stretch so far, but the women were bright in spring dresses, the men smart in their Sunday suits. Out here there were no constraints and they cheered and whistled.

Gerry Shanks was bending to his work, tying a string of tin cans to the back bumper of the rented but very posh Bentley Continental. A crudely hand-lettered sign, JUST MARRIED, had been wired in place. The capped and gauntleted driver finished his cigarette and held the back door open. As was customary, the short walk to the waiting cars was flanked by men from the Ballybucklebo Highlanders, colourful in full dress uniform. At a signal from Dapper Frew, the estate agent, the great Highland bagpipes roared out "The Minstrel Boy"—in two-part harmony no less.

The happy couple stopped and Kinky hurled her bouquet to be caught by Jeannie Kennedy. There were gales of laughter and some joker yelled, "Look out, Colin Brown. Jeannie's going to be looking for a husband." The laughter redoubled. Jeannie was fourteen and apparently as enterprising as Colin when it came to missing school for something as important as the wedding of Kinky Kincaid to Archie Auchinleck.

Archie helped Kinky into the Bentley and a second car, a humbler Morris Oxford, awaited Rory Auchinleck and Flo Bishop and Bertie.

O'Reilly waited until the bridal cars had left for the drive to the Crawfordsburn Inn then, followed by Barry, piloted Kitty across the road to where his long-nosed Rover waited.

"I think," Kitty said, "you are a very lucky man, Fingal. Living in Ballybucklebo for years."

"I am," said O'Reilly, "and I'm all the luckier for having you to live here with me—"

The rest of his words were drowned by a strangled yodelling coming from his back garden.

O'Reilly stopped at the garden gate, where Arthur Guinness stood with his front paws on the top, tongue lolling from his great square Labrador's head.

"Not today, lummox," O'Reilly said, patting the dog. "Back to bed."

Arthur's sigh would have softened Pharaoh's hard heart, but the big dog obeyed.

"Right," said O'Reilly. "Everybody into the car. Party time today." He climbed into the driver's seat and turned on the engine. Party time indeed today. But it would be back to porridge tomorrow with Fingal and Barry running the practice. Next week things would get more interesting when young Doctor Jenny Bradley, her training under Doctor Graham Harley of the Royal Maternity Hospital complete, would be starting her first well-woman clinic.

"Fingal," Kitty said as they moved onto the main road, "drive carefully, please, and watch out for cyclists."

4

Only the First Step That Is Difficult

O'Reilly glanced up, his attention caught by the sun's rays being re-flected from the cut-glass chandelier over the bog oak dining room table. The table had stood in the dining room at Number One Main Street, Ballybucklebo, long before he'd come here as an assistant twenty-eight years ago, just a year before the war. "Those poor divils have been in the wars," he said, nodding at the remnants of lunch.

The heads and bones of three brown trout, one each on his plate and those of Barry Laverty and Jenny Bradley, were mute testimony to the meal's success. Barry had caught the fish two days ago from the beat on the Bucklebo River where the marquis owned the fishing rights. There was a distinctly piscine aroma in the room, which prob-ably was why twice during the meal Jenny had had to ask Lady Mac-beth to get her little, white, feline self off Jenny's lap—the second time with a certain amount of force.

"I must ask Kinky for the recipe for the sauce," Jenny said. "Any-one can grill fish, but that sauce—"

"Anyone?" O'Reilly said. "With Kitty at work and Kinky away on honeymoon, I'll have you know that anyone was me." O'Reilly smiled broadly at Jenny and, still seated, made a deep bow and extended his left arm.

"Ta-da. Drum roll please, maestro," Barry said.

"Less of your lip, Laverty," O'Reilly said, chuckling, delighted by how the youngster's self-confidence was growing. "But you're right, Jenny, the sauce is a different matter. I know Kinky uses horseradish, but what else is in it is a mystery. Good thing she keeps a jar in the fridge. You'll have to wait for her and Archie to come home on Saturday from Newcastle, where," O'Reilly sang,

. . . the Mountains of Mourne sweep down to the sea.

"I was so sorry to miss the wedding, but it was a very important last couple of days on the course," said Jenny. "Nice to think of Kinky only a couple of hours away in Newcastle. The town's got the loveliest beach."

O'Reilly looked over at Jenny's shining young face, her obvious pleasure in thinking of Kinky off on her honeymoon. God, but it was good to be here in County Down in early spring with Jenny fresh from her three months of training at the Royal Victoria Hospital under the aegis of Doctor Harley, raring to start her well-woman clinic, and Barry back from trying specialising, choosing general practice instead, and fitting nicely into his new role as partner.

Barry added, "Did you know that Percy French, who wrote that song, was quite the watercolourist too? I've seen some of his paintings in the Slieve Donard Hotel in Newcastle. I don't suppose Kinky and Mister Auchinleck are staying there, are they? I mean, it's awfully grand."

O'Reilly was silent and Barry looked over at him. "Is it a secret, then?" said Barry, laughing. "Come on, Fingal."

O'Reilly cleared his throat. "Kitty and I gave them a wee wedding present—their last four nights at the Slieve Donard Hotel, but let's just not let the whole village and townland know about it, all right? And let's change the subject, shall we?" O'Reilly picked up his pipe and put it down again. He'd not wanted any fuss over the gift. It was the least he could do for someone who had been such a part of his life for almost two decades.

"Did you really grill the trout, Fingal?" Barry said. "As Donal Donnelly might say, 'Dead beezer.' They were excellent." Barry pursed his lips and cocked his head to one side. "But, fair play, you did get much better last year in the kitchen when Kinky was sick and we had to do a bit of cooking."

"Well done, Fingal," Jenny said. "I think all men should be able to cook. I'm teaching my boyfriend, Terry."

"Different generation," O'Reilly said. "In my day, men didn't, except for professional chefs and cooks in the armed services." He wiped his mouth on his napkin and rose. "Now," he said, "I know you've home visits to make, Barry. Don't let me stand in your way."

"I'll be off," Barry said.

"Jenny, I know this is your very first well-woman clinic since your training," O'Reilly said. "Would you mind if I sat in? Saw how it works?"

Jenny frowned, inhaled, clicked her tongue on her teeth, and said, "Fingal, it's really important to get this thing off to a good start. It's not long ago that we went through the 'lady doctor' thing here about women physicians not being acceptable to country patients. And didn't we find out that quite a few of the younger ones actually chose to see me?"

"That's true." It hadn't fazed O'Reilly, and it was true that the practice of medicine was changing, as well as attitudes toward its practitioners.

"So if you don't mind, I'd prefer to run the inaugural one all by myself."

"Hmmmm," said O'Reilly, thinking quickly. He could understand her point of view but was hesitant to relinquish his position as undisputed boss of this practice. "I can certainly see why you'd feel like that, but I'd be surprised if any of the patients haven't already seen me before or would mind me being there, and I'd really like to know how the system works. Doctors aren't immune to illness, Jenny, and if you got sick or wanted time off, somebody'd have to fill your shoes." He had to hand it to the lass. She wasn't slow replying, "You'd look daft in my dress high heels."

O'Reilly bellowed with laughter. "Touché, but what do you say?"

"Let's compromise, Fingal. You have another cup of tea. Smoke your pipe. I'll ask those in the waiting room if any have a particular need to see me on my own, get them taken care of, then come and get you to join me. It's just to get the thing started."

O'Reilly fished out his briar, shook his shaggy head, grinned, and said, "If you ever get tired of medicine, Jenny Bradley, I have a friend in the Foreign Office."

"Whatever for?"

"You'd have a stellar career in the diplomatic service. Go on, get the first ones seen to and then come and get me." He sat, lit his pipe, and called to Lady Macbeth, who came out from under the table and jumped up on his lap. "What does Kinky call you, madam? 'A wee dote'?"

He found a few slivers of trout on what had been Barry's plate. "Here you are."

Lady Macbeth wolfed them down then began to purr. She was easily satisfied.

O'Reilly looked across the hall to see a smiling Jenny showing a young woman into the surgery. He'd been around long enough to know that nearly every doctor would be excited when they started a new programme, but Jenny Bradley was a very smart woman. She had graduated from medical school with honours. Doing nothing but routine physical examinations, taking cervical smears, and giving contraceptive advice must surely be going to pall after a while? Making difficult diagnoses or doing surgery were the constant stimuli of specialty practice. Knowing your patients, and all the variety of complaints, were what made general practice so attractive to O'Reilly and, he knew, to Barry. But repetitive routine, day in and day out? He wondered if Doctor Jenny Bradley was going to be happy with her new position or whether after a few months she'd move on. He blew a magnificent smoke ring and invoked one of his favourite sayings. It was a bridge they'd cross when they came to it.

"Doctor O'Reilly." Jenny stuck her head round the door. "Will you join us?"

He put his pipe in an ashtray, decanted her ladyship onto the floor, and headed for the surgery. Once inside he closed the door. Jenny sat in the swivel chair at the rolltop desk. "How are you, Mrs. Beggs?" O'Reilly said to a short, slim, fair-haired woman wearing a light raincoat over a simple dress. She occupied one of the two patients' seats.

"I'm grand, sir, so I am. Your nice Doctor Bradley's going til do one of them new- fangled smears for me, so she is. I seen Eileen Lindsay— her that won the Christmas raffle at the Rugby Club party . . ."

Whose son, Sammy, had had Henoch-Schönlein purpura and was now quite recovered, O'Reilly thought.

"Anyroad, she told me all about getting one so you'd not get cancer of the neck of the womb. We come in together, so we did. She's next."

"Eileen's right about the test," O'Reilly said. "We're very lucky to have Doctor Bradley and the clinic here." He was rewarded by a smile from Jenny and said to her, "Irene's been a patient from almost the first day I started to practise here when I came back from the war. She was eight in 1946 and had tonsillitis. Had them out in '48." He smiled at the woman and said, "Isn't that right?"

"You're dead on, Doctor," Irene said.

"And apart from a few coughs and colds she's been feeling fit as a flea since, haven't you?"

"I've always kept myself rightly," she said, "and I get enough til keep me busy with my two weans." She directed her next remarks to Jenny. "Doctor O'Reilly delivered wee Albert in '62 and Doctor Laverty looked after me for Vera in '64, so he did. Gertie Gorman's minding them this morning for me. And Doctor Laverty had me in for an examination a year after wee Vera was born. Nothing til worry about. Just routine, he said."

Jenny was scribbling on a form of a kind O'Reilly hadn't seen before, presumably a standard record for a well-woman visit.

Not quite routine, he thought. Barry had sought O'Reilly's advice during Irene's postpartum visit in '64. He'd found a mass about the size of a golf ball that seemed attached to the front of her uterus, the presence of which Barry had asked O'Reilly to confirm. It wasn't difficult. Irene Beggs was slim with little abdominal fat and O'Reilly had concurred with Barry's diagnosis of a small fibroid, a benign swelling of part of the uterine muscle, and was satisfied it was not of ovarian origin. X-rays were of little help in the diagnosis of pelvic lesions, and the only way to be absolutely certain was to open the patient's belly, a pretty radical procedure for something that probably wasn't going to give the patient trouble.

They had decided that discretion was the better part of valour, to say nothing, and simply keep her under observation. Which was why Barry had reexamined her and had happily, as expected, found no change. O'Reilly knew that about 20 percent of women had been found to have fibroids of which they had been blissfully unaware. He had been convinced they were not putting Irene at any risk and saw no reason to worry her by telling her about it as long as it was asymptomatic and her doctors kept a regular eye on her.

"Don't mind me," he said, grabbed the other patients' chair, swung it round, and sat legs astraddle, arms draped over its back. He waited while Jenny completed the standard social history concerning her age, twenty-eight; occupation, housewife; and religious persuasion.

Jenny went on to ask about illnesses in the patient's family, previous illnesses, had O'Reilly's information about her tonsils confirmed, and rightly sought details of the two normal pregnancies.

"Last thing, Mrs. Beggs." Jenny swung in the swivel chair to face the patient. "I need to know about your periods."

"The monthlies? You could set your watch by them, so you could. Every twenty-eight days, a few cramps on the first day or two and they last for five days."

"And," said Jenny, "when was your last one?"

Irene frowned and started to count on her fingers, then she smiled. "It was four days after them Frenchmen fired one of them statamelites intil outer space."

O'Reilly kept a straight face. Ulster folks were prone to producing pronunciations of their very own, like "bisticks" or "biscakes," both of which meant "biscuits." "That was on the seventeenth. So your last was the twenty-first of February?" he asked.

"Aye." She smiled. "I'm pretty sure I'm up the spout. See my Davy? See him?" She lowered her voice. "He only has to hang his britches at the end of the bed and I'm in the family way again. I was going til ask about it while I was here, but I wanted a smear too."

Jenny must have been doing the necessary calculations while Mrs. Beggs rambled on about her ease in falling pregnant. "That means you are eight weeks pregnant now and due on November the twenty-eighth," Jenny said.

"Aye. I guessed it would be about then." She smiled. "We're looking forward to it. Davy and me loves weans, so we do."

O'Reilly was trying to decide whether knowing the woman had a fibroid should force them to examine her now. Probably not unless it was causing pain, and she hadn't complained of any. "Now we know you're pregnant you'll need more than a Pap smear, Irene, but doing a full antenatal checkup for you now would take too long. I know Doctor Bradley doesn't want to keep her other patients waiting." He looked at Jenny, who nodded.

"Could you come back in four weeks and we'll arrange for you to have both at once? I'm sure we can get Doctor Laverty to see you for the pregnancy, and Doctor Bradley, if you'd not mind . . ." Young doctors could be touchy about their spheres of influence. "I'm sure he's learned to do smears and could save you the trouble."

Irene frowned. "Right enough, you could kill two birds with one stone, like."

"We could," O'Reilly said. He put a reassuring hand on her shoulder. "You come and see us or send for us before that if you're worried about anything."

"I will," she said, "and thanks very much." Irene rose. "Bye for now," and let herself out.

He watched her go and as she did the sun as it moved around the firmament began blazing in through the bow windows.

He heard Jenny cough, turned, and could tell by the way she was frowning and shaking her head that he had ruffled her professional feathers by suggesting Barry take over the case.

"I can do antenatal visits perfectly well, you know, Doctor O'Reilly. I fail to see why we need to involve Doctor Laverty . . ."

"Whoa, Jenny." O'Reilly held up his hand. Lord, he thought, preserve me from professional sensitivity. "You can indeed," he said. "But there are two things you need to think about. First, you'll not be doing her ongoing care or delivery . . ."

"But I could. I'm fully trained."

"Jenny, you're here to run a clinic, not run obstetric services." O'Reilly kept his voice quite level.

"I suppose." She sounded a bit less tense.

"And second, she has a small anterior fibroid that you don't know about and that Barry and I have both had the opportunity to examine."

"Oh," said Jenny, clearly distressed. "I should have—I could have—"

"No, you couldn't. You haven't seen her old notes because the patients don't make appointments in advance, and you'd no idea who was coming today and couldn't look at her medical history beforehand. And like an eejit I'd locked the filing cabinet after morning surgery the way I always do. You'd no reason to suspect anything much in a healthy young woman and reckoned you'd find out about anything unusual when you took her history for the well-woman form."

"You're right. And if I'd been worried I'd have asked you to unlock the files," Jenny said.

"I'm sure you would. Now look, because it's not going to make any difference to her care, it didn't really matter that you didn't know. And I didn't want to mention the fibroid in front of her. There's no reason to worry her."

"Oh," said Jenny. "I see. That makes sense." She nodded, smiled. "Sorry, Fingal. Sometimes I can be a bit touchy."

"I understand." And he did. It would have been much harder for a young woman at medical school. She'd have had to fight her own battles, he was sure, but Jenny was not using that as an excuse now. He admired that. "Warm in here," he said, and he wasn't only referring to the heat of the sun. "Let's get a bit of fresh air." He went to the window and opened it. For the moment there was no traffic noise on Main Street and from the trees of the churchyard opposite a series of twice-repeated notes rang loudly and sweetly. "Hear that?" he said. "The song thrush is back."

"It's a beautiful song," Jenny said.

"It is that," said O'Reilly, "and I'd be happy to listen to it all day, but I think, Doctor Bradley, perhaps I'd better go and get your next patient."

"Thanks, Fingal," she said quietly, and he knew what he was being thanked for.

As he left, the bird began again and the purity of its song reminded him of a caged bird in a hotel lobby, long ago.

5

Cry "Havoc!" and Let Slip the Dogs of War

Fingal had finished handing his suitcase and their coats to the cloakroom attendant. The caged budgerigar in the lobby of Belfast's Midland Hotel tweedled, pecked at its cuttlebone, and for no apparent reason announced, "Get up. Get up."

"Poor wee thing," Deirdre said as they passed it on their way to the hotel's palm court dining room.

"Indeed it is," Fingal said. "And far from home. Its ancestors came from the Canary Islands, the Azores, and Madeira."

"And you're going to be far from home too, Fingal," she said.

He was. Nazi Germany's jackbooted armies, panzer columns, and squadrons of stukas with their "Jericho Trumpet" dive sirens screaming had smashed into Poland on September 1, 1939. The United Kingdom and France declared war on Germany two days later. By early October, Poland had been carved up between Hitler and Stalin. The Russians, signatories of a secret pact with Germany, had taken the hapless Poles from the rear. Polish cavalry against tanks. By November, mobilization in Great Britain was still in full swing and Doctor Fingal Flahertie O'Reilly, Royal Naval Reserve, was one of the hundreds of thousands being called up. Today, he would be leaving Ulster. His friend of Trinity days, Bob Beresford, had already volunteered and been accepted into the Royal Army Medical Corps.

Fingal held Deirdre's chair, saw that she was seated, took his own place, and as soon as the waiter arrived ordered a cream tea with assorted pastries for two. "I never thought I'd be wearing my bloody uniform again," he said, glancing down at his undress jacket with its three groups of three gilt buttons and a single gold stripe on each cuff. "I told you, Deirdre, I'd only joined the Royal Navy Reserve for the money. Back then, in 1930, I was twenty-two and needed cash to go to medical school. And we really did think the Great War had been the war to end all wars. I reckoned joining up was money for old rope. Never *ever* expected to be called up." He looked fondly at her.

"You look very handsome in blue, Fingal," Deirdre Mawhinney said, her own blue eyes smiling.

The waiter reappeared and set Delft cups and saucers, a silver teapot, hot water jug, and sugar and milk on the table's pristine damask cloth, then placed a multiple-tiered silver cake stand between Deirdre and Fingal. She poured. He offered her a pastry. She took a scone with clotted cream and strawberry jam. He helped himself to a fig roll then sipped his tea.

She leant forward and covered his hand with her left one. It was warm on his and the little gold band with its tiny solitaire diamond encircled the third finger.

Fingal looked at it for perhaps a moment longer than necessary. It had been a bright, cloudless July day when he'd put it on her finger. While they'd walked hand in hand through Strickland's Glen and back to the car they'd happily made plans for a May wedding in 1940 when Fingal would have saved enough. Mister bloody Hitler and his gang of nasty Nazis—in his head Fingal pronounced it "Naaahzees," the way Winston Churchill did—had put the kibosh on that, and he knew how much it was costing Deirdre to try to be cheerful on this their last time together until—until when?

She followed the direction of his gaze. "And we thought," she said, "that when Mr. Chamberlain announced 'Peace in our time' last year that things were going to settle down in Europe. I know the Japanese have been at it in China for years. Nobody knows how that's going to end. But it's an awfully long way away and doesn't really concern us, and yet . . ." She shrugged. "Not many people, except perhaps Mister Churchill, expected this horror to happen so close to home. Not again." She took a small bite from her scone.

"True on you," he said. "Too bloody true." And because of the war today he must say good-bye—no, damn it, not good-bye, *au revoir*—to the girl he loved, and God alone knew when he'd see her again or the familiar things of his home in Ulster. He finished his fig roll and glanced around the palm court of the fashionable hotel, where other couples and family groups were taking afternoon tea. Several aspidistras, each in its brass pot, were arranged around the walls. The scent of expensive cigar smoke flavoured the air. As was expected in polite society when dining out, conversations were kept hushed. Over the low murmurings he heard a little boy in short pants and a Methodist College blazer yelling, "But I wanna Jaffa cake, so I do," and the stern masculine admonition, "Little boys should be seen and not heard. You've already had one. Put it down, Patrick."

Fingal grinned. He wasn't a little boy. There was a chocolate éclair on the top tier of the silver cake stand. It would go nicely with the Jacob's fig roll he'd just finished. He remembered how the girls who worked for the factory in Dublin had been called Jacob's Mice when he'd been a student there in the early '30s. It might be some time before he saw another chocolate éclair. He reached for it, put it on his plate, and finished his tea.

A string quintet serenading the patrons finished a sedate rendition of last year's hit "Flat Foot Floogie (with a Floy Floy)" and moved into Franz Lehar's "Vilia," a piece that Fingal found too saccharine. Afternoon teas, string bands in palm courts, school blazers, he thought. On the surface here in Ulster in November 1939 life appeared to be going on as usual, but already the shipyards at Harland and Wolff were on a wartime footing, with full slips and riveting guns hammering twenty-four hours a day. Short's Aircraft factories were turning out Sunderland flying boats for antisubmarine patrol, and despite the "Careless talk costs lives" posters drawn by a cartoonist known as Fougasse and scattered all through the city, he'd heard rumours that Short's was developing a four-engine bomber called the Stirling.

"Another bloody war," he said, scowled, and took an enormous bite.

The British Expeditionary Force was in France on the Belgian border and Whitley and Wellington bombers from the Royal Air Force had dropped millions of propaganda leaflets over Germany. The Royal Navy was at war stations and many vessels were already escorting convoys bringing vital supplies to Britain. A group of cruisers hunted the German *Admiral Graf Spee,* which was loose somewhere in the vastness of the South Pacific, bent on commerce raiding.

"Still," he said, "it's not as if I'm going to the far side of the world." He knew enough not to mention his exact destination—"careless talk" and all that. "Scotland's not far."

"It'll feel a world away to me."

"I'll write," he said, "but I know it's not the same."

"No. It's not," she said quietly. He noticed that her cup was empty. "More tea? Another scone?"

She shook her head. "No, thank you." She looked away into the distance. "I've never been to Scotland. Maybe I could go there for a long weekend and you could get a few days off?"

"I honestly don't know," he said. "Might be possible." He'd received orders and a travel warrant from the Admiralty to report to his ship at the naval base of Greenock on the River Clyde in Scotland. The Home Fleet had been moved there from Scapa Flow in the Orkney Islands after what they had thought was an impregnable anchorage had been penetrated by a U-boat. The old battleship *Royal Oak,* a twenty-five-year-old *Revenge*-class ship, was torpedoed and sunk on September 14 by the German U-Boat Ace Günther Prien. It had been a morale-shattering start to the war. "I'm sure I'll get a bit of leave and be able to get back to Ulster."

"I do hope so," she said. "I'm going to miss you, Fingal."

He squeezed her hand. "And I you, pet." He forced a smile. "And cheer up," he said, "it'll be a pretty safe billet."

He was to join HMS *Warspite,* a super-dreadnought. In light of his earlier naval experience, their lordships said, and his medical qualifications, he had been promoted from sub-lieutenant to surgeon lieutenant with four years' seniority and an expectation of another rise in rank to surgeon lieutenant-commander within one year or so.

"And I'll be getting a promotion soon and that'll mean a bit more cash to be put by for when we can get married." He glanced at his single cuff ring with its central upward loop called a curl. Once he'd reported on board, he'd get a second plain ring added beneath and red cloth between them to signify medical branch. Good thing he'd kept his old 1930 uniforms. Bloody war, and just when he was finding his way in a practice in Ballybucklebo that he loved, with marriage to the woman he loved supposedly in their very-near future.

He felt the pressure of Deirdre's hand on his. "You will take care of yourself, darling, won't you?" Frown lines marred her usually smooth forehead.

He tried to make light of it and to soothe her fears. He glanced round to be certain he was not being overheard. "My ship has a fourteen-inch armour belt and eight fifteen-inch guns. Each shell weighs nearly a ton. And she's got a great gross of secondary armament and antiaircraft guns. There are one thousand two hundred men on board, not counting me yet." He wondered if his old friend, Tom Laverty, was still on her as a navigating officer. "It's not me that'll have to take care. It's bloody Adolf Hitler's navy. His nice new *Bismarck* won't dare show her face. Not to my ship." He laughed.

"I suppose it sounds encouraging. I mean, all those guns and armour and so on. And you'll hardly be alone." She smiled, looking a little reassured. "But I'll still worry."

He turned his hand so he held hers and looked into a pair of piercing blue eyes. "No need. Honestly. I promise." He saw no reason to tell her that in the First World War at the Battle of Jutland in 1916, *Warspite* had sustained massive damage, fourteen killed, and sixteen wounded. His smile faded. "But maybe I was wrong asking you to marry me with the world getting more topsy-turvy every day," he said. "I never thought I'd be going off to fight in a world war and we'd have to delay things."

She shook her head. "Fingal Flahertie O'Reilly. Since the day I met you in Dublin's Rotunda Hospital I knew I was going to fall in love with you." She squeezed his hand. "But you were such a shy, hesitant old bear. The other trainee doctors weren't so bashful." Her laugh was throaty.

My own ineptitude cost me my first love. Kitty O'Hallorhan, as far as he knew, had stayed on in Tenerife after the Spanish Civil War ended in April, continuing at an orphanage for children who'd lost their families in that war. She'd kept in touch with Virginia Treanor, one of her nursing cronies in Dublin, and she, an old friend from their student days, had told Donald Cromie, now a trainee surgeon at the Royal Victoria Hospital. He'd mentioned it to Fingal en passant. After he and Kitty had parted, Fingal O'Reilly had decided to emulate his bachelor brother Lars and have nothing to do with the fair sex—until that summer day in 1937 when a student midwife with the most amazing blue eyes—all he could see of her face over her sterile mask—had walked into the delivery room.

In the background, the ensemble had switched to "I'll Be Seeing You," and Fingal sang along for a bar or two.

I'll be seeing you in all the old familiar places,
That this heart of mine embraces . . .

Then he said, "We danced to that in the Gresham Hotel in Dublin last year, the September night I finally plucked up the courage to tell you I loved you," and he looked at her and saw a petite, newly qualified midwife crying softly at their table and saying, "Oh Fingal, I'm so happy."

"I always will love you, Deirdre, no matter how far away I am." And he wondered how many times men—men on both sides—had said that to dear ones. War? Bloody lunacy. Fingal popped the rest of his éclair in his mouth and glanced at his watch. His train for Larne would be leaving in half an hour. There he would catch the *Princess Victoria* ferry or her sister ship *Princess Maud* to Stranraer in Scotland on the first leg of his journey to Greenock. It was a good thing the Midland was a station hotel and he'd have no distance to walk. "Would you like anything else, pet?"

She shook her head.

Fingal attracted the attention of a passing waiter.

"Yes, sir?"

"Just my bill, please." He noticed that the man had a distinct kyphoscoliosis, a hunchback.

Deirdre waited until the man had departed then said, "I'll write, Fingal. Every day."

"And I'll write too." Fingal felt a lump in his throat.

The quintet had shifted to a version somewhere between andante and adagio of "September Song."

He squeezed her hand. "Thank you for saying that you'll wait."

"I love you, Fingal," she said. "I always will."

"Thank you, my love," he said softly, "and I will come back. Promise." He wanted to kiss her, but it wasn't done to be too emotional in public.

"Your bill, sir." The waiter had returned.

Fingal consulted it, took out his wallet, and paid. "Keep the change."

"Thank you, sir." The man hesitated. "May I say something?"

"Fire away."

"When I was a wee lad I had TB of my spine."

That explained the hunch.

"They'd not take me for the army, but I'd just like for til say that me and my mates here, us waiters and waitresses, like, all want for til thank you, sir, so we do, for going off til do your bit." He turned to Deirdre. "And, missus? We all hope your brave sailor-man comes home safe and sound, so he does. Begging your pardon." The man was blushing.

"Thank you," Fingal said, and felt the lump in his throat grow bigger. "Thank you very much."

"If you'll excuse me, sir?" The waiter began clearing the table.

O'Reilly rose and held Deirdre's chair. "Now," he said to her, "no arguments. I'm getting a taxi for you."

"Thank you, Fingal," she said, rising. "I'm not good at waving damp hankies on platforms." He saw how her eyes shone, heard the catch in her voice.

Bugger convention. O'Reilly, who towered over her, swept her into his arms, lifted her off the floor, and after remarking, "I love you, Deirdre Mawhinney, and we will get married—one day," kissed her long, hard, and with all the longing in him. He set her down and was amazed by a small round of applause and a man's voice saying, "Bon voyage, captain."

"Come on," he said, "out of here," and blushing and taking her hand hurried her to the door.

They collected their coats and his suitcase from the cloakroom and Fingal helped Deirdre into hers. She turned and faced him as he shrugged into the new duffle he'd bought this morning. "Last hug," she said, then moved into his arms and held him tightly. "Look after yourself. Please."

He held her hand and together they went out onto York Street.

As he settled her into one of the recently established W. J. McCausland's Auto Taxis and paid the driver, he looked at the love of his life, into sad, brimming blue eyes, at her soft lips, her trim figure, and said, "You look after yourself, darling. I'll get leave one day and until then I'll write. I promise."

"I'll not say 'good-bye,' Fingal," she said. "Just, 'until the next time.' I love you, *a cuishle*. Take care."

And Surgeon Lieutenant Fingal Flahertie O'Reilly, not wanting to see her tears, heart like lead in his chest, closed the taxi door, clenched his teeth—and went to war.

6

Come Cheer Up My Lads, 'tis to Glory We Steer

Thank the Lord the open motorboat, a thirty-six-foot pinnace *Warspite* had sent to collect Fingal from Greenock Docks, had three dodgers. The canvas screens were in place and each at least provided some protection from the elements. He sat amidships on a bench behind the shelter nearest to the stern and shivered, paying little attention to any possible view ahead. He was tired, cold, and distinctly out of sorts.

The ferry crossing last night from Larne to Stranraer had been rough and the Scottish boarding house there damp and draughty. A six A.M. train, which had covered the hundred miles to Greenock at a crawl, was crowded. He'd missed lunch, and the couldn't-care-less-sir petty officer in charge of arranging transport seemed to think that delivering junior officers to His Majesty's battleships ranked a good deal lower on the scale of importance than sending a month's supply of toilet paper to an armed trawler. Fingal had languished cold and bored in a rickety dockside hut.

Spray struck his cheek. He hunched his shoulders, but his convoy coat (naval jargon for duffle), provided little protection from the wind. The coat was so new he'd not even had time to put his rank shoulder straps on.

He shivered. What had been a breeze had kicked up to a gale

howling down from the mist-shrouded Rosneath Peninsula across the upper Firth of Clyde. All he could hear was the puttering of the engine, a whistling noise as the tempest tore over some projection on the boat, and the constant slapping against the hull of a vicious chop. Spray was being torn in tattered streamers from the wave crests. The little vessel was making heavy weather of the last part of the shore-to-ship voyage.

"Hang on, sir," a deep voice roared. "Not much longer." The boat's cox'n was a leading seaman. The killick badge on his left upper sleeve, an anchor fouled by a rope wrapped loosely round it, denoted his rank. He was the possessor of one of the biggest ginger beards Fingal had ever seen. The man stood at the helm as unconcerned as if he'd been on a parade ground ashore.

The pinnace pitched and rolled and took water green over the bows to be smashed into wind-driven spume against the canvas screen. Fingal pitied the able seaman who crouched behind it there. Another AB of, O'Reilly guessed, nineteen or twenty shared the space aft. Those two sailors' main function was to handle the bow and stern lines when docking or casting off.

Fingal tasted salt mixed with a suggestion of bile in the back of his throat. There was a churning in his guts. Perhaps it was no bad thing he'd not eaten for a while. He'd last had sea legs in 1931 and hoped he wasn't, like Admiral Lord Nelson, going to be seasick in harbour. Fingal knew from his previous nautical experience that fixing your eyes on something immobile, like a horizon, could help avert seasickness. He moved along the bench to the port side and stuck his head around the dodger.

He had to grab his cap before the wind took it. The gale stung his cheeks and made his eyes water. The sight he saw made them widen and his mouth gape. "Holy Mother of God," he said, and was barely aware he had spoken. The earlier sea mist that had shrouded his view from the dock had been whipped away. Tail of the Bank, the main anchorage in the Firth of Clyde, lay open to his gaze and before him were more ships at anchor than he had ever seen collected in one place. Lines from Henry Newbolt's "Little Admiral" came to mind.

> Brag about your cruisers like leviathans—
> A thousand men apiece down below

How many and who were the men in those grey, grim giants? Some would be career navy, but many would be conscripted "hostilities only" ratings, civilians drafted to serve in the war. They'd be barely trained, resentful, scared, and, like him, missing their loved ones. And yet, he suspected, they'd also be not a little proud, as deep down he was, to be following in the footsteps of Admirals Nelson, Howe, Bowen. And every man jack, volunteer or conscript, would be facing immersion in the ocean, fire, explosion, flying metal fragments, bullets, and disease, all things that might kill—or horribly wound. Nor would they be immune to the regular ills of the flesh.

He took a deep breath. And it would be his job, with the two other doctors and one dentist of *Warspite*'s medical branch, to tend to the 1,200 crew of the battleship, and any casualties brought aboard. What the hell did I ever learn at medical school to prepare me for that? The half of sweet bugger all. He hoped he'd be up to the job.

He studied more closely the largest ship he could see and recognised the Home Fleet's flagship from seeing her description in *Jane's Fighting Ships*. Shore boats fussed round her. HMS *Nelson,* where Admiral Sir Charles Forbes, GCB, DSO, flew his flag, was an imposing if unusual sight. She carried her main armament of nine sixteen-inch guns on an elongated foredeck ahead of the tall bridge tower and single funnel.

The anchorage was full to overflowing and she was surrounded by cruiser squadrons and destroyer flotillas. Nearby he saw a single pip-squeak among the bigger ships, a Flower-class corvette, about two hundred feet overall. Many of these escort vessels were being built in Belfast. Seeing her, small among giants, but from his own home country, gave Fingal a twinge of homesickness, even loneliness.

In the merchant anchorage, a convoy was forming with ships anchored in lines. Part of one bound for Halifax, Nova Scotia, perhaps? And that little corvette was going to help escort them across the Atlantic? Good luck.

He staggered as a higher-than-usual wave made the pinnace heel, but managed to grab hold.

Around them and among the anchored fleet were harbour craft, drifters shuttling crew back and forth, launches, supply boats and, he noticed, an admiral's barge putting out from *Nelson*—all battling the waves. The wind was freshening.

He watched as the pinnace rounded the battleship's stern, and as it did another great grey warship slowly was unmasked. Grey, yet of a lighter shade than the other vessels of the Home Fleet. HMS *Warspite* was still wearing her Mediterranean colour scheme. She'd been there at the outbreak of hostilities. They were approaching her at an angle from astern on the ship's port side. Fingal knew that the aft starboard gangway was reserved for admirals. To his relief, the great hull was acting as a windbreak and the waters in her lee were relatively calm. His nausea began to settle.

His gaze was attracted to the ship's aft fifteen-inch turrets, designated X and Y. The measurement referred to the diameter of the rifles' bore. The barrels were nearly fifty-five feet long. The pinnace was close enough so he could make out the tompions, plugs that were kept in the guns' muzzles to keep salt water out. On each was embossed the ship's emblem, the green woodpecker or "spight." The first HMS *Warspite* had actually been *Warspight* and had been Sir Walter Raleigh's at Cadiz in 1596.

This modern *Warspite*, the seventh to bear the proud name, would be his home for God only knew how long.

The cox'n answered a hailed challenge from the deck above and brought the pinnace alongside a boarding platform. Fingal craned to look up at the battlewagon's towering cliff of a side. It seemed a very long way up. His job was to get out of the pinnace without falling overboard—and it did happen—and scale the stairs. Fingal realised that he'd now have to remember and use the arcane language of sailors. It was called an accommodation ladder even though it was a staircase. At the top he'd stand at attention, salute the bridge, salute the officer of the day, and report himself. After that, naval routine would take over.

Surgeon Lieutenant Fingal Flahertie O'Reilly smiled, thanked the pinnace's coxs'n, and stepped onto the platform. One of the ABs followed, carrying Fingal's suitcase.

As he climbed, he slipped a hand into his duffle coat pocket. His pipe and tobacco pouch were still there, but when he thrust his hand lower, he found something beneath that he'd not noticed before. He hesitated on a stair, pulled out an envelope, and read, *To my darling Fingal,* in Deirdre's neat handwriting. She must have slipped it there during their last embrace in the hotel lobby. He'd open it the minute he was alone, but the officer waiting on deck for the new arrival would not be pleased if Fingal spent any longer coming aboard. He started to climb, sad but accepting that, for the duration at least, love must take second place to war.

How in the hell would he ever find his way around this floating maze? The young seaman who'd brought Fingal's suitcase from the pinnace had been detailed by the officer of the day to "Take this medical officer and his luggage to his cabin and then to the PMO. He'll be in the sick bay."

Principal medical officer—PMO. O'Reilly had to remind himself of the term as they walked away along the quarterdeck from the stern through a doorway. O'Reilly corrected himself—hatch. "Upper deck," said the young man. "There's another deck, the foc's'le deck, above this and a couple of gunnery control towers above that again. Going for'ard there's the funnel, then the command bridge." They went past watertight hatches along a corridor.

Over all hung a pervasive, ever-present stink of fuel oil. And the sounds: the humming of intake fans supplying air to the machinery spaces, a metallic ringing of hammers, the soughing of the wind through rigging, the splashing of bilge water being discharged and, neverendingly, although her motion was not nearly as lively as that of the pinnace, the great ship rose and fell as the seas rumbled under her keel.

His guide, a stocky, bowlegged young man who Fingal now knew was AB Alfie Henson from Harrogate in Yorkshire, seemed to have overcome his initial shyness and was providing a running commentary. The younger man's tone was slightly patronising. He reckons I'm a naval innocent from the Royal Naval Volunteer Reserve, Fingal thought. They were amateurs, and mostly had been yachtsmen in civvy life or a few needed professionals like doctors, lawyers, and chaplains. In 1939, they'd only have had ten weeks' basic training at HMS *King Alfred,* a shore base in Sussex. When Fingal had enquired of Henson about his service, he had replied, "Five years I've been in the Andrew . . .' He'd paused to see if the naval slang had been understood. Not one to let the patient, or in this case a junior rating, get the upper hand, O'Reilly said, "The Grey Funnel Line?" the other irreverent title used for the Royal Navy.

"Right, sir." A little more deference. "I joined the navy as a lad. I was fifteen." He grinned to reveal a missing lower incisor. "I do like it, sir. I want to make a career of it."

"I'm glad to hear it."

They went down a staircase—companionway. The old lingo was

returning to him, along with a cascade of memories from nine years before. "We're on the main deck, now, sir. Port side. This big bugger amidships is the barbette of X turret." Henson pointed at an arc of a steel cylinder that clearly continued beneath the deck on which they stood and on above the deckhead overhead. "And this, over to port," he walked to a bulkhead, along which was a row of doors spaced at regular intervals, "officers' berths. You're a lucky bugger for a junior officer."

It was a reasonable assumption. All newly commissioned medical officers were granted the rank of acting surgeon lieutenant. Fingal wasn't acting and he had four years' seniority.

Henson opened the door. "They've given you one with a bit of daylight, like, not like the other buggers inboard where the sun never shines."

Fingal looked into a small, Spartan, grey-painted room with a corticene "sole," as the flooring of a ship was called. The space held a cot, a chair and metal table, and a wardrobe, all bolted to the sole. On the far side of the room, a circular porthole of salt-streaked glass let in a faint light. AB Henson put the two suitcases on the bed as Fingal shrugged out of his duffle coat and hung it in the wardrobe. He wanted to open Deirdre's envelope. "Wait outside for a minute, will you, Henson?" Fingal noticed Henson glancing at the ring on Fingal's now-visible uniform jacket sleeve. Regulars' rings were solid, Royal Naval Reserve officers' insignia were like thin chains, and Royal Navy Volunteer Reserve had wavy stripes on their cuffs. Hence "Wavy Navy."

"Here," Henson said, "you're not Wavy Navy. The principal medical officer, Doctor Wilcoxson, he's Royal Navy, but the two junior pills and the dentist are all Volunteer Reserve."

Fingal laughed. He really would have to brush up on his navalese. "Pills" and "sawbones" were slang reserved for junior MOs. "I'm a pill myself, Henson, but I've a second stripe to keep that one company. Just haven't had time to put it up yet."

"So? You've been in the navy, sir?"

"Merchant service for three years. Year on the old *Tiger* in '30." Fingal reached into the duffle's pocket. "Now, Henson, give me a couple of minutes, please."

"Aye, aye, sir." The AB left and closed the door.

Fingal ripped the envelope open. It contained a green silk scarf, a trace of her perfume—Je Reviens—and a single page of notepaper. He read. *You gave me this scarf for my birthday and I loved it then. Please wear it when the weather is cold and let my love in the scarf keep you warm until you come back to me. Yours eternally, Deirdre.*

He took a deep breath, waited for the prickling in his eyes to stop, took a deep breath, put the letter and scarf under the pillow on the cot, and went and opened the door. "Next stop sick bay, I think," he said, struggling to keep his voice level.

"Right, sir." Henson led the way. "You were on *Tiger,* and I did a year on *Hood,* sir." He smiled his missing-tooth grin. "You and me's— if you don't mind me saying so, sir, seeing we're both old battle-cruiser hands—nearly old shipmates. I hope you'll soon feel at home on *Warspite*. She's a happy ship."

"Thank you, Henson," Fingal said, remembering how lonely he'd felt back on the pinnace when he'd noticed the Belfast-built corvette. "I'm starting to feel that already."

"I hope so, sir. The owner—"

"You mean the skipper?"

"Aye. Captain Victor Crutchley, VC. He's a proper gent."

"I've heard," said Fingal, "and you sound content."

"I am." He frowned. "But there are one or two right sods."

Fingal reckoned it would be surprising if there weren't, with more than a thousand men on board. A shrill piping noise filled the air. It was coming from loudspeakers of the SRE address system. A tinny voice said, "Liberty men close up. Liberty men close up at port fore and aft accommodation ladders. The drifters will be leaving at four thirty." The message was repeated.

"Jammy buggers," said Henson. "I'd not mind a run ashore myself even if we only get four hours, but my turn's coming."

O'Reilly nodded sympathetically.

Henson pointed up. "There are six-inch guns on the upper deck immediately above here, sir, and the same to starboard." Fingal heard the pride in the man's voice. "I'm the loader on six-inch gun four, starboard side."

"A responsible job." Fingal became aware of cooking smells. His mouth watered.

"Main galley and main kitchen's in there," Henson said, pointing inboard. "The wardroom galley for officers is farther aft on the deck above and the wardroom, where you'll be dining—"

Soon, I hope, thought Fingal.

"—is just ahead of X turret on the upper deck."

Fingal's tummy rumbled.

"More guns in that turret," Henson said. "I hope to be a leading rate soon. If I can, I want to go to the Whale Island gunnery school, HMS *Excellent,* at Portsmouth. Specialise in gunnery." There was not only affection. The lad was bubbling with enthusiasm.

"Can I help—" Fingal cut himself short. He wasn't in a Dublin tenement trying to find work for an unemployed cooper. It was none of his business. "Sorry, Henson. I'm sure your divisional officer will be able to advise you."

"You're right, sir. He's a decent enough bloke, Mister Wallace." He paused at another stair. "Down here, sir." Henson led the way down an amidships companionway into a lobby. The aft bulkhead was curved like the one astern near Fingal's cabin. Another big gun barbette, he assumed.

"That's A turret," said Henson. He pointed to the ship's port side. "Dispensary's in there if we need medicine and—" He walked to starboard and stopped at a door. "—sick bay and all medical spaces are through there, sir." He pointed for'ard. "Next space ahead of the sick bay is the chief petty officers' mess." He frowned and curled his lip.

"You don't like CPOs, Henson?"

Henson shrugged. "Most of them are decent blokes, but there's one, Gunnery Chief Petty Officer Watson?" Henson's eyes narrowed and he shook his head rapidly. "That bugger's a right bastard."

"I'm sorry to hear that," Fingal said, his curiosity piqued.

"I shouldn't be going on about it." Henson knocked on a door in a bulkhead. He saluted. "I'll be off then, sir."

Fingal returned the salute. "Thank you and good luck with your gunn—"

The door was opened by a sick berth attendant to whom Fingal said, "Surgeon Lieutenant O'Reilly to see the principal medical officer."

A soft, very English voice from behind the SBA said, "Lieutenant O'Reilly? Surgeon Commander Wilcoxson. Do come in and let me show you the shop."

7

Move from Hence to There

"It is very good to have the pair of you back, Kinky, Archie," O'Reilly said from his usual place at the head of the table. He sipped a nearly finished after-lunch tawny port. Seeing it was a Saturday and he was not on call he saw no reason not to have a tot. He'd have preferred Jameson, but Kitty in her usual tactful, but irresistible way had hinted some months ago that perhaps he should not be starting on the hard stuff until the evenings. He lifted his glass to her where she sat on his right talking to Barry and Archie, who faced each other at the dining room table. He was rewarded by her smile.

Kinky sat on his left looking rested and a little tanned after three weeks away. "It did be a very pleasant drive home in Archie's motor-car from Newcastle yesterday. We went over on the Strangford-to-Portaferry ferryboat and up along the coast by Ballywalter and Millisle and Groomsport, so."

"It is a pretty run," he said. "On a good day you get a great view of the Copeland Islands."

"And it was a very good day, bye," she said. "We had a lovely lunch in Donaghadee overlooking the harbour. But Doctor O'Reilly, sir, after you spending all that money on us at the Slieve Donard hotel, there was no need for this homecoming luncheon." She lowered her voice. "And if you don't mind me remarking, Kitty does be a very fine cook, if I do say so myself. There was a time I'm sorry to tell you that I misjudged the lady."

"That's water under the bridge, and," said O'Reilly, "I consider myself a very lucky man," he lowered his voice, "because she's nearly as good a cook as a certain Kinky Auchinleck."

"Go away with you, sir," she said, but her grin was huge.

"And having lunch here simply makes sense. Didn't you go round your quarters like a bee on a hot brick the week before the wedding, tidying, organizing, cleaning, packing all the clothes and such you'd not need on your honeymoon, taking them round to Archie's?"

"I did."

"And didn't we agree that you'd come here today and that we'd all help you pack up all the heavy things? So why would you not come here for lunch?" He didn't wait for an answer. "Donal Donnelly's coming round with a van so we can get them round to your new home."

"Thank you, Doctor. I'm grateful." There was an impish quality to her smile. "Whatever would people have said, though, if I'd taken everything round there before the wedding and moved in with Archie? I'd never have been able to hold my head up. Thank you for letting all my things rest here, sir, but the sooner they are out the better now." She turned to Barry. "Doctor Laverty, I will be back here first thing on Monday to give my old home—" She sighed. "—to give my old home a final dust and a polish and then you can move in."

"Thanks, Kinky," he said. "It'll be good to have more space and my own TV, but please don't think I'm rushing you out."

"I'd think no such thing," she said, "but it will be strange for me at first. I've lived here since 1928, that's thirty-eight years." She smiled at Archie. "And I know you'll not be offended, dear, if I say I'll miss it for a while no matter how grand it's going to be being with you, bye."

"Why would I take the strunts, Kinky? There's not a soul living who'd not miss their old place if and when they had to move," Archie said. "And don't forget, you'll not be leaving completely. You'll still be working here, anyroad."

"We couldn't let you go entirely, Kinky," Kitty said. "Fingal needs you during the week to answer the phone and the door. I couldn't keep on nursing and do all the things you do here, and that includes those lunches you make for the doctors and some of those wonderful ready-to-heat dinners." She chuckled. "Knowing how much grub means to you, Fingal, I'm surprised you gave Archie permission when he asked for your hand, Kinky."

Everyone laughed.

"Thank you, Kitty." Kinky cocked her head and beamed at Kitty. "I'm the luckiest woman in all of County Down and that's no lie, so, to have friends like the O'Reillys and yourself, Doctor Laverty."

"Bless you, Kinky," Barry said. "I'll always be your friend."

O'Reilly simply smiled at her. Some things were a given as far as he was concerned and needed no comment. "And," he said, finishing the last of his port, "if all of us friends are going to get you moved today, we need to start getting the job done. Here's what I propose." He looked straight at Kinky. "You'll be skipper. Or if you prefer you can be 'the hat,' the foreman of the job. We need you to direct operations."

"I'll do that, sir," Kinky said.

"Kitty? Packing of breakables? You've a softer touch than Barry or myself."

"I do have lots of newspaper and tissue paper for padding, so," Kinky said.

"Aye, aye, sir," Kitty said, and threw a mock naval salute.

"Doctor Laverty, Donal Donnelly when he arrives with the van, and I will be the muscle, humping boxes out to the vehicle. But I think," he looked at Archie, "I think, Archie, you should go home and be ready to meet us there. It's not that long since you had a very bad back and I'd not want you to put it out again lifting boxes."

"That's considerate, sir. Is that all right with everybody?"

"You run along, dear," Kinky said.

"If you're sure I can't help, I'll be off, then. There's still lots to do at the house," Archie said.

Kinky gave him a kiss and said, "I'll see you soon, back at home, *muirnín,* and make sure the kettle's on for I'm certain we'll all need a cup of tea when we get there, bye. I'll come in the moving van."

O'Reilly smiled to himself. It was the hallmark of all professional moving men that they seemed to run on a fuel of limitless cups of tea provided by the homeowners. "So," he said, "lead the way, Mrs. Auchinleck."

Kinky indeed took charge in her quarters. "Everything's gone from the bedroom and I've washed the bed linen and made the bed for Doctor Laverty."

"Thanks, Kinky," he said.

"But all my pictures and ornaments have to go, and a couple of pieces of my own furniture like . . ." She pointed to a mahogany fire screen, embroidered with a galleon in full sail that she'd done herself in the late '30s and early '40s. It stood in front of the fire when not lit. "My books are in boxes already so, Doctors, if you'd not mind waiting for a shmall-little minute, I'd like to get Kitty started first then I'll tell you what to do."

"Of course," O'Reilly said.

"And I'll give you a hand, Kitty," Kinky said, "but I'd like you to start with . . ." She pointed to two ornate brass candlesticks on the mantel and a glass, water-filled ball with a tiny village inside. ". . . the candlesticks. They were my own ma's and she had them from her ma, and she from her ma before her. I do love them dearly, so." She handed them to Kitty. "And Fidelma, my sister, gave me this"—she shook the glass ball and it looked as if the little village was in a snowstorm—"for my tenth birthday. It still delights me yet." And she giggled like a little girl.

O'Reilly swallowed. Hard. He'd given one just like it to Deirdre for Christmas 1940, and like Kinky she'd giggled in simple, unalloyed delight and clapped her hands. He glanced at Kitty and smiled when she said, "I'll be very careful with them, Kinky, I promise."

"And I'll pack this." Kinky moved to a model in a whiskey bottle of a fully rigged *Cutty Sark* that sat on her sideboard. "My first husband, Paudeen Kincaid, God rest you, Paudeen, and if you can see me now . . ."

O'Reilly felt the hairs on his forearms rise.

". . . you'll be happy to know I took your advice and have remarried. And your *Cutty Sark* is coming with me to my new home." She lifted it. "It was two whole years in the crafting and Paudeen gave it to me as an engagement present." She joined Kitty at the table, where they both bent to wrapping the treasures before putting them in boxes. "Gentlemen, could I ask you to take down those paintings first?"

"Come on, Fingal," Barry said. "We'll start with this one."

"That does be of the home farmhouse in Beál na mBláth," Kinky said. "Tiernan, who was here at the wedding, farms it now. He's a powerful man for the road bowling to this day."

O'Reilly saw her eyes mist.

"It's beautiful, Kinky, a very well-rendered watercolour," Kitty said.

"And bloody heavy," Barry muttered sotto voce.

O'Reilly hoped that the remark had been hidden by the rustling noise of wrapping paper. They started removing the next one.

"That's Lios-na-gCon," Kinky said. "The ring fort of the hound, near Clonakilty. I went to a dance on Lughnasadh there one August when I was sixteen." She inhaled. "That night the moon was so low I thought I only had to reach out and I could touch it. Those two pictures—Ma sent them up to me for my new home here—did give me great comfort when first I came to work for Doctor Flanagan and was missing County Cork and my family, so." She pointed to some faded sepia photos in frames. "Those ones are my family and that one is the County Cork camogie team. That's me, the thin one on the left." She shook her head. "Long, long ago now." She smiled and said, "But those dried flowers in their circular frames, I did pick them fresh in the soft springs and warm summers here in Ballybucklebo and preserved them. I embroidered the samplers when the winter nights were bitter, and the gales howling through the village, but I was snug at my own hearthside here."

"What's that one?" Barry asked. "I don't have the Gaelic."

She smiled. "It's called 'Pangur Bán.' It's a poem written by an Irish monk in the ninth century to his white cat. I did it when Doctor O'Reilly got Lady Macbeth." She took it down and offered it to O'Reilly. "I'd like for you and Kitty and her ladyship to have this as a memory of me here in this house."

O'Reilly glanced at Kitty, who was smiling and nodding. "Thank you, Kinky," he said. "May I leave it on the wall right here where it's been these past two years so there'll always be a memento of Kinky Kincaid in what was her old home and Barry can see it too?"

"I'd like that very much," Barry said.

"I do think," she said, "that would be a very fitting thing, so."

Kitty leant over and kissed Kinky's cheek. "Thank you so much, Kinky. For everything."

And for a moment no one spoke.

Silently, O'Reilly returned the sampler to its original place, then said quietly, "Come on, Barry, let's get the rest down and wrapped."

As each decoration was removed, the darkness of the paint behind contrasted starkly with the lighter sun-faded surrounding cream. When Barry took his first holiday O'Reilly would have the room repainted or perhaps papered—with a rose wallpaper. He liked roses on walls and Barry was a man of taste. Hadn't he been most admiring of the flowers Donal Donnelly had painted in the waiting room after Kitty had repapered it? With the personal belongings gone and the signs of her pictures covered, it would be almost as if Kinky Auchinleck, once Kincaid, née O'Hanlon, had never been there. But for the presence of the sampler.

In his mind, O'Reilly recalled the next-to-last verse of the poem:

> So in peace our task we ply,
> *Pangur Bán,* my cat, and I;
> In our arts we find our bliss,
> I have mine, and he has his.

And, he thought, wasn't that Kinky and me for all those years. I had my art and she had hers? He shook his head and smiled, carefully lifting her framed School Leaving Certificate from the wall. It was dated 1927. O'Reilly knew how fiercely proud she was of it. "You'll have memories of this room all right, Kinky," O'Reilly said.

"And mostly good, so," she gestured at the boxes waiting to be transported, "and I'm taking all those ones with me," she smiled, "and starting three weeks ago I'm on the road to new memories, and Archie's on that journey with me."

It was how O'Reilly had felt last April when Kitty had said "I do." "Good for you, Kinky."

"And please remember, Kinky," Kitty said, "you are welcome here always as our friend." It was only then that O'Reilly saw the hint of a tear in his old friend's eyes.

There was a knock on the door.

"Come in," Kinky said.

Donal Donnelly's carroty mop and buck teeth popped in with the springiness of a jack-in-the-box going sideways.

"Come in, Donal," O'Reilly said. "I do appreciate your volunteering to help."

"Och sure, wouldn't everybody in the village and townland walk on hot coals for our Kinky? Welcome home, Mrs. Auchinleck."

"Thank you, Donal," she said.

"It's not a bit of bother, so it's not, and hasn't Mister Bishop loaned us a van, and all?"

"He had to," said O'Reilly. "Flo told him to, and you know how Flo can be."

"I do that," said Donal. "She can be a right ould targe when it suits her."

"Mister Donnelly," said Kinky sternly, hiding her smile behind a sheaf of wrapping paper. "I'll have you know—"

"*And,*" said Donal, "*and* she can have a heart of corn when her friends are in need. But our Flo can be the right taskmaster, make you no mistake."

"And so can I," said O'Reilly with a mock scowl. "I want the three of us men to get all the boxes into the van and take them round to Archie's."

"Archie and Kinky's," Kitty said.

"So jump to it, *Miss*stah Christyun," said Barry in an uncanny impression of Charles Laughton's Captain Bligh in *Mutiny on the Bounty*. It made O'Reilly laugh so much he nearly dropped the box of books he'd just picked up. He set it down. "Gentlemen," he said. "I'm sure we can pull this job off smoothly if Doctor Laverty refrains from acting the lig. There'll be more help unloading at the other end. Archie's son Rory is coming down from Palace Barracks to give a hand."

"I promise. And it'll be great to see Rory," said Barry.

"And," said O'Reilly, "once the job is done, it will be my pleasure to treat the gentlemen of the moving crew, those who want to come, to the first pint of the evening in the Mucky Duck. I regret, ladies, that I am not responsible for Ulster's archaic licensing laws, so you won't be able to join us."

"That's perfectly all right," Kitty said. "I'll not be coming in the van if that's all right, Kinky? I have a date with a black Lab for a walk in the dunes on Ballybucklebo Beach."

"Grand, so. Arthur Guinness will be a happy dog and I'll be settled and content in our new home with Archie."

"So, you run along and play with your friends, Fingal," Kitty said, and gave him a wicked smile, "but don't think that now Kinky has moved you can be late for your dinner."

8

Brave New World

"Come with me," Surgeon Commander Wilcoxson said, heading for a curtain to the right.

Fingal finished the salute he'd begun when his superior officer had appeared and followed him into what he assumed was the sick bay. Instead he found himself in a small alcove. Directly ahead, double doors led to what must be another room on the ship's starboard side. The sick bay attendant had disappeared through a screen behind and to Fingal's left.

"He's just gone into the sick bay proper," Wilcoxson said. "I'll show you round later." He held open yet another curtain and stepped through. "In here's the surgeon's examining room. Doubles as my office." He waited until Fingal had gone in, and followed. "Take a pew and the weight off your feet." He sat at a kneehole table and indicated a simple seat, onto which Fingal subsided. Wilcoxson pointed at double doors in the far bulkhead. "Operating theatre's in there and the isolation ward's behind the doors on the other side of the screen we've just come through."

"I see." He didn't really, but no doubt it wouldn't take him long to find his way around, at least in his own bailiwick if not throughout this floating behemoth.

"We're very well set up medically," Wilcoxson said, stretching his legs out under the table. "Now tell me, is this your first time on a battleship, Doctor O'Reilly?"

"Not quite, sir. I served on the old *Tiger,* battlecruiser. I'm ex-mercantile marine, Royal Navy Reserve. Navigating sub-lieutenant. Believe it or not I can actually use a sextant and sight reduction tables. Or I could." He laughed.

"Excellent. Excellent. And are you familiar with our ship at all?" said Wilcoxson.

"Not really, although I was on *Warspite* once, in Gibraltar. Just for the afternoon in 1931, when the Atlantic Fleet had combined exercises with the Mediterranean Fleet. I was boxing. Light heavyweight championship."

"Who won?"

Fingal hesitated before saying, "I did, sir," and tugged at the lobe of his cauliflower ear.

"Good for you." Wilcoxson, a grey-haired man in, Fingal guessed, his early fifties, had a ruddy complexion and an aquiline nose that separated two brown eyes. Crow's-feet etched their corners, which Fingal hoped bespoke a sense of humour. The dark circles underneath told of weariness. The principal medical officer wore a white shirt under a V-necked blue sweater with rank shoulder straps, no tie, and navy blue trousers. He smiled. "Nice to have a doctor with naval experience on board, and perhaps you could take a noon sight," he frowned, "but you've forgotten some service etiquette. No need to salute me. I'm not wearing headdress so I can't return the compliment."

"Sorry, sir. It's been nine years so I am a bit rusty," he said, "and my naval experience didn't include anything medical. I certainly know nothing about treating war wounds."

"I like a man who knows his limitations." Wilcoxson pointed to a bookshelf.

It was full of medical textbooks and leather-bound copies of the *Journal of the Royal Naval Medical Services.* The reference works would be needed. Getting a consultation in mid-ocean would be problematical.

"Help yourself to anything on there. The practical wound experience will come—I promise." He shook his head and said quietly, "I started getting mine at Jutland in 1916 and I've taken courses between the wars at Haslar Naval Hospital in Gosport near Portsmouth. I'll be able to advise. The rest of my staff is Volunteer Reserve and still have a lot to learn. A fine young physician and a dentist. They're both a bit green. The dentist's on a week's leave.

"There should be two surgeon lieutenants on establishment, so we can do our work in the day, and with one on call at night the others can get a bit of sleep. There's a sleeping cabin in the sick bay so if he needs to, the duty officer can stay in the bay but have a zizz if he's free. Sometimes we split the night work into two four-hour watches starting at eight P.M. After ordinary eight-hour nights, the duty physician has eight hours off the following day—unless we are at action stations, then it's all hands on deck for as long as we're needed. You're replacing young Johnson. Broke a leg on our trip here."

"Poor man."

"Hmm," said Wilcoxson noncommittally, then said, "You'll meet the chaps in the wardroom anteroom aft for drinks before dinner."

"Still served at quarter to eight when in harbour?" Fingal's long-empty tummy growled.

"Still the same," he said with a smile. "The Royal Navy's a creature of habit and routine, O'Reilly," the PMO said, suddenly serious. "And that applies to our customs too, so please don't mind me correcting you on form. Some of the more senior regular officers, particularly in the executive branch, gunnery, torpedoes, navigation—"

Fingal wondered if his old friend Tom Laverty was on board, but refrained from asking. Since 1931 they had maintained a desultory correspondence, and the last letter Fingal had had was from this ship and had been posted in Malta. Tom had been going to get married.

"—that kind of thing, they're very old school and can be sticky about etiquette and naval customs. Can't have my staff getting a dose from the bottle for some trivial infringement. Rather ironic, don't you think, considering we're the ones giving out doses?" He chuckled.

"I'll remember, sir." And Fingal recalled that a "bottle" was a reprimand, not a medication.

"Good man, and while we're at it, in here we aren't usually formal except in front of the lower-deck patients, and we're quite democratic with our sick berth attendants too." He offered his hand, which Fingal shook. "I'm Richard."

"Fingal."

"Trinity, Dublin, I believe, Fingal. Fine school."

"Yes, sir."

"It's Richard."

"Sorry, sir. I mean sorry, Richard. That's going to take some getting used to when I'm sure the other officers will expect the deference due to their rank."

"They will, but you'll not forget."

Fingal nodded. "I am Trinity," he said. "And you're?"

"Cambridge for my university and Guy's, actually, for my teaching hospital."

Fingal smiled. Already by the man's Oxbridge accent he'd given himself away as upper-crust English, and it seemed impossible for any graduate from the famous London institution to answer questions about their alma mater without tacking on "actually" to Guy's.

"Joined the navy straight after I graduated in '07. Destroyers first, then light cruisers. HMS *Galatea*."

Fingal whistled. "She first reported sighting the German ships at the battle of Jutland in 1916 and she took a hit from an enemy shell that didn't explode. I was born in '08 and only vaguely aware there'd been a naval battle eight years later, but I read a fair bit of naval history when I was on *Tiger*."

"*Galatea*'s where I started getting my trauma schooling." Richard Wilcoxson's earlier good-natured tone then took on an edge and, as was often the way of old warriors, he changed the subject. "Be grateful for your youth, Fingal. I don't want to discourage you, but we can have our moments at sea even if nobody's shooting at us." He yawned mightily.

"I think I understand." Fingal saw again the dark bags under his senior's eyes.

"I don't mean to sound patronising, but I doubt it. We've had a pretty rough time—literally—since the beginning of the month."

"Oh?"

"We were in the Med when war broke out. Admiral A. B. Cunningham used us as his flagship for the Mediterranean Fleet. Not much happened. We were based in Alexandria."

"His father was a professor of anatomy at Trinity. He was before my time, but we used his dissection manuals."

"So did we. I had no idea he was ABC's dad. Interesting. Anyway, we were ordered to join the Home Fleet. We left Gibraltar on November the sixth for Greenock, but were redirected to Halifax, Nova Scotia, for escort work. In all my thirty-two years at sea I've never seen a series of storms like it. Both outward and inward bound. Non-bloody-stop screeching winds, huge waves, and *Warspite*'s a notoriously wet ship. Spray was thrown so high it was hitting the bridge. Because of the oil in the tanks flowing about when they're only half full, she does a double roll to each side. Poor old Johnson fell down a companionway. Bust his tibia and fibula. Precious little sleep for any of the crew and the medical department were kept busy. Johnson wasn't the only one to get knocked about."

"Sounds pretty hellish." Fingal had no trouble remembering North Atlantic winter gales.

"It was. Before the war, the RMS *Queen Mary* could do Southampton to New York in about four days. It took us nine to get from

Halifax to here. Whole damn convoy had to heave to for two days so some of the smaller ships could ride out the gale. We made eighteen miles—sideways. Still," he managed a smile, "weather like that keeps the U-boats at bay so I suppose we should be thankful for small mercies. We only got into the anchorage yesterday. Sent Johnson and some of the more badly battered cases that were better dealt with by specialists ashore."

A head appeared around the curtain. It was the chief petty officer who had opened the door to the sick bay when Fingal had arrived. "Excuse me, sir, can you take anudder look at Engine Room Artificer Stewart please, sir? His temperature's gone up." The man had a thick Dublin accent.

Commander Wilcoxson rose. "CPO Padraic O'Rourke, I'd like you to meet Surgeon Lieutenant O'Reilly. He's joining us."

There was of course no question of a handshake. The middle-aged, thickset man smiled at Fingal. "Welcome aboard, sir." He cocked his head to one side. "O'Reilly? Irish?"

Fingal nodded.

"Dere was a young fellah of dat name once worked for Doctor Phelim Corrigan in Dublin—"

"In Aungier Place." Fingal laughed.

The CPO's grin was vast. "I'm from Frances Street in the Liberties meself. My cousin, John-Joe Finnegan, lives there too, on High Street. Him and me have a jar or two together when I'm home on leave. He bust his ankle a few years ago. I remember him saying he knew a Doctor O'Reilly. Said he was a good skin."

"I left Dublin a couple of years back. I'm in County Down now. But it's a small world," said Fingal, who was warmed inside by being remembered.

"It is dat. And saving your presences, Doctors, it'll be grand altogether to have another Irishman—even if you are from the wee north, sir—among all the Sassenachs on this ship. Most of the lower deck are from London, the Midlands, and we even have some hairy-kneed Scotsmen. There is another northerner. CPO Thompson, a gunner from Holywood."

"Not far from my home in Ballybucklebo," Fingal said, "but I can't claim to know him."

"And I thought one bog-Irishman was enough, Paddy," Wilcoxson said, and they both laughed.

From that exchange, it was clear that his superior officer was no martinet and allowed his staff a fair bit of leeway. He turned to Fingal. "And if you take my advice, Fingal, if you're ever stuck medically, ask CPO Paddy O'Rourke."

Fingal had learned as a student that it was an *amadán,* an idiot, who ignored the advice of senior nursing sisters. The sick berth attendants, particularly the petty officers, would fill the same roles here. "I'll remember."

"Fair play til you, sir, I t'ink you'll fit in grand altogether."

"And I think, Paddy, that you and my young colleague here are a couple of . . . what's the word?—um—bletherskites. Perhaps we should see the victim?"

"Right dis way, sir."

"And I'll explain a bit more about the medical facilities as we walk," Wilcoxson said.

Fingal followed them through the room he'd first entered and into the sick bay proper.

Richard Wilcoxson pointed to where the curtain they had just passed was continued to Fingal's right. "Sick berth staff's mess is in there."

From where they stood, the large open space in front of them was L-shaped. Fingal could see a row of scuttles in the far bulkhead, so that must be the farther side of the ship's hull. Lockers, a table, benches, washbasins, and shelves took up this part of the L. At its far end, where the room extended aft, he could see another curtained-off area astern.

"Bathroom," said Wilcoxson, who must have been watching Fingal's eyes. Between it and the for'ard bulkhead were four two-tiered swinging cots arranged two abreast. Three were occupied, presumably by the not-so-badly damaged victims of the storm and the patient under discussion. "If we were to get more than eight patients we have room to sling nine hammocks. And if all that ever became full, we'd overflow into the mess decks, but so far it hasn't happened—so far." The tone of his voice was not confident. "And this isn't the only medical space. We use the sick bay unless we are in battle." He stopped walking, forcing Fingal and Paddy O'Rourke to do the same.

Paddy, who must have heard it all before, waited.

"If we are likely to be shelled," said Wilcoxson, "the idea is to protect the medical staff and most of the equipment and supplies behind more armour, more deeply inside the ship."

"Like the surgeon working on the orlop deck well beneath the waterline in Nelson's navy?" Fingal said. He'd been a devoted follower of C. S. Forester's Captain Hornblower novels.

"Exactly. There are two spaces called medical distributing centres amidships, one fore, one aft on the middle deck, that's just below this one, but it's four decks down from the open air. They are always partially set up and supplied. One MO; the dentist, who can give anaesthetics; and three sick bay attendants work aft. You, and me now that you've joined, and the other five SBAs will work for'ard if the ship gets into a fight—and she will sooner or later. There are first-aid parties detailed to look after the wounded where they fall, mostly bandaging and giving morphine, and stretcher parties to bring them to us. The ship's bandsmen double up as stretcher bearers. We're meant to stay below and not go on deck except under exceptional circumstances." He laughed. "Apparently we're more use alive than dead."

"Comforting thought," Fingal said.

"Isn't it?" Wilcoxson chuckled. "Anyway, I'll show you the distributing centres some other day. Now we've a patient to see." He led the way to the nearest cot, where a young man lay in the lower berth.

"For your information, Lieutenant O'Reilly, Engine Room Artificer Stewart, the patient, is twenty-t'ree," Paddy said, "never been sick before. Commander Wilcoxson saw him this morning when the patient reported sick with vague pains in his belly, loss of appetite—"

Fingal's tummy gurgled. He himself was not suffering from that particular symptom.

"—and a low fever of ninety-nine point two and that was about the length and the breadth of it. Dirty tongue, he smokes, and a bit of bad breath, but there were no real physical findings, so he was admitted for observation. There wasn't much change until I took his temperature before I reported, sir. It'd gone up to a hundred, and although there was nuttin' else in particular I could find"—he screwed up his face and shook his head—"I don't like the look of him."

When a senior nurse felt like that it was time to take heed, and already Richard had praised CPO O'Rourke's acumen. Fingal paid attention.

The party arrived at the cot where a young, fair-haired man lay. Fingal noticed a sheen of sweat on his forehead and how pale he looked. The man stiffened and Fingal realised that the patient was trying to lie at attention.

"At ease, Stewart," Wilcoxson said. "How are you feeling?"

"Pretty bloody peely-wally, sir."

Fingal heard the lowland Scots burr. "Peely-wally" was not a strange expression to him. Ulster folk also used it to mean feeling rotten.

"This is Surgeon Lieutenant O'Reilly," Wilcoxson said, then sat on the cot and stopped it swinging by bracing his foot on the ship's sole. "CPO O'Rourke's been telling me you've not got any better since this morning."

"I have not, sir. My belly's awfully sore there." He pointed to his epigastrium, the inverted V where the lower ribs and breastbone met.

Wilcoxson nodded. "Have you thrown up?"

"No, sir. But I could not eat a gnat."

"Anything else?"

"No, sir."

Wilcoxson turned. "Lieutenant O'Reilly? Opinion?"

"ERA Stewart," Fingal said, and smiled at the man. He didn't want the patient to feel as if he were being discussed like an anonymous lump of illness. "I'm sorry you're not feeling too sharp."

"Aye, it's not so grand, sir, but I think I'll live."

The lad had spirit. "I've no doubt you will, and I have to say"—he divided his attention between the ERA and the principal medical officer—"I'm not sure what ails you, Stewart. There are absolutely no other symptoms?"

Wilcoxson shook his head. "Nary the one."

"Would you like me to examine him, sir?" Although what he was hoping to find was unclear to Fingal.

"I examined him fully this morning. Really nothing to go on," Wilcoxson said, and stood. "I don't expect there'll be anything new to find."

Vague pains in the belly could presage a host of developing disorders, Fingal thought, and any discussion of them would take place out of the patient's hearing.

Wilcoxson turned to Paddy. "Keep an eye on him and let us know if anything important changes. You'll know where to find me, Mister O'Rourke."

"Aye, aye, sir."

It was important to be formal in front of the patients, and CPOs, less formally called Chief, were entitled to the title of Mister.

"Just try to rest, Stewart."

"Thank you, sir."

"Right, Lieutenant O'Reilly, come with me."

They had to walk halfway across the sick bay to get to the door leading to the lobby outside and the companionway up. Once they were out of the patient's hearing, Wilcoxson said, "Stewart's apparently a good lad. I've spoken with his divisional officer and we don't think he's swinging the lead, trying to be excused duties. I think he is sick." He stopped for a moment. "Are you a betting man, Fingal?"

Fingal laughed. "I've been known to risk a bob or two."

"Right then, a pink gin says he's going to blow up acute appendicitis before midnight."

"You're on, Richard." Fingal offered a hand, which was shaken. He agreed with his senior's opinion, but thought the price of a pink gin worth it, if only to further an early developing friendship.

"Good." Richard opened the door. "We'll settle that bet later, once we've made a final diagnosis. For the time being, when we get to the wardroom anteroom I'll introduce you to my other staff. And as a welcome aboard, the first drink's on me."

Fingal grinned. From what he'd already seen of his senior, it would seem unlikely he'd take umbrage at a request for something other than the naval officers' preferred tipple of sweet Plymouth gin with a hint of Angostura bitters. "I don't suppose you'd be willing to buy me a Jameson instead?"

"Bloody bog-trotter," Richard Wilcoxson said, but his grin was relaxed and natural. "I think Paddy was right, Fingal." He produced a mangled stage-Irish impersonation. "Fair play 'til you, sir. I t'ink you'll fit in here, grand altogether."

9

He Had a Fever

"Four pints, please, Willie," O'Reilly said, "and can you bring them over when they're ready?" He inclined his head to where Barry, Donal, and Rory Auchinleck sat in the midst of the packed pub. Saturday evening and every table in the Mucky Duck was taken, with men standing shoulder to shoulder at the bar. The hum of conversation, bursts of laughter, clinking of glasses on the bar and on tabletops rose and fell.

"Aye certainly, Doc." Willie Dunleavy had to raise his voice to be heard. He started to pour the black ale into four straight glasses. "Did youse get Kinky moved in all right, the day?"

"We did indeed." O'Reilly smiled. The only way to keep anything confidential in Ballybucklebo was to tell no one but yourself . . . and even then it might get out.

"That's good. Councillor Bishop come in earlier for a wee jar. He was blowing til everybody how he'd loaned youse a van for free. He's not the boy til hide his light under a bushel, so he's not. Mind you," Willie lowered his voice until it was just audible, "and no harm til Mister Bishop, but he's been a much nicer man since he took that wee turn last Halloween and scared the living bejasus out of himself." Willie let the Guinness in the glasses settle.

O'Reilly laughed. "Bertie isn't a shy man. He's always believed in credit where credit's due—particularly when it's due to him." He fished out his briar and lit up, adding to the tobacco fug that struggled with the smell of beer for supremacy in the low-ceilinged single room. "I'd better get back to my table, Willie."

"Run you away on, Doctor." Willie made the second pour into each glass. "I'll bring them over the minute they've settled and are ready."

O'Reilly passed a table where Gerry Shanks was telling a joke to his friends. Gerry nodded to O'Reilly but didn't break his stride. ". . . so there's your mountaineer man on a ledge a hundred feet down, both arms broken, and this other climber higher up throws him down a rope and says he, 'Grab you on til that there with your teeth and I'll get you up here, so I will.' "

O'Reilly saw the grins on the men's faces, heard their chuckles already beginning. Gerry had a reputation as a storyteller.

"So the one at the top starts pulling away and pulling away." Gerry accompanied his words with the motions of a man hauling hand over hand on a rope. "He's working like blue blazes."

O'Reilly had to hear the punch line.

"And then, as your other man's head appears level with the safe ground, the one pulling gasps, takes a big deep breath, and says, 'Are you all right, Paddy?'

" 'I aaaaaaaaaaaaaaaam,' says Paddy," and as Gerry spoke he let his voice fall from a yell to a whisper.

Every man in the group guffawed loudly. So did O'Reilly.

"That was a right cracker, Gerry. Nice one." Charlie Gorman, Gerry's best friend, banged his nearly empty pint glass on the table, allowed a suitable pause to let everybody relish the humour, and said, "Now, did youse all hear the one about the fellah from Alma Street?"

"Is Alma that wee narrow back street off the Falls Road in Belfast?" Fergus Finnegan, the bowlegged jockey, asked.

"Aye, you're dead on. Well, your man gets a powerful skinful and wins an elephant at the coconut shy at the August Lammas Fair in Ballycastle—"

"An elephant," said Gerry, rolling his eyes and looking sceptical. "Pull the other leg. It has bells on."

"Come on, Gerry, we all know there's about as much chance of seeing an elephant as there is of a grown man hanging on to a rope with his teeth, but that's what made your yarn work. Now give me a chance, it's only a gag, so hould your wheest."

"Fair play," said Fergus. "Give Charlie the floor."

"Go ahead, Charlie," Gerry said.

"Thank you, and you'll all have to be patient. This is a bloody good story and takes a wee while til tell right. Soooooo, anyroad, your man brings this bloody great pachyderm back til Alma Street and tethers it til a lamppost and goes off til bed . . ."

O'Reilly chuckled. When some Ulstermen got into competive storytelling it was like two gunslingers in the Wild West shooting it out. He'd have liked to hear the end of the yarn, but his friends were waiting.

O'Reilly'd barely taken his seat when Willie, pursued by Brian Boru, the pub's feisty Chihuahua, appeared with the pints. O'Reilly paid with a ten-shilling note, which would exactly cover the cost.

"Cheers, Fingal," Barry said, and raised his glass to the accompanying toasts of two of the others. Rory nodded but did not drink.

"*Sláinte*," said O'Reilly, drinking and relishing the beer's bittersweet taste. "And thank you all for your help."

Barry simply smiled, but Donal said, "No bother, and sure wasn't it a great pleasure to see the Auchinlecks settled? I mind how excited Julie and me was when we moved intil our wee house." He chuckled. "You all know about the Stone-Age grave on the site at Dun Bwee? The National Trust have it open til the public now—and I got permission from one of their highheejins for her to do it, so Julie's going a humdinger selling afternoon teas in the back garden for the visitors, so she is, and I'm carving wee hairy-looking men with spears and clubs for the customers til buy for souvenirs, like. And I've another wee sideline going too." He winked at O'Reilly.

O'Reilly laughed. Trust Donal to find a potential for profit. He wondered what the "wee sideline" might be, but refrained from asking.

Charlie Gorman's voice could be heard over the buzz, and by his inflection it sounded as if he'd finally got to the punch line. "'Och, missus,' says your elephant man who's woke up with a ferocious headsplitter, 'don't be ridiculous. My elephant couldn't possibly do that to your wee pussy cat.' And she says, 'It did so.'" Charlie paused for effect. "'It took its big foot and went—'" He stamped his foot on the floor to a momentary pause, then gales of laughter and a round of applause.

O'Reilly laughed. He'd missed too much of the story to understand the joke, but the laughter of the Ulsterfolk was terribly infectious.

"Your man Charlie Gorman's the quare gag, so he is. He'd make a cat laugh," Donal said.

"He's a comedian, all right," Barry said, "but you're no slouch yourself when you're telling a story, Donal. I still remember the one about the Kerryman and the dead greyhound."

"Away off and chase yourself, Doctor Laverty," Donal said, but O'Reilly could tell by the man's buck-toothed grin he was delighted to be complimented.

O'Reilly sank another third of his pint.

Rory said nothing, barely raised a smile, and toyed with his pint.

For a moment, O'Reilly wondered if Archie's son was all right. He'd been sluggish about lifting boxes back at the Auchinlecks' home and had nearly declined O'Reilly's offer to come for a pint.

O'Reilly looked more closely. Rory was sweating like a pig and pale as parchment, but before Fingal could ask how he was feeling, a man stopped at the table and said, "Excuse me, Doctor O'Reilly."

O'Reilly recognised Hall Campbell, the fisherman who'd moved here from Ardglass last year and was buying Jimmy Scott's fishing boat. Jenny had made a very astute diagnosis of patent ductus arteriosus, a congenital heart defect, which had been successfully repaired surgically. "Yes, Hall?"

"I've not seen Doctor Bradley about the place for a brave wee while, but I heard tell she's come back to us. When you see her, would you tell her I'm going round like a liltie since I got over the operation and say thanks very much."

"I'll do that. She was off taking a course, but she's back now. She'll be pleased to hear."

"She done me a power of good, so she did, sir. I've more energy than I've had for years." He laughed. "I need it. The herring's running great this year, so they are, and we've been netting the odd mackerel this week. They should be coming in in shoals soon too."

"I'm very glad to hear it, Hall. Very glad," O'Reilly said.

"Aye," said Hall. He tilted his head to one side. "Jimmy tells me you like an evening at the mackerel fishing, sir."

O'Reilly, who had just finished his pint, said, "I do that."

"If you'd like I'll let you know when they're in and I'll take you out."

"That would be wonderful," O'Reilly said, "and if it would be all right I'll bring Mrs. O'Reilly too?"

"More the merrier," said Hall. "I'll be running on now, sir, but I'll see you soon."

Now that was something to look forward to. An evening out on Belfast Lough, lines in the water trolling for the silver-and-blue fish— and they were great eating too. He glanced at his watch. Better not be late for dinner.

Another roar of laughter came from Gerry Shanks's table and Charlie Gorman yelled, "Five more pints, Willie." An adjoining table had been pushed over to join Gerry's and the evening was beginning to develop the attributes of a spontaneous party. A voice said, "Maybe we'll get Alan Hewitt to give us a tune?"

O'Reilly'd not mind hearing Helen Hewitt's dad. He had a great voice. There might be time to listen and have another pint before Kitty expected them home. O'Reilly was about to signal Willie, but Rory said, "Excuse me, sir, I don't want to spoil the fun—"

The man's pint was hardly touched.

"—but could Donal maybe run me back to barracks? I just come over funny there now. I thought it was just a wee turn. Jasus," he said, "I'm weak as a bloody kitten. I was feeling grand this morning so I'd no reason to go on sick parade, but I'm bollixed now, so I am."

O'Reilly reflexively reached for the man's wrist to take his pulse. The skin was hot and clammy and when he counted for fifteen seconds and multiplied by four, Rory's pulse was 112 instead of a steady 88. "You have a fever, Rory."

The noise from the party, the people at his own table, seemed to have vanished as O'Reilly concentrated on trying to discover how sick Rory was.

The man's teeth chattered. "I have something, sir, for I'm bloody well frozen." He shivered.

Probably a summer flu, O'Reilly thought. It wouldn't take long to run him up to Holywood and get him under the care of his regimental doctor, but something made O'Reilly ask, "Have you ever had anything like it before?"

"Aye, twice now."

"When?"

Rory made a brrrrr noise, shivered, and said, "The regiment'd been back from thon peacekeeping in Cyprus for about two months, that's about ten months ago. The doc said it was flu. I was like this for four or five days. I'd sweat something ferocious at night—"

O'Reilly made a mental note of that.

"—then about six months ago I'd another go for about a week, just like the one before. We'd a new MO then, young fellah just out of Queens and basic army training. He said it was flu too." Rory shivered again. "And this attack's come on like the first two."

"Everything all right, Fingal?" Barry asked.

"No. Rory has a fever. I'm trying to sort him out. Just be a minute." That he was doing it in a pub was irrelevant. A sick patient needed care on the spot, be it in a familiar pub or outside a blazing bomb crater on a stricken battleship. "We may have to take him back to Number One, so hang on a tic, please." O'Reilly concentrated on the job in hand. Two recent attacks of flu? This would be a third bout in less than a year. That wasn't right. "You were in Cyprus for how long?" he asked.

"A year, sir."

"Been stationed anywhere else abroad?"

"No, sir."

If Rory had been, O'Reilly would have suspected malaria, whose victims kept on having relapses, but to his knowledge there was no malaria in Cyprus. Still, three bouts of flu? He shook his head. He supposed a poker player *could* fill three full houses in three consecutive deals, but he'd not bet on it. "As I see it," O'Reilly said, "you may have flu, but it could be something else." Recurrent fever, rapid pulse and chills, and night sweats over a short time frame after returning from the Mediterranean? O'Reilly had a fair idea of what was wrong. "You need to be examined properly."

"You're the doctor, sir." Rory shuddered.

"I can nip home, get my car, run you up to the barracks, let your MO take care of you, or, and it's closer, head for my surgery, get a good look at you and see if we can work out what ails you."

"I'd like that, sir." He took a deep breath and said, "And if you'd have an aspirin, sir? My head's pounding fit to beat Bannagher."

"I have in the surgery," said O'Reilly. "Can you stand up?"

"Aye." Rory staggered to his feet and O'Reilly put an arm round the man's waist. He was heavy and O'Reilly recognised that he was going to need help getting Rory to Number One. He lowered Rory back into his seat. "Donal, Barry, Rory's not well and I want to get him to the surgery. Donal, fetch the van and come right up to the front door."

"Right, sir." Donal, presumably believing in waste not, want not, sank the remains of his pint and trotted off.

"We'll give Donal a few minutes, Barry, then you help me oxter-cog Rory out to the van."

"Right."

"I'll explain what I'm thinking once we get him home."

"Fair enough," Barry said, clearly stifling his professional curiosity.

"Willie. Gentlemen," O'Reilly roared in his best force-ten-gale voice, "your attention please." He was not going to submit Rory to the spectacle of being half-dragged out of the Mucky Duck without an explanation. Otherwise it might be all over town the next day that Rory had been stocious. And the poor man hadn't even had a sip of his beer. The conversations died. Every eye was on O'Reilly.

"Rory here's not very well—"

A chorus of "och" and "oh dear" and "poor lad" sounded throughout the pub.

"He's not infectious so you've nothing to worry about and Doctor Laverty and I can manage, so don't let us spoil your fun. But I just wanted you all to know." He nodded to Barry and between them they each got one of Rory's arms round a shoulder, lifted him to his feet, and with him trying to take short steps headed for the doors that Gerry was holding open.

By the time they had Rory loaded into the van O'Reilly too, was sweating, but not sufficiently to distract him from trying to formulate a diagnosis. It was the combination of Rory's having been in the Mediterranean followed by three apparent bouts of flu that had given the clues. Lord knew O'Reilly'd seen enough cases when *Warspite* had left the Atlantic and been based at Alexandria in Egypt later in the war. A few confirmatory physical findings and a simple blood test he could do at Number One would clinch the diagnosis— and to do so would get Rory on the road to recovery and give a great deal of professional satisfaction to a simple country GP.

10

My Belly Was Bitter

"Sorry to interrupt, gentlemen," Richard Wilcoxson said from a few feet away. "Finish what you're saying, but then can I have a word, Fingal?"

Fingal, his first glass of Jameson in hand, had been in the middle of a lively conversation with Bangorman and old friend Lieutenant-Commander Tom Laverty, *Warspite*'s navigating officer. Tom had worn well, his fair hair thick but cut short, his eyes blue and alert. There were deep lines at their angles. The one thing that had changed was that Tom had married in March 1938, but that was as far as the two men had got on personal matters in the crowded room.

"Excuse me, Tom, Davy." Surgeon Lieutenant David Jones, the other member of the conversational trio, was a dark-haired Aberystwyth native and a fierce supporter of the Welsh rugby team. Quite naturally, the Welshman answered to "Davy" and took good-naturedly the inevitable jokes about his mythical Davy Jones's locker, where it was believed dead sailors fetched up. Sometimes, Davy had told Fingal, it was even suggested that sailors might end up there with a bit of help from a certain sawbones of the same name.

The mess anteroom he crossed was furnished and functioning like a gentleman's club with a highly select membership, which in many ways in the peacetime navy it was. There was, O'Reilly thought, something essentially British about having a piano in a room near the aft main fifteen-inch armament, and that an Oërlikon antiaircraft gun was mounted on the deck immediately overhead. They'd be some percussion section when they opened up, an event which sooner or later was going to happen. In late 1939, the war was fairly static, but things were bound to start heating up. "Yes, Richard," Fingal said, after taking a few steps away to where the senior waited.

"Paddy O'Rourke's been along to tell me that Stewart's taken a turn for the worse."

"So you'd like me to go and see him?" Fingal coughed. His pipe was adding to the tobacco smoke fug in the room. The wardroom anteroom and immediately adjoining wardroom for officers above the rank of sub-lieutenant was on the port side on the upper deck just ahead of X turret. Sub-lieutenants, midshipmen (known as snotties), and clerks had their own mess on the same deck on the starboard side. The anteroom hummed with the pre-dinner chatter of the off-duty officers, many of whom Fingal had now met and most of whose names had already become lost. No matter. In the weeks and months to come, he'd be getting to know them better.

Richard smiled. "Both of us will go. Judging by the report, I think I'll be getting that pink gin from you later. Seems he's chucked up and says the pain's in his right lower belly now."

"Sounds like appendicitis." There were other diagnostic possibilities, but as one of Fingal's teachers used to remark, "If you saw a bird on a telegraph wire in Dublin, it was more likely to be a sparrow than a canary." Common things occurred most often. Fingal was glad that, contrary to his usual approach, he had sipped his first Jameson slowly, knowing he might have to work.

"I've told Paddy and Leading Sick Berth Attendant Barker to prepare the operating theatre. It'll take a minute or two, but we'd better get back to the sick bay, take a look at the patient. I'm pretty sure we'll be operating." He turned to David Jones. "You stay and enjoy yourself, Davy, and try to get an early night. I want you to take the morning watch tomorrow. Give Fingal a chance for some shut-eye and with a bit of luck, you'll not be disturbed between four and eight A.M. You've earned a breather, Davy. Fingal and I can manage between now and then."

Fingal was sure that they could. He'd not eaten since breakfast and with only a small amount of whiskey aboard his knees felt a bit rubbery, but he knew he was far from drunk. If he had been, he'd have apologised to Davy Jones—but asked him to do the work.

Wilcoxson turned back to Fingal. "You can anaesthetise, can't you?"

Fingal swallowed. Certainly as students they'd all been made to give a few, but he was no expert. "Yes." He tried to sound confident. He'd assumed he'd be assisting.

"No rest for the wicked, eh, Fingal?" Tom Laverty said. "Nor for me. I'm going to be busy tonight, then I've got a week's leave. My wife Carol's staying in a boarding house here in Greenock . . ."

Fingal's friend needed to say no more and he envied him. "Lucky devil," Fingal said. "Enjoy your leave, give my love to Carol, and we'll get a chance for a blether once you're back. A lot's happened to both of us since the year of our Lord 1931. I want to hear what you've been up to." Fingal put down his unfinished drink. He turned to the PMO. "Ready when you are, Richard."

He sighed as together they began the walk back to the sick bay. Talk about being chucked in at the deep end? Only on board for a few hours, not yet able to find his way around the labyrinth of passageways, hatches, and lobbies, and now about to give an anaesthetic, something for which he was hardly trained. Still, what did the lower-deck sailors say? "You shouldn't join if you can't take a joke," a way of expressing that all sailors were expected to take everything the service threw their way and deal with it. He just hoped he could.

To add insult to injury, dinner was going to be served in ten minutes and almost certainly by the time they'd finished with the patient the meal would be over. Unless things had changed since the last time Fingal O'Reilly had set foot on one of his majesty's ships, tonight he was going to have to settle for a late supper of bully beef sandwiches and hot greasy cocoa.

"Any change?" Wilcoxson asked Paddy O'Rourke, who had met them in the sick bay.

"He's thrown up twice more, sir, and his temperature's one hundred and one point eight."

"Come on then," said Wilcoxson, "let's take a look at the victim."

"Ronnie Barker's setting up next door," Paddy said.

When they arrived at the patient's cot, Fingal became aware of a smell of vomit and the man's clearly worsening condition.

"The doctors have come back to see you, Stewart," said Paddy O'Rourke.

Commander Wilcoxson stood beside the cot looking down. "How are you feeling?"

"Pretty crock, sir. Pain's down in my right side and it's a damn sight worse now."

"You've upchucked?"

"Aye, sir. Three times."

"Stick out your tongue."

O'Reilly could see how furred it was and even from where he was standing on the far side of the bed he could smell the patient's halitosis.

Wilcoxson sat on the cot and was taking the man's pulse. "Hundred and twenty," he said. "Now let's see your belly." He pulled the blankets down, opened the patient's pyjama jacket.

O'Reilly noticed a likeness of Popeye the Sailor Man tattooed on the patient's chest and "Janet" in a scroll underneath a heart pierced by an arrow.

Wilcoxson undid the trousers string, and began a running commentary. "No obvious abnormalities. Abdominal wall moves on respiration."

So, Fingal thought, there's probably no generalised peritonitis. If the membrane lining the abdominal cavity was infected, breathing would cause the patient severe pain and he would tighten up his abdominal muscles to prevent that.

"No visible peristalsis . . ."

The bowel was not obstructed.

Wilcoxson put the earpieces of his stethoscope in his ears and the bell on the patient's belly. "Plenty of borborygmi."

So, the bowel was contracting and making its usual rumbles and gurgles, more evidence that it wasn't paralysed because of infection of the entire peritoneal membrane. If that were the case, the belly would be as silent as the tomb, and if a sulphonamide couldn't cure the infection, it would indeed be Davy Jones's locker for the victim. Fingal gave an involuntary shudder and was grateful that Stewart's condition was not so dire.

"Tell me if this hurts," Wilcoxson said, and began gently to palpate the abdomen, initially avoiding the right lower quadrant. The patient lay quietly until Wilcoxson's questioning fingers reached there, then Stewart sucked in his breath. "Bit of guarding," Wilcoxson said, and suddenly released the pressure.

"*Yeow.* Jings, sir, that hurt like the very devil."

"Sorry, Stewart."

So there was localised peritonitis over the spot where the appendix lay. The patient, by tightening his muscles, was trying to protect himself from pain—called guarding—but the sudden movement when the fingers' pressure was released caused the muscles to spring out, thus moving the undoubtedly inflamed membrane. It was called rebound tenderness and the finding of it in that precise spot, taken in conjunction with the other symptoms and signs, was pretty conclusive of a diagnosis of—

"Appendicitis," Wilcoxson said. "You were right, Paddy."

The CPO inclined his head.

"It'll have to come out," Wilcoxson said.

O'Reilly was surprised to see the width of the patient's grin, which he quickly hid. "So will I have to go to the Glasgow Royal Infirmary, sir?"

Where Robert Lister had first described aseptic surgical techniques in 1860 and revolutionised the whole discipline of surgery. Fingal had a sudden memory of being back at Trinity College, sitting in Professor Ball's classroom.

"Or mebbe the Royal Alexandra Infirmary in Paisley?"

"'Fraid not, Stewart. It's a pretty simple procedure. Doctor O'Reilly here will give the anaesthetic."

O'Reilly inhaled deeply.

"And CPO O'Rourke will assist and look after the instruments."

"Och, and I'm from the Gorbals, sir."

A tenement district of Glasgow as notorious for its squalor and poverty as was the Liberties in Dublin.

"I thought I could mebbe have recovered at home." Stewart's voice was crestfallen.

O'Reilly could feel for the man and was going to ask why that couldn't be arranged. After all, some of the injured after the last convoy had been sent ashore. But a look from Wilcoxson killed the unspoken words. "Regulations. Sorry about that," Wilcoxson said. "Now, CPO O'Rourke, will you see to the prep, please?"

"Aye, aye, sir."

The unfortunate would need a pubic shave and the painting of his belly with an antiseptic before he was taken through to the operating theatre.

O'Reilly thought it was pretty cavalier not letting the man go to a civilian facility, especially as his home was nearby. It was a matter O'Reilly was going to raise when the patient and CPO were out of earshot.

"Come along, Doctor O'Reilly, and we'll change and start getting ready." Wilcoxson walked to the curtain at the end of the sick bay.

O'Reilly now knew what was in there. He closed the curtain.

"We change in here," Wilcoxson said, stripping off his sweater. "Lockers beside you have surgical whites and you can hang your clothes in the left-hand locker."

O'Reilly began to strip. "Commander Wilcoxson," he said. It was always tactful to show deference to rank if you were going to question the judgment of a senior officer. "I'd have thought it would have made a lot of sense to transfer the man ashore, and it would be a kindness to let him convalesce at home. He is entitled to sick leave after all." As he spoke, O'Reilly asked himself, Are you honestly consumed with compassion for the man or trying desperately to get out of giving the anaesthetic?

"No," Wilcoxson said, hauling on a pair of white trousers, "we'll operate on board, and"—he pointed at a set of double doors directly ahead—"the isolation ward's through there, remember?" He lowered his voice. "We'll nurse Stewart in it postoperatively."

O'Reilly frowned. "Why, sir? I thought postappendicectomy cases were usually looked after on the general ward."

Wilcoxson laughed as he hauled on a white linen top. "First of all, Fingal, it's Richard. Secondly, I never mind younger doctors questioning my judgment. Shocking as you may find it, even surgeon commanders can be wrong from time to time, and remember, the patients' welfare always outranks the feelings of anyone with a medical degree."

"Thank you, Richard," O'Reilly said, and thought, I admire that attitude. It's not one often found in senior surgeons.

"You're wondering why do him here and why isolation? Because

I don't want him talking to anyone. I want him kept incommunicado. He can't have his mates visiting him in there. If he's all right by postop day three we will quietly send him home for a few weeks' recuperative leave—as long as we are still in port."

"I don't understand, sir. I mean, Richard."

"Lord, Fingal, if word gets out before we've gone to sea again that appendicitis, which is easy enough to pretend you have, is a sure ticket to Glasgow or Paisley, we could have every last man-jack or—" He smiled. "—perhaps since I'm in Scotland I should be saying every man-*jock*, reporting sick, clutching his belly, and hoping to get sent ashore too. We've no time for that."

"I'd never have thought of it." Fingal laughed. "And a friend of mine used to call me the Wily O'Reilly. I admire your reasoning."

"Experience, my boy. Experience. It'll all come to you with time, but now," he strode to the double doors, "let me show you the anaesthetic gear we have here. I'm sure you'll do perfectly fine with that."

O'Reilly followed his chief's example, tied on his own mask, and followed. His laugh faded. He wished he felt as confident in his abilities.

11

Nuisance of the Tropics

"Thanks, Barry," O'Reilly said. They were both breathing heavily. Rory Auchinleck was no featherweight, but with Donal's help they got him up on the examining couch in the surgery.

"Do you need me, Doctors? Should I be driving Rory anywhere once you've done your doctoring?"

"That's kind, Donal," said O'Reilly, "and thanks, but we'll take it from here. You get that van back to Bertie Bishop's builder's yard before his milk of human kindness starts to curdle."

"Right you are, Doc. Good luck, Rory; you're in grand hands with these two learnèd men, so you are." Donal tipped the brim of his duncher to the trio, turned on his heels, and left the surgery.

"Aspirin, aspirin," said O'Reilly, rummaging in a drawer of the rolltop desk. "Here." He shook two from the bottle and filled a glass with water. "Get those into you, lad."

"Thanks, Doc," Rory said.

"To bring you up to date, Doctor Laverty—I couldn't in the Duck or in front of Donal in the van—Rory was stationed in Cyprus for a year with the British contingent of the United Nations peacekeeping force that was making sure the Greek and Turkish Cypriots weren't at each other's throats."

"Your dad's delighted to have you home, Rory," Barry said, "and, coincidentally, so is his back."

Rory gave a short laugh, but his voice was weak. "Dad's been taking cricks in his back since I was a wee lad. It's all the lifting with his job, so it is." He grimaced and sucked in a breath.

"Anyway," O'Reilly said, "since Rory's been home in Ulster he's had two bouts of high fever, shivering, night sweats. Both were diagnosed as flu, by two different MOs. Today he's started to have a third attack. Without examining him, have you any notion what might be wrong, Doctor Laverty?"

"No," said Barry, "and to be honest I don't think examining you, Rory, would help me much either." He must have seen the man's frown. "But don't be worried," Barry said. "It's not because you've got something terrible, it's because Doctor O'Reilly made a point of telling me you were in a foreign country. I'd be willing to guess that he thinks you've picked up some foreign disease. Doctor O'Reilly knows much more about them than I do. My textbook of medicine only had fourteen pages on tropical diseases. They're pretty rare in Ulster so I didn't pay much attention."

"Aye," said O'Reilly, "things like kwashiorkor, beriberi, and bilharzia aren't exactly ten a penny here. But Doctor Laverty is being modest, Rory. He has diagnosed a tropical disease and his patient was most grateful." O'Reilly could tell by Barry's smile that he was remembering Alice Moloney's amoebic liver abscess. "And he's right about my thinking you picked up something in Cyprus. I just need to take a quick shufti at your neck and belly and do a simple blood test and we'll have a pretty good idea."

Rory shuddered. "Just go ahead, Doc. I feel foundered, so I do."

"I can believe it," O'Reilly said. "A high fever will make you feel cold." He moved to a small instrument cabinet. "I'm going to take a blood sample before I examine you. Usually we do the tests last, but this one needs time to develop. Can you roll up your left sleeve?"

O'Reilly took out a small syringe and deftly went through the steps to fill the barrel with blood, then removed the needle, put the swab over the puncture, and said to Rory, "Hold that there for a few minutes."

"Right, sir."

"Good." O'Reilly removed the rubber stopper, squirted the blood into the sample tube, and restoppered it. "It'll take about five or ten minutes and while that's going on I'll have a look at you, Rory. I'm sorry, I know you're cold, but I'm going to have to ask you to take off your pullover and shirt."

"Let me help you," Barry said, and did. "You do have a fever, Rory," he said.

Meanwhile O'Reilly left the sample tube on his desk and washed the syringe. He held his hands under a stream of warm water from the sink's tap. "Might as well get my paws warm before I start." He dried his hands and approached the couch. "Now," he said, "I'm going to give Doctor Laverty a running commentary, but don't let it worry you, Rory, because it won't take long and as soon as I've done I'll explain everything. One quick question. Were the bugs bad in Cyprus?"

"Aye. There were wee buggers called sand flies. The bites stung like bejizzis and you got a hell of an itchy bump."

"Mmmm," said O'Reilly, "we had those flies in Egypt too." He started to palpate Rory's neck. "No enlarged lymph nodes," he said. "If I'm right about what ails you, swollen nodes would be a rare finding anyway." And, he thought but didn't say, almost invariably present in cases of the lethal cancer of the lymphatic system, Hodgkin's disease, which, with its propensity to causing fevers and night sweats, could perhaps be confused with what O'Reilly sought. His hands moved into Rory's armpits each in turn. "No axillary nodes either." Even better. The diagnosis of Hodgkin's was becoming progressively more remote.

He listened with his stethoscope to Rory's breathing and heartbeat.

Although both were rapid, as was to be expected in a patient with a fever, there were no abnormalities of either.

"Tummy now," he said, and, starting at the top right, rapidly percussed the belly wall using his bent right index and middle fingers to rap the backs of his left middle and ring fingers. These were laid on the skin and produced a hollow sound except for a more dull note in an area extending about six inches below the margin of the left ribs. "Hear that, Barry?"

"I do. Is it the spleen?"

"I think so." O'Reilly laid his right hand flat, with his fingers pointing to the ribs on Rory's belly at a level slightly below the lower margin of the area that had been dull to percussion. He exerted pressure so his fingers pushed the abdominal wall inward. "Take a deep breath."

Rory did. Nothing touched O'Reilly's fingers. "And out." He moved his hand upward as Rory exhaled. "And in." This time the expansion of the young man's lungs and accompanying downward excursion of the diaphragm, the sheet of muscle that separates the chest from the abdominal cavity, pushed something solid inside against O'Reilly's questing fingertips. "It's spleen all right," O'Reilly said. That organ did become enlarged in Hodgkin's but usually late in the course of the illness. He repeated the examination on the patient's right side. "Liver's not enlarged." He handed the clothes back to Rory. "Put these on. You must be freezing."

While Rory got dressed, O'Reilly summarized the situation for Barry. "So we have a relapsing fever that started coming on several months after Rory left an area where sand fly bites were common, headache, shivering, night sweats, no enlarged lymph nodes, splenomegaly, but no hepatomegaly." He saw Rory's eyes widen. "Don't be scared, Rory. I promised I'd explain and I will in just a minute. The main thing is it's not cancer." Old Doctor Micks had drummed that into his students. Every sick patient had one overwhelming, usually unspoken, fear and as soon as any physician was certain that the patient was cancer-free it was the doctor's responsibility to allay those fears.

"Thanks, Doc," Rory said.

"Any ideas now, Barry?" O'Reilly asked.

Barry was frowning. "You've pretty well told me it's a tropical disease and the one that I can think of that half-fills the bill, recurrent bouts of fever and an enlarged spleen, is malaria, but it's spread by mosquitoes, not sand flies."

"You're right about the mosquitoes and close to being right about the condition," O'Reilly said, "but I know for a fact that Cyprus is the only foreign country Rory has been to, isn't that right?"

"Yes, sir."

"And malaria is not present in Cyprus."

"Then I'm stumped," Barry said.

"And I would be too if I hadn't served in the Mediterranean." He turned to Rory. "Doctor Laverty made a pretty good stagger at making a diagnosis. I doubt if many GPs in Ireland could put their finger on what I think you've got, but I was lucky to have seen a number of cases during the war. Those bloody sand flies. The female sand flies need proteins from blood from some animals, and that includes us humans, to ripen their eggs. When the flies bite, they inject an anti-coagulant, something to keep the blood flowing. That anticoagulant is what makes the bite swell up and itch. Sadly, though, the bugs carry a tiny wee beastie called *Leishmania donovani,* and they usually inject some of the wee beasties too, when they bite. When they multiply inside you, they're what give you a fever and make your spleen, the organ that removes old dead blood cells, get bigger. That's what 'splenomegaly' means. 'Hepatomegaly' means an enlarged liver and the disease can cause that too, but you don't have it."

"I'll be thankful for small mercies," Rory said. "But have I still got the wee buggers inside me?"

"I'm pretty sure you do," O'Reilly said. "If the test I'm doing is positive, I'll be ninety percent certain and we'll get you up to the fever hospital at Purdysburn where a specialist will take a sample from your bone marrow or possibly your spleen. I'll not lie. It'll sting for a minute or two when it's being done, but the only way to be absolutely certain is to look for the *Leishmania* there."

"And can you cure it, Doctor O'Reilly?"

"I used to when I had a sick bay where I could admit patients, but now we'll leave that up to the specialists at the hospital and let them do the curing. Now," he said, "Doctor Laverty, could you nip up to the hot press and get a blanket so we can keep Rory as comfortable as possible."

"I'm feeling a wee bit better," Rory said. "Them aspirin's working, so they are."

"Good," said O'Reilly. "Hang on and I'll start the other part of the test." He went to collect the sample tube. There was a dark brown-red clot at the bottom and a layer of yellow-coloured fluid, the serum, on top. If there was an increase in the level of globulin, a serum protein, as there would be in cases of visceral leishmaniasis, adding one drop of formalin to one millilitre of serum would render the mixture opaque in about ten minutes.

He busied himself pouring the serum into a fresh tube and adding the formalin, wrinkling his nose at the pungent fumes of the chemical used to preserve bodies in an anatomy dissection lab. O'Reilly couldn't ever smell it without in his mind being transported back to Trinity College and sharing lab time with Bob Beresford, Charlie Greer, and Donald Cromie, his closest friends. Those had been great days. The thirtieth class reunion they'd been planning for this year was approaching and there was still planning to be done.

Barry reappeared with a blanket and busied himself making Rory comfortable.

"If I've to go til Purdysburn, would I have to go now, I mean like right away? Is it an emergency?" He swallowed and O'Reilly had a quick flash of what Rory Auchinleck must have looked like as a little boy. He was frightened and who could blame him.

"It's not an emergency, and you're not in any immediate danger, but the sooner we get those little buggers out of your system, the better."

"So you'll tell my da and Kinky?" He blushed and giggled. "I'm very fond of her, so I am, but I just can never call her Ma."

"I hear you," O'Reilly said, "and I will of course let them know. And I'll tell them not to worry and that you're going to get better."

Rory snuggled down under his covering, still with a childlike look, but now somewhat more reassured. "Huh," said Rory, "some welcome home, me getting sick and all. Thanks for the blanket, Doctor Laverty. It's taking the edge off the chils."

O'Reilly stole a look at the tube. The pale yellow serum was a milky colour, so the Formol-gel test was positive. Unfortunately, it wasn't entirely specific for visceral leishmaniasis, or kala-azar, as the disease was also known, but it gave O'Reilly all he needed to say, "Bingo. It's the Purdysburn Fever Hospital for you, young fellow, one more test then you'll have to be given a drug called sodium antimony gluconate intravenously for three to ten days, but it'll marmalize the invaders."

"I'll be glad til get better." Rory frowned. "And will you let my platoon officer know too, please, sir?"

"I have to, in fact; I'll give your duty officer a call in a minute. I'm not altogether up with military protocol, but I'm sure he'll agree with what I'm proposing."

"Thank you, sir."

"Och, you'll be on your feet in no time," O'Reilly said, inwardly blessing all the extra experience his time on the old *Warspite* had given him. Of course by the time he'd been seeing cases of kala-azar in Egypt he was no longer the wet-behind-the-ears young surgeon lieutenant who had joined the ship at Greenock—and got pitched in at the deep end.

12

Emptied Some Dull Opiate . . .
and Lethewards Had Sunk

The ship's operating room looked to Fingal as if it could have been onshore—if it hadn't been rolling gently side to side. In here the smell of fuel oil was masked by the odour of disinfectant. The operating table was arranged fore and aft immediately in front of where Fingal stood with Richard Wilcoxson. Above it hung a huge multi-lensed operating light. A hand basin for scrubbing up was attached to the bulkhead to Fingal's left and two tiers of shelves stacked with instruments and sterile towels were on the farthest bulkhead. It would have been silent, but for the incessant rumble of machinery in the ship's bowels, the gentle whirring of an air supply fan in the lobby outside, and the sounds of a man's voice as Fingal came through the door.

"Appendix then, sir?"

"Leading SBA Barker, meet Surgeon Lieutenant O'Reilly. He's just joined and he'll be stunning the patient, and yes, it is an appendix."

"Hello, Barker," Fingal said, looking at a wiry, auburn-haired lad of about twenty-five. His eyes above his mask were green. The left one had a slight squint.

"Hello, Doc. Pleased to meet you, and welcome to *Warspite*."

"Thank you," Fingal said. "Londoner?" The man must have been born somewhere within the sound of Bow Bells. His accent was pure Cockney.

Wilcoxson said, "You should hear Barker and his oppo using—"

"Sorry, sir," O'Reilly said. "Oppo? I've forgotten."

Wilcoxson smiled. "Goes right back to the days of tarry pig-tails. Sailors paired off to help each other tie theirs so each had, in the parlance of the time, an opposite number, shortened to oppo."

"Oh, right."

"But Barker here would probably call Sick Bay Petty Officer Fletcher his old china—china plate. It means mate. You should hear the pair of Cockneys using rhyming slang. You'd think they were yam-mering away in Greek."

"I'll teach you some if you like, Doc," Barker said.

"Like up the apples—apples and pears—stairs, but that's all I know. A foreign language is always useful in the navy and I'm always happy to learn something new," Fingal said, but his smile faded. Something new, like giving an anaesthetic for an open abdominal operation. Something he'd never done before. He had to tell Wilcoxson. He couldn't pretend he knew what he was doing, could he? He was well aware that in some of the best hospitals in Britain and Ireland, it was quite common for medical students and even porters to be pressed into service as anaesthetists—with the surgeon, if necessary, provid-ing helpful hints.

"I've finished setting up the instruments, sir," Barker said.

Fingal saw an instrument table covered in a white sterile towel standing near the operating table. All the necessary scalpels, forceps, clamps and needle drivers, ligatures, sutures, the tools of the sur-geon's trade, would be under it.

"I've your gowns and gloves beside the wash-hand basin. Just a couple of things more to do."

"Thank you, Barker. When you've finished, go and give Paddy a hand bringing the patient in."

"Righty-ho."

"Have you any preference for the anaesthetic you're going to use, Fingal?" Richard Wilcoxson asked as he started to scrub.

Fingal hesitated. He'd rather not be giving one at all, but needs must when the devil drives. He wasn't the first junior doctor to give an anaesthetic without knowing quite what he was doing. He realized he had to. Fingal cleared his throat. "Would ether be all right?"

"Of course, my boy." His senior smiled. "And we do have a Boyle's machine."

Fingal was familiar in principle with the apparatus that carried cylinders of oxygen, nitrous oxide, and a device for vapourising ether. It had been introduced in 1917 and steadily improved by such additions as a soda lime container to remove the carbon dioxide that the patient exhaled and a rebreathing circuit. In practice he'd not the faintest idea which knob to twiddle or even what the proportion of gases should be. He vaguely remembered one doctor's unhelpful guidance at Sir Patrick Dun's, where there had been no specialist anaesthetists on the faculty. "You start with nitrous oxide and let the patient breathe freely until he turns blue." Fingal shuddered. He could remember nothing more and had no wish to suffocate a patient to sleep—or to death. He'd not use the Boyle's machine. He preferred something simpler, but it was comforting to know a supply of oxygen was handy on the machine if he needed it.

"Or would you like to use chloroform? We have a Vernon Harcourt apparatus."

Fingal remembered his senior in Dublin, Doctor Phelim Corrigan, draping the device round his neck so he could anaesthetise a wealthy young woman in her own home for the removal of an ovarian cyst. But Fingal had never actually used such equipment himself. He'd better stick to the tried and true—well, occasionally tried. The last time had been in '35 for a five-minute procedure, the removal of a large sebaceous cyst if memory served, in the surgical outpatients at Sir Patrick Dun's Hospital. He took a deep breath. "I think I'll use an open Schimmelbusch mask, Richard, if you don't mind. It's really the only thing I've used before."

Clearly Richard Wilcoxson was unconcerned. "Sounds fine to me," he said, "and don't be afraid to ask for advice."

That was a comfort. "I'll not."

"All shipshape and Bristol fashion now, sir," said Barker. "I'll nip off and get Paddy and the patient."

"We'll need a mask and ether for Lieutenant O'Reilly. Can you get them before you go?"

"Righty-ho, sir." It clearly was second nature to Barker, who immediately went to one of the sets of shelves and took down a contraption that looked as if it might have suited Alexandre Dumas's *Man in the Iron Mask*. A fat oval with an outer thin rim surrounding an open space, it had a handle that looked like a duck's bill at one end. Two thin, convex metal bars, one running north–south, the other east–west, crossed in the middle of the aperture. Barker produced a thick wad of lint sheets. "There's ten of them there, sir, that's routine."

It dawned on Fingal that Barker and probably the other SBAs knew how to give an anaesthetic. And that possibly Barker was well aware of Fingal's inexperience. The thought was far more reassuring than humbling. It had ever been thus with senior nurses and junior doctors. No reason it should be any different afloat.

Barker stretched the lint sheets over the frame and locked them in place with a device that was hinged to the handle and which conformed to the shape of the oval frame. He handed it to Fingal. "There you are, sir. Bob's your uncle." He produced a bottle of ether with a glass stopper, "and Fanny's your aunt."

"Thank you, Barker," Fingal said. Everything indeed was as it ought to be.

"I'll be off, then." Barker left.

"Tie up my gown, will you, Fingal?" Wilcoxson had already dried his hands on a sterile towel and shrugged into a white gown.

"Of course." As Fingal tied the strings at the back, Wilcoxson slipped on a pair of sterile rubber gloves.

The door opened and O'Rourke and Barker carried the patient in on a stretcher.

Fingal saw the young man's wide-open eyes peering round the room.

"Alley-oop," said Barker, and the two SBAs loaded Stewart onto the table.

For a moment Fingal thought he was in a C. S. Forester novel about Nelson's navy with the victim about to lose a leg at the hands of a barber surgeon. The two attendants were now securing Stewart with leather straps across his chest, arms, and legs. He'd seen it before in Dun's hospital. The anaesthetic didn't always put a patient under completely, and a half-awake sailor could thrash about. At least poor Stewart was going to have the benefit of ether, not like Nelson's men who had to make do with rum and a leather strap to bite down on.

"How are you feeling, Stewart?" Fingal asked.

"Not too grand, sir," the seaman said.

"We'll have you fixed in no time," Fingal said, trying to exude a confidence he did not feel. He was vaguely aware that the two SBAs had removed the stretcher. Paddy O'Rourke, who was to handle the instruments and assist, jobs that would have required a nurse and another doctor onshore, was getting scrubbed, gowned, and gloved. Fingal took a deep breath, looked at the mask, and with the glass stopper halfway into the neck of the ether bottle, started to drip the pungently smelling liquid onto the gauze. "I'm going to start putting you to sleep, Stewart. Don't be frightened."

"Is that laughing gas, sir? I once had that at the dentist. It wasn't so bad."

"No," said Fingal, "this is ether." He wished fervently he knew how to use nitrous oxide. Some eighteenth-century chemist, whose name escaped Fingal at the moment, had called it laughing gas—and for good reason. It was a kinder way of putting the patient to sleep. "I'm afraid ether doesn't smell very nice. Try not to let the pong and the mask bother you and just take deep breaths." He put the mask over the man's nose and mouth. Engine Room Artificer Stewart's gaze never left Fingal's face. Eventually his eyelids drooped and closed and the man seemed to be unconscious. If Fingal remembered correctly, that was the first stage of anaesthesia. Stewart started to mutter incoherently and Fingal ignored his string of expletives. Stewart began to cough, hold his breath, and for several minutes the ERA struggled against the straps, trying to move his right arm, no doubt in a half-conscious attempt to pull the mask away. Those reactions typified the second stage.

The struggling stopped and Stewart's breathing became slow and perfectly regular. His eyeballs, which Fingal had observed by lifting the upper lid, had stopped rolling about in their sockets and were steady in central positions. This was plane one of the third stage, or what was known as "surgical anaesthesia." There were three more ever-deepening planes and it was Fingal's job to juggle between them so that the patient felt no pain but did not descend into the fourth stage that followed, namely the cessation of breathing, cardiac failure, and death. Never in his short medical career had the clichéd "Their life is in your hands" been so horribly true. He knew he was sweating. "I think you can start, Richard." Fingal crossed his fingers. Painting the belly with more antiseptic solution and draping him with sterile towels shouldn't cause any response, and when it didn't Fingal felt himself relax—a little.

"I'm making the incision," Richard said.

The patient twitched and held his breath. Fingal saw the man's eyes start to move.

"Needs to be deeper, Fingal," Richard said. "Belly's rigid as a rock. I need more muscle relaxation."

"Right." Fingal, who had himself jumped when the patient did, dropped more ether on the gauze. But how much was enough and how much was too much? He waited. The respiratory rate stabilised, the eyes stopped moving.

"That's better. Off we go."

Fingal was too busy keeping watch over ERA Stewart—it helped Fingal to think of the patient by name, not simply as "the patient"—to be able to pay much attention to how the surgery was progressing. He was able to guess from the exchange between surgeon and assistant.

"Clip that skin bleeder."

"Got it."

"Hold up the peritoneum so I can cut it. Thanks." They had nearly entered the abdominal cavity.

Concurrent with Stewart's eyes starting to move came, "Damn it, Fingal, take him down some more. He's all tensed up again. Put more ether on the gauze." Richard's voice softened. "You're doing fine, lad."

Fingal could understand the surgeon's irritation, and was grateful for the advice and support. It was well nigh impossible to operate if the abdominal muscles were rigid. He dropped ether onto the gauze.

"Better. Lord, would you look at that?"

Fingal peered along the table to where Paddy was holding up the appendix prior to Richard ligating its base and cutting it free. The normally pink, wormlike structure was a horrible bluey-green, infected, and gangrenous. "Better an empty house than a bad tenant," Fingal said, feeling less stressed now that the critical part of the operation had been completed and all that remained was to close the incision. Perhaps he could start letting the anaesthetic wear off?

Not quite. As Richard reached the stage where he was starting to sew up the skin, Stewart began to moan and try to thrash. Fingal was glad of the leather restraining straps. "Hang on, please," he said, dropping more ether, then, "okay, carry on." He lifted the right upper eyelid. Christ, the pupil was dilated and the breathing was becoming shallow. Fingal ripped the mask away. The lips had a blue tinge. Cyanosis. He'd overdosed the man, who now desperately needed oxygen. "Quick, Barker. Bring over the Boyle's machine. Turn on the oxygen."

"Everything all right, Fingal?" Richard asked. "I'm putting in the last stitch now."

"He's gone a bit deep," Fingal said. A bit? He was damn nearly dead.

"Here, sir." Barker had shoved over the trolley with flow meters and gas cylinders. He offered Fingal a rubber mask connected to the machine by two corrugated rubber hoses. "I've got the oxygen on full blast." There was no flippancy now.

"Thank you." Fingal clapped the mask over Stewart's nose and mouth. Thank you? Fingal could have kissed the Cockney. God bless him. Fingal hadn't a clue which knurled wheel controlled the flow of oxygen.

"Finished," Richard said. "You can wake him up now."

And because the man's pupils were now normal sized, his respiration slow and deep and regular, Fingal knew it was true, he could let Stewart wake up, but he nearly wouldn't have been able to. The Duke of Wellington's remark about Waterloo being "A damn near-run thing" certainly had applied today.

Already Richard Wilcoxson had stripped off his gloves. "Undo my strings, Barker, there's a good lad." He shrugged off the gown. "You happy enough with him, Fingal?"

Stewart's eyes were rolling and he moved his head from side to side. His breathing was regular and his pulse was—a hundred. "He should be all right now," Fingal said, handing the mask back to Barker, "but he may throw up so please keep an eye on him."

"I will, sir."

"Good," Richard said. "All right, Paddy, you and Barker know what to do. Take him along to the isolation ward. Make sure he does wake up all right. Keep him on his side in case he vomits. Give him a quarter of a grain of morphine and repeat the dose six hourly."

"Aye, aye, sir," Paddy O'Rourke said. "And Doctor O'Reilly?"

"Yes, Paddy?"

"Well done, sir."

"Thank you." Fingal knew he shouldn't feel gratified. Damn it all, he'd nearly killed ERA Stewart, but there was a satisfaction to having given his first-ever anaesthetic for an open abdominal operation and having got away with it.

"Come on, then," said Richard to Fingal, heading for the changing room, "we'll get changed and head for the mess." The door to the operating room closed behind them.

"Bit hairy, was it, gassing the victim?" Wilcoxson asked.

"Honestly? It was bloody terrifying," Fingal said, stripping off his surgical shirt.

"I know and I'm sorry. None of us knows much about anaesthetics, I'm afraid. But look, if you're interested I may be able to change that." He dropped his slightly bloody white trousers round his ankles. "They've set up a training scheme for military doctors in Oxford. I hear it's very well subscribed. I'd like one of my medical staff to be absolutely up to date with the latest in anaesthetic techniques."

"I didn't know about the unit in Oxford," Fingal said.

"Mmm. And the navy's going to do the same at Haslar."

"The hospital at Gosport near Portsmouth?" Fingal struggled into his uniform pants.

"Right. How'd you feel about going on a course there?"

"Me?" Fingal's mind was spinning. "For how long?"

Richard knotted his tie. "Dunno. Could be two or three months if we added your learning a bit about the treatment of battle trauma."

"I'd love it, but why me? I'm the new boy?"

"Because I'm expecting Davy Jones to be promoted out of *Warspite* soon. He's earned it and I'll be sorry to see him go. But if I start working on the skipper about this right now, he can arrange for you to stay here with me when you're fully trained. In any fleet action, battleships act as hospital ships. We'll need the best-trained personnel. And," he added, "it won't hold up your promotion."

"I see." Fingal's mind raced. Three months would be long enough to get married if he could get Deirdre over from Belfast. He continued dressing. "I have a little surgical experience already, Richard. I did one year of gynaecology training, but I'd like it very much to be better qualified all round."

"Good. I'll see what I can do. Mind you, it might not be for a year or so. These things take time." He shrugged into his jacket and glanced at his watch as he picked it from a nearby shelf. "And there are more pressing things at the moment. Like that pink gin you owe me."

Fingal put on his jacket. He'd only been parted from her for two days, but what had he said in the Midland Hotel? "I'll write." He'd get his first letter off to her as soon as he'd eaten. He missed her and wanted to write, but the travelling and the work had yet to give him much of an opportunity to put pen to paper.

"We'll take one more quick look at the patient, then we might even be able to get a bite." Richard strapped on his watch.

Fingal's stomach gave its imitation of one of the bubbling mud pots of New Zealand. "I hope so," he said, "I truly do."

Fingal sat at the table in his cabin, staring at a blank sheet of writing paper. How to begin? Every piece of mail, even the officers', was opened and censored lest information of use to the enemy's military intelligence would slip out. The slogan "Loose Lips Sink Ships" was everywhere throughout the navy. He couldn't even tell her where he was. Next time he was home he'd be sure to have worked out a code for them along the lines of, "Give my love to Aunt Jessy," who did not exist, to mean that *Warspite* would be crossing the Atlantic. "Can you get Ma a birthday present from me?" *Warspite* in the Med. And he'd certainly not want the censoring officer reading any intimate thoughts. Perish the thought.

But for this one? He started,

My dearest darling, I've got to where I was going. My boss is a gentleman and I think I'm going to enjoy working here. I gave an anaesthetic this evening and he says in perhaps a year I may get a chance to go on a course in England for three months so I can become a better anaesthetist and I hug the thought as I think of hugging you, I think we could get married then. I am missing you so dreadfully already and . . .

He hesitated, knowing how much more he wanted to say, then got up, rummaged in his suitcase, and brought out her photo. He stared at it, whispered, "God, I do love you so much, Deirdre," and turned back to his writing of the first of what would become a torrent of letters.

13

Plan the Future by the Past

"My turn to be late, Fingal, Charlie. Sorry," Sir Donald Cromie said as he entered the booth in the Crown Liquor Saloon on Great Victoria Street. "Shove over, Fingal."

O'Reilly slid along the cubicle's horseshoe-shaped black leather benches. He brought his half-finished pint with him. "It's good to see you, Cromie," he said. None of the three practising physician friends would ever ask for an explanation of tardiness. It often unavoidably went with the job.

"Fit and well you're looking," said Charlie Greer. "And you've a pint in the stable. Fingal set up the first round. I'm sure Knockers recognised you as soon as you—"

"One pint of Mister Arthur Guinness's elixir of life, Sir Donald," said the barman, Knox Ritchie, known to one and all as "Knockers." "I'd just finished pouring this one for a fellah I've never seen in here before when I seen you come in. The young lad can wait a wee minute, no sweat."

Typical, O'Reilly thought. All good Irish pubs looked after their regulars first, and as far as he was concerned, rightly so.

"Thank you, Knockers," Cromie said. "I should let you get back to your customers, but how's the back?"

Six months ago when they'd met in here, Knockers had wrenched his back manoeuvering a full keg of Guinness.

"Och, it gives me the odd twinge, but a couple of them Panadol you give me, sir, and I can thole it rightly, so I can. Nice of you til ask."

"You'd expect an orthopaedic surgeon to be interested in bones," O'Reilly said absently.

"It's still nice of Sir Donald to ask, sir." Knockers made to leave, but before going said, "Just buzz if youse need anything."

"When we do, it'll be for three more pints," Charlie said. "My shout."

"Right, Mister Greer." Knockers left.

"Your job to ring, Fingal," Cromie said. "You're nearest the bell push."

The ceramic-and-brass bell push was mounted in one of the vertical posts supporting dark wooden panels inset at their tops with small stained-glass windows. Several other booths were occupied. A snatch of an unusually loud conversation came from the one next door.

"See them Americans? See them? They put an unmanned spaceship called *Surveyor* on the moon yesterday, so they did."

"Bully for them. Do you think it is green cheese?"

"Nah. Probably acres of dust and a wheen of boulders like my mother-in-law's front garden in Lisburn." The speaker cleared his throat. "Do you think they'll make Landing on the Moon Day, June the third, a holiday from now on? Like their Groundhog Day in February?"

"They might. Them Americans, they're powerful ones for holidays, so they are. I hear tell they celebrate Saint Patrick's Day with parades and green beer and all."

"Green beer? Away on." The scorn in the man's voice was palpable. "I tell you, never mind green beer, roll on the Twelfth Fortnight here. That's a *real* holiday, so it is."

Traditionally most places of work in Ulster, particularly the two big industries, shipbuilding and linen, closed for the two weeks sur-rounding the Twelfth of July, when the victory of the Protestant King William over the Catholic King James on that day in 1690 was celebrated with parades and bonfires. Over in Scotland, the city of Glasgow and the Clyde shipyards ground to a virtual standstill at the same time, and many Scots holidayed in Ulster.

"Did you hear that about the Twelfth?" Cromie asked.

Both O'Reilly and Charlie nodded.

"Last year I'd a patient I'd to tell he'd only got two weeks to live."

"Och dear," O'Reilly said. "I hate to hear that kind of thing."

Cromie took a pull on his pint. "Actually he took it rather well. Do you know what he asked me?"

"No." O'Reilly was intrigued, and it wasn't until Cromie contin-ued that Fingal realised he and Charlie were having their legs pulled.

"'Two weeks? Boys-a-dear, that's desperate, so it is,'" said Cro-mie, assuming a Belfast working-man's accent. "'Look. It's Decem-ber now, so if it's all right with you, sir—could you please make them the Twelfth Fortnight next year.'"

"Eejit," O'Reilly said, but his and Charlie's laughter rose to mingle with the hum of conversation from other booths and the men stand-ing at the bar below an etched-glass pane announcing *Bonders of Old High Class Whiskies and Direct Importers of Sandeman's Port.*

"All right, all right," said Charlie. "Enough codding about." He produced a file. "Here's where we're at in the reunion planning. It's pretty well put to bed."

O'Reilly and Cromie leant forward.

"We agreed last time that we'd hold the affair on the weekend of September twenty-third," Charlie said.

O'Reilly, whose job it had been to arrange accommodation, said, "And I've got a tentative block booking for those dates at the Shel-bourne Hotel on Saint Stephen's Green." He paused. "And you may be interested to know that it was built by putting together three adjoining townhouses, by Martin Burke in 1824. Alois Hitler, the Füher's half brother, once worked in the place, and the Irish Constitution was drafted there in 1922."

"Lord," said Cromie with a chuckle, "if the *Encyclopaedia Britannica* ever goes out of business we can get answers from Fingal O'Reilly."

"You'll never change, O'Reilly," Charlie said, "but more to the point, it looks like you can change that tentative booking to a definite because we've had thirty-two affirmative replies, and considering that we started in '31 with forty-one men and six women, that's a pretty good percentage. I'm happy to say that one of those women is Hilda Bronson."

"Who?" Cromie asked.

"She was Hilda Manwell, remember? Married an Australian bloke," Fingal said. "She's the one who wrote to Charlie to suggest the whole thing."

"It'll be great to see Hilda again and the rest of the mob . . ." Cromie said.

"I'm almost afraid to ask, but is Ronald Hercules Fitzpatrick coming?" O'Reilly took a pull from his pint.

"He is," Charlie said.

"Well, perhaps it won't be so bad. Last time I saw him was at a party and the old gobshite was cracking jokes," O'Reilly said. "He's still a dry old stick, but I suppose we'll be able to put up with him."

"Or lose him in the crowd. I never thought we'd get that many out," Cromie said.

"I estimated we'd get about twenty-five. I'll have to ask the Shelbourne for more rooms."

The three men had been sipping their pints. All their glasses would soon be empty. O'Reilly quietly shoved the bell push and lit his pipe. His blue tobacco smoke drifted up to join the cirrus cloud from cigarettes and more pipes.

"The hotel will lay on a welcoming cocktail party and dinner too, on Friday night. Black tie of course, long or cocktail dresses," O'Reilly said, "and uniforms," thinking of how much use he still got out of his old number-one blues.

Cromie nodded.

"We've had a pretty good response from our more academically minded colleagues," Charlie said, "so we'll be able to put on a full day's programme of talks on the Saturday."

"Which," O'Reilly said, "should keep the tax man at bay when we all claim the thing as a deductible scientific meeting and write it off."

"Maybe youse can, sirs," said Knockers, coming in with the three pints, "but this here'll be seven and six, please." As he set the glasses on the table, Charlie counted out three half crowns. "Thank you, Mister Greer," Knockers said, and left.

"The hotel will provide a conference room, projectors, pointers, that kind of stuff," O'Reilly continued. "We'll pack it up at three thirty, give folks a bit of time on their own, then I've booked the banquet, black tie too, on the Saturday evening. Cocktails first, then grub. The folks at Trinity will be letting us use one of the dining halls and doing the catering. The main hall was built in the eighteenth century, in case you two don't know," O'Reilly said.

"And I suppose you were there personally for the grand opening, Fingal, you old fart," Charlie said.

O'Reilly laughed, shook his head, and took a pull on his pint. "Maybe, Greer, it's time we put on the gloves again. Had a rematch." He rubbed his bent nose, which Charlie had broken in a boxing match back in their student days.

Charlie shook his head and patted a not inconsiderable potbelly. "I think," he said, "those days are over."

"Aye," said Cromie, reflexively rubbing his pate, which was merely fringed by a corona of greying hair. "Hard to believe it's thirty years since we qualified."

For a long moment no one spoke, each man, O'Reilly guessed, lost in his own particular memories. Finally Cromie broke the silence. "I'll not bore you with the details, but I've managed to whip up the funding to pay for the social events, and that includes a farewell breakfast on Sunday morning. Several of the pharmaceutical companies have been generous—they will of course receive full recognition on the printed programme, and I'll be taking care of getting that done. Now," he said, "this was your job, Charlie. How about a guest of honour? Have you managed to get one?"

"Indeed," Charlie said. "I tried Doctor Micks first . . ."

The mere mention of his name made O'Reilly purse his lips. Doctor "Robbie" Micks had looked after O'Reilly's father during his terminal illness in 1936.

"Unfortunately while he was very flattered to be asked, he won't be able to make it. He's got another conference that weekend. Seems the class of '41 are having their twenty-fifth and got to him first."

"Did you try Vincent Millington Synge?" O'Reilly asked, remembering the ENT surgeon's primrose Rolls-Royce and private aeroplane.

"No luck there either," Charlie said. "He's seventy-three now and completely retired from matters medical and is living in Rockbrook, County Dublin, but I think you'll be pleased to hear that Mister Kinnear, the surgeon from Sir Patrick Dun's, will be delighted to come and give the after-dinner address."

"Mister Kinnear?" O'Reilly said. "He let me do my first appendicectomy."

"And he's not going to be Mister much longer," Cromie said. "He'll be appointed Regius Professor of Surgery next year."

"Good for him," O'Reilly said.

"A remarkable man," Cromie said. "I found out recently he's Jewish . . ."

"I don't see what being Jewish has to do with anything," Charlie said pointedly.

"In which case, old chum, you'd be wrong. This time it means a great deal," Cromie said. "Nigel Kinnear volunteered for the British Army in the war—"

"Lord," said O'Reilly, "that really took courage."

"You fought, Fingal," Charlie said.

"Yes, I did. And I'd have been a prisoner of war if I'd been taken. If Mister Kinnear had been captured, he'd have been sent straight to the concentration camps if not simply shot on the spot."

"I hadn't thought of that," Charlie said.

"He did go there," Cromie said. "He was one of the first British officers into Bergen-Belsen in '45 when the British and the Canadians liberated the camp."

"My God," O'Reilly said, setting down his half-finished pint from which he had been going to drink. "How absolutely awful for him." And O'Reilly thought about how it wasn't only the Nazis who had been guilty of atrocities. His best friend and the man who had been the fourth of the Four Musketeers of Trinity days, Bob Beresford, had died of starvation and brutal ill treatment at the hands of the Japanese after the fall of Singapore. The wealthy, debonair Robert Saint-John Beresford had had an eye for the ladies, a weakness when it came to the racetrack, and a dry wit that O'Reilly missed to this day. He'd also been a kind and devoted friend and a first-rate medical research worker.

"Aye," said Cromie. "Nigel told me about it a couple of years ago at a Royal College meeting. He is a remarkable man."

"I was thinking," said Fingal, "about another remarkable man, our old friend . . ."

"Bob Beresford," Charlie said, who must have been pursuing a similar train of thought.

"Aye, and I've a notion." O'Reilly paused. "I think if this reunion's a success there'll be others."

"Most likely," Cromie said.

"It's up to Mister Kinnear what he talks about, but I reckon his address should have a title," O'Reilly said.

"And?" Charlie said.

"What would you feel about calling it the 'Robert Beresford Memorial Oration'?"

O'Reilly watched Cromie look at Charlie and Charlie look back. Finally Charlie said, "I think it's the best idea I've heard all night."

"Hear, hear," Cromie said.

"Fine," said O'Reilly very quietly, and raised his glass. "To absent friends," he said, and drank. "We still miss you, Bob."

"To absent friends."

14

I Must Go Down to the Sea Again
to the Lonely Sea . . .

O'Reilly was lighting his pipe in the shelter of Y turret as he stood beneath the massive guns' barrels. The tobacco was burning well. It needed to be because *Warspite* was making twelve knots, and here on the exposed quarterdeck, with nothing but a narrow twin 20 mm Oërlikon antiaircraft cannon for shelter, the wind of her passage would have defeated any attempt to relight it. He'd been told this part of the ship's upper decks was reserved, apart from the crew whose duties brought them there, for off-duty officers, and in warmer climes could be a pretty crowded place. Today he and Tom Laverty had it nearly to themselves. Tom had moved to the port side of the taffrail.

Fingal recognised the single gunner manning the Oërlikon. AB Henson, the Yorkshireman with the missing tooth, had carried Fingal's suitcase aboard. "Afternoon, Henson," Fingal said. "I thought your station was on one of the six-inchers."

"Normally it is, sir, but CPO Watson—"

Fingal remembered that Henson had said there was friction between himself and the petty officer.

"He reassigned me to up here last week so the bloke that normally mans this gun could go on a gunnery course at HMS *Excellent,* the lucky duck."

"Any chance you'll go next?" He knew of Henson's ambition to specialise in gunnery and attend the course on Whale Island near Portsmouth.

"Dunno, sir. Depends on my CPO."

"Well, good luck." But the man sounded discouraged, and there really wasn't much Fingal could do. He nodded and said, "Carry on, Henson."

"Aye, aye, sir."

Fingal moved to beside Tom. The early December day was clear and crisp rather than bitterly cold and he'd not bothered to put up the hood of his duffle coat so he could relish the fresh air tousling his hair. He grabbed the railing. It would take some time to become fully accustomed to the ship's motion as she rose and fell to the long slow Atlantic combers.

Tom Laverty stood, clearly at ease with the ship's slow rolling. This was the first opportunity they'd had for a chat since the night they'd met in the wardroom anteroom ten days ago. Fingal was free and Tom had come off watch after piloting the great ship away from Tail of the Bank and down the Firth of Clyde; past Holy Loch to starboard and the Cloch Point light to port, on between the Isle of Bute with its snow-dusted hills and Great Cumbrae and Little Cumbrae Islands, then dropping the Isle of Arran to starboard and rounding the Mull of Kintyre.

Now the battleship, her escorting destroyers, two light cruisers, and a fast convoy of forty-eight merchant ships, had begun to steer a prearranged zigzag course. The first jog to port had brought the leading ships to within two miles of Rathlin Island. In four minutes it would be time to turn onto the opposite zag. They were heading across the wide Atlantic for Halifax, Nova Scotia, and on the next leg the Mull of Kintyre would drop beneath the horizon and the ships would be a widely spread phalanx ploughing west through a boundless sea.

Warspite herself was vulnerable to submarine attack and so was stationed in the centre of the columns of merchant ships. The escorting naval vessels were posted ahead, on the flanks, and astern of the columns of ships. No matter which way Fingal looked, ships stretched to the horizon. Over the churning of *Warspite*'s propellors, the never-ceasing rumble of the turbines, he could make out a rhythmic, high-pitched pinging. The ship's ASDIC operators, like those of every escort, would not cease their constant probing with sound waves for an enemy lurking below. In this war, from day one when a U-boat had torpedoed and sunk the SS *Athenia* near Rockall in the North Atlantic, it had become apparent that the Nazis were going to wage unrestricted warfare against British merchant ships and that naval escorts were, of course, fair game too.

Apart from searching, *Warspite* herself was much too cumbersome to be an antisubmarine vessel, unless by some fluke she surprised one on the surface and engaged it with gunfire, but the very real possibility of encountering German pocket battleships like the *Scharnhorst* or the *Gneisnau* that were bent on commerce raiding meant that the convoy must be accompanied by what the navy called "a ship of force." And *Warspite* was most certainly that.

Tom had to speak loudly to be heard over the low rumble of the ship's four propellers turning the sea into a tumbling, frothing wake immediately beneath where he and Fingal stood. Above them a blue sky that should have looked freshly washed and scrubbed was sullied by the smoke from fifty funnels, and even here in the open there was a smell of fuel oil.

"That's home over there," Tom said, nodding to Ireland. "We're not far from Cushendun on the coast. There's a young sub-lieutenant on board, Wilson Wallace. He's a gunnery officer on the starboard six-inch battery."

Fingal glanced at AB Henson. The six-inch guns were his normal station. If Fingal had a word with this Wallace about Henson and his CPO . . . He shook his head. He wasn't in the Liberties anymore. It was none of his business—and yet . . .

"He'll be feeling homesick if he knows where we are. Portstewart, his hometown, is only about thirty miles from here."

"Might as well be on the far side of the moon," Fingal said, aching in the knowledge that Deirdre was only fifty miles away as the crow flies. "How was your leave?"

Tom looked at Fingal and said, "Wonderful. I can fully recommend marriage."

"I'm sorry I couldn't get to your wedding last year, but it's a bit of a trip from Ireland to Malta."

"Carol and I understood and we did appreciate the canteen of cutlery." Tom looked at the grey seas. "Malta was wonderful, Fingal. Magnificent scenery and history, warm weather, inexpensive. But we got there much later than we expected."

"Oh?" Fingal took a long pull from his pipe and chuckled. "What happened? Don't tell me the navy played havoc with your wedding."

"On this old ship, things don't always go according to plan. I think you know *Warspite* was almost rebuilt in the mid-'30s. She was an old lady then, launched in 1913, and long overdue for a refit. She was supposed to be recommissioned in June 1937. I was with her then. Everything seemed to be going all right, but a month later we ran manoeuvering trials at high speed and the steering jammed." Tom laughed. "It's been the bane of *Warspite*'s life. She's rammed more than one ship because her steering failed, and I know it got stuck at Jutland in '16 too."

"I read about that," Fingal said. "Can't have been much fun steaming in circles while the whole German High Seas Fleet used the ship for target practice."

"I'm told it wasn't. And things got worse after the refit. Nobody was shooting, but it was breakdown after bloody breakdown. We finally got everything sorted out and reached Grand Harbour in Malta in January '38, six months late. Carol joined me and we got wed."

"But she's home now?"

"Well, in Greenock anyway." Tom got a dreamy look on his face. "When it looked like war might break out and Admiral Cunningham moved the Med Fleet from Malta to Alexandria in Egypt, I was able to get Carol home from Malta to Bangor, and the minute it looked like we were going to be based in Greenock instead of Pompey . . ."

"Pompey?"

"Sorry. Sailor talk for Portsmouth. I was able to get digs ashore in Greenock. You know it only takes a couple of days to get there from Ulster, so I sent her a telegram and she arrived the night you did. I was on watch that night, but the skipper's pretty decent about letting married officers sleep ashore if the ship's orders aren't for imminent departure. He gave me leave." Tom glanced at AB Henson, who appeared to Fingal to be minding his own business, then said, "We've been trying to make a baby, if you know what I mean?"

"I *am* a doctor," Fingal said, and chuckled, as much to disguise a certain amount of embarrassment—such things were rarely talked about openly—as to hide the ache in him when he knew how much he longed to make love to his Deirdre.

Sharp cracking noises sounded overhead and Fingal looked up to see strings of coloured flags soaring up the halliards. At the same time, signalling lamps on the bridge began flickering.

"That's the 'prepare for course change' signal," Tom said. "We'll give every ship time to read them and acknowledge, then the minute the flags are hauled down—that's the 'execute' signal—all the ships will simultaneously turn ninety degrees to starboard."

Down they came and immediately *Warspite* and every other vessel began to swing, the great battlewagon heeling slightly into the turn as she came round. The wakes curling behind met and tossed in a tumult of waters that Fingal knew would soon disappear, and the sea would go about its business as untroubled as if the ships had never passed.

He took a long look astern at Rathlin Island. "That was where, in 795, the Vikings first raided Ireland, Tom."

"I didn't know that," he said, looking thoughtful. "I sometimes wonder you didn't become a scholar like your old man, Fingal. I was so very sorry to hear about his passing. And I'm glad you made your peace with him. I was based in Trincomalee in Ceylon when your letter came."

Fingal nodded and looked out to stare at an oil tanker making her turn. She was clearly empty by the way her red antifouling paint made a bright, sharp contrast to the grey seas. "Thank you, Tom." A streamlined white bird with a cream head and viciously pointed beak was flying level with him, but about fifty yards away. It closed its wings and plummetted down like, like one of those bloody stukas he'd seen on a Pathé news reel. Father had been right—the year before he died he'd predicted that war with Nazi Germany was inevitable.

"Gannet," said Tom, interrupting the silence between them. "What amazing fishermen they are."

Tom looked ahead. "We should be settled on our new course soon. It's pretty straightforward from here on unless we hit a storm or U-boats, so I'm happy to leave the nav to one of my juniors, at least in the daytime. Rank has its privileges."

"You've done well, Tom," Fingal said. He nodded at Tom's shoulder straps, two wide stripes separated by one thin gold one. "Lieutenant-Commander Laverty, your professional life is on track. Thirty-two and navigating officer on a bloody great battlewagon."

Tom blushed. "I've been lucky—"

"I don't believe it," O'Reilly said with feeling. "I'm damn sure you earned it." He looked down. "I'm afraid," he said, "I wasn't as good as I might have been about keeping in touch after I left HMS *Tiger.* Sorry." He looked at his old friend. "Ten years? Where did they go? Mind you, as they'd say in our part of Ireland, you're sticking the pace rightly, oul hand." And Tom was. Same full head of fair hair, blue eyes. Maybe more crow's-feet at the corners and deeper bags beneath. Cheeks as ruddy as those of an Ulster farmer. Living a life exposed to the elements would do that.

"I was hard to keep track of," Tom said, "but there's no need to bore you with my various postings. I'm sure your career kept you busy too. I'm happy at what I do, my career is moving ahead, and I told you I like being married even if the bloody war does get in the way." He looked ahead. "That's us on course." And as he spoke Fingal noticed that the ship was back on an even keel, and coincidentally his pipe had gone out. He stuffed it in his coat pocket.

"What about you, Fingal? I know you qualified in '36, but what happened after?"

Fingal shrugged. "I qualified, fell in love—" For a moment he wondered if Kitty O'Hallorhan was still in Tenerife. "—Dad died, Ma moved to the North to be closer to Lars. I, well, I fell out of love, tried GP in Dublin, tried specialising, went back to GP in Ulster— and I love it. Got called up. "

"There is a war on."

"I had noticed," O'Reilly said. He hesitated then said, "It put a bit of a spanner in my works too. I got engaged this year. Deirdre Mawhinney's a wonderful girl." He closed his eyes and saw her, heard her laugh. "She's a midwife. We've had to postpone the wedding." He didn't want to tempt Providence, but then said, "Surgeon Commander Wilcoxson may be going to send me back to Pompey"—it was so easy to slip back into the naval jargon—"for a three-month course. I hope we can get wed then." And to use Tom's term, try to make babies too.

"I'd like to meet her," Tom said, "and I wish you luck, Fingal, but it won't be soon. Skipper's told me to get my North Atlantic, Canadian, and American seaboard charts up to date. I reckon we're in for a lot more convoy work after this one and then scuttlebutt has it we'll be headed back to the Med."

Fingal shrugged and sighed. "Can't be helped," he said, "but I reckon I will get my chance. Richard Wilcoxson strikes me as someone who keeps his word."

"He is that," said Tom. "One remarkable man." He smiled. "The crew call him Hippocrates, but not to his face. You should have seen him on our last convoy. We left Halifax on November eighteenth with convoy HX 9. About fifty merchant ships and a naval escort. Took us six utterly miserable days to get to the southern tip of Greenland, and then we were detached to search the Denmark Strait between Greenland and Iceland." He lowered his voice. "Our armed merchant cruiser *Rawalpindi* had been sunk the day before north of the Faroes, poor devils, by a German surface raider. No armour and little six-inch pop-guns against something chucking eleven-inch bricks?" He shook his head. "Admiralty thought the German pocket battleship *Deutschland* was loose, but we never found her." He shuddered. "I'll tell you, chum, the North Atlantic and the Denmark Strait in the winter are not for kiddies."

"I've heard the rumour," O'Reilly said, vividly remembering a trip from Scapa Flow to Saint John's Newfoundland in 1929 on *Tiger*.

"We'd some pretty serious injuries what with severe lacerations, bones broken, two stokers scalded, a ham-fisted gunner's mate who amputated his own left thumb by closing a breech block on it, paralysing seasickness. Even one of the MOs bust a leg. If Hippocrates slept for any time for more than an hour on end I'd be surprised."

"Aye," said O'Reilly. "I've met doctors like him before. They are to be admired." And thought, I hope I can live up to Hippocrates'— he liked that nickname for Wilcoxson—Hippocrates' standards.

"I'd have to say I was pretty banjaxed myself. The weather was so foul, not a snowball's chance of getting sun or star sights."

A bugle boomed from the loudspeakers. Bosun's pipes shrilled.

"Good Lord," said Tom, "that's action stations." A voice boomed over the loudspeakers, "All hands close up to action stations. Close all watertight doors. All hands . . ."

"See you soon," Tom yelled as the two men ran for'ard, Tom on his way to the conning tower, Fingal to his place below.

One of the ships in *Warspite*'s convoy, a sleek destroyer, rushed by with a bone in her teeth and a white rooster tail of wake high above her stern. Fingal saw the cylindrical depth bombs arc high into the air from the destroyer's midships and heard the multiple cracks of her depth-charge launchers before the charges splashed into the sea about three cables' lengths or six hundred yards away. He slowed his pace and watched another team of men on the destroyer rolling more charges off stern-mounted racks. They must have an ASDIC contact and believe a U-boat had penetrated into the middle of the convoy—probably trying for a shot at *Warspite*. And in broad daylight. Cheeky buggers.

Just as the waves caused by the charges had flattened out, the sinking bombs exploded at preset depths. There was a sonorous booming against *Warspite*'s hull, and the ocean boiled in vast white plumes towering higher than the ships' decks before crashing back to an ocean littered with dead fish.

In the fifteen minutes it had taken him to reach his action station four decks down, their escort ships had loosed five more depth-charge attacks on the unseen German sub. Each time the shock waves struck, *Warspite* shuddered like a retriever shedding water and Fingal had to grab for support.

He shook his head. He knew the charges were aimed at an enemy hell-bent on sinking British ships and killing British sailors, perhaps even him. That risk was over now. No U-boat skipper in his right mind would try to launch a torpedo when he knew his boat had been detected. He'd be too busy trying to escape. For a moment Fingal's heart bled for those German sailors somewhere deep below in a stinking, damp, claustrophobic steel tube, bracing themselves and trembling at the thought of what the water pressure would do to frail flesh if their submarine's hull were breached. Then he took a seat in the for'ard medical distributing station to do nothing—he hoped—but wait until the *Warspite*'s captain deemed the emergency to be over.

He'd surprised himself by the power of his feelings for the enemy and it occurred to him that before this war was over he might well be having some very intense moments. He smiled, knowing he was no academic, but thinking it might be worth trying to record those thoughts and keep a kind of a shorthand diary of the war's more important times too. One of his treasured books was *Recollections of Rifleman Harris,* a firsthand account of a private soldier's experiences in the Peninsular War with Napoleon in the 1800s. For once it would be a paperwork job Fingal would not mind doing. He opened a drawer in his table and rummaged about finding a ruled notebook. With nothing else to do, today was as good a time to start as any.

15

The History of Class Struggle

"If," said Kinky from the dining room doorway, "if you'd kindly move yourself, sir, and take your coffee to the upstairs lounge, I'll get a start made to the hoovering of the dining room, so. And take her ladyship with you, please."

Barry would be leaving soon to make after-lunch home visits, but he was talking to someone on the phone in the hall. Jenny had come down from Belfast this afternoon—it was a Wednesday—to run her clinic. And the empress of Number One, Main Street, was lying on her back on a dining room chair with all four paws in the air, her eyes closed and the tip of her pink tongue sticking out.

O'Reilly stood, finished his coffee, grabbed the white cat from the chair to the accompaniment of a curt "mraah" and tucked her under his arm like a rugby football. "You carry on, Mrs. Auchinleck."

"Mrs. Auchinleck," Kinky said, and grinned. "Now there's a lovely thing." She pushed an upright vacuum cleaner into the room. "Fine day," she said, "for late May, and grand it is to be back in Ballybucklebo, getting my new home with Archie organised, and still being able to do most of my old job here too." She unwound the flex and plugged the machine in.

"It's good to have you back, Kinky. We missed you."

"It was a lovely holiday, so. Archie is a grand man for the hiking.

He near had the legs worn off me charging right up to the top of Slieve Donard, but the view from up there?" She looked dreamy. "You'd think you could reach up and touch Heaven."

O'Reilly wondered how Kinky might feel if she ever went up in an aeroplane. "It's impressive," he said. "On a fair day you can see a goodly bit of southwestern Scotland." But not quite as far as Greenock and the Firth of Clyde, he thought.

"You can, so, but it does be good to be back home and to have Rory on the mend too. It was a frightful shock to Archie and me when you told us, sir. It's not right that a good Irish boy should get a foreign disease that I can't even pronounce. Them people should keep their ills to themselves. We've plenty enough of our own to go round and *we* don't be giving them to foreigners, so." She managed a small smile. "It was a great comfort, sir, to have you explaining all about it so that Archie, God love him, could rest easy until we got Rory home. He's been home a week now. The nice doctors at Purdysburn said he'd need three weeks' convalescence so he still has two to go."

"How's he doing?"

"He has been very well looked after, so, and he's to report back to his own medical officer in two weeks. There'll be some kind of panel to see if he's fit to return to duty." She inhaled. "He's concerned that they'll not pass him A1, and he does love his soldiering."

"I'm sure he'll be fine," O'Reilly said. "The army looks after its own."

"Thank you, sir," she said, "that's good to know. And now I'd better get going with my work." Kinky lowered the vacuum cleaner's handle to the sweeping position and switched it on. The machine roared. Lady Macbeth screeched. The machine's bag inflated. Lady Macbeth's tail did the same. She wriggled, howled, and clawed at O'Reilly's jacket.

"All right," he said, "all right," and set her on the floor. Howling like the banshee, the little cat rocketed off, heading for the kitchen.

"Sorry, your ladyship," he said. "I'd forgotten you had a thing about vacuums."

Barry was still on the phone. "I'll speak to Fingal. See you on Saturday, love." He hung up and turned to Fingal. "Got a minute?"

"Sure." He headed upstairs. "Kinky has banished me from the dining room."

Barry followed. "That was Sue," he said. "She's in a bit of a pickle. Needs help."

"Then off you go, Barry," said O'Reilly, "I'll make the home visit for you." He wondered what could be upsetting Sue Nolan, who was usually a very self-contained young woman.

Barry shook his head. "I'd like you to go round to the school and see if you can help her," he said.

"Me?" said O'Reilly. "Why me?" He and Barry had stopped on the landing beside a framed photo of his old battleship.

Barry pointed at the black-and-white picture. "Because I think she needs backup from some big guns and in Ballybucklebo, Fingal, that's you. It's about Colin Brown—again."

"Colin? Oh-oh." O'Reilly shook his head. "What in the name of the wee man has that rapscallion been up to this time?"

"Nothing," Barry said. "We all know Colin's as bright as a button. Very bright. It's probably why he gets into so much mischief. He'll be finished with his elementary schooling and moving on. Sue says he's one of the smartest kids she's ever taught. Thinks he should be sitting his Eleven Plus. She's sure he'd pass and have a chance for a better education. I agree. Apparently the necessary application forms for the next exams arrived at school yesterday."

O'Reilly whistled. In Ulster the powers that be divided youngsters whose parents could not afford to send their offspring to fee-paying schools into those who should excel academically and those better suited for the trades. The two groups were educated differently. The kids, if their parents wished, could take an exam, the Eleven Plus, between ages eleven and twelve. Based on the results, the top 25 percent were offered places at grammar schools and given an academic education with the state paying. Most went on in six years to win university places or at least could get jobs like bank tellers or other white-collar occupations. The others went to secondary or technical schools for more practical training in the trades, also at the taxpayers' expense. "She certainly could be right," O'Reilly said. "He deserves a chance."

"And Colin really wants to," Barry said, "but the trouble is, Sue naturally assumed his parents would agree. She asked him to mention it to his folks when he went home for lunch. Said she'd drop in after school this afternoon and bring the forms if Colin thought that was convenient." Barry scowled.

"And?"

"And it wasn't—convenient, I mean. According to Colin, his mother's all for it, but Lenny, Colin's da, was definitely not. He wants Colin to go into one of the trades. Lenny's adamant. Won't even consider having him sit the exam." Barry sighed. "Colin went back to school after lunch absolutely gutted. Seems he's got his heart set on being a veterinary."

"Good Lord. Hope he hasn't told his father that."

"No, Colin's too smart. He can see what's happening. But Sue said he was very upset. He's clutching his tummy and making hideous moaning noises. She reckons it's all a sham but it would be a good reason for a doctor . . ."

O'Reilly cocked his head and smiled at Barry before saying, "Good plan. Where are Sue and Colin now?"

"There was some kind of concert going on and no classes so she got permission from the headmistress to take him home. Sue wanted me to go with her round to the Browns. Try to talk sense into Lenny." He looked at O'Reilly. "You've taught me that being a GP here involves more than looking after the ills of the flesh. Our job's to—" He looked down and up again. "—to look after the whole ruddy community. Sue'll probably get told to mind her own business if she goes by herself." His smile was rueful. "I imagine so would I, but—"

"You think we need what the navy used to call 'a ship of force,' and that I fill the bill?" O'Reilly laughed. "Right. You go and see your patient and I'll nip round to the school and take Sue and Colin to see his folks."

"Doctor O'Reilly," Connie Brown said when she answered O'Reilly's knock from the brass lion's head on the front door. "And Miss Nolan. What's wrong? Is it Colin?" She moved to her son, who was wiping his nose with the sleeve of his school blazer. "Colin, use your hanky."

"Colin's fine," O'Reilly said. It had taken little for him to pretend to examine Colin at the school and then pronounce with all the authority of an expert adult, "There's not a blooming thing wrong with you, Colin Brown," for Colin to quit his moaning. O'Reilly said, "He's a bit unhappy, but he's not sick and he's not in any trouble. I promise."

"That makes a change," she said, the words clipped. "Sorry, Doctor, but it's been a bit hectic round here. Len's home from the shipyard. They had a work slowdown today."

"We wondered if Miss Nolan and I could have a word with you and Lenny, seeing as he's still home?"

"Yes, of course, come in. He's in the front parlour." Connie stepped aside. She lowered her voice. "It's about that there exam, isn't it?"

O'Reilly nodded.

"Just a wee minute," Connie said, and turned to Colin. "Away you out into the backyard and play with Murphy, son."

"Yes, Mammy," Colin said, and ran down the hall and into the kitchen. O'Reilly knew that the back door led to a walled yard where

Murphy, a dog of indeterminate breed from one of Sonny and Maggie Houston's bitches, would be overjoyed to see his master.

Connie looked at Sue. "Miss Nolan, I'm awful sorry. I know you mean well, so you do, and want what you thinks is best for Colin. I think you're right, but my Lenny, and he's the man of the house, can be terrible thran when he gets his mind made up."

Just as the Ulster sense of humour was ingrained, so was the tendency in some Ulstermen to congenital bloody-mindedness.

"He's calmed down a bit, but—well, I'm glad you're here, Doctor. Begging your pardon, miss, but I know how Lenny respects the doctor, and all."

Lenny's voice came from the front parlour. "Who the hell is it, Connie?" The words were not dripping with honey.

She led the way. "Doctor O'Reilly and Miss Nolan have just popped in, like."

Lenny rose, as was proper when a lady entered a room.

"Please sit down, everybody," Connie said. "Would anybody like a wee cup of scald in their hand?" Her tones were those of a hostess greeting welcome guests with the offer of tea, and O'Reilly knew she was trying to pour oil on Lenny's troubled waters.

"There's no time for tea," Lenny said. "I want for til know now what all this palaver's about, so I do. Right now."

O'Reilly and Sue sat. Connie remained standing. O'Reilly hesitated. He would help where he could, but Colin was Sue's pupil and, after all, education was her speciality. "Miss Nolan?" he asked.

"Mister Brown, I'm a young teacher, I don't want to interfere in your family's business, but I have never, *ever* met such a smart young man as your son, Colin." Sue's voice was low and encouraging, not pleading, the voice O'Reilly thought she probably used to encourage slower learners with difficult problems.

O'Reilly saw Connie smile. "That's very nice of you, Miss Nolan, isn't it, Lenny?"

Lenny frowned, ignored his wife. "Go on, miss."

"I believe he could be anything he wants; a lawyer, a doctor, a—"

"He's going til be a plater like his daddy, and that's that," Lenny said with a flat air of finality. "Right now, Harland Wolff shipyard is working on a deep-sea oil rig, the *Sea Quest.*" The man said the words with pride. "And the first supertanker, the *Myrina,* ever built in the UK. There'll never be no shortage of work there and the wages is dead good. A man can take pride in a job like that." He emphasised his point by stabbing his own chest with his index finger.

Sue looked at O'Reilly.

He said, "It's been five years since the last liner, the *Canberra,* was finished here."

"Aye," said Lenny, "that's true. With all them airyplanes now there's not the demand for liners no more, so there's not." He wagged the same finger at O'Reilly. "But our managing director's got a loan from the government, and Harland's is modernising the yard. We'll be building ships as big as thirty-three thousand tonnes, so we will." He folded his arms across his chest and looked O'Reilly straight in the eye. "No son of mine's getting ideas above his station, so he's not. There's been a Brown at the yard since the first Mister Harland bought it from his boss, Mister Hickson, in 1861. That's more than a hundred years, so it is, and there'll be one there when I'm long past it and eating bread and milk."

O'Reilly, not missing the reference to Lenny's toothless dotage, strained to catch the nuances in the man's voice. Certainly there was a hard-to-shake, ingrained class consciousness, and definite pride in the shipyards, but underneath O'Reilly detected a tinge of worry. Despite Lenny's bluster about government loans, in the wider community there was serious concern about the long-term future of shipbuilding in Ulster. The Japanese and the Koreans were able to build much less expensively in a world where now the war was over the demand for ships had diminished massively. The loss of orders was further exaggerated by a move to bigger container ships and fewer general cargo vessels. Was Lenny somehow insisting that Colin follow in his father's foorsteps to reinforce his belief—or perhaps more accurately his fervent hope—that the shipyards would remain in business indefinitely?

"Even so, a profession—" Sue said, then a puzzled look crossed her face.

O'Reilly clenched his teeth, recognising, as she must have, just how thin was the ice under her. Any suggestion that a profession was a step up in life would be an immediate slap in the face to a proud tradesman. He glanced at Lenny and saw the man's fists tightening and how he was starting to rise from his chair.

"Take it easy, Lenny," Connie said. "Miss Nolan thinks she's trying to help Colin, and it is her job as his teacher, like, just like it's Doctor O'Reilly's."

O'Reilly, watching Lenny subside, smiled at Connie. "I think what Miss Nolan means," he hastened to say, "is that maybe we should give Colin a chance for more of a choice?"

Lenny frowned. "Like what? She already said she wanted to send him for to be a doctor or a lawyer. Being a bloody fine plater's good enough for me. The apprenticeship's longer than going for a doctor, but he can start earlier."

That was true. Most apprentices began their training at sixteen and would already have been taught basic trade skills if they'd gone to a technical school.

"He'd still be at the yard if he was, say, a naval architect," said O'Reilly slowly, "but he'd need different qualifications for that." Colin, at the ripe old age of eleven, thought he wanted to be a vet, but who could predict what career the boy might choose six years from now. That was up to Colin. All O'Reilly was after was getting Lenny to agree to his son sitting the exam so his options would be open.

Lenny frowned and stared at his callused hands, the dirt under his fingernails that no amount of scrubbing could get out, the white puckers of burn scars that were the badges of honour for platers and riveters.

Sue looked as if she was getting ready to say something and O'Reilly caught her eye, hoping she noticed the merest shake of his head. Let Lenny make up his own mind.

Finally the man spoke. "Suppose he passes the exam. Does he have to go to grammar school with all the kids of the toffs?"

The class thing again, O'Reilly thought.

"No," said Sue. "Only if you want him to."

Lenny pursed his lips and looked at Connie.

O'Reilly said, "You like the odd bet on the horses, Lenny?"

"Aye."

"Letting Colin write the exam's like backing a horse both ways—to win or place. Gives him two chances of winning."

Lenny nodded slowly, ponderously, before saying, "When do them forms need filling in by?"

Sue glanced at O'Reilly before saying, "September the first."

Lenny stood, went to Connie, and put his arm around her shoulder. "The missus and me'll think on it, all right? I'm making no promises, so I'm not, but we'll talk it over."

Connie smiled and patted her husband's hand.

"I think that's very wise," Sue said. "After all, it is your decision."

Well done, Sue, O'Reilly thought. As far as he was concerned, any attempt to try to sway Lenny farther at this point would probably push him into rearing up with a flat refusal. Let the hare sit. "Come on, Miss Nolan," he said. "I think Mister and Mrs. Brown would like to be alone."

"Thank you, Doctor O'Reilly, Miss Nolan," Connie said. "I'll show you out—and I'll get you a cuppa and wee jam piece, Lenny, when I come back."

16

The Hours of Light Return

The sound of the bo'sun's pipes shrilled through the Tannoy system. Fingal, perched at a table in the sick bay doing a job he hated, didn't need to look at his watch to know it was eleven o'clock. While he was filling in requisition forms for pharmaceuticals, *Warspite*'s petty officer of the day would be collecting the keys to the spirits room to start the daily ritual of issuing the rum ration: one-eighth of a pint per petty officer and every man over the age of twenty and not under punishment. There was no issue for officers; they had the bar in their mess. The next pipe would be at noon when the measured quantity would be ready for general distribution. O'Reilly smiled at the thought of this arcane practice surviving into the twentieth century. There'd been talk over the years in Parliament of abolishing the men's grog, but nothing had happened. Trust the navy to hang on like the devil to its archaic ways.

Rituals like these had become a fixture of Fingal's life, but today they marked the passage of time aboard ship in an entirely new way. Unless there was some unforeseen event, *Warspite* should be dropping the hook at Tail of the Bank by two P.M.—four bells of the afternoon watch. The ship needed maintenance and wouldn't be ready for sea until two weeks after she'd anchored.

Which meant he would start his first long leave, of fourteen days—time enough to get back to Ulster and see Deirdre. Deirdre. He hugged the thought to him. As soon as the first liberty drifter was alongside he'd be off—unless, as Tom Laverty had remarked at breakfast, there was some "excitement." Although they were nearly home, safety was by no means guaranteed. O'Reilly knew very well that only last month, the minesweeper HMS *Gleaner* had depth-charged and sunk a U-boat here in the seemingly protected waters of the Clyde Estuary, *Warspite*'s current home base. The havoc an enemy submarine might have wrought among the ships anchored here did not bear thinking about.

Since O'Reilly had joined the battleship in November, three nearly nonstop months of bleak midwinter convoy escort duty had been his initiation back into the navy. In the final six return runs from Halifax they had lost eight merchantmen to enemy action.

The weeks of ceaseless noise, ship's smells, constant wetness, incessant motion, and sleeps interrupted by calls to readiness or action stations had run one into the other. At least in the medical department, O'Reilly and the rest didn't have to contend with the savage cold on deck or the brutally high temperatures in the engine and boiler spaces. Their lot was treating the endless rounds of cuts, bruises, sprains, and broken bones occasioned by the weather.

The grinding monotony was punctuated by periods of horror when a ship within their convoy was torpedoed or struck a mine. At those times, the sea would stink of bunker oil and men would be tossed into the sea like flotsam or grimly hang on in lifeboats or on Carley floats. *Warspite* was too valuable to risk stopping to rescue survivors—she could be hit by a torpedo too. O'Reilly would pray for the half-frozen men to be picked up by one of the smaller escort vessels.

There was some relief to be had in port with occasional four-hour runs ashore to Greenock, when O'Reilly and Tom and sometimes Davy Jones or the young gunnery officer Wilson Wallace would dine on meals prepared from the limited choice of wartime rationing.

Once they had attended a concert given by the singer and comedienne Gracie Fields. O'Reilly still chuckled when he remembered her singing "The Biggest Aspidistra in the World" and "Walter, Lead Me to the Altar." After these brief shore leaves sick bay would inevitably be busy treating crew members for the damage from bar brawls or doses of venereal disease.

And, once in a while he'd been able to telephone Deirdre. Just hearing her voice had warmed him through.

Then back to sea, where *Warspite* would pitch and roll horribly in force-nine gales, the winds roaring at more than forty knots and the thirty-foot-high Atlantic waves marching across the ocean from horizon to horizon. More often than not, Fingal would be safe belowdecks on the big ship, but sometimes, when the claustrophobia and blighted air would overcome him, he'd go out on deck and watch the wind tearing spindrift off the combers and listen to the banshee keening in the big ship's rigging. She was more than thirty thousand tons, but the seas treated her roughly. It was madness to be at sea in such conditions. But the convoys had to get through or Britain would starve, run out of fuel—and lose the war. All that could be said in favour of the weather was that it made the task of the enemy submarines well nigh impossible.

O'Reilly grumbled to himself, finished the last of the forms, stretched, and stood. "Nearly home," he said to Ronnie Barker and Bert Fletcher.

"We are that, and if it's all right with you, sir, I think we can let Chief Barker go a little early," Fletcher said. "I can hold the fort until the afternoon watch comes on if you'd like to get your packing finished."

"I'd appreciate that, Fletcher," O'Reilly said. "I'd appreciate it very much. See you both in two weeks."

"Ta very much, Fletch," Barker said. "I'll do the same for you soon, and you have fun back home, sir."

"I will," O'Reilly said, grabbing his cap and heading for the way out, "believe me I will."

It had taken the remains of yesterday, last night, and this morning, all the while consumed with impatience, but he'd made it to Belfast. Now, after running half the length of the platform and hurrying through the ticket barrier, O'Reilly couldn't find her in the throng of men in uniform. Like him, they were home on leave and being greeted by family and friends. Belfast's Midland Station was noisy with their joy and laughter, with the hissing of steam and the clattering of iron wheels on luggage trolleys being pushed by uniformed porters across concrete platforms. The incomprehensibly garbled voice over a loudspeaker system presumably was announcing the arrival of the Larne boat train. The air was heavy with the smells of coal smoke and engine oil.

And then he saw her twenty paces away. Deirdre was struggling to get past a portly man and his four small children. She waved and called, "Fingal. Fingal," and his heart hiccupped.

The other people, the station itself, faded into a misty blur, and all he could see was her face, her eyes smiling, lips open. She was bundled in a long brown overcoat with slightly padded shoulders held shut by a loosely tied belt and her shining hair was tucked up under a silky green scarf.

He dropped one shoulder and, as if he'd been back on the rugby field, battered his way through the scrum, oblivious to a yell of "Watch where the hell you're going, admiral, you great glipe." As *Warspite*'s bows cleaved the ocean, so O'Reilly carved his path. He dropped his suitcase and enfolded her in a huge hug. "Deirdre. Deirdre." He held her at arm's length, drinking in the wonder of her, then pulled her to him. "I'm home," he whispered into her hair. And then he kissed her. Damn it, there was a war on and old conventions about displays of emotion in public could go to hell. "I love you," he said and kissed her again, her lips soft against his.

"I love you, Fingal, and I've missed you terribly." She kissed him, eyes shining with tears and laughter. "I suppose you better put me down, though. All these people here, and Lars is waiting outside."

"All right." He set her down lightly like a man putting fine porcelain on a sideboard, lifted his suitcase, and took her hand. "Come on." He started striding toward the way out.

"Good Lord, Fingal," she said, "did you have a drink or two on the train?"

"No," he said, "why?"

"Because you're swaying as you walk."

He laughed. "It always happens when we've been at sea. I'll have to get my land legs again and," he laughed again and said, "we've nearly two whole weeks for me to do it before I have to go back."

"And I've got two weeks off too," she said, trying to match his swaying gait with her own.

"Bloody marvellous," he said, but anything more would have to wait. He squeezed her small hand in his.

"It's wonderful you're here," she said. "Darling, I've missed you so much."

They were on York Street in the chill of a damp March afternoon in Belfast, the air sooty from the smoke from the linen mills and factories. O'Reilly's big brother Lars, dapper in a fedora hat, long grey Ulster overcoat, and brown leather gloves, was waiting on the steps. He stripped off his right glove and offered his hand, which O'Reilly shook with vigour. "Welcome home, Finn. How are you?" Lars's narrow moustache, worn in the style of the film stars Errol Flynn and Douglas Fairbanks Jr., curled into a grin. "Good to have you home."

O'Reilly let go of his brother's hand. "It's good to be home. Good to see you, Lars. How's Ma?"

Lars grabbed his brother's suitcase. "Ma's fine. She'll be feeding you the fatted calf tonight. She and Bridgit have been getting it ready for days when she's not working like Billy-o with Lady MacNeill from Ballybucklebo raising money for the Spitfire fund . . ."

"Lady MacNeill? I know her husband, the marquis. He's off with his Irish Guards tank regiment, God knows where—"

"Sorry, Deirdre, I didn't mean to monopolize Finn." Lars, who had dumped the suitcase into the boot, held open the back door of Ma's huge Armstrong Siddeley for her.

She laughed that wonderful contralto chuckle that always melted Fingal. "Lars O'Reilly," she said, "you and Fingal are family and you've a lot of family stuff to chat about. I'm not family—"

"Yet," O'Reilly said, "but as soon as the bloody war permits, you will be."

"I know," she said, "but for today, Fingal, you sit in front with Lars for the run down to Portaferry. I'm happy just to have you home—and I'm sure neither your mother nor Lars will expect to monopolise your time for the next ten days until you have to start your journey back."

Ten days with no bugles calling to action stations, no false alarms, no ships torpedoed, no screeching gales, no corned beef sandwiches. O'Reilly heard the promise in Deirdre's voice of time together to come—of laughter, and softness, and love, of walks through little green hills, and lunches in small pubs, dinner at the Widow's in Bangor if he could borrow Ma's car and the petrol ration would stretch. With an enormously contented sigh, he let himself into the passenger's seat. "Home, James—and don't spare the horses." He half-turned as Lars put the car into gear, and stared at Deirdre. "Apparently Queen Victoria used to say that," O'Reilly said, and he inhaled deeply when she mouthed, "I love you, Fingal."

There was nothing left to do but say silently back, "And I love you too."

17

The Mackerel-Crowded Seas

"Be careful on the last step, Kitty. That green seaweed can be bloody slippy when it's wet." O'Reilly held on to her left hand and helped her down the final step of the Ballybucklebo jetty.

"Thank you, Fingal." She took a deep breath and sighed. "An evening's mackerel fishing is exactly what I need. I've had better weeks at work. You've met one of my senior surgeons, Mister John Roulston. Ordinarily he's a sweetheart, but this week? Oh boy. He's had us running round like chickens with their heads cut off."

"The week's over, love," O'Reilly said, giving her hand a squeeze, "and Hall's waiting. Let's go and have some fun."

Hall Campbell had brought Jimmy Scott's thirty-foot open fishing boat to the stone jetty and was now clutching a rusted ring in the granite to hold the craft alongside. He took Kitty's right hand with his free one. While keeping the boat against the step, he took his time waiting for just the right wave to bring the boat's gunwale exactly level with where Kitty stood.

The boat's engine, currently in neutral gear, puttered and gurgled, ejecting intermittent gushes of seawater mingled with exhaust fumes. The sea's surface beneath was rainbow-hued as unburned oil reflected and refracted the sun's rays. O'Reilly could smell the exhaust over the salty tang of the waters of Belfast Lough.

As promised last month in the Duck, Hall had called round at Number One yesterday evening, the second Friday in June, to say that the mackerel were running. Would the O'Reillys like to go out on Saturday evening?

"Bloody right we would," O'Reilly'd said. "Thanks, Hall. That's very generous of you." Kitty wasn't the only one who needed a break from patients. Not an hour before Hall had appeared last evening, O'Reilly and Barry had nipped out to the Duck for a quick preprandial. They'd been standing at the bar supping their pints, passing the time of day with Willie Dunleavy, when Lenny Brown had come in.

"Evenin', Doctors," Lenny said, clearly avoiding meeting O'Reilly's eye.

"Evening, Lenny. How's Connie and Colin?" O'Reilly asked.

"They're grand." He turned away. "I'm meeting Alan Hewitt, so I am, so if youse'll excuse me?" He quickly headed off down the bar room.

"Away you go," O'Reilly said to the man's retreating back. "Has Sue said anything about Colin doing the Eleven Plus, Barry?"

Barry shook his head. "I'm afraid not. The Browns have been mum on the subject, and Sue says Colin is quite subdued these days. And you know that's not like Colin."

"It certainly isn't. I thought as much. If Lenny'd given the go-ahead he couldn't have waited to tell me. And Colin certainly wouldn't have kept it quiet. I think Lenny's dug his heels in. Damn. He sounded like he was coming around when Sue and I talked to him a couple of weeks back."

"So what are you going to do?"

"Damned if I know—yet. But we still have a few weeks."

"Come on ahead now, Mrs. O'Reilly, don't wait any longer," Hall Campbell was saying. "This wave's just the job." O'Reilly watched as his wife stepped onto the boat with the grace of a dancer. "There you are, ma'am. Dead on. Just like a pro," Hall said, guiding her over the gunwale and into the cockpit. "Nice til have you aboard, Mrs. O'Reilly." Hall turned. "Take a hold of that there, sir." He offered his hand to O'Reilly.

"I'm all right," O'Reilly said, "I was in plenty of boats in my navy days." He planted one foot on the boat's side and pushed off with the other, only to have it skid on the very eel grass he'd been at pains to warn Kitty about. The force of trying to regain his balance shoved the vessel away from the quay and broke Hall's grip on the iron ring. As the ship-to-shore gap widened, O'Reilly began to do an ungainly split, which could only have one soggy and frigid outcome. "Hoooooly thundering mother of—" He whirled his arms like a demented semaphore signaller and managed to totter over the side and into the boat's cockpit, grabbing at Kitty as he tumbled aboard.

The action dumped them both in a heap and the little boat tossed and bobbed like a Flower-class corvette in a force-eight gale.

His stream of profanity, caused partly by his embarrassment and partly by his concern for Kitty, was cut short by her laughter as she hauled herself to her feet. She offered him her hand and helped him stand. "Welcome aboard, admiral," she said, and to her credit, O'Reilly thought, refrained from making any more obvious remarks about his assurance that he'd been in plenty of boats.

"You'd not be the first to slip on them there steps, sir," Hall said. "I think maybe if you and Mrs. O'Reilly got yourselves sat down?" He indicated a bench that ran round the inside of the hull to provide seating round the cockpit. The fore end, one-quarter of the length of the clinker-built wooden boat, was decked over to provide some shelter and storage space for nets and fishing gear beneath. O'Reilly was aware of the strong smell of fish coming from the forepeak.

Hall took the tiller, bent to the gear stick, and moved it to "ahead." O'Reilly heard the change in the engine note and felt the thrust of the propeller pushing the boat through a swell, which she rode easily.

The wind of their passage ruffled his great mop of shaggy hair sticking out from under his tweed Paddy hat. He had no idea where Kitty had bought her peaked navy blue skipper's cap, but sitting at a jaunty angle it suited her. Just the right touch to set off her white Arran sweater and her navy blue stirrup pants.

"Where the hell did you get that hat, Kitty? Very fetching if I do say so."

"Where did I get it? That's for me to know and you to find out," she said, inclining her head and raising an eyebrow. "A woman has to have some secrets, you know."

In other words, he thought, none of your business, O'Reilly. He chuckled.

She let a few seconds lapse, then said, "Fingal, you great glipe. Do you not remember buying it for me in that wonderful outdoor market in Rhodes, just a few blocks from our hotel?"

"Did I now? I'll be damned. I must have had other things on my mind during our honeymoon."

He heard a great guffaw from Hall, who was studiously looking out to sea. "Where are you taking us, Hall?" O'Reilly asked, smiling at Kitty.

Hall Campbell pulled out a packet of Capstan Full Strength cigarettes, politely offered one to Kitty while saying to O'Reilly, "I know you smoke a pipe, sir." After she refused he took one and lit it with a Zippo lighter. "My da got that there," he said, showing them the lighter, "from a Yankee GI when they were here waiting for D-Day in 1944. It's a great yoke. Even if it's blowing a half gale it lights." He let go a cloud of smoke that was dispersed by the wind. "Where are we going, sir?" Hall said. "Well, there's been a brave run of herring fry for the last week. The mackerel are after them and they've been coming in near Grey Point, so we'll head down thonder." He pointed ahead. "If you could mebbe steer, sir? I'll get the fishing lines ready for you and the lady."

"Fair enough." O'Reilly slid aft and took the tiller while Hall went for'ard. "This'll be your first time out in the lough, Kitty," O'Reilly said. "Enjoying it so far?"

"A lot," she said, "but I'd like to know where we are."

"Right. We've just left Ballybucklebo and are heading east. Directly across to port if you look over the waters to the far shore . . ."

Tonight the lough was lightly rippled and a deep blue, reflecting the sky's summer shade. An oil tanker so laden and low in the water that her deck was nearly awash made her way to the Port of Belfast. Overhead, puffy clouds played a slow-motion game of follow-my-leader.

"Those are the Antrim Hills that we can see from our lounge."

"And I know that's Carrickfergus Castle," Kitty said, pointing to the massive motte-and-bailey edifice that had squatted grim and menacing on the Antrim shore since Norman times.

"Right. Now if you look astern past me—" He'd already glanced back to see a fleet of racing Fairy-class yachts. Their multihued spinnakers ballooned and collapsed, only to fill again on the light airs as the boats raced downwind. "Those fellahs are out of Royal North of Ireland Yacht Club in Cultra and it's on our side of the lough."

"I know Barry and Sue sail," she said, "but they race out of Royal Ulster down in Bangor."

"Which is a fair stretch up ahead, past where we're going." He nodded his head in that general direction. "Now to your right, to starboard, is the County Down coast. Those big houses with the long rambling gardens running down to shore are where some of the better-off live, including Bertie and Flo Bishop. And that big pile inland, halfway up the hills, is the Culloden Hotel."

"We've been there," she said. "Funny how things look so much different when you see them from out here." She smiled up at him. "It really is a lovely evening to be afloat."

Kitty had to grab the gunwale as the wake from the tanker hit the boat beam on and it rolled four times before settling on an even keel.

The motion didn't bother O'Reilly. It had been more than twenty years since he'd served on *Warspite,* but it was as if no time had gone by at all, so well he knew this feel of the pitch and roll of the deck. "Pity old Arthur couldn't come."

"It's no fun for a dog on a boat. Let's take him down to Strangford tomorrow," she said. "The forecast's good and Barry's on call. I'll make a picnic. There's some cold roast beef in the fridge and I'll have time to make some Scotch eggs in the morning."

"Done," he said. "I think I've a bottle of claret."

"Do you know, Fingal," she said, "I think for a picnic I'd prefer a couple of bottles of Harp lager."

"Then you shall have them, madam," he said, and smiled, damn sure she'd prefer wine, but knew his tastes. He'd bring both.

Hall had reappeared from under the covered forepeak. "I know you know what to do, Doc, but mebbe I should show Mrs. O'Reilly?"

"Go right ahead." O'Reilly watched as Hall set two mackerel fishing hand lines on the bench.

There was neither rod nor reel, but rather a square frame made from four pieces of wood laid so the ends of each overlapped by a couple of inches. Wound round the frame were numerous turns of grey whipcord, to the end of which was tied a wicked-looking barbed hook. There was no fine leader between the stout line and the hook as there would have been on a trout or salmon rig. Belfast Lough fishermen had used the simple setup for as long as anyone could remember.

"There's nothing complicated, Mrs. O'Reilly," Hall said, taking out his packet of cigarettes and removing the silvery foil that lined the packet. He folded it into a strip half an inch wide and four inches long. "The mackerel thinks that this here's a herring fry." He ran the barbed end of the hook twice through the shiny strip close to one end.

"I see," Kitty said. "Clever."

Interesting the things you could use as bait, O'Reilly thought.

Just took having the right appearance and many a fish would be hooked.

"Now." Hall lifted a heavy oval-shaped lead weight with split copper rings at each end. He worked the whipcord through the rings so the weight was now attached to the line about four feet from the hook. "Nearly all set."

O'Reilly reckoned he'd better pay attention to his steering. Coming up ahead was Grey Point, which jutted out into the lough, and the sea itself was not uncluttered. Hall Campbell had no monopoly on fishing for the migratory mackerel. Four herring boats like Hall's, several small cabin cruisers, and even a red-and-white half-open kayak were all trolling off the point. He passed close enough to the kayak to see that the young man in it, who needed both hands to paddle to maintain trolling speed, had taken a turn of whipcord round his naked big toe. Presumably he'd be made aware of a strike by the sudden tug on his toe.

Behind the boats, a flock of herring gulls, the adults grey and white, the adolescents tawny and speckled, hovered over the wakes, swooping and screeching. Periodically they would alight upon the water to bicker over the fish guts that had been thrown overboard from boats already cleaning their catch. Gliding above the herring gulls, a solitary black-backed gull, too aloof to indulge in petty squabbles, waited until one of the smaller birds tried to fly away with a beakful of food. The big robber swooped on its victim until the terrified bird opened its beak, at which point the scavenger caught the entrails in midair and made off.

"Put her out til sea past everybody else, Doc," Hall said.

O'Reilly put his helm down and swung the boat's head.

"Do you know about Grey Point, Mrs. O'Reilly?" Hall said. "We're just passing it."

"Please tell me."

"Used til belong til Lord Dufferin, but the army bought it and built a fort there in 1907. They put two breech-loading six-inch guns in for til defend Belfast Lough. They only ever fired once in two world wars, and that was a warning dummy shell across the bows of a Belfast-bound freighter that hadn't been warned about the guns and didn't pay attention til a challenge from the fort."

"The folks who lived round the lough'll tell you the guns made ferocious rows practising twice a week shooting at drogues towed by tugs," O'Reilly added.

"Aye. And apparently they usually missed them," laughed Hall. "The powers that be took the guns out in the '50s and closed the fort." He lifted the prepared fishing set. "Now, Mrs. O'Reilly," he said, "we're on the fishing ground. Time for work. There's only one important thing til remember. Always, *always,* put the hook in the water first. Never the weight. If it goes in and you're holding the line between it and the hook, the pressure of the flow of water on it will rip the line through your fingers and you'll hook yourself. And we don't want that."

"No, we don't," she said. "I may be a nurse, but I wouldn't have the faintest idea how to remove a fishhook."

"Hall told Jenny Bradley last year how to do it. It sounded painful."

"Sit here, Missus," Hall said, indicating a place on the bench at the stern on the port side. When she did, he took the gear, put the hook over the side, then the weight, then unreeled about thirty feet of line. He handed her the line. "Hold you that there and if you feel a tug, jerk hard to set the hook, then haul the line in hand over hand." He stood beside O'Reilly. "I'll take her now, Doc. We'll get you set up, sir, once Mrs. O'Reilly catches her first fish."

O'Reilly surrendered the tiller, happy to let Hall deal with bringing the boat on a parallel course with all the others yet avoiding the other boats and the lines that, like Kitty's, would be streaming out behind. O'Reilly watched Kitty sitting facing aft, hand held in front of her, the line running from the wooden square, up through her fist, and out over her bent index finger. He smiled to see the look of concentration on her face.

She whipped her arm back so her hand was level with her ear. "Got one." Her smile was enormous and she bent to hauling in the line hand over hand, letting the wet coils fall into the boat's cockpit. The lead weight came over the taffrail, the highest plank of the vessel's stern.

O'Reilly glanced into the water to see a silver, torpedo-shaped fish being pulled along, then leaving the water as Kitty hauled. Its silver scales flashed brilliantly and its dorsal stripes were that intense blue-green seen only on a mackerel or the head of a mallard drake in bright sunlight.

She boated the fish at Hall's feet. It thrashed, making a rattling noise on the deck, and gasped. Single scales like sparkling sequins patterned the deck's planks. Hall bent and thumped it once on the head with a short wooden cudgel that O'Reilly knew was loaded with lead at its tip and known locally as a "priest" because it gave fish the last rites. The mackerel lay still. "Nice fish, Mrs. O'Reilly," Hall said.

"Golly," Kitty said, "that was exciting." She grinned, then her smile faded. "I can't help feeling just a bit sorry for the fish, though."

"Aye," said Hall, "but you'll get used to it, Missus, particularly after you've grilled one or had it smoked and eaten it cold."

"We'll ask Kinky," Kitty said. "We didn't catch many mackerel down in Tallaght, so I don't have a clue." She must have seen Hall's puzzled look. "It's an inland suburb of Dublin where I grew up."

"I heard you were a Dubliner, Mrs. O'Reilly. Well, welcome to the wee north," said Hall, then looked at O'Reilly. "Can you steer again, Doc?"

O'Reilly took the tiller, and Hall unhooked Kitty's mackerel, then produced an old Erinmore Flake tobacco tin and from it took a single safety razor blade. The silver paper on the hook was in tatters so he ripped it off and threw it away. He used the razor blade to slice two thin strips from the fish's silvery belly, put one on Kitty's hook and gave the other to O'Reilly. "You know what to do, sir."

"I do in soul," said O'Reilly.

"I'll take her," Hall said, reaching for the helm.

O'Reilly set to work baiting his hook. Soon he and Kitty had their lines in the water. "Thanks for taking us out, Hall," O'Reilly said. He felt the steady pressure of line on finger, the gentle motion of the boat, heard her engine and the cries of the gulls, both plaintive and belligerent. In the cusp of the low hills of both sides of the lough, the waters and all they contained lay calmly waiting for the soft gloaming as the summer sun slid down the gentle sky. The last quarter of a waning moon swung gently, waiting in the wings to play her bit part after the night had come. "Got one," O'Reilly yelled as the line jerked and tugged at his finger.

As he happily hauled his first fish in he thought, All it takes is the right technique and the right bait. Then a kernel of an idea began to form. He'd come here to relax to put the concerns of the practice behind him for a few hours and had done, but it was the second time he'd thought of bait, and fish weren't the only animals that might be lured.

The shining, twisting mackerel had mistaken a strip of belly for a herring fry and been hooked.

How could O'Reilly devise a bait that would catch Lenny Brown and get it through his stubbornness that the best gift ever he could bestow on Colin was the opportunity for a scholarly education? He'd been off to meet Alan Hewitt last night. Alan was a workingman, but his daughter, Helen, was a medical student who'd just completed her first year. Could that be used in any way?

O'Reilly boated his fish and thumped it with the priest. And if bait wouldn't work with Lenny, he thought, might there be another way to drive sense into his head?

18

Fathom Deep I Am in Love

Ma wore a green cardigan over a ruffle-fronted white blouse. She and the armchair she was in were as straight-backed as the Victorian lady she was. "Come and sit beside me by the fire, Deirdre. It's horrid outside," Ma said.

The burning turf was cosy and filled the lounge with a peaty smell that pleased Fingal. All the electric lights were on to banish the gloom.

"Thank you, Mrs. O'Reilly." Deirdre moved from Fingal's side where they had been standing in the bow window of Ma's lounge watching the gale. It was blowing through the old elms at the bottom of her garden, making them thrash and fight back with bare-clawed branches that tried to rake the lowering sky.

"It's been so nice having you, Deirdre, and you, Fingal, to stay. It's just terrible how the time flies. I can't believe it's been nearly two weeks since you came."

Fingal was back in uniform for the first time in ten days. "It has, Ma," he said, listening to sheets of rain rattling against the panes. The sound reminded him of *Warspite*'s quadruple half-inch machine gun mounts letting go. "And it's been ten wonderful days of your cooking and Bridgit's. I'm going to miss that . . ." And, he thought, I'm going to miss pre-dinner pints with brother Lars in the Portaferry

Arms. Two brothers, old friends, catching up. Eleven marvellous nights in a soft bed, no bugle calls and alarms in the middle of the night, no stink of fuel oil. Nothing tossing and pitching underfoot. "And I'm going to miss you, Ma."

"Thank you, son," she said.

And ten wonderful days with Deirdre. Fingal looked at her sitting demurely, knees together, feet firmly on the ground, her hands in the lap of the grey skirt of her tailored suit. She'd not been so demure when they kissed and caressed on their long walks over the drumlins and round the shore. They'd cuddled in the back stalls of the Art Deco Tonic Cinema in Bangor where they'd gone to see *The Dawn Patrol* with Errol Flynn and David Niven and *The Ghost Goes West* with Robert Donat and Jean Parker.

He sighed then smiled as he pictured her delight on the day when they'd startled a pair of teal from a brown peat pool practically underfoot. In return the birds' sudden noisy appearance had startled Deirdre. Their wings had clattered as they sprang into the air, the little drake with his chestnut head and iridescent green teardrop round his eye venting his displeasure with a harsh quacking. Deirdre'd squealed, then clapped her hands, and giggled like a ten-year-old getting an ice cream. God, he thought, but I'm going to miss how she takes limitless pleasure from the simplest thing. How she can laugh at herself.

"Your father used to say it, Fingal, usually at the end of a holiday, 'All good things must come to an end.'" Ma inhaled deeply. "He was right of course, but I hate you having to go back to the war." She pursed her lips and looked at an ormolu clock on the mantel. "Lars should be here soon."

Fingal walked to Ma's chair and dropped a hand on her shoulder. "You'll still have Lars and Bridgit and all your new friends here, and your work with Lady MacNeill."

Ma nodded, brightened, then said, "We'll be presenting a Spitfire to 602 (City of Glasgow) Squadron, next month. You've both seen the newsreels of what those horrid stukas did in Poland last year. Laura and I think raising five thousand pounds to buy a first-class fighter is well worth it."

"Good for you, Ma," Fingal said. "From what I've read and heard on the radio, not much is happening except at sea. Our side call it the 'Phoney War' and the Nazis the 'Sitzkreig.' But Hitler's going to have to move against France soon and when he does we'll need all the fighter planes we can get. Thank you, Ma."

"Don't thank Laura and me. Thank all the others who've contributed time and money to our Spitfire fund," she said, turning to Deirdre and changing the subject. "I hope, Deirdre, while Fingal's away, you'll not be a stranger even if it is a fair journey from Belfast to Portaferry. There'll always be a bed for you here."

"I will try to get down, I promise," Deirdre said.

The phone in the hall rang. Brigit would answer it, Fingal knew.

"I think," Ma said, looking Fingal straight in the eye, "that you are a very lucky young man. I'm just sorry you'll not be able to make me a mother-in-law soon, but I understand."

Fingal looked at Ma then to Deirdre. "It's a sentiment we all share, Ma, and we've been talking about it. Haven't we, pet?"

Deirdre nodded. "Fingal's hoping to be sent on a course to learn about anaesthetics. He might be home, at least in England, for three months and—"

"Seize it," Ma said. "Life's too short. If you mean to get married then, do it. Do it the minute you can." She cocked her head and grinned at Fingal. "The sooner you make me a granny the better."

He swallowed. Was Ma, straight and proper Ma, was she hinting what he thought she was?

She became serious. "Being in love is wonderful and everything, and I mean everything, about love is wonderful. I envy you young people. Don't waste it."

Fingal nearly whistled. He certainly blushed. Ma could hardly have been more explicit if she'd said, "Hurry up and make love to the girl." He said, "Thanks for everything, Ma," and was relieved when Bridgit, who was now more a companion for Ma than a maid, came into the room and said, "Mister Lars was on the telephone. He is coming in his motorcar to run the lieutenant and Miss Mawhinney to Belfast."

Fingal didn't want Deirdre to go back to the nurses' home tonight. They could breakfast together tomorrow before he caught the boat train to the morning ferry. The plan was for Lars to drive straight to Belfast today, where Fingal had reserved two rooms at the Midland Hotel. It would be unreasonable to expect his brother, in these days of petrol rationing, to make the detour to Ballybucklebo where Fingal and Deirdre were going to visit Fingal's old principal Doctor Flanagan. Once they had registered, he and Deirdre would take the train. Fingal wanted to keep his option open to return to the practice after the war, and was very aware that the old adage "Out of sight, out of mind" was true.

Bridgit said, "He says it's still bucketing down out so he'll honk when he arrives and will you please go straight out."

"Thank you, Bridgit," Fingal said.

She shyly offered him a brown-paper-wrapped parcel. "It's one of my cold pork pies, sir," she said. "It'll maybe do for your lunch, bye, on the train in Scotland, hey." That soft Antrim brogue she'd never lost was in pleasing familiar contrast to the Babel of English and Scottish accents on *Warspite* to which he would be returning.

"That's very thoughtful, Bridgit," O'Reilly said. "Thank you again."

She smiled and bobbed her lace-capped head.

Ma stood. "Give me a kiss, Deirdre."

Deirdre rose, hugged Ma, and pecked her cheek. "I will come and see you, I promise, Mrs. O'Reilly."

"And I think," said Ma, "we know each other well enough by now. Please call me Mary."

"Thank you—Mary."

Fingal hugged his mother. "So long, Ma. I hope it won't be too long until I get home again. I'll write."

"See you do."

There was a blast of a car's horn from outside.

"Now run along and both of you take care of yourselves."

As Fingal stood aside to let Deirdre go first, he heard his mother say sotto voce so only he could hear, "And I meant what I just said. Don't waste time. There's a war on."

"Doctor Fingal O'Reilly, as I live and breathe, and Miss Mawhinney." Deirdre had been invited to Doctor Flanagan's home several times for a meal since Fingal and she had become engaged in July. "As welcome as rain in a summer of drought you are, so."

"Mrs. Kinkaid," Deirdre said. "How are you?"

"Grand, so." Mrs. Kinky Kincaid, Doctor Flanagan's house-keeper from County Cork, stood in the open doorway of Number One, Main Street, Ballybucklebo. Her silver hair, as ever, was done up in a tight chignon, her floral pinafore dusted with flour and, Fingal thought, the beginnings of a double chin seemed to have increased since he'd left here last November. She beamed, and dimples came to her cheeks as her agate eyes looked Fingal up and down from head to toe, frowned, then said; "But those uniform trousers could use a pressing, bye."

Fingal laughed and shook his head. "They'll need it a lot more after I've been on the Scottish train for hours, and anyway, Deirdre and I came to visit Doctor Flanagan and yourself, not to have my trousers ironed."

"Well, come in. Come in." She stood aside, closed the door after them, and helped hang their sodden hats and coats on the coatstand. "Doctor Flanagan was so pleased when you phoned yesterday and he'll be sorely vexed that he's missed you, sir," she remarked. "He said to apologise, but you'll remember Agnes Alexander?"

Fingal frowned then said, "Red-haired lass. I saw her once or twice last year. Early on in a pregnancy. Husband's Fred, a shipyard plater?"

"That's right, sir. You've a powerful memory, so. Anyroad, she did go into labour six hours ago and the midwife sent for Doctor Flanagan an hour since."

"Oh," said Fingal, rather at a loss. He had wanted to pay his respects to his senior colleague, but not spend too long. This, after all, was his last time with Deirdre and he wanted her to himself. No one could predict how long a labour might take, so there was not much sense hanging about for what could be hours. Perhaps they'd made the trip for nothing.

"And you've come all the long way from Belfast City by train." Kinky shook her head and tutted.

It was only about six miles, but to country folk, who mostly walked or cycled, it would seem a long way, and he knew from experience that villagers always found the big city intimidating.

"But I knew what time to expect you, so, and I have the kettle on and it'll only take a shmall-little minute to toast and butter the barmbrack. I only baked it this morning. If himself gets finished soon you might still see him, but there'll be a Belfast train in about forty minutes so if he's not back you could catch that."

And be back at the Midland Hotel with Deirdre all to myself before high teatime, Fingal thought. "That would be wonderful, Kinky," he said, and hesitated. It was not customary for servants to dine with guests of the master, but in the months Fingal had worked here he'd come to know big, motherly Kinky Kincaid as much as a friend as the housekeeper. "Will you sit down with us, Kinky?" he asked. "We'd really love to hear what's been going on in the village since I left."

She frowned and said, "I would like that, so, but only if I could entertain you in my kitchen, sir. It does not be my place to dine in the master's quarters."

"That would be lovely, Kinky," Deirdre said.

"Lead on," said Fingal, and took Deirdre's hand.

Past the surgery, the waiting room, and into the big warm kitchen where amazing cooking smells were coming from a pot bubbling on a black cast-iron range and a kettle was coming to the boil.

Kinky pulled out three chairs from her wooden table and said, "Please sit down." Fingal held Deirdre's chair. He was aware of her faint perfume and longed to have her to himself. As he took his own seat he noticed a needlework frame over which was stretched mesh canvas. Already the hull of a Spanish galleon had been completed in coloured wools which must have come from a nearby box of threads and needles.

Deirdre must have noticed it too. "That's a beautiful tapestry you're stitching, Mrs. Kincaid," she said.

"Thank you, Miss Deirdre." Kinky finished making the tea. "I intend it for a fire screen that'll sit in front of the hearth in my quarters when the fire's not lit. It does be of the *Falco Blanco* from the Spanish Armada. She went aground in Galway Bay."

"In 1588, I believe," Fingal said. "Eight years before the first *Warspite* was built. The finished tapestry is going to be lovely."

"Thank you, sir," Kinky said, setting the teapot, sugar, milk, and three cups on the table.

"I usually work on it in my room, but sometimes on a cold day like today the warmth of the range in here saves me from having to light my own fire." She turned to Deirdre. "Now, Miss Deirdre, would you pour, please, while I get the 'brack out of the oven?"

Fingal spent the next thirty minutes munching warm wedges

of the buttered dark spicy loaf, sipping his tea, listening, and questioning.

Kinky was the font of all knowledge about the village. Young Bertie Bishop's building company had secured a contract to erect Nissen huts for the army, so he was coining money hand over fist and he was already a junior office holder in the local Orange Lodge. Talk was that in a year or two he might run for the Council. His wife Flo was, with Kinky and Cissie Sloan, active in the Women's Guild. Two months ago Declan Finnegan had volunteered for the Tank Regiment. Mrs. Doreen Donnelly had had a miscarriage, but she and her husband Michael wanted a wee boy and were going to try again and if they succeeded were going to call the lad Donal. The Ballybucklebo Highlanders had been given new sets of pipes and drums by Laura, Marchioness of Ballybucklebo.

". . . and," Kinky said, "t'was very sad, so, but Willie Dunleavy's father took a stroke, and him only sixty-six, and passed away last December and now son Willie's owner and landlord of the Mucky Duck."

Fingal realised how much he missed village life and was certain that he wanted to come back here once the war was over. He glanced at Deirdre. She was a country girl. He knew she'd love it here too. He glanced at his watch. It would take only five minutes to walk to the station, but it was time they were moving. He rose. "Kinky, thank you for the tea and 'brack. I'm sorry we missed Doctor Flanagan. Please give him our best."

"I will, sir." Kinky rose. "I'll show you out."

And to Fingal's delight the gale had blown over. "Take care of yourself, Kinky," he said. "The Lord knows when, but I will be back—one day."

"And I know, Miss Deirdre, you'll be by his side."

Kinky had been one of the first people Fingal had told of his engagement last year.

"I would have dearly loved to come to your wedding here, but I'm sure you'll not have to wait for the war to end." She fixed Fingal with an eye-to-eye gaze that lasted a moment too long and he felt the back of his neck tingle. Kinky Kincaid had the sight. And he recalled Ma's parting words. "Remember what I just said. Don't waste time. There's a war on."

⬧

Fingal acknowledged the head-bobbing from one of the Midland Hotel's uniformed chambermaids, straightened his tie, and knocked on the door of Deirdre's room. "I'll come and get you in twenty minutes for high tea," he'd said after the taxi from Queen's Quay Railway Station had left them at their hotel. He'd only managed to wait for seventeen. He inhaled and smelt the aged fustiness that must have been an aroma common to hotel corridors worldwide.

The door opened an inch. "I'm not quite ready, darling, but please come in."

He did and closed the door behind him. She'd left an aura of faint musk behind her as she walked back to sit on a backless stool in front of an Art Deco dressing table topped with a huge semicircular mirror. "Won't be a minute," she said, and began brushing her hair that had been cut to have a wave on the crown and fall to curve up at shoulder height.

"You'll remember our code for letters?" Fingal said. "I want you to know where I am and not be fretting about it."

"I will. 'Can you buy Ma a present' means you're in the Med. 'Speak to Kinky' means the Far East. I have it all written down. Now stop worrying and let me finish getting ready."

He watched her. She was wearing a black dress, belted at the waist. The shoulders were padded and the back cut low across her shoulder blades. He noticed that the upper buttons were undone. In the mirror he could see that the bodice was of a dark material cut in a V. On top of it, from waist to neck, was transparent stuff, chiffon perhaps or maybe this synthetic material newly invented by DuPont that was being made into women's stockings as well as parachutes. Whatever it was, the effect of showing, but as through a glass darkly, her cleavage and the upper swelling of her breasts was hellishly erotic. Fingal took a deep breath and swallowed.

"I'm sorry I'm not on time," she said, her breasts rising and falling with each brush stroke.

"I'm early," he said.

"Be a pet and button me up."

Just, he thought as he crossed the floor, like an old married couple. He had to squat behind her to reach and began to fumble for the lowest button. As he did his fingers touched the warm skin of her back and she made a throaty noise.

To his surprise, she stood, walked round the stool, and waited for him to rise. "Fingal O'Reilly," she said, and he heard the huskiness, "I love you very dearly." Before he could speak she kissed him. Long, tongue tinglingly, and hard. She stepped back.

He was breathless. Tongue-tied.

She turned her back and said, "My buttons."

"Yes," he said.

"Undo them."

"What?"

"Undo them." She half-turned and smiled, before saying, "Undo them, Fingal darling. I want you to make love to me, just like your mother hinted. I've been thinking about it all afternoon. I want to own you and you to own me, and I need that before you go back to this hateful war."

His fingers shook as first one then another button slipped from its hole.

It was only because he'd asked that both rooms be given an early morning call that they managed to get to breakfast.

And after they'd eaten, Surgeon Lieutenant Fingal O'Reilly RNR chastely kissed Nurse Deirdre Mawhinney good-bye, still trembling with the taste of her, the warmth, and the softness of her. The unreserved love of her. Surgeon Lieutenant Fingal O'Reilly, hugging the memories to himself, boarded the morning boat train for the Larne to Stranraer Ferry and for the second time went to war.

19

He Smelleth the Battle Afar

"Best as I can tell, people, all hell's going to break loose in about two hours." Surgeon Commander Wilcoxson was sitting at his desk in the sick bay surrounded by his staff—two medical and one dental officer and eight SBAs. "The executive officer, Commander R. A. Currie, has briefed me fully and I've to pass the word to you about the upcoming action." He frowned and looked CPO Paddy O'Rourke straight in the eye. "The ships' boys have been instructed to bathe and put on clean underwear and overalls. We assume the rest of the crew know to do that and you are all well aware of what it means."

Paddy nodded and pursed his lips.

Lord, Fingal thought, since the days of Nelson's navy, those instructions had been given before an action, because bits of dirty clothes, if driven into a wound by a projectile or splinters, increased the risk of infection. The instructions were an indication that those in charge expected there to be casualties aboard *Warspite*.

Fingal shuddered. Since rejoining the ship after his leave in March, he'd not been faced with treating any wounds, but things in the wider world had been moving rapidly, and it was unlikely that he could avoid doing so for much longer. He had it all in his ruled notebook diary and would have more to add today. Germany had invaded Denmark and Norway on the night of April 9, 1940, four days ago.

Today the big ship, for reasons that were not clear to Fingal, was going to be in the thick of things in a Norwegian fjord called Westfjord that led to the harbour of Narvik. He paid close attention to what his senior officer was saying. Some of this would be worth recording too.

"To bring you up to date tactically," Wilcoxson continued, "Vice Admiral Whitworth was at sea on HMS *Renown* with the Twentieth Destroyer Flotilla chasing the Germans' *Scharnhorst* and *Gneisenau*. Unfortunately, they didn't catch the two battlecruisers. Meanwhile the Nazis, as part of their invasion plans, sent ten destroyers and we don't know how many U-boats to attack Narvik and to land troops to occupy the place. I'm told that strategically they want the port so they can export Swedish iron ore to the Fatherland, but that's not really our concern. Our job is simply to stop the buggers. The admiral detached the Twentieth Destroyer Flotilla under the command of Captain Bernard Warburton-Lee. By the end of the day, April 10, he and his ships had carried out a brilliant attack in Westfjord in a snowstorm, but the Germans fought back. Two of our ships were sunk and one was badly damaged. A shell hit the bridge of his destroyer, HMS *Hardy,* and Warburton-Lee was killed."

"He was a Welshman," Davy Jones said with pride in his voice.

Fingal wondered how many more men had died. Men on both sides.

"The Germans lost three destroyers sunk and four seriously damaged—"

"Sounds like our side out-scored the Jerries," Davy Jones said.

"God Almighty, Jones, it's not a bloody rugby match," Wilcoxson said.

"Sorry, sir." Davy studied the toecaps of his shoes.

"Be that as it may," Wilcoxson said, "as far as we know the Germans have managed to land two thousand troops, and it's going to be our job to clear out the rest of the Kriegsmarine ships still in there so our army can land and get the Huns out. The Germans have had three days to effect what repairs they can to their damaged ships so there may be a lot of trouble. The whole of the Westfjord has smaller fjords entering it from both sides. Even a damaged, moored destroyer, hiding in one of them, can fire torpedoes at short range. We can't manoeuvre in here to avoid the bloody things. It's too narrow. So our guns' crews are going to have to be on their toes to knock out any enemy ships first. This is going to be an all-out effort."

"And is dat why Vice Admiral Whitworth came aboard at sea from *Renown* yesterday, sir?" Paddy O'Rourke asked.

"It is," Wilcoxson said. "He's taken overall command of *Warspite* and nine destroyers. We're his flagship. Apparently *Renown*'s too valuable to risk in the narrow waters of a Norwegian fjord. At the moment, we're about one hundred miles from Narvik. Shortly we will start our run in."

"What's the screen like, sir?" Petty Officer Barker asked.

"There'll be three destroyers in line astern leading up the middle of the fjord. They'll have mine-sweeping gear rigged out. Next, we'll have six destroyers divided between two lines of three, one out to port, one out to starboard. They'll be looking for U-boats and taking on any German surface ships. We'll be sending up a Swordfish spotter plane soon too. Our smaller ships' disposition will look like a giant tuning fork proceeding handle first. And we, good old *Warspite*, we'll be smack in the middle between the tips of the tines at the arse end of everything. Our job's to back up the destroyers, and pulverise any shore batteries."

"And we're going today, sir?" an SBA asked. "Because if anyone's superstitious, it's Friday the thirteenth."

"Och sure," said Paddy O'Rourke, "pay no heed. With Lieutenant O'Reilly and me on board and Mister Laverty from Bangor and Mister Wallace from Portstewart, aren't we sure to have the luck of the Irish?"

The laughter, Fingal thought, was forced, but he felt the men were in good spirits.

"All right," said Wilcoxson, "settle down. I have a rough timetable. By twelve thirty we should have passed the island of Baroy to starboard and be entering Westfjord proper. We should get to Narvik, the Lord and the Nazis willing, or shoved aside if they are unwilling, at between four and five P.M." Wilcoxson scratched his chin. "We all know where our battle stations are in the for'ard and aft medical distributing stations. I don't think we need rush there just yet. There's to be an early lunch and then we'll probably close up for action stations once we're well into the fjord."

Fingal overheard Paddy O'Rourke mutter to Petty Officer Fletcher, "Lunch? More bloody bully beef and hard-boiled eggs. Always the same if it looks like we're going to have to fight." He was probably right, and with the constipating effects of the eggs there'd usually be a lineup at the dispensary the next day asking for laxatives.

"Now, two more things," Wilcoxson said. "One, it has been arranged, for the sake of most of us in the ship's crew who won't be able to see what's going on, that an officer up on the bridge, who's privy to reports from aircraft and destroyers, will give a running commentary over the Tannoy system."

Bloody good idea, Fingal thought. Good psychology to keep the crew informed.

"And two, I want to thank you all. I know that since we received orders to sail with the prospect of imminent surface action I have been completely satisfied that everything that can be prepared in the medical department has been, by your efforts. Well done."

There was a general muttering of assent and Fingal, who had been thinking about how much Richard Wilcoxson's leadership was responsible for that, suddenly became aware of a sudden change in the sounds around him. The whine of the fans in the lobby outside became higher pitched as they increased their speed. The constant thundering of the ship's turbines grew louder. The Tannoy announced, "HMS *Warspite* and her destroyer escort are now proceeding into Westfjord to seek out and engage the enemy. Vice Admiral Whitworth is confident that, with God's help, we will achieve a great victory." Barely had the speaker stopped than the roar of the ship's turbines grew louder yet and even in the sick bay the forward motion was obvious.

There was a cheer from the assembled men.

Fingal felt a stab of impatience, now that things were under way. He wanted to see where they were going, watch how the destroyers deployed, try to get a sense of time and place. "Permission to go on deck, sir?"

"Don't see why not, O'Reilly," said Wilcoxson, "but the second they sound action stations, make a beeline for the for'ard medical distributing centre. I'll be there."

"I will." Fingal, who had hoped for such an opportunity and so had brought his duffle coat, slipped it on, as usual reaching in the pocket for Deirdre's green silk scarf to wrap round his neck, hiding the gossamer fabric beneath the rough wool of the duffle's collar. He was grateful she'd not know and so not have to worry that he might soon be under fire. He left the sick bay and made his way aloft.

The open forecastle deck was covered in snow, and two groups of sailors were having a snowball fight among the flurries. Fingal assumed by their white asbestos antiflash hoods and gauntlets that the men were the crews of A and B turrets. He glanced up. Those long rifles above his head might be bellowing very soon. Certainly their tompions, with their green woodpecker crests, had been removed.

He was distracted by the roaring to full power of an aeroplane engine. *Warspite* carried two spotter aircraft in hangars on her decks aft of the funnel trunking. They were launched by a steam catapult that ran across the ship from side to side, athwartships. There was a hissing of steam from the catapult and a loud thud as it reached the end of its run. The biplane contraption of wings, struts, and canvas-covered fuselage lumbered into the grey lowering sky bearing its crew of three in open cockpits. Rather them than me, Fingal thought. It's bloody well cold enough down here and they're not exactly in a wingèd chariot. The plane, a Fairey Swordfish torpedo-bomber, affectionately known as the "Stringbag," had a maximum speed of 129 miles per hour and only two machine guns. The design had been obsolete before it came into service, but such was the need for a torpedo bomber that the navy had accepted it anyway pending delivery of a more modern type. Yet today she was the eyes of the little fleet and for good measure carried a full load of antisubmarine bombs. "Godspeed," Fingal said, saluted, and whispered, "Come home safely."

As he watched the biplane move ahead and into the fjord, it cleared the rearmost destroyer of the centre column, HMS *Hero*. Ahead of her, the funnel smoke of her two companions was streaming off to the side. Long wakes churned the grey sea's surface behind the sterns of the rearmost ships, HMS *Eskimo* and *Forester*. All around, the leaden sky bore down on the snow-covered hills and cliffs of the fjord. They had been torn into the Earth by the last ice age and today hung scowling as if bent on the destruction of the ships that dared to invade this domain of ogres and trolls.

He was blinking away the tears brought on by the Arctic wind of their passage when he heard from ahead the staccato crack of a destroyer's 4.7-inch guns, the deeper bark of German 5-inch gun replies, and, over the Tannoy, a bugler sounding the charge, the call to action stations.

It had begun.

He set off at a good pace, the crashing of the other ships' rifles and the bellowing of *Warspite*'s turbines filling his senses, surrounding him with noise. He was two decks down when a loudspeaker announced, "There is a German destroyer to starboard. She is burning, but her crew can be seen preparing torpedo tubes. She will be taken under fire."

There was a short silence. He knew what was happening above

him. The gunnery officer's team, way up in the fifteen-inch control tower, would be feeding range and bearing data to the turrets, where the nearly one-ton shells and their cordite charges would be loaded into the rifles. The gun's crew would take aim. When the guns were on target, firing gongs would sound and—Holy Mother of Jesus. He had to grab on to the handrail as *Warspite* heeled to the blast of one, then another gun. The sound even down here was deafening. Nothing could have prepared him for the noise that surrounded him like an impenetrable wall and by its force seemed to be crushing his chest. Dear God, how did the gun crews survive even one firing? The row was infernal, inhuman. In moments the stink of burnt cordite assailed his nostrils. He could picture the vast tongue of fire leaping from the gun's barrel and the all-enveloping cloud of brown fumes belching from the muzzle. They were firing at almost point-blank range on an already damaged vessel many times smaller, a killer whale devouring a penguin with a broken flipper.

The Tannoy's voice rang, flat, expressionless, as unexcited as if it were announcing, "Up spirits. The enemy has rolled over and is sinking."

As the battleship's fifteen-inch guns and six-inch secondaries fell silent, Fingal spared a thought for the German sailors, but his reverie was interrupted by the squawk of the Tannoy. "Our Swordfish spotter plane, that we've nicknamed Lorna, has identified and sunk, by bombing, a German U-boat in Herjangsfjord, which is up ahead off our port bow."

He was greeted by cheering of the announcement as he opened the door and went into the medical distribution centre. Inevitably, the casualties would start arriving soon. Although *Warspite* was still unscathed, other British ships had been hit, some hard. The only question was when the medical staff's work must start.

Nobody would feel like cheering then.

He sat down at his desk and opened the notebook with lined

pages, now well thumbed from use. There was time to bring his war diary up to date.

> *April 13, 1940. Second Battle of Narvik under way. Have heard the fifteen-inchers fired at an enemy destroyer. It was an absolutely devastating assault on all the senses and I'd better get ready for more because that initial duel was only the beginning. There are several German ships up ahead. Nothing seemed to faze Richard and the SBAs, but I find it claustrophobic down here knowing that all the watertight hatches between us and the open air four decks up are dogged down. It would have been the same for many of the crew on the sinking German ship.*

He looked at the grey steel walls and imagined the room filling with freezing oily water from sole to deckhead. Stop it, he told himself. Your imagination is far too vivid. He reached inside his jacket and pulled out her last letter, which had been waiting for him in Greenock after the most recent convoy. There was still the faintest trace of the musk she always wore. He would try to read it from beginning to end.

> *My Darling Fingal,*
>
> *I wonder where you will be or when you will get this? Probably when you return to home base in . . .* the next word was smudged over by the censor's blue pencil. He smiled. Even though she knew perfectly well about censorship Deirdre from time to time seemed to forget, and for that matter so did Lars and Ma when they wrote. *I hope you will be well and able to get some rest.* She never stopped worrying about him, bless her. *I am keeping myself very busy to help me try to ignore how terribly I am missing you and cannot wait until your next home leave so we can continue our sweet explorations, my pet.* He smiled as he

had done the first time he'd read it, cherishing his memories of their lovemaking, hurried the first time, then sweet and langorous. The softness of her and the urgency and—

The whole ship shook as the great rifles roared their hatred at the Germans, and Fingal slipped her letter back in his pocket, took a deep breath, and settled down to wait for what the day might bring.

20

Grim-Visag'd War

At last the guns had fallen silent. The battle was over. "A, B, X, and Y guns' crews may go on top of turrets," the Tannoy announced. "Guns' crews may go on top of turrets."

For the first time in the four hours since he'd last been on deck, Fingal didn't have to strain to hear the words over the din of war. Even here, deep within the ship where the medical team was effectively locked up with all the watertight hatches sealed, the racket had been horrible. It hardly bore thinking about how deafening it must have been inside the gunhouses when the guns fired. And how suffocating as cordite fumes leaked back each time the breeches were opened. No wonder the crews were being let out into the fresh air.

No one had been injured on *Warspite* and not a single casualty had been received so far from any other ships. Two portable operating tables were set up and waiting. Boxes of presterilised instruments were stacked against the bulkheads. A steam autoclave for sterilizing instruments was plugged into a power supply. All the other necessities for patching up wounded humanity were here, ready and waiting.

Fingal was relieved and, he had to admit, shocked, that no one on *Warspite* had been hurt. The constant and unearthly din of the guns had given him the impression that topside things would be hellish and chaotic. And yet not a single man had been wounded. He knew from the running commentary of the Tannoy, however, that eight German destroyers had been sunk and at least two British ships were "badly damaged" and another "damaged." He wondered where the dividing line between the two descriptions lay and if other ships had been hit.

"I'm sure we're going to be busy soon," Commander Wilcoxson said, "and so will Davy Jones's crew aft. So does anyone want to go on a short sightseeing trip, get a breath of fresh air?"

Fingal nodded his yes. He felt claustrophobic in this porthole-less room down on the middle deck. He needed to breathe some air. And he needed a smoke.

He was not alone. Before he could say anything, all five SBAs said they'd appreciate the opportunity. "Me too," said Fingal.

"Right," said Wilcoxson, "everybody back in half an hour. I'll phone Davy's lot too. Tell them to take a break."

Fingal had his pipe in his pocket filled and ready to go when the little party emerged onto the foc's'le deck. Paddy O'Rourke offered Fingal a Player's Navy Cut cigarette. One did, even if you knew the other man was a pipe smoker or didn't smoke at all.

"No thanks, Paddy. Pipe." As Fingal lit up and gratefully inhaled he looked up to see the crews of the big guns clambering out from the hatches on top of their turrets. Some of the men were already munching on what he guessed was another round of bully beef sandwiches and hard-boiled eggs.

He and CPO Paddy O'Rourke walked along the deck past A turret to get a better view.

Warspite had anchored at five P.M. in the oil-stained waters of Westfjord off the town of Narvik. Immediately to starboard, at the mouth of Beisfjord, one of the smaller fjords that joined the main one, the hulks of three German destroyers poured columns of greasy smoke to defile the sky, which was now the clear blue of an early evening above the Arctic Circle. The sun wouldn't set for another three and a half hours. Black snowflakes from the fires, like smudges on clean paper, defaced the firmament. The surrounding snow-covered hills sparkled in the rays of a still high sun, but what should have been the tangy saltiness of the frigid air was overwhelmed by the stink of burning oil and paint—and of something roasting. He'd never smelled it before, but he was sure it was human flesh. Fingal gagged and took a deep pull on his pipe.

Paddy O'Rourke grimaced. "Doze Jerries must have taken a hell of a pounding, poor sods," he said. "And our lads, sir." Paddy pointed astern to where a British destroyer had run aground. "There'll be wounded coming off that ship. Her fore end's a feckin' shambles."

"I think that's *Cossack*," Fingal said. "She was hit hard early on. But," and he jabbed much farther for'ard with his pipe stem, "that's Rombaksfjord. You remember that our ships went in there—"

"*Eskimo* was torpedoed, and she's in rag order too, but we did for four Huns, the gurriers." Paddy shrugged. "I think we've won this one, at least at sea." He nodded toward the town. "How do you reckon we're going to winkle the German buggers out of there, sir? I reckon they'll be all over the place like clap on a heifer's arse."

Fingal chuckled, cheered by the words from home, and let go a blue cloud that hung motionless. "No idea," he said, "and be grateful it's not our problem. See there?" Two destroyers, their names on their bows, *Forester* and *Bedouin,* were finishing coming alongside and mooring with their bows secured against *Warspite*'s quarterdeck. "I reckon they'll be offloading casualties from the other ships to us. Maybe some German wounded too." He took a final pull on his comforting briar. "I don't mind telling you, Paddy, I'm worried about how I'm going to manage." Although, he thought, the general surgical principles he had been taught in his year studying obstetrics and gynaecology would be of some help.

Paddy grinned, and said, "Och Jasus, sir, look on the bright side, at least you'll have me and ould Hippocrates keeping an eye on you."

"I've been aft, Fingal," Richard Wilcoxson said when he and Paddy O'Rourke returned to the medical station. "We're going to be taking wounded from five of our damaged destroyers."

Five? That answered Fingal's question about how many other ships had been hit. He wondered just how many cases that would mean. Again the worm inside nagged at him. Would he be able to cope?

Richard continued. "I've been able to free up all but one of our fully trained sick berth staff to work here or in the aft medical centre on the patients who need us most. We're not actually at action stations, but we might get bombed so we'll continue to work below. The MOs of *Forester* and *Bedouin* will act as triage officers, spare us that duty. You remember, Fingal, I told you battleships serve as hospital ships after major actions. They'll send the walking wounded to the various mess decks on the main deck and the MOs and their SBAs will pitch in there until it's time for the destroyers to leave. Some of the wounded will have already been patched up on the way here. A lot of them can be cared for by our first-aiders. Others will only need a few stitches or wounds dressed. They'll have to wait. We'll be putting the surgical cases on the seamen's mess deck both pre- and postoperatively. I've detailed one of our SBAs to work with that group. The other four on our team will work with us. "

"I'll go there now, sir," Paddy said, "and come down and let you know when the first surgical cases start arriving."

"Good man," Richard said, then, taking a deep breath, pursed his lips. "Those badly wounded for whom all we can offer is morphine . . ." Wilcoxson frowned and shook his head. "The poor devils will be made as comfortable as possible in the seamen's mess too. The chaplain's trained to give the medication and he'll stay with them and offer what support he can. He'll have two bandsmen/ stretcher bearers to help."

Fingal understood but hated what must be done. In wartime, brutal decisions had to be made, and the limited medical resources put to where they could do the most good. The hours of surgery spent on one patient who would still probably die were better invested in caring for men with lesser wounds who could be saved. Some men must be left to die. "I see," he said, and his heart ached.

"Simpler cases, uncomplicated fractures, lacerations, minor burns, will be treated in the aft medical distribution centre by Davy Jones, the dentist, and their team, and," he clapped Fingal on the shoulder, "the tougher ones will be brought here."

"You're the most senior surgeon," Fingal said. "I understand."

"Paddy O'Rourke will assist me . . ."

And I'll give the anaesthetics, Fingal thought, and shuddered.

"Barker will assist you."

"Me?" Fingal's voice rose. He was, he thought, between the devil and the deep blue sea. On one hand, he was still terrified at the prospect of having to give anaesthetics, and also relieved that it didn't look as if he was going to have to.

"You've had a year of gynaecological surgery training, you told me. The basic surgical priciples are the same in men and women."

"I have." But, Fingal thought, there would be a huge difference between performing a simple hysterectomy and treating someone with a belly full of shrapnel.

"You'll be fine."

Fingal swallowed and said, "Aye, aye, sir." Needs must when the devil drives. Fingal felt his stomach turn over.

"The two other SBAs can use the mask and ether like you did the day you arrived. We're going to need all the surgical hands we can get. Pity we're not connected to the mess decks by phone. The SBAs and us will be too busy between cases getting ready for the next one so we'll keep one stretcher bearer here as a runner to get his mates to take away each case back to the mess decks when we've finished. Have them bring the next one," Richard said, "and we'll all pitch in to get the dirty instruments washed and resterilized." He clapped Fingal on the shoulder. "It's going to be a long night and God knows when we'll get finished tomorrow—if then. If you think you're going to drop on your feet tell me. I have some benzedrine."

Fingal had heard of naval surgeons and indeed deck officers keeping going on the amphetamine stimulants. "I'll ask if I need it," he said.

Richard nodded. "Good." Then he said to Paddy, who had reappeared, "Well, what have we got so far?"

"I spoke to the *Bedouin's* MO. He reckons that between them and *Forester,* the other destroyer, they're going to bring us at least two hundred casualties—"

"Bloody hell," Richard said, and frowned.

It startled Fingal. He'd not thought anything could rattle Richard Wilcoxson.

"Only about fifty of those will need to be looked after, either here with us or by Lieutenant Jones and his crew. The rest aren't seriously hurt."

"Still, that's fifty surgical cases, right?" Fingal said, and heard his voice rise. "Fifty?"

"Don't worry, Fingal," Richard said, and his voice had returned to its usual unflappable tone. "With God's help we'll cope."

The words were a comfort. Fingal had already learned that Richard Wilcoxson was a Christian who kept his faith to himself. Fingal, whose own beliefs tended much more to the agnostic, couldn't help but remember a remark he'd overheard a patient make at Sir Patrick Dun's. A nursing sister had been reassuring her patient that God loved him and that he would come through his operation with flying colours. "Indeed God *is* good, Sister," the Corkman had said. "But a wise man never tries to dance in a shmall narrow boat, so." In other words, don't expect the impossible under unreasonable circumstances.

All Fingal could hope for was that they would manage. And after all, he smiled to himself, *Warspite* was a very large and beamy vessel.

21

Thus Must We Toil

Barker, already gowned and gloved and ready to assist, faced Fingal across the operating table where his first case lay. Not AB Smith. Not CPO Jones. Not a real person, it seemed, merely a nameless case. Overhead lights glared down. The smell of ether mingled with the bitter aroma of Dettol and the coppery tang of blood. The SBA seated at the table's head lifted one of the patient's eyelids and said, "He's out, sir."

Fingal watched as Barker poured disinfectant on a shattered right thigh where a rubber tourniquet controlled the bleeding. There was no time for personal niceties. In the next few hours three doctors would have to perform more than fifty operations, and Fingal could feel the nausea of anticipation deep in his belly. The bone end, the femur, nacreous and jagged, stuck through the skin and muscle. The man had no foot and the lower leg and thigh were a mangled mess held on by a strip of skin.

"Right," said Fingal, and bent to his work, concentrating on the surgical steps. Cut the remaining skin and drop the wreckage into a bucket. Take off the tourniquet and clamp the spurting blood vessels. Ligate the arteries and veins. Use a scalpel to create hemi-elliptical flaps of muscle and skin in front and behind the bone. Saw off the jagged bone and take a file to smooth off the femur's end. The rasping set his teeth on edge. Sprinkle sulpha powder on the insides of the flaps and sew them closed over the bone. Dress the stump. "Done," he said. "Give him a quarter grain of morphine before he comes to, then wake him up." He turned to the waiting stretcher bearer. "Please go and get your mate. You'll be taking this poor bugger to the seaman's mess then bringing the next patient."

"Aye, aye, sir." The man left.

Fingal began to strip off his glove.

"I'd keep them on, sir, if I was you," Barker said. "Remember the boss said we all help out washing the instruments?"

"Of course." Fingal looked over to where he could see Richard using a carpenter's brace and bit to drill a hole in the skull of a sailor who had been hit on the head and, according to *Bedouin*'s medical officer on the basis of his clinical findings, probably had a blood clot on the brain. The senior surgeon's actions were rhythmic, unhurried. Fingal envied the man his experience.

"Good diagnosis," Richard said, and Fingal could see the dark blood flowing from the burrhole. That patient now had an excellent chance of recovery.

Barker took the bucket with the shattered leg to a corner and deposited the contents in a large galvanised tub. Fingal bundled up his instruments in a towel and took them to a sink where he started to wash them. He was barely aware of the bustle around him, of tables being cleaned, stretchers coming and going.

"I'll finish off and pop them in the sterilizer," Barker said. "Your next one is arriving. He's been shot in the guts."

Bullet wounds to the bowel were not like a case of straightforward appendicitis. Fingal was trembling as he approached the table where a fair-haired young man was being strapped down. A plasma bottle suspended above his head was dripping into an arm vein and a narrow rubber tube for sucking out stomach contents disappeared up one nostril.

"Mutti. Mutti. Fur Die liebe Gottes. Mutti." He was moaning and trying to twist free from his bonds.

A German prisoner of war calling for his mother, for the love of God. It brought a prickling to Fingal's eyes. The wounded man couldn't have been more than twenty. He was a frightened child, but his mummy couldn't kiss a perforated bowel better. It wasn't clear that Surgeon Lieutenant O'Reilly could make it heal either.

"Bitte, wasser. Wasser zu trinken. Bitte."

A drink of water was the worst thing to give such a patient.

"Come on, Fritz," the SBA said, putting the mask in place. "Couple of deep breaths like a good Kraut." He dropped ether on the gauze and said to Fingal, "I don't think much of the master race. 'Cepting they talk funny, they're not much different from us, are they, sir?"

Fingal nodded and thought, "If you prick us do we not bleed?" The pity was that none of this carnage should have been necessary in a so-called civilised world. God damn Adolf Hitler and his megalomaniacal crew, the Goerings, the von Ribbentrops, the Goebbels, and the rest.

Fingal went to scrub and met Richard, who had finished his first case. "What have you got, Fingal?"

"Man with a bullet in the bowels."

"Can be a bit tricky. Call me if you're worried and I'll look over your shoulder and talk you through it, but remember it's quite easy really . . ."

Easy for you to say, but thanks for the offer of help, Fingal thought.

"Fish out the small bowel, run it through your fingers like you would a bicycle inner tube looking for punctures. Any you find, sew shut in two layers. Large bowel. Same thing. I don't think you need worry about damage to the great vessels. If they'd been torn, he'd not have made it here. But if anything else like a kidney or the spleen's been hit, there'll be a fair bit of blood so you'll have to search for the source, fix it or take it out . . ."

Fingal shuddered. He'd be asking Richard for help if such were the case.

"When you've got everything repaired or removed, wash out the belly cavity with saline, dump some sulpha in. If you find the bullet take it out, but if not just leave it. Once he's got over this operation and we've got him to facilities where they have time to do X-rays and the like it can be removed then . . ."

Another reminder of how everything under battle conditions had to be done in a rush, Fingal thought.

"Then bring a loop of bowel at a level closer to the stomach than the highest perforation out through the abdominal wound and shove a glass rod between the loop and the belly wall. Sew up the bullet wound and your incision. Incise the loop so the contents can leak into a bag. That'll rest the gut and give the inner gut wounds a chance to heal until he's better."

We hope, Fingal thought.

Richard shook water off his hands and said, "Good luck. Yell if you're stuck."

"Thank you, Richard." I'll need all the luck I can get, Fingal thought, and stared at the PMO's departing shoulders. That's where the man carries the medical woes of the whole damn fleet. Thank God he's here.

Fingal did have good luck. By the end of the arduous procedure, the young German had been patched up satisfactorily and the bullet removed.

And so it went case after case; bodies on and off the table, groaning men being anaesthetised, yelling men awakening. The Germans weren't the only ones begging for their mummies. Blood had flowed in rivers—thank the Lord for plasma. He must have stitched enough to have, under different circumstances, woven a Persian rug, and used enough dressing to stuff a mattress.

Fingal knuckled his eyes. It was as if the entire sandy beach at Ballyholme had crept under his eyelids. He put a hand in the small of his back, which was knotted from bending and felt like all the eight forwards of the Welsh rugby team had trampled on it. "Wake him up and bring the next one." He'd finished another amputation, this time of a foot only. It was an abhorrent procedure, he thought, turning a healthy young man into a cripple, but it was better than letting him die. At least Fingal was becoming more skilled in removing limbs.

"Begging your pardon, sir, but Commander Wilcoxson says we've dealt with the most urgent cases. It's ten to three in the morning," Barker said.

"Is it, by God?"

"Yes, sir, and the boss's sent for sandwiches and hot cocoa. We've all to take a breather. And don't worry about these instruments. I'll see to them."

"Thank you, Barker." Fingal stripped off his gloves and gown and went to sit at his desk. His war diary lay where he'd left it after making his last entry about coming into Westfjord at noon. Not now, he thought, but later, later he'd try to record his feelings for what he'd been doing for—he did a quick calculation—the last nine hours. Pity, revulsion, anger were there, and so was pride. An enormous pride in the medical branch of HMS *Warspite* and their complete dedication. And what about Fingal O'Reilly, who had always tried to think of his patients as individual human beings, not bullet wounds or amputations? Was he becoming hardened? Inured? He shook his head. He didn't know, and while he'd never burden her with all his worries, at that moment Fingal wished Deirdre were here so he could tell her about his fear, and be comforted. He'd write it all down later so when next they were together, he'd be able to remember, at least tell her some of it. She was a nurse. She'd understand.

Someone knocked on the door and Fingal saw a mess steward appear and hand Barker a steaming tray. "Here you are, mate, K-eye and dorks."

Which translated meant cocoa and sandwiches.

"Ta very much," Barker said. As he neared Richard, the SBA paused while the PMO tipped something from a bottle into each mug.

Barker offered the tray to Fingal, who gratefully accepted the first grub he'd had since noon yesterday. Tonight the tinned Uruguayan salted beef would taste very good, and the cocoa? He sipped and looked up to see Richard Wilcoxson, smiling with his mouth and eyes, their crinkling for a moment smoothing the deep bags beneath.

"Ah," said Richard, "I keep a little something for moments like this. The malt whisky will give us all a boost, because we're not done by a long chalk." He plumped down on a chair beside Fingal. "Once we're finished, we'll go and take a look at our recent handiwork and what else needs to be sorted out."

And it will be, Fingal thought, until the last man-jack is seen to or Richard and I drop in our tracks. Or at least until I drop in mine. Richard Wilcoxson, twice my age, seems to be an indestructible man of steel like that new American comic book hero, Superman.

After they'd left the medical distribution centre, Fingal and Richard had to climb up one deck to get to the mess decks, which were serving as temporary sick bays for the two hundred casualties aboard. They'd gone only halfway when the turbines roared into life and the great ship was once again steaming ahead, presumably out to sea.

Fingal glanced at his watch: three A.M. Three hours into the new day, April 14, 1940.

"I reckon," Richard said, "that the admiral's worried about air attack or U-boats in the fjord. I'll bet we're bound for the Norwegian Sea."

"I'll take your word for it," Fingal said as he stepped over a coaming and through the hatch leading to the seamen's mess. He stopped in his tracks. Rows of hammocks all swinging in unison were slung overhead above ranks of mess tables. In the hammocks off-watch sailors snored, mumbled in their sleep, and farted.

Amidships, the trunking of A and B turrets ran from sole to deckhead. At the for'ard end on both sides of the A cylinder, men sat at mess tables tucking into the same sort of meal that Fingal had just finished. Farther aft and closer to where he stood, the sole and the tabletops had been pressed into service as beds, where the wounded lay, the healthy crew members stepping round and over the victims.

"The sooner we can get back into our proper sick bay, the happier I'll be," said Richard. "At least get the worst cases into proper cots." He looked round. "Right," he said, "the pre-op cases still waiting are to port with our SBA. I'll go and have a word with him. See what's yet in store." He yawned mightily. "Then I'll phone up to the bridge, find out what's going on." He stifled another yawn and that set Fingal off.

"The post-ops are to starboard. Take a quick shufti at them. See they're as all right as can be expected."

"Right," Fingal said, and began his work. The nearest case, lying under a blanket on a mess table, was the young German with the perforated bowel. Fingal quickly checked the man's pulse and breathing, then made sure the plasma was running freely. Lifted the blanket. The dressing was clean and there was no blood staining. He consulted a chart where the SBA had recorded the same signs and the blood pressure. The patient seemed to be holding his own.

The young man opened two blue eyes and stared at Fingal through morphine-constricted pupils. *"Danke schön, Herr Doktor. Danke."*

"Bitte. Denken sich nichts dabei," Fingal said. "Thank you" and "think nothing of it" were the only German he knew, and he smiled at the notion that in this circumstance, it was all he needed to know. It was all that was important. Between now and the young man's leaving the ship, Fingal vowed to find out his name. He moved on to the above-knee amputee.

Finally Fingal had finished his rounds. Apparently so had Richard, because he was walking toward Fingal.

"Everything under control?" Richard asked when they met.

"So far they're all doing reasonably well," Fingal said.

"Good," said Richard, "but I'm afraid there are going to be three burials at sea in the morning, and we're not going to get much rest I'd reckon until at least noon, another nine hours or so. How are you bearing up?"

"I'm fine, Richard. And much the better for knowing that the post-ops are all doing well."

"Good man. Now, come on. Back to the salt mines."

Together they walked along the passages and down the companionway.

"On a brighter note," Richard said, "we're going to get more of a respite. I spoke with Captain Crutchley. While the War Office and the Admiralty work out what to do about the German occupation of Norway in general and those still in Narvik in particular, *Warspite* will remain on patrol out here. And as soon as possible we'll rendez-vous with the hospital ship *Franconia* and transfer the walking wounded. Then, in another twelve days, we'll offload the cot cases to HMS *Isle of Jersey*."

He opened the door to the temporary operating theatre, where Fingal immediately saw that both tables had patients on them and that the SBAs were at their posts.

"Time to scrub again," Richard said. "No rest for the wicked." He looked Fingal straight in the eye. "I'm proud of you, Fingal. You've probably been feeling pretty terrified for most of the night, but you haven't shown it. You've kept your nerve and you've been doing a bloody fine job."

Fingal blushed. "Thank you, sir."

"But look here, it's just not right expecting someone, anyone, only half trained, to do what you did tonight. And one day you're going to have to start giving anaesthetics for more complicated cases too. So, that training course?"

Fingal stopped scrubbing his nails, hardly daring to hope.

"I didn't get a chance to tell you before this Narvik campaign, but I had a letter in Greenock. We've got a place for you on a course at Haslar Hospital, starting in the autumn."

"That's wonderful, Richard. Thank you." Fingal, tired as he was, felt as if all his birthdays had come on the same day.

"Might be a bit tricky getting you there, though." Richard shook the surplus water from his hands. "The scuttlebutt is that *Warspite*'s going back to the Med soon."

"I see," Fingal said, feeling his heart sink. He too turned from the wash basin. "I'll just have to be patient," he said, "and speaking of patients, right now there's more work to be done."

22

*Caveat Emptor (*Buyer Beware*)*

"Thanks for coming over on a Saturday, Kinky," Kitty said as O'Reilly ushered the Corkwoman into the upstairs lounge. "It's much appreciated." Kitty patted the armchair beside the one in which she was sitting. "Now, have a seat, Mrs. Auchinleck, and tell me all your news."

"Thank you, Kitty, dear," Kinky said as she settled herself comfortably in the upstairs lounge. "And I'll say again, it's no bother at all. Sure isn't Archie taking Rory to the British Legion for a pint or two and a few games of darts and snooker tonight?" She hesitated before saying, "At least Archie will have a pint, bless him, but poor old Rory." She sighed. "Lemonade for him."

"We can't blame the fever doctors for telling Rory he'd have to stay off the grog for a year. That kala-azar has affected his liver," Kitty said.

Kinky nodded, but managed a smile. "At least he's completely cured, and he passed his medical board this week so he can stay on in the army. We're all tickled pink for him, so."

"So are we," O'Reilly said, thinking how natural it seemed to include Kitty in his reply. He loved the "we-ness" of it.

"I'll leave you two to have a blether," O'Reilly said. "I've got a f—" He bit back the adjective that came to mind. "—a form to finish filling in. I'll join you later." He only had until Monday to get the blasted thing to the ministry and because he'd let procrastination be the thief of time, it would have to be completed today or tomorrow. He started to leave, but hesitated when he heard Kitty ask, "Is that a new book you have there, Kinky?" New books always intrigued him.

"It's for me to read when you all go out." Her eyes twinkled and her dimples appeared when she said, "It's by an American woman, Jacqueline Susann. It's called *Valley of the Dolls*—and it does be a bit racy, so."

O'Reilly's head jerked back when she winked at him. Kinky reading racy books? Yet why the hell not? He recovered his composure and said, "I hear it's selling like hotcakes."

"Oh, it's a real corker, all right," Kinky said with a laugh. "The mess some people make of their lives is not to be believed. You know," she said conspiratorially, "it's said it's based on the writer's own experiences in Hollywood."

"Must make life in Ballybucklebo look a little dull," said O'Reilly.

"I wouldn't have it any other way, sir."

"I hear you, Kinky. Nor me neither. Now excuse me, ladies. Won't be long." He trotted downstairs. Jenny had said she'd be happy to take call once in a while, particularly on weekends, but this Saturday she had an unbreakable family commitment and so it had fallen to him.

O'Reilly didn't mind. After all those years of single-handed practice, only having to be on call every third weekend was pure luxury, but he had wanted to take Kitty, Barry, and Sue to the Culloden for dinner this evening. The young fellah was out sailing with the light of his life this afternoon. And there was no reason why they all still couldn't enjoy dinner, but of course the perennial problem would then arise. He glanced at the phone as he passed it on his way to the surgery where the unspeakable form lurked on his desk. With no one in the house who would take urgent calls?

Good old Kinky, he thought, you could always count on her. Who else?

The form lay right where he had left it. Muttering imprecations he sat down at his desk. Where was I?

O'Reilly chewed the end of a Bic ballpoint and stared at the June 1966 version of a form that as principal of the practice he had to complete on a bimonthly basis to satisfy some faceless bureaucrat in the Ministry of Health and Welfare. "Roasting over a slow fire and being basted with boiling lead while his toenails are pulled out one at a time would be too good for whoever designed this blasted instrument of the devil," O'Reilly said aloud, and wondered, not for the first time, if there was any way he could delegate the work to Barry, who should be getting here soon.

"Hellfire, brimstone, and damnation," he growled. "I did not spend five years at medical school and thirty years building up a successful practice to become a glorified clerk in a counting house." He read the instructions aloud, " 'Take the total in column A and add to the subtotal in column C which is derived from the lesser of the two figures on lines B12 and E14 overleaf unless E14 has been deleted from this form.' " Balderdash. It's like one of those games: "Think of a number, divide it by three, add the first digit from the day after your birthday, and subtract nine, and that's your weight in stones to the nearest stone." Damn it all. Why not just ask me in plain English?

He felt a dull ache starting behind his eyes and yet his irritation with the form in question had reminded him of a moment of naval administration and the memory brought a smile. Once a document he'd signed had been returned with the instructions, "This document was not for your eyes. You should not have signed it. Kindly ink out your signature—and initial your inking."

The phone in the hall rang and he leapt to his feet with the grin of a killer bound for the noose who's been told a reprieve has been granted.

"Hello?"

"Doctor, it's me, Donal. We hate to bother you on a Saturday, like, but it's wee Tori. She won't stop gurning and she's just come out in a rash on her face, so she has."

"It's okay, Donal. I'm glad you called. I'll be right round to take a look at her."

"Thanks, Doctor. Julie's that concerned about the wee mite and I don't like the look of her one bit neither. See you soon."

A pandemic of rubella, German measles, had started in 1962, and while he'd not jump to conclusions, he'd already made a shrewd guess. Its rash always started on the face, and fortunately it was a mild disease. He put down the phone, turned, and yelled upstairs, "It's Donal Donnelly. Wee Tori's come out in a rash. I'll just nip over. Won't be long."

Bag in hand, O'Reilly trotted through the back garden, called to Arthur—he'd give the big Lab his run after the home visit—and put him in the back of the old Rover. Free from Kitty's usually restraining influence and released from the Kafkaesque government form, O'Reilly, like the recently retired British racing driver Stirling Moss, roared down the Belfast to Bangor Road singing lustily,

> Over hill over dale we will hit the dusty trail
> as the caissons go rolling along . . .

"Settle down, Arthur. I'll not be long," O'Reilly said.

The big Lab, as he always did when the car bounced down country lanes, was thrashing his tail and making throaty, excited noises. With a final "aaaargh," and a deep sigh, Arthur put his head on his forepaws.

O'Reilly had to stop because the Donnellys' lane was blocked by a chain from which hung a National Trust sign that read, DÚN BUÍ SIDTHE, DUN BWEE PASSAGE GRAVE, CLOSED TO THE PUBLIC. Donal, with a sick child in the house, probably simply did not want to be disturbed, and it was just as well he had closed the site. It would have to be done if Tori had an infectious disease, at least until the period of probable transmission was over. As he unhitched the chain O'Reilly remembered Donal mentioning in the Duck that Julie was selling cream teas to tourists and that Donal had two sidelines going, one of little Celtic figures that he carved and painted, and the other more mysterious. O'Reilly drove through, reattached the chain, and as he went to park was greeted by a waving Donal.

"Thanks for coming, sir," Donal said. "Julie has the wee one on her lap in the parlour."

O'Reilly grabbed his bag and followed Donal. "Has Tori been with any other kids lately?"

"Aye," said Donal. "Two weeks ago we went to Rasharkin to visit Julie's folks. Her big sister has two kids, so she has. She phoned us up a week ago to tell us her lot were all down with the three-day measles."

That sounded like confirmation of O'Reilly's initial suspicions. Rubella had an incubation period of fourteen to twenty-one days, and the rash came and went within three days, hence its local name.

Donal went into the tidily furnished little lounge.

"Doctor O'Reilly," Julie said from where she sat on a small sofa. "Thanks for coming. Tori's not too grand." She cradled the infant, who snivelled and sobbed.

"I can see the rash. What are her other symptoms?" O'Reilly asked, gently touching the tiny hand with his big paw. The wean's skin was warm to the touch.

Julie sighed. "She wasn't at herself this morning. She was hot and had a runny nose. I took her temperature and it was one hundred. I thought she was teething again so I rubbed her gums with whiskey and give her a baby aspirin, but she'd not settle and then about half an hour ago that there rash," Julie pointed to a pinkish disfiguration that covered the child's face, "started til come over her face."

O'Reilly bent and peered at the child's mouth to see if there was a pale area surrounding it. There was not. Good.

Julie turned Tori and lifted her nightie. The child's back from above the waist of her waterproof panties right up to her neck was covered in a pinkish blotchy rash.

O'Reilly leant forward and examined the nape of Tori's neck. Sure enough, he could feel enlarged lymph nodes. He hardly needed to run a mental checklist—the Lord only knew how many rashes of childhood he'd seen in more than thirty years—but to do so was ingrained. The rash wasn't intensely red enough to be that of red measles, morbilli, and too pale to be that of scarlet fever, which in any case would be accompanied by the paleness round the mouth he'd looked for earlier and accompanied by a sore throat.

O'Reilly straightened and smiled. "Not much to worry about here," he said. "She's got German measles, that's all." He kept his voice reassuringly low.

"German?" Donal said. "They should keep their flipping measles to themselves, so they should. We won the wars—twice."

"It's just a name, Donal. The German doctors didn't invent it. It's called that because the first doctors to describe it in the middle of the eighteenth century were from the country we now call Germany."

"Oh," said Donal, sounding more mollified. "And it's not serious, then?"

O'Reilly shook his head. "Not in kiddies. She'll be over it in no time." He said to Julie, "She'll probably have a temperature for about three days and you'll need to keep her in bed for a week after that, then she'll be fine."

"Thank you, sir," Julie said.

"Actually," said O'Reilly, "it's not a bad thing for girl children to have German measles. It means they'll not be at any risk of getting it again when they grow up."

"And would that be bad?" Donal asked.

"Only if they catch it in the first three months of a pregnancy, then it can hurt the baby. So you'll not need to worry about that now because Tori will be immune." He looked at Julie. "I know Doctor Laverty attended when you were pregnant with Tori, Julie, but just as a matter of interest, have you had them?"

"Me?" She laughed. "Och, aye. When I was wee whatever was going around, I caught it."

"Good," said O'Reilly. "You'll be immune too."

"I think," said Donal, "that *is* good because it's about time Tori had a wee brother isn't it, pet?"

Julie smiled and nodded.

"Indeed," said O'Reilly. "Anyway, there's nothing to be frightened of. I'll pop in in a few days, but if you're worried—"

"We know to call, Doctor," Julie said, "and thank you very much."

"Right," said O'Reilly, "I'll be off."

"I'll show you out, Doc," Donal said.

O'Reilly's eye was caught by something on a small table. On a piece of newspaper there were some tools, a paintbrush, and a pot of wood stain. The side of a log shone white where pieces had been chipped away. A small pile of white sticks about the size of matchsticks kept company with a much bigger heap of pieces of the same dimensions, but stained a dark brown. "What on earth's that all about, Donal?"

Donal's left eyelid drooped slowly. "I'll tell you on the way to your car, sir, but do you know your man, Brian Boru?"

"Ireland's last *Ard Rí,* High King? Not personally, but I know he won the battle of Clontarf against the Norsemen in 1014, but was killed in the battle. His harp's in the Long Room in Trinity College." O'Reilly waited until Donal had closed the back door.

"Aye," said Donal, and lowered his voice, "but did you know about his war club, *marfóir mór dubh,* the great black killer?"

O'Reilly shook his head. "Never heard of it."

"Very few people have." Donal's toothy grin was feral and that wink appeared again. "It was passed down through the County Donegal Ó'Donnghaile, and their ancestor was Donnghaile Ó Néill who died in 876 before Brian Boru was born, and Donnaghaile, a descendant of Eoghan, son of Niall of the nine hostages, and his—"

"Enough, Donal," O'Reilly said.

"Right enough," Donal said. "I'll go and take the chain down." He walked the few paces, did so, and waved O'Reilly on.

As O'Reilly got into his car and told Arthur to be quiet he vividly pictured Donal giving this dissertation to a group of entranced tourists as they sipped Julie's cream tea. He'd be explaining that the old Irish way of naming was to prefix the first name of the grandfather with Ó'. The descendants of Donnelly (Donnghaile) O'Neill would become the O'Donnellys. O'Neill himself had been a grandson of Neill (Niall).

O'Reilly motored to where Donal stood, stopped to say good-bye, and wound down his window.

Donal bent and said. "Anyroad, the great club, much battered by time and wars, finished up with the last of the Ó'Donnghaile—me, so I am, at least until Tori gets a wee brother."

O'Reilly shook his head. "You're not telling me those stained matchsticks on your table are chips from the original great club?"

Donal held one finger beside his nose. "I'd never try that on with you, sir."

"But you would with the English and American tourists?"

Donal at least had the courtesy to blush. "Fair play, sir, for one pound ten they get a chip and a wee certificate of authenticity. You sussed it out quare and quick, sir, so you did. You'd not tell nobody?"

"Not at all," he said. "I just didn't know there was a branch of the Ó'Donnghaile family in Alexandria, Egypt."

Donal scratched his carroty head and frowned. "I never knew about them," he said, then asked with his face set in a serious question, "Would them lot be related to the County Tyrone branch, like?"

"No. Definitely the Down clan, of which I believe you truly are the last," O'Reilly said as he put the car in gear. "In 1940, one of the Alexandrian Donnellys, I think his name was Abou ib'n ben Donnelly, tried to sell me a piece of the True Cross from Calvary—and a certificate of authenticity to go with it."

As he drove off laughing, O'Reilly thought it was because of the war and being stationed in Egypt that he'd met the Arab peddlar. Thousands of miles away but up to exactly the same kind of tricks as Donal. O'Reilly's laughter faded. Come to think of it, there wasn't a hell of a lot to choose from between a crafty Arab on the make and a scheming Ulsterman, and they both probably were doing it to have a bit more cash to help raise their familes. O'Reilly inhaled deeply. Maybe, he thought, just maybe, if the human race could spend a bit more time concentrating on what makes us alike rather than our differences, like that black American clergyman Martin Luther King Jr. was trying to do in the States, maybe we could make war a thing of the past?

23

On the East of Eden

Fingal, waiting in his cabin on the main deck for Tom Laverty and Richard Wilcoxson, scanned recent entries in his war diary.

April 24, 1940, ordered back to bombard town of Narvik. Some of wounded still on board screamed when they heard gunfire. Very distressing for them and me. April 25th to Scapa Flow. April 27, Captain Crutchley relieved by new skipper, Captain D. B. Fisher, CBE. April 30 Warspite *leaving Scapa Flow. Uneventful run to Med. Dropped anchor Alexandria, Egypt, Friday, May 10. Now flagship for Vice Admiral A. B. Cunningham, ABC to his men. Same day Germans smashed into the Netherlands, Belgium, and Luxembourg.*

It was three days since *Warspite* had dropped anchor in the West Harbour, Alexandria. What little news there was coming out of Europe was gloomy indeed. The Germans, it seemed, after eight months of inactivity on the western front, were waging Blitzkreig, lightning war, with their tank and motorized armies in the Ardennes. Their aim: to outflank the French Maginot Line. Everyone, of course, believed the Allies would prevail—of course they would. They had to. They had more men, guns, tanks, and aircraft. Fingal slowly closed the diary and laid his hands flat on its cover.

There was a knock on his door. He took a deep breath and set aside the unsettling thoughts. "Come in."

Tom Laverty stepped over the raised sill. "Ready?" He, like Fingal, was wearing number two tropical rig of white open-necked short-sleeved shirt with rank shoulder straps, white shorts, knee-length white stockings, and white shoes. Much more comfortable for the climate. Temperatures here in May could rise as high as 113 degrees Fahrenheit.

"Tom." Fingal rose. "Where's Richard?"

"He'll meet us at the portside aft accommodation ladder. Had a last-minute something to do in the sick bay."

"Right." Fingal grabbed his cap. "Let's go."

Together they began to pass along the corridors and companionways, now all familiar to Fingal. "So," he said, "what's the inside gen from admirals' country?" Tom, as navigating officer, was often privy to much more recent news.

Tom laughed. "It's an ill wind that blows nobody any good. We're going to be staying in the harbour for several days for repairs to damage—"

"Damage? What damage? We've not been shelled or bombed."

"Self-inflicted wounds. Happens more than you might think. Those massive jolts you felt down at your station when the guns were fired at Narvik last month knocked a few things out of kilter."

"Good Lord. I knew the rifles sounded like the clap of doom, but it never occurred to me the concussions were affecting the ship."

Tom smiled. "They can, all right. If we ever have gunnery practice and aren't closed up at action stations, I'll see if I can get you up with me to watch. Then you'll understand."

"I'd like that," Fingal said as they climbed the companionway to the quarterdeck.

They emerged into bright sunshine. Knots of officers stood in two groups. Those right aft near the taffrail would be off duty on board and were smoking and chatting. The shore party, which Fingal and Tom joined, stood close to the head of the accommodation ladder. There was no sign of Richard.

Tom pointed directly astern. "See there, on the mainland? That cluster of buildings on the shore is the commander in chief's headquarters, HMS *Nile*." He must have seen Fingal's puzzled look. "All naval shore establishments, we call them stone frigates, are designated as one of His Majesty's Ships and are given a name."

"Even though it's a building—on land," said Fingal.

"That's right," said Tom, looking somewhat affronted.

"The good old Andrew certainly has its own way of doing things," said Fingal with a laugh. "Please carry on with your tour, Tom."

"Okay, well, immediately to the left of *Nile* from our perspective, that area under the gantries is the harbour's Gabbari Dock. It's the biggest one, but it's only large enough to take a cruiser. The shipwrights'll have to come out here. Skipper reckons the work'll take about five days."

"So with a bit of luck this won't be our only run ashore?" Fingal said.

"Probably not." Tom waved his arm around in a semicircle. "So what do you think of this anchorage?" He pointed out to sea. "The breakwater out there is five miles long."

"The bay's huge." And even out here, over the smell of fuel oil, an offshore breeze brought scents of a foreign land, not entirely unfamiliar to Fingal, whose ships had visited the Red Sea when he'd been a merchant marine apprentice. "And that's a bloody great fleet anchored in here." More numerous even, he thought, than the ships he'd first seen at Tail of the Bank in Scotland. Was that really six months ago?

Ranks of grey warships of all sizes swung at anchor. Smoke rose lazily from the many funnels of ships that must be on notice to be ready to raise steam quickly. *Warspite*'s funnel was not smoking. "Furnaces out. Tom?"

"Right. Skipper reckoned we might as well give her a boiler clean while we're stuck here."

"Makes sense." Fingal surveyed the scene. Small craft, pinnaces, captains' barges, liberty boats, and supply boats motored back and forth. Their wakes crisscrossed the waters, churning them to a constant chop. Gulls swooped and screeched where ships were taking provisions on board.

Nearby on *Warspite*'s deck a group of sailors wearing nothing but white-topped round caps and shorts were loading fifteen-inch shells into the after shell room. He was alarmed to notice that the supervising petty officer was smoking.

Fingal glanced away and watched a boom defence vessel (BDV) at the harbour's narrow mouth, which was closed by heavy antisubmarine nets hanging from floating booms. The busy little boat hooked onto one of the booms and dragged it aside to open a gateway to let three destroyers enter in line astern. The leading vessel's Aldis lamp was sending messages in Morse code to the C in C's headquarters. The destroyer let go a series of joyous "Whoops" on its whistle. When the last ship was safely inside the BDV would close the gate.

"Cheeky bugger, that destroyer skipper," Tom said with a grin, and went on, "Our capital ships, those that aren't at sea, are at this end. But see over there, up ahead, behind the land that the breakwater starts from?"

"Near the lighthouse?"

"Yes, just to the left. That's the cruiser anchorage. We've ships in there and so have the French. Their battleship *Lorraine* is over there. They have battleships at Oran in Algeria too."

"*Vive la France,*" Fingal said, and shook his head. "It sounds like their army and air force in Europe are taking a terrible pasting, the poor devils."

"They'd better win, that's all I can say," Tom muttered, "because if they lose, Cunningham and their Lordships of the Admiralty will have to decide what to do to stop the French warships in the Med from falling into German hands."

"A cheerful thought for such a sunny day," a familiar voice said.

Fingal turned to see Richard Wilcoxson. "Sorry I'm late, gentlemen. I had to stop a nosebleed."

"You've time to spare," Tom said. "We're still waiting for the next boat ashore."

Richard stared at the anchorage and nodded. "I see old *Barham*'s back."

"Part of a convoy escort to and from Malta," Tom said. "Got in early this morning."

Fingal stared at what was nearly *Warspite*'s doppelgänger, which was not surprising. They were sister *Queen Elizabeth*–class battleships. "Altogether, Tom, just how many ships are under ABC's command?" he asked.

Tom counted on his fingers. "Four fifteen-inch-gun battleships, but three really need massive refits. *Warspite*'s the only fairly modern one. The aircraft carrier HMS *Eagle* and her Fleet Air Arm Swordfish torpedo bombers, the Seventh and Third Cruiser Squadrons, both made up of six-inch-gun-armed vessels, twenty-five destroyers, and twelve submarines and their depot ship HMS *Medway*. I'm not counting things like boom defence vessels, motor torpedo boats. Can't give you an exact number, but it's enough for the present."

"And the Italians?" Richard asked. "Lord knows how Il Duce will jump, but if he did form an alliance with Germany, how big a threat would the Italian navy be?"

Tom shook his head. "We'd have our hands full. The Regia Marina has, in commission or ready for service, several modern battleships that all outclass the old vessels at Admiral Cunningham's disposal except *Warspite*. And its cruisers have eight-inch rifles. Ours have six. I know, because I saw the Italian ships when we were on goodwill visits before war broke out."

Fingal shook his head. "I don't think I'll ever understand politics. Italy was on our side in '14 to '18."

"But then they got the Fascisti and Mussolini." Richard nodded toward the harbour where a pinnace was approaching *Warspite*'s port quarter. "That's our boat, and right on time." He glanced at his watch. "Benito Mussolini made Italy's trains run on time, they say. So does the Royal Navy with its liberty boats." He stepped aside, outstretched one arm. "After you two," and then in a fair imitation of Leading SBA Barker's Cockney accent remarked, "All ashore what's going ashore, gents, hif you please."

A dappled grey horse that looked to Fingal to have nearly terminal swayback was solemnly clopping ahead, pulling their gharry along a bustling thoroughfare. It was noisy with the racket of hooves and wheels, the engines of ancient motorcars, horses whinnying and donkeys braying, all accompanyied by an endless symphony of honking horns. An Arab in flowing white robes guided a single-humped camel along the street.

"I can never remember," Tom said, "if that's a dromedary or a bactrian camel."

"Dromedary," Richard said. "The bactrian ones live in China. They're the ones with the twin hump mount."

Fingal inhaled. The most overpowering smell was of animal dung mingling with roasting coffee, and dashes of spices that he could not begin to identify. Their conveyance was bringing the three men from the dockside through the native quarter along the notorious Rue des Soeurs, the red-light district, to the more salubrious city centre. Alexandria's red-light district was out of bounds to all service personnel unless in transit, but Fingal was sure he'd seen a couple of sailors ducking back into an alley. They must have seen two regulators, as the naval police were called, marching along the street looking for men breaking the rules. Sailors cooped up at sea for months would pay little attention to out-of-bounds orders, and in about a week sick parade would be dominated by cases of the clap, or, worse, syphillis.

A thought struck him. "Suppose there's a sudden emergency. How do we get all the crews out of these warrens and back to their ships?"

Richard said, "Combination of things. The Jaunty—"

"What?"

"The masters at arms of the ships with men at liberty. The nickname's the Jaunty, a corruption of the French *gendarme*. Their naval police do a round-up and before that the ships' sirens will sound." Richard smiled. "Sorry. Should have told you before we came ashore."

Fingal stared around. On each side of the road, plastered square buildings were apparently built on top of each other with no obvious rhyme or reason. Some had domes and balconies. Some protruded onto the street. Most were open-fronted housing, small shops, coffee-houses.

"Those scruffy-looking blokes are Egyptians," Richard said, nodding at a group of men sitting round a table. "You can tell by their loose smocks and fezzes. They sit all day drinking Turkish coffee. In Nelson's navy they'd have been called 'idlers' because they send their missusses out to earn the crust while the men take their ease. Upper-class Egyptian men favour Western dress, and although the working-class women often wear the veil, their better-off sisters don't."

The gharry stopped abruptly. The way was blocked by a man riding a donkey and one pushing a hand cart in a heated dispute over who had the right of way. Fingal had a flash of memory of old Lorcan O'Lunney, the tugger he'd befriended in Dublin.

The pavement underfoot was littered with horse apples from the innumerable draught animals, and flies swarmed around the ordure. Fingal had seen locals using fly whisks and determined to get one at the earliest opportunity. People on foot jostled by. He noticed one man of about fifty being led by the hand. His eyelids were scarred shut and puckered, and Fingal made a diagnosis of trachoma, better known as Egyptian opthalmia, the leading cause of blindness in the world. The human race would be a damn sight better off looking for a cure for it and other debilitating illnesses, than shooting at each other.

He was distracted by their driver yelling something in what Fingal assumed was Arabic and using his whip to threaten the donkey rider. Eventually the gharry was able to proceed. The driver shrugged, smiled, and said, *"Insha'Allah,"* obviously by way of apology.

"It means, 'It's the will of Allah and can't be helped,'" Richard explained.

"I see," Fingal said, drinking in with delight the sights and sounds. This really would be something to tell Deirdre about when next he saw her.

From somewhere farther inland, a voice began calling, *"Allahu akbar, Allahu akbar . . ."* and was echoed from several different directions.

"It means 'God is good,'" Richard said. "Those are the *muezzins,* the men of the mosques who call the faithful to prayer. It's late afternoon so that's *Asr,* the third of the five daily devotions. The religions rub shoulders here and funnily enough, there's very little friction."

Not like Ireland, Fingal thought, but stifled the idea.

"It's a pretty cosmopolitan place," Tom said. "There are Egyptian, French, Italian, Greek, Jewish, and Armenian districts."

"And English," Richard said.

"Off-work you'll find them and their memsa'bs at one of the two sporting clubs," Tom said. "Naval officers have automatic memberships." He produced a leer that came as a surprise to Fingal, winked, and lowered his voice. "Used to be quite the places for a bit of the old Somerset Maughams."

The English writer's short stories were rife with tales of colonial extramarital dalliances.

"—before I met Carol, of course."

Fingal laughed. Interesting to know, but Deirdre was at no risk of his being tempted by bored, rich, excitement-seeking English wives who'd be waited on by servants at home and who, apart from their social whirl, had little to do to pass their days. "I'd not mind a day at the horses," he said, and thought fondly of trips to Leopardstown racetrack with Bob Beresford in their student days. Bob was in the Royal Army Medical Corps attached to a light tank regiment now, somewhere in Europe.

"We're here," said Richard, paying the driver a few piastres. "The famous Cecil Hotel. I suggest we nip in for a cold beer, then pick up another gharry or even do a bit of walking to sightsee before we come back here for dinner."

"Fine by me," Tom said, dismounting. "Fingal?"

"As they'd say in our part of the world, I'm yer man." Fingal got down. He was immediately accosted by a street vendor in a red striped jellaba, fez, and sporting a huge drooping moustache. The man tugged at Fingal's short sleeve and said, "I am having a wonder of the East for sale, *effendi*."

Fingal laughed. "Oh," he said, knowing full well he'd been advised to avoid street vendors. "A wonder of the East?" He expected to be offered dirty postcards or perhaps a woman. It might make a good story for telling later in the wardroom. It was reputed that when one such mendicant had been told by a very upper-class Englishman that he did *not* want the man's sister, he wanted the British consul, the answer had been, "Very difficult, sir—but I'll try."

"The master is a Christian?"

Fingal chuckled. It made a change from the Ulster, "Are ye Catholic or a Protestant?"

"I am."

"Come on, Fingal," Richard called.

"Just a tick." Fingal bent his head to hear what the man was whispering. It was all he could do to keep from bursting out laughing before he straightened and said, "No, no thank you. I'm most grateful, but I really don't need a piece of the true cross from Calvary. No, not even if it does come with a certificate signed by Pontius Pilate himself."

Richard Wilcoxson and Tom Laverty were being besieged by ragged urchins yelling for "*Baksheesh, baksheesh*," or alms. The hotel doorman shooed the beggars away and Fingal, running his fingers inside his open collar and feeling the sweat, followed his friends into the Cecil heading for the bar. That beer would certainly hit the spot.

24

A Stranger in a Strange Land

Fingal followed his friends into the Cecil Hotel's foyer and through to a lounge bar. Richard was speaking to a waiter and Tom had already taken a seat at a circular filigree brass table.

"I for one," said O'Reilly, dropping into a comfortable rattan chair beside his friend, "can take this climate after Norway and the North Atlantic. I'm sure all this is old hat to the pair of you, having been in Alex often before, but it's all new to me."

"I like the place," said Richard Wilcoxson. "It really is a cosmopolitan city. Some of the buildings like the Morsi Abou el Abbas Mosque and Saint Catherine's Cathedral are well worth a visit. And the place oozes history. Founded in 332 BC by Alexander the Great—"

The Egyptian waiter, smart in white jacket and red fez, coughed discreetly and said, "Your drinks, *effendim*." He set three bottles of Blue Light Ale and glasses on the tabletop. There were beads of condensation on each glass.

"Used to get this stuff in Malta," Tom said. "Tuppence halfpenny a glass. It's not a bad drop."

Fingal lifted his bottle and glass, the cold welcome on his palm, and poured. Already there were damp patches on his shirt beneath his armpits, and he was looking forward to the chilled ale. Overhead, electrical fans circled soundlessly. Though civilians occupied a few tables the bar was largely full of officers; naval colleagues in whites, Royal Air Force men in slate blue, and army types whose shorts were much the same cut as Fingal's, but of faded khaki. There were French naval officers too, probably off the cruisers he'd been shown earlier. It was officers only here. There were plenty of pubs and clubs along a big thoroughfare, the Corniche, for "other ranks." The murmurings of conversation rose and fell, punctuated by occasional bursts of laughter. Turkish tobacco smoke had its own distinctively acrid smell.

"Cheers," said Richard, then lifted his glass and drank.

His sentiments and actions were mirrored by Fingal and Tom.

Fingal, who, like all naval personnel, had been repeatedly warned that many Egyptians were German sympathisers, was determined to keep the conversation in here on neutral subjects. "Careless talk costs lives," after all. "You started to tell us a bit of the history of the place, Richard."

"I did. When we were here before the war I read up on it. After Alexander died, one of his generals, Ptolemy, founded an Egyptian dynasty in 305 BC and they ruled here as Pharaohs until the Romans came in 80 BC."

"Cleopatra was one of the Ptolemaic lot, wasn't she?" Tom said.

"That's right," Fingal said. "Quite the lass, if you believe half the stories. Had affairs with Julius Caesar and Marc Anthony. Did for herself by clasping an asp to her bosom." He fished out his pipe.

"It must have been quite a hotbed of Greek culture back then. But sadly, most of the ancient Grecian buildings like the famous Library and Alexander's mausoleum are gone. One of the seven wonders of the ancient world, the Pharos lighthouse, stood not far from here. Earthquakes did for it. The palace of Ras el Tin is on that site now, beside the yacht club and not far from the coastal forces base. Actually it's a reasonable walk from here and the place is worth a look. I suggest that when we've finished these, we go out there."

"Let's do it," Fingal said, and drank.

"Tom? You in?"

"Suits me."

"Fine," said Richard.

A young, round-faced surgeon lieutenant came in peering around as if he were looking for somebody he knew. His uniform was spotless and the two stripes on his shoulder straps were wavy, indicating he was Royal Naval Volunteer Reserve. The cloth between the gold was red—medical branch—and Fingal noticed that, like his own legs, those of the newcomer were white. Troops who had been out here for some time were wont to belittle newcomers by listing their own service postings and ending with a scornful, "And *my* knees are brown," implying that they'd been here long enough to get a suntan.

"Can we help you?" Richard Wilcoxson asked as the young man moved nearer.

"Thanks. I'm a bit lost, actually." His smile was engaging. "Just got here the hard way from England and it seems my ship has left."

"You're one of us. A sawbones," Richard said. "Join us if you're all alone."

"Thank you." The young medical officer took a chair.

Richard introduced himself, Fingal, and Tom, and told the young man that, just as in the mess, titles of rank were not used among officers on shore leave. He explained that they were all off *Warspite*. He beckoned to the waiter, who materialised with all the speed of a genie popping from his lamp. "Four more Blue Ales please."

"Yes, *effendim*." The man vanished.

"Steptoe. Patrick Christopher Steptoe," the young man said. "HMS *Hereward*—or at least I'm supposed to be." He laughed. "She left for the—" he hesitated. "Well, for points unknown and won't be back until later this month." Fingal guessed that he and the newcomer were about the same age. His accent though, like Richard's, was strictly upper-class Brit.

"*Hereward?*" Tom said. "H-class destroyer. Launched in '36, I believe. Four quick-firing four-point-seven-inch guns."

For a second Fingal glanced at the civilians. He'd been surprised by Tom's disregard for security, but then it dawned on him that the destroyer, built in '36, would have been described in detail in *Jane's Fighting Ships,* which annually listed and described every warship worldwide. The Germans' naval intelligence service, the Abwehr, would already know all about her specifications.

"Apparently, but I've never been aboard her." Patrick laughed again. "I'm a bit new at this. I qualified from Saint George's Hospital Medical School in London last year. Did a locum, but then I really thought I should volunteer when war broke out."

"Good for you. Tom and I are regulars and Fingal's a reserve officer."

"I see."

"And?" Tom prompted.

"After a bit of preliminary training I was told to report to *Hereward.* I got here yesterday so I'm billetted at the Naval Base Hospital. They expect to have a job for me by tomorrow, at least until my ship comes back."

The waiter appeared with the beer.

"Cheers," Patrick said, "and thanks. This is very welcome. The beer and the company." He drank.

"So," said Richard, "you're at a loose end this evening. We're going for a walk after we've finished these drinks, then back here for dinner. If you'd care to join us?"

"That would be terrific. I'd like that. I'd like that very much."

"If you've just left Blighty, you must have up-to-date news from home," Fingal said.

"'Fraid not. I came by ship. Took me quite a while to get here. Ages in fact, and most of it was a bit boring to be honest. Lots of waiting with not much to do. So I don't have anything to report."

He looked around and said, "But I've hardly been out of England before, and from what I've seen, this Egypt's a most interesting place."

Overhead, the sun baked down and after the coolness in the hotel the heat outside, even at this hour, hit Fingal; and then there were the flies. They buzzed everywhere.

On the pavement outside the hotel, a *gulli-gulli* man in jellaba and fez had attracted a small crowd and was performing feats of sleight of hand, hoping for a few coins. Similarly dressed dragomen, the official interpreters and guides of Alexandria, offered their services in barely accented English.

Fingal's group didn't need a guide. They had Richard. "This square that we're crossing is Saad Zaghloul Square. Two of Cleopatra's needles once stood here before they were shipped off, one to London and one to New York. Actually they had nothing to do with Cleopatra. They were erected a thousand years earlier by Thatmose III."

"I believe," Fingal said, "that massive concrete road between us and the sea is the Corniche." Across the road he saw a shore where date palms swayed.

"Right, and that's the inner or eastern harbour ahead," Richard said. "It's too shallow for ships."

The sheltered bay was full of moored dhows and feluccas. Fingal and his friends had to dodge the traffic to get across the Corniche to the promenade.

"It's about a mile-and-a-half walk to the palace," Richard said. "I suppose I wouldn't do it in the heat of the day, but it's not too far for late afternoon."

" 'Mad dogs and Englishmen go out in the midday sun,' " sang Fingal. "Ooops. Sorry, sir."

"No offense taken, Lieutenant," said Richard, laughing. Then Richard himself began to sing in a surprisingly rich baritone. " 'It's such a surprise for the Eastern eyes to see, That though the British are effete, they're quite impervious to heat.' Noel Coward."

"In my case," Patrick Steptoe said, "I suppose I should start singing his 'Has anybody seen our ship? The HMS *Peculiar*.' "

All four men laughed. "Are you musical, Patrick?" Tom asked.

"Actually, yes. At one time I was going to be a musician. Piano."

"Terrific," Tom said. "We'll have to invite you aboard, let you loose on the one in the wardroom anteroom." He smiled at Richard. "Sorry, didn't mean to interrupt the guided tour."

The three men continued walking and Richard took up his commentary. "The Corniche runs up the right side of the Ras el Tin peninsula and continues west past where we're going. The peninsula divides the eastern harbour from the western one where the dockyard and the fleet are."

A train's whistle screeched as a small locomotive hauled several freight wagons along a single rail line running along the dockyard side.

A sea breeze was blowing in from the main harbour, for which Fingal was grateful. He inhaled a heady mixture of smells: cinnamon, the salt of the nearby sea, drying fish, horse apples from the beasts hauling innumerable gharries. "Where's the spicy scent coming from?"

"The Ramsis Bazaar's a couple of streets over and to our left. They sell lots of spices there," said Tom.

It really all was very exotic. He thought of Dorothy's line in last year's wildly successful film *The Wizard of Oz*: Something like, We're not in Kansas, Toto. And he chuckled. War, it seemed, had some compensations. He'd certainly never have had the chance to visit Egypt if it weren't for the navy.

Fingal fell into step with Patrick, letting Richard and Tom lead the way through strolling knots of people.

In the harbour, a felucca had hoisted a dazzlingly white lateen sail on a yard lying at thirty-five degrees to the short single mast and was scudding across the water.

"I saw great big two-masted versions of those called *boums* in the Indian Ocean on my way out from England," Patrick said.

"You said it took you a while to get here, Patrick?"

"Mmm." That smile again. "Troopship in convoy from Liverpool, stopped in Santa Cruz de Tenerife—"

And for a moment Fingal's thoughts strayed to a certain Kitty O'Hallorhan who had gone to Tenerife to work with orphans of the Spanish Civil War. He wondered if she was still there and hoped she, like him, had found a new love.

"Then on to Durban."

"How long did that take?"

"Liverpool to Durban? Six weeks. Convoys, as you know, have to zigzag. Adds hundreds of miles to the trip. About ten thousand miles to Durban, I estimated. And then we had to get to the Suez Canal from there."

"God, it must have seemed like a lifetime."

Patrick shrugged. "For a fellow who'd never been out of England . . ." His voice trailed off. "To be honest, I've been feeling pretty homesick. But there were some compensations. Have you ever seen a whale?"

"No."

"Lots of them off Tenerife, especially. Mammoth blue whales and smaller black-and-white ones called orcas. Beautiful creatures."

"I'd have liked to see that," Fingal said.

"Golly," Patrick said, "they sing. It's a most eerie noise and they can keep it up for twenty-four hours at a stretch. Then there's the tropical nights and the sunrises and sunsets." His eyes widened and Fingal heard the awe in the man's voice. "You have to see them to believe them." He smiled. "We did get a couple of days to go ashore in Durban. Spectacular beaches."

Fingal thought about his promised trip back to Blighty. It was going to take a while, but perhaps, like Patrick, he'd have some memories to share with Deirdre.

"They finally landed me in Port Tawfiq in Suez City. Then I managed to hitch a lift in an Avro Anson with an RAF squadron leader who was heading this way."

"How long did the whole journey take?"

"Two months, twenty days, eight hours," he said, raising an eyebrow, "but I'm not quite sure how many minutes. It really did rather seem to go on and on, but it appears that there are German U-boats in the Med and their Lordships of the Admiralty felt the long way round was preferable for all the soldiers on the ship and one junior MO—me."

"And you did make it. Good for you. I'm happy to know you, Surgeon Lieutenant Patrick Steptoe." Fingal lengthened his stride. "Let's catch up with the others and take a look at this Ras el Tin Palace. I can see its dome quite clearly. Then get back for dinner. I'm starting to feel a bit peckish."

After onboard meals, the bounty of Egypt had produced a wondrous feast at the Cecil. Another gharry ride through the red-light district had offered new sights and sounds. Flashing neon lights were everywhere; clearly no blackout was in force here. Pimps beckoned from shady doorways, and two soldiers were having a punch-up and being wrestled apart by two of the ever-present red-capped MPs. Provocatively dressed, heavily made-up women leered invitingly, and a man in a jellaba and fez ran alongside the gharry yelling, "You want my sister, *effendi*. Very clean, very pretty." Fingal smiled. At least no one was offering a piece of the true cross. His ears were assailed by blaring jazz, and from somewhere came the rhythm of small drums and the tinkling of finger cymbals. Presumably someone was belly dancing.

Fingal had been glad of the quiet as the pinnace headed back to the ship, the only sound the puttering of the boat's engine and the slap of small waves against the hull. Overhead, inset in a sky carved from ebony, the constellations looked uncaringly down on Fingal and his friends. The same stars would have shone on the Egyptians, the Macedonians, the Persians, the Byzantines, the Mamelukes, the Ottoman Turks and their Bashi-Bazouk mercenaries, and the British, each race in its turn, ruling Egypt and this city.

Now he sat at his table. His cabin's porthole was open and the ship was rowdy with the whirring of innumerable fans trying to circulate the hot air. A tiny breeze wriggled into the room, panted, and expired. *My darling Deirdre*, he wrote, *please do me a favour and get Ma a present*. That would let her know roughly where he was. *The weather today is sunny and some friends and I*—the censor would not permit the use of names—*had a wonderful run ashore. I met a very friendly young MO newly out from England. I'd love to have had you with me to see the sights. I'm told that there are some marvellously private beaches here and all I could think of was swimming there with you*—and, he thought, making love on the beach in the warm sun. He closed his eyes and pictured her reading it, God knew when, because getting and sending mail was no easy business in the middle of a war. She was far too clever not to be able to read between the lines. He wrote two more pages of uncensorable trivia and, damn the censor's prying eyes, finished with *and this comes to you with all my longing and all my love. It won't be long until autumn when I'll hold you and kiss you and tell you I love you, my pet. Fingal.*

25

He Haunts Wakes, Fairs

"Come on, Fiona, you can do it," O'Reilly said with a grin as a chubby girl of twelve astride a small, equally rotund, piebald pony approached a low jump. Fingal wondered how the pony could even see the red-and-white-striped cross bars. Its silky mane hung in front of its eyes much like the fringe of an old English sheepdog. Girl and pony could have been subjects for the cartoonist Thelwell, whose sketches of such sights had given the English language the expression "Thelwell Pony." She'd already taken two of the obstacles. "Think she'll clear this one, Kitty?"

As was traditional, the Marquis of Ballybucklebo had loaned his ten-acre field for the annual Ballybucklebo Garden Fête and Horse Show. By long-hallowed custom, it was held during the famous Twelfth Holiday Fortnight on the first Saturday in July. The garden fête was organised jointly by the Presbyterian and Roman Catholic churches with the proceeds being split.

Kitty said, "I hope so. She seems to have a good seat."

O'Reilly surreptitiously patted Kitty's behind and whispered in her ear, "So do you, Mrs. O'Reilly. Great legs too."

"Stop it, Fingal, you eejit," she said, but laughed, shook her head at him, and then applauded as the pony and rider cleared the hurdle. "Well done, Fiona," Kitty called.

Although a detachment of the Saint John's Ambulance Brigade had a tent here if first aid was needed, the local doctor, one Fingal Flaherty O'Reilly, had always made a point of being available too. He enjoyed wandering round all the exhibits and the horse show, accompanied this time by Kitty, and by Barry, who was temporarily Sueless.

"Having fun, love?" O'Reilly asked.

"I certainly am. This is much better than the Dublin Horse Show. Much more personal."

"The local branch of the North Down Pony Club arrange the equestrian competitions. This jumping is being judged by the marquis, his sister Myrna, and Sue Nolan," he said. "She's been very active with the pony club since she came here to teach."

"She's going to join us later in the refreshments tent when the judging's over," said Barry.

O'Reilly had wondered why Sue, despite O'Reilly's advice to Barry not to leave things too late, still wasn't wearing an engagement ring, but thought it politic to mind his own business.

The little girl, to the accompaniment of applause from O'Reilly and Barry, and a little pleased whoop from Kitty, cleared the final jump. The child wore the club's livery of a white shirt and dark tie, cream jodhpurs, gloves, and under her black-velvet-covered hard hat, a hair net.

"Seen enough, you two?" said O'Reilly. "We ought to visit the fête. It's always a lot of fun and Kinky has one of her rhubarb-and-gooseberry tarts entered in the fruit-pie-making section of the pie competition."

"Think she'll win?" Barry asked.

O'Reilly guffawed. "She has for as long as I can remember. Then it's always a toss-up between Cissie Sloan, Aggie Arbuthnot, and Flo Bishop for runner-up."

"Good thing they're all such friends," Kitty said. "There was a pie contest at a local fair in Tallaght when I was a teenager. The

Hatfields and McCoys were bosom buddies compared to the enmity between Bridie Murphy and Rosie O'Grady over a pumpkin pie beating a lemon curd tart for best in competition."

"Wars have been fought for less," O'Reilly said, and chuckled. "Come on, let's take a dander over."

They walked away from the flat, grassy arena that was roped off for equestrian events. July was at its kindest with barely a cloud in the sky. O'Reilly had slung his tweed jacket over his shoulder. Wood pigeons cooed and burbled from the top of an enormous oak that had probably been a sapling when the eighteenth marquis, who had fought on King William's side at the Battle of the Boyne in 1690, had been living in the big house. The old peer might even have planted the tree himself. It was reputed that he was a very keen arborist, his enthusiasm for that pursuit coming second only to his unswerving attention to fathering children out of wedlock on his dairy maids.

Cattle lowed on the side of a hill, and from deep in the covert that marched from the wall, a cock pheasant *kek-kekked* harshly. A horse in a paddock on the far side of a low blackthorn hedge gave a ferocious whinny, kicked up its heels, and charged across the field. Bitten by a horse-bot fly or simply in high spirits? O'Reilly recognised Myrna's gelding, Bramble. Not long ago the animal had thrown Myrna and she had bust her femur which, thanks to Sir Donald Cromie, had healed nicely.

Shrill cries of children; dogs barking; the loud, whistling, off-key music of a steam-driven roundabout organ; and a defiantly bellowed "heeeee-haaaaw" came from the end of the field where the fête was in full swing. The last would be from one of the little jackasses giving rides for sixpence to the smaller children.

O'Reilly inhaled deeply and frowned. Was he smelling knapweed mixed with clover and gorse? Not that a precise identification mattered. He smiled. The air was perfumed and a tonic to the senses.

He had an immediate desire to skip like a spring lamb, but as Father O'Toole and Mister Robinson, the Presbyterian minister, were approaching, O'Reilly considered the dignity of his position and stifled the urge.

Father O'Toole, clearly comfortable in his loosely fitting cassock, said, "The afternoon is grand altogether now that I for one have no further official duties, so."

O'Reilly smiled to see that the priest was eating a huge swirl of pink candy floss mounted on a wooden stick.

"And are you enjoying yourselves, Doctor and Mrs. O'Reilly and Doctor Laverty?" As ever the man's Cork lilt was music to O'Reilly.

"You two," Kitty said to the two men of the cloth before her, "both deserve medals and a gold clock each for the work you do bringing the communities together here in Ulster." Despite her earlier levity, her voice was serious.

"Kitty's right," O'Reilly said.

"Och, now," Father O'Toole said, "I think there's some mention in the Book about loving your neighbour, and besides," he looked sideways at Mister Robinson, "who else could I beat at the golf every Monday, so?" He laughed.

O'Reilly was not surprised to see that so did Mister Robinson. "If I'm still alive next Monday we'll see about that, Father." The man's black jacket and tight dog collar were making his forehead perspire and glisten in the sun. "I'm afraid *my* official duties are not over. Those of us on the committee drew lots and I lost. I've to judge the fruit pie–making contest."

O'Reilly whistled. So that's why Father O'Toole was looking so smug and Mister Robinson assessing his chances for survival.

"Oops," said Barry. "I don't envy you, Your Reverence."

"Perhaps," said O'Reilly, "you'll be able to invoke some divine inspiration." It was, after all, his job to try to comfort those in distress, but inside he was hearing William Congreve's, "Nor hell a fury like a woman scorned." And there could only be one winner. "Good luck," he said.

"Good luck indeed," said Kitty, and turning to O'Reilly, she said, "We mustn't miss that. It could be the highlight of the show."

"How's about youse, Doctor and Missus and Doctor," Colin Brown called as he charged past with his friend Art O'Callaghan and the faithful Murphy at his heels. "We're going til the Punch and Judy, so we are," and they were gone, Colin's young legs twinkling as he ran with, as usual, both knee socks down round his ankles.

"Sue told me there's still no word from his parents about his being allowed to sit the Eleven Plus," Barry said.

O'Reilly shook his head as some of the day's bright pleasure became a little tarnished. He knew he should have been trying harder to find a way to persuade Lenny. O'Reilly was still musing on the subject when they entered the fête proper, a veritable town of canvas. The tall, narrow, red-and-white-striped Punch and Judy tent was faced by ranks of children, including Colin and Art, sitting on the soft grass laughing or yelling, "Behind ye," and pointing as Mister Punch said in his raspy voice, "There's no crocodile," while the puppet beast in question, its jaws snapping, was making its entrance behind his back.

"I loved Punch and Judy shows when I was a little girl," Kitty said.

And I love you, Kitty, O'Reilly thought, but kept the thought to himself.

Farther on, a coconut shy rubbed shoulders with secondhand book stalls, crafts, confectionaries selling dulse and yellow man, candy floss and toffee apples.

O'Reilly sang to himself.

> . . . with gingerbread and spices to accommodate the ladies
> and a big *cruibín* for thruppence to be pickin' while
> you're able.

He walked past a stall labelled "Bring and Buy," cluttered with all kinds of bric-a-brac. It was being run by Miss Alice Moloney, the dressmaker. She waved at O'Reilly and he waved back. A woman he didn't know, who was probably down for the day from Belfast, was saying, "I brung three pairs of my oul fellah's red suspenders and a right wheen of carved clothes pegs I got off one of the travellers. I don't need pegs no more since the ould lad bought me a tumble dryer."

O'Reilly could remember ever since he'd been a boy how the *Lucht siuil*, literally the walking people, made money carving such pegs and selling them from door to door. The tinkers among them mended pots and pans and sharpened knives on treadle-powered grindstones. They did still to this day, though their caravans were more likely to be modern commercially sold ones pulled by Land Rovers than gaily painted wood-and-canvas affairs drawn by horses.

He waited to hear the rest of the transaction.

"That's very generous," Miss Moloney said. "Thank you. I'm sure we'll get a few bob for them." It was customary for people to give things for the stall to sell—the "bring" in its name.

"And I can't make up my mind between that there cuckoo clock or thon wee carved Celtic man." Here comes the "buy."

O'Reilly said to Kitty, "It's one of Donal Donnelly's hand-carved souvenirs like the ones he's selling at Dun Bwee."

"Is there anything our Donal can't turn a profit at?" she said. "He really is one of a kind."

"Mebbe," O'Reilly said, "but I think Colin Brown will be giving Donal a run for his money in a few years."

O'Reilly noticed money changing hands and saw the Belfast woman leave with the clock and the figurine. "Come on," he said. "There's more to see."

They had stopped where Donal Donnelly stood in front of a huge wheel of fortune calling, "Come and spin, come and spin, try your luck and see if you win. If you do you'll wear a grin. Buy some beer to wet your chin." He was sweating from the effort of working the numbered contraption. At the top of the wheel, a leather flap hung down. It was presently in the number 10 slot.

"Roll up, roll up," Donal yelled. "Have a go. Every time she bumps, she bounces."

He must, O'Reilly thought, have picked up his patter from a barker at the travelling fun-fair that visited the village each August.

Donal spotted O'Reilly and winked. "Step right up, Doc. Step right up." He was shouting to be heard over the steam organ's rendition of "Marching Through Georgia."

Why not? It was only a bit of fun, and the money went to the churches.

There was quite a little crowd, many men with their jackets off, perspiring like O'Reilly, the women in their best dresses and hats.

O'Reilly looked at the chequered board, selected a square, and put down a ten-shilling note on 15. "That's for you, pet, if we win," he said to Kitty.

She made a little curtsey. "Thank you, kind sir."

Mister Coffin, the undertaker, put half a crown on 8.

More squares were covered with money from strangers who, like the cuckoo clock buyer, would be down from Belfast.

"That it?" Donal asked, and as no one else had bet, counted, "One, two . . ." the little crowd chanted along, "threeee," then Donal gave a mighty heave and set the wheel in motion. The leather flap chattered as it flipped from pin to pin.

"Round and round the big wheel goes. Where she stops nobody knows," Donal cried.

The clattering grew slower until it was a tap—tap—tap. The flap hesitated over 15 and O'Reilly held his breath, but exhaled as it flipped past a few more numbers to stop in the 8 slot. "Well done, Mister Coffin," O'Reilly said as the undertaker collected his winnings.

"Here y'are, sir," Donal said. "Now don't you be spending it all in the one shop."

"I shan't," Mister Coffin said and started to turn away. "Doctor," he said. "How are you?"

"I'm fine," O'Reilly hastened to reassure the undertaker. Any time the man asked that question, it always sounded a bit too professional, as if he had an eye out for business. "And yourself?"

"Very well, thank you," he frowned, "but a little puzzled."

"Oh?"

He lowered his voice. "Yes. I've been here at the wheel for quite some time and I've observed a most unusual phenomonon. The strangers rarely win and then it's only if there is no local person betting." His frown deepened.

"I'd not worry," said O'Reilly, looking hard at Donal and wondering, How the hell are you pulling that one off, Donnelly? "The Lord moves in a mysterious way—and it's all for a good cause."

"Well—I suppose so." He brightened. "Anyway, I must be off." He giggled. "I've entered a blueberry pie in the fruit pie contest and I don't want to miss the judging."

"Good luck," said an astounded O'Reilly. To the best of his knowledge, no man had ever entered before. "And neither do we. Shall we?"

"Let's," said Barry, "and support Kinky."

"It'll surely set the cat among the pigeons if Mister Coffin wins. I'd hate to miss that," Kitty said and she lengthened her stride.

26

They Would Ask Him to Dinner

Fingal slipped his white uniform shirt over his head and down across the beginnings of a potbelly that hadn't been there in his rugby-playing days. Getting exercise wasn't always possible on *Warspite,* although he did, in emulation of his nautical hero, C. S. Forester's Horatio Hornblower, try to get a long to-and-fro walk on the quarterdeck as often as he could. Since Tom Laverty had mentioned the possibility on the gharry ride to the Cecil three weeks ago in May, Fingal had taken out an honorary membership to the Alexandria Sporting Club. Founded in 1880, it lay in the Al Ibrahimiyyah district with Omar Lotfy and Sidi Gebir Roads to the northwest and Abou Quer Road to the southeast, and only two blocks from the sea. A large part of the complex was an eighteen-hole golf course bisected by the El-Gaish Road.

None of his *Warspite* friends was free this Saturday evening, so he'd taken a taxi here to see if he could get a game of squash and then have a meal on the terrace. Even though *Warspite* had been based in Alex for nearly a month now, the sights and smells were still exotic to him. Perhaps his penchant for stopping to buy baklava from street vendors was contributing to the tightness of his waistband, but he had to admit to himself, Fingal Flahertie O'Reilly, you always did have a sweet tooth.

He did up a couple of top shirt buttons. The changing room was humid with steam from the showers and smelled of fresh and not-so-fresh sweat. He'd finished having a badly needed post-game shower and was getting dressed. Face it old boy, he told himself as he patted his tummy. It's 1940 and you're thirty-two years old—not as young as you used to be. He'd lost a brutal first-to-nine-points game in the third set, nine to seven, to an RN Lieutenant John Collins whose home was in the village of Bourn in Cambridgeshire and who did something hush-hush in the signals section at headquarters. They'd met last week in the bar here. A cold beer on the terrace with my new friend, Fingal thought, would hit the spot.

Across the aisle John was hauling on his shorts. "Thanks, Fingal. Great game. You really pushed me hard."

"Bollix," Fingal said, but grinned. He stood in front of a mirror and ran a comb through his still-wet shaggy locks. Time for a haircut. "You ran the legs off me."

"But stationed on shore I pretty much work banker's hours. So I can get a game in almost every day before I go home to Michelle, the missus." The man's accent was upper-class English. Although he'd never heard it referred to as such in the navy, Fingal had begun to believe that their officer class underwent what the army called the "chameleon effect," all acquiring the same clipped tones. Mind you, Tom Laverty and Wilson Wallace hadn't, and Fingal wasn't going to lose his brogue for anybody. "Having the missus here must be nice," he said, thinking of Deirdre and missing her.

"A lot of us were able to bring our better halves out before the war. Can't do it anymore of course since the war started, and now after Dunkirk . . ."

The horror of the Dunkirk evacuation was still fresh in Fingal's mind five days after the last little ship had limped back to England across the English Channel. Fingal had made some terse entries in his war diary:

May 26, Operation Dynamo *has begun. Evacuation of the British Expeditionary Force and some French troops from beaches and through town of Dunkirk. June 2nd. Little ships under attack by stukas and Heinkels still gallantly getting troops off the beaches. June 4th evacuation called off. Almost 350,000 men out, but all equipment lost. How long can France hang on alone?*

He wondered if Bob Beresford had got out.

John was saying, "Michelle'll be joining us soon. She's playing tennis with a woman who'll be our hostess at dinner tonight. If I'd known I was going to bump into you—"

"Perfectly all right," Fingal said quickly. "There's always a bit of *craic* at the Cecil." He smiled and took in his very civilised surroundings. "I suppose," he said, "there's a fair bit of dining out?"

"It's not a bad billet," John said. "There's the permanent English colony of administrators, bankers, railway officials, that kind of thing too. They stayed on after the Anglo-Egyptian Treaty was signed in 1936 granting semi-independence to the country. And of course there are their ladies and daughters." His neatly cropped head of brown hair slipped through the open neck of his shirt. His brown eyes sparkled when he said, "It can get a bit 'Change partners and dance with me.' Most of the younger eligible local chaps have joined up. But there's rather a lot of dashing naval bachelors who spend a good deal of time with men only, and then when they come ashore, well, you know what I mean."

Fingal did. He remembered Tom's *craic* about things being a bit W. Somerset Maugham. "I'm engaged," he said with a touch of smugness. "I'll be leaving for Blighty next month to do a course. My fiancée and I are getting married in Portsmouth when I'm there." And he hugged the thought and felt aroused at the mere thought of Deirdre.

"That's in the future, my friend. But I wish you every happiness,"

John said. "A cold beer or two now are on the immediate agenda." He finished tying a shoelace. "Beer's on me."

Together under a cloudless sky they strolled through a large park where the red-roofed two-storey clubhouse dominated the golf links, three swimming pools, red clay tennis courts, a football field, and a polo ground where a chukka was in progress. He could hear the horses panting, their hooves pounding, the creak of harness, and the "thwack" of mallets on the wooden ball.

Everywhere palm trees swayed in the hot June breezes. The noises of the city were faint and its malodorous vapours were as likely to have been granted entrance to this preserve of the British upper classes and their superior native friends as a couple of unwashed, jellaba-wearing *fellahin* peasant farmers would be offered memberships.

The two sailors found seats at a table in the shade of a large umbrella on a tiled terrace some reasonable distance from two occupied tables. The other patrons' conversation was, as it ought to be, quite inaudible. Beer was ordered. Fingal lit his briar and John a Player's Navy Cut cigarette. He left the packet open on the tabletop and Fingal could read the motto on the inside of the lid's flap: *It's the tobacco that counts.* Glasses and two bottles of Ind Coope's Burton Pale Ale were delivered and John signed a chit.

"Thank you," Fingal said, then, forgetting that his companion was not Irish, *"Sláinte."*

"Um? What?" John frowned, then as Fingal drank smiled and said, "Oh, quite. Jolly good. Bit of the old Gaelic? Well, as we Sassenachs say, 'Cheers,' or, if you prefer today's toast—"

It hadn't taken Fingal long to learn the traditional naval daily toasts. Saturday's was, and he raised his glass, "To our wives and sweethearts."

John added the unofficial, "May they never meet," and both men chuckled.

"Hello, darling. Good game of squash?"

Fingal half-turned to see a young woman in a short tennis dress holding a racquet in one hand and standing beside their table. She was accompanied by the lass she must have been playing.

John and Fingal scrambled to their feet. John pecked his wife's cheek and said, "Mrs. Michelle Collins and Mrs. Eleanor Simpkins, may I present Surgeon Lieutenant Fingal O'Reilly, a hell of a squash player."

It was not customary for men and women to shake hands.

Michelle smiled. "Delighted."

Eleanor Simpkins's smile was radiant and the sun made a halo of her shining blonde hair, done in the roll fashion of the day. "Lieutenant O'Reilly," she said in a rich contralto, "it's a great pleasure to meet you."

Fingal pulled out a chair and waited for her to be seated before he sat and said, "Miss—I mean Mrs. I'm sorry, please forgive me—" Why the hell are you getting tongue-tied, O'Reilly? He noticed red lips smiling under a retroussée nose and high cheekbones. Damn it, but she was lovely. "Mrs. Simpkins. The pleasure . . ." He took a deep breath. "The pleasure is all mine." Stop grinning like an *amadán*. She's a married woman and you're engaged and deeply in love with Deirdre.

"Please call me Elly. Everybody else does." She sat and crossed her legs; long, well-muscled legs barely covered by her short white skirt. Her shirt was open at the neck and when she leant forward to put her racquet on the ground the collars parted and Fingal's breath caught in his throat.

"And you're Fingal," she said, helping herself to one of John's cigarettes. "Such an unusual name. Wasn't it one of Oscar Wilde's middle names?"

Fingal dashed to light it for her. "My father was a Wilde scholar," he said.

"Fingal's not just a pretty face," John said from where he was sitting with Michelle. "He's an ex–Irish rugby international."

"Impressive," she said, blowing a smoke ring then turning to John with a mock frown. "Ex-Irish? I thought once a man was Irish he was always Irish."

Everyone laughed.

John chuckled and said, "She never stops teasing, do you?"

"Why on earth should I?" she said, lifting an eyebrow. Then, turning a radiant smile on Fingal, she asked, "What position did you play?"

Fingal melted. He generally kept his athletic career under wraps, but—though he knew he shouldn't—he wanted to impress this vivacious young woman. He blushed and said, "Second row." Her blue eyes had an intensity that matched the cloudless Mediterranean sky.

The club steward appeared.

"Your usual chotapeg, Michelle?" John asked.

Fingal never ceased to be amazed by how much Hindi had come from India into the lingo of the British armed forces. "And Elly?"

"You know," she said, "I'd really love a snake bite." She must have seen Fingal's frown. "It's a kind of shandy. Half beer, half cider."

"Gin fizz and a snake bite, please, Mahmoud," John said.

The steward left.

"How's Chris, Elly?" John asked.

She shook her head. "Sometimes I think that husband of mine fancies he's a reincarnation of Hornblower himself. Chris cares more for his bloody *Touareg* than he does for me. He went off to her an hour ago. Won't be back for ages." She took a drag on her cigarette.

Another of the new Tribal-class destroyers, Fingal thought.

"He's left me one short for dinner tonight and"—she turned to Fingal—"our houseboy is an absolutely wizard chef. He's putting on a traditional Alexandrine spread tonight. John and Michelle are coming. I don't suppose you'd care to make up the numbers?"

"Well, I—" Damn it she was attractive, and he'd love to try the native cuisine. Gyppy tummy was prevalent, so apart from tasting the baklava, he had avoided eating in native establishments.

"Come on, Fingal, be a sport," John said.

What would Deirdre say? Nothing, he told himself. She'd laugh and tell him to have a good time. She was so trusting and, besides, why shouldn't an officer and a gentleman go out with mixed company and enjoy dishes he'd never tried before? "I'd love to," he said.

"Oh goody," she said, recrossed her legs in that angled-to-one-side, calves-tightly-together way that Fingal found was at once prim and yet erotic. And then she winked at him.

27

Would Not Give His Judgment Rashly

O'Reilly, Kitty, and Barry arrived at a series of tables, each displaying an array of pies on its tablecloth-covered top. Behind each was a pole with a placard reading BEST CREAM PIE, BEST MEAT PIE, and—the créme de la créme in the world of Ballybucklebo pie making—BEST FRUIT PIE.

The contestants—Kinky, Flo, Aggie, Cissie, Gertie Gorman, Connie Brown, Mister Coffin, and several more of Ballybucklebo's pie-making artistes—were lined up in front of the table and staring expectantly at Mister Robinson. He sat behind the table regarding a row of pies, each missing a tiny wedge. He was sweating profusely and patting his stomach.

Possibly by a prearranged signal, the calliope stopped in the middle of "Stars and Stripes Forever" and Mister Robinson got to his feet. "Ladies and gentlemen, ladies and gentlemen, it is my great honour to have been chosen to judge the fruit pie entries. To paraphrase the late Sir Winston Churchill, 'Never in the history of fruit pie making have the works of so many, to produce so much culinary magnificence, been judged by so few.' Me."

A giggle ran through the crowd.

"Nice one," O'Reilly said sotto voce to Kitty, who stifled a laugh.

"I was instantly reminded of the Judgment of Paris in Greek mythology."

Typical Presbyterian, O'Reilly thought. Never miss a chance to preach.

"Three Greek goddesses all claimed a golden apple inscribed 'To the fairest,' and asked Zeus who should win. Your man Zeus, as we'd say here, was no dozer and he juked out by selecting a mortal called Paris to pick. All the goddesses offered Paris inducements, and one offered him the most beautiful woman in the world. Paris gave that scheming Jezebel the apple and he got—he got Helen of Troy, who unfortunately was already someone's wife. And that was the start of the Trojan War."

A wave of laughter rippled through the crowd.

"I," Mister Robinson said, "am a great believer in one of the beatitudes, 'Blessèd are the peacemakers,' but I am not myself blessed with the wisdom of Solomon."

"Come on, Your Reverence," a voice called. "Who won?"

The minister took a deep breath, exhaled, then said, "For the first time in the history of the competition I am declaring . . ."

"Lord," O'Reilly said to Kitty, "has Kinky's reign finally ended?"

"I am declaring—a four-way tie."

"Ooooooooh," murmured the crowd.

"The winners are, in alphabetical order, Aggie Arbuthnot, Kinky Auchinleck, Flo Bishop, and Cissie Sloan."

"Crafty bugger," O'Reilly said as the four winning friends hugged and kissed and the crowd roared its approval.

"Smart man if you ask me," Kitty said.

"And," said Mister Robinson as the applause died, "this precludes there being any runners-up, but an honourable mention is awarded to Mister Coffin for an absolutely delectable blueberry pie."

The crowd cheered.

"Good for Mister Coffin," Barry said. "I suppose, seeing he's a bachelor man, he's had to learn to cook."

"I think more men should learn the art," Kitty said, "and, Fingal Flahertie O'Reilly, one word out of you about not 'buying a dog and barking yourself,' and I'll not make that special meal I was planning for tomorrow." She put one hand on her hip and pretended to glower at him.

"Would I actually say such a thing? Really, Barry, I ask you. But you're not cooking tomorrow anyway, love. We're having a night on the town, you and I. And you know why, Kitty O'Reilly, and Barry knows why too."

"I do indeed," Barry said. "Tomorrow is your first wedding anniversary. Congratulations to you both from your best man, Fingal."

"Thank you, Bar—" Kitty started saying, but O'Reilly grabbed her and planted a kiss firmly on her open mouth. "I don't care who was looking. Thank *you*, Mrs. O'Reilly. Thank you very much. Now," he didn't wait for a reply from Kitty, "my tongue's hanging out. We've to meet Sue in the refreshments tent. I suggest we head that way now."

"Actually Sue's teaching me to cook," Barry said as they began to walk. "She's of your opinion, Kitty. That it's time women and men weren't forced into predetermined roles about who does what job." He frowned. "Sometimes she can bang her drum a bit loudly, but a lot of the time she makes a great deal of sense. She's a great debater."

"I should think she'd have to be, to hold her own against the likes of young Colin Brown," said Kitty with a grin.

Barry nodded. "I went to a boys' school and I had to learn to fight my own corner too. And the cooking's been great fun. I make a wheeker pot roast and I'm going to graduate to steak Béarnaise next week. Remember when Kinky got sick last year? The well-known culinary team of O'Reilly and Laverty might have got some horrible deficiency disease if it hadn't been for the kindness of neighbours. That's when Sue thought a few cooking lessons might be in order."

"Good for you and Sue, Barry," Kitty said, and looked sideways at O'Reilly.

"No. Thank you, but no. I'm too old a dog to learn new tricks. Between Kinky and you, Kitty, I'm as well fed as any man can and should be. Now if only I could say the same about this thirst."

"Oh all right, you old bear," Kitty said, and took his hand. "You'd probably burn the kitchen down trying to make a pot roast anyway."

As they passed back the way they had come, it was clear that the afternoon was drawing to its close. The crowds had thinned out and shadows were moving round. The Punch and Judy man was striking his tent. The roundabout was still going round, its steam organ happily piping "I've Got a Lovely Bunch of Coconuts," but more than half the herd of carved and garishly painted horses, each rising and falling on its pole, was riderless.

"Before we get our drinks, there's something I want to tell you and Kitty," Barry blurted out as they passed the Bring and Buy table. "It's about Sue and me. We don't spend all our time running a friendly 'war between the sexes.'"

"That sounds like the caption for a James Thurber cartoon," O'Reilly said, then saw that his young friend was looking like a mooncalf with a grin from ear to ear.

"I'm a lucky fellah. It's not every girl that's as smart as Sue Nolan, can sail as well, has a great seat on a horse, and is so restful on the eye too, if you don't mind me saying so, Kitty?"

"It's only the truth, Barry Laverty," Kitty said, turning to him. "Sue is a lovely-looking lass and what woman doesn't like a sincere compliment?"

"She's certainly all of those things and very beautiful to boot, and we know you love the girl dearly, so why haven't you asked her to marry you, you buck eejit?" O'Reilly said.

"Fingal. Really," Kitty said, stifling a laugh. "Sometimes you go at things like a bull in a china shop. It's none of your business."

"Yes, it is." He knew Kitty meant well, but the hare had been started from its form, the depression in the grass where it liked to lie, and O'Reilly meant to course after it until the finish. "Well, *are* you going to—"

"Hush, Fingal. There's Donal," said Kitty.

"Bout youse, Doctors? Mrs. O'Reilly?" A bored-looking Donal Donnelly was idly pushing his wheel of fortune back and forth and making the flap go tap-tap-tap. "Fancy another go, Doctor O'Reilly, sir?"

O'Reilly shook his head. "Ten bob was enough, Donal. We're heading for the refreshment tent. I've a thirst that would drain the Bucklebo River."

Donal winked, then said, "I'm sure you'd be luckier this time, Doc. Honest to God. And what about you, Doctor Laverty? This marrying business is expensive. A little extra do-re-mi could come in handy."

O'Reilly saw Barry's eyes widen as the lad took a step back. "Donal Donnelly, how in the hell did you know? Good Lord. I haven't even told Doctor and Mrs. O'Reilly yet. I was just going to."

Donal grinned his buck-toothed grin. "How long back is it since you first asked me for directions to Doctor O'Reilly's house, sir?"

Barry frowned. "That was in the summer of '64."

"Aye," said Donal, "so if we subtract the six months you spent in Ballymena, you've had eighteen months til get used til Ballybucklebo." He picked at a tooth with the nail of his little finger. "I'm not too good with the scriptures, but I seem to remember a bit about not even a sparrow could fall—"

"Without your Father's permission," O'Reilly said.

"Aye, well this here place is like that too. Not much goes on but it's through the place like grease through a goose," Donal said. He scratched his head. "I think the women here have some kind of institution, so I do."

Barry shook his head and laughed. "I think you mean intuition, Donal, and, yes, you're spot on. We're going to get married. I did propose last week and—" Barry took an enormous breath, smiling all the while. "—and Miss Nolan said yes. But we were going to wait before we make it public."

"I doubt," said Donal, "the cat's not so much out of the bag as halfway through the back door by now. But if it's any comfort til you, sir, the news isn't likely til get til Broughshane, where Miss Nolan's people are from. And it isn't likely til get all the way to Australia, so it's not. Isn't that where your da and ma are?"

Barry laughed, shook his head. "Can you give me their address there too?"

Donal became serious. "Not the day, but if you'll give me a week, sir."

"You're a hopeless case, Donal Donnelly," O'Reilly said, and chuckled. "You keep all this under that hat of yours so that informed speculation doesn't turn into fact. You hear me, Donal?"

"I do, Doctor. I do. And that's just what Doctor Laverty and Miss Nolan—"

"Enough. Now," O'Reilly said, eager to change the subject, "how's that little lass of yours? Tori's well? Over her German measles?"

"Och aye. She's her wee self all over again, so she is. She made a full remuneration."

"Remu—? Aye. Right. Good. I'm glad to hear it. Say hello to Julie for us, Donal. Now we'd best be moving on to the refreshment tent. I'm as dry as one of Mister Robinson's Sunday sermons."

After they'd put some distance between them and Donal, Kitty said, "It's wonderful news, Barry. We're delighted, aren't we, Fingal?"

"Damn right." He stuck out his hand and he and Barry shook. "Every happiness to you, my boy. But why the hush-hush? Surely you're not going to elope or anything like that, are you?"

"No. Nothing like that. It's just that Sue is pretty ambitious about her work and she's got this great opportunity. She's been awarded a teacher exchange. A teacher from Marseilles will be coming to Ballybucklebo and Sue'll be going there. I'm all for it."

"Why, that's wonderful, Barry," Kitty said.

"Isn't it?" He grinned. "She'll take up her position in mid-September and she'll stay for six months. We'll be able to have a holiday there together and we'll get wed when she gets back. Not much point being married if you both have jobs hundreds of miles apart, but get home for Christmas."

"Makes sense." O'Reilly decided there was nothing to be gained by telling Barry that it was exactly what had happened to him during the war. "But there's still one thing."

"What?"

"I don't understand why that's stopping you giving her a ring now. I'd want my fiancée to be wearing one in a city full of randy Frenchmen. And a bloody great big ring at that."

"She will," Barry said, and laughed. "But Donal was absolutely right. My dad and mum are still in Australia. They'll not be coming home to Bangor until August, so we thought we'd announce our engagement then and then go up to Broughshane to tell Sue's people." His smile was rueful. "That is if Ulster's answer to the jungle telegraph hasn't got the word there already. I think," he said, "I'd better have a word with Sue about letting our parents know right away. I'd not want them to think we were being devious."

"That would be wise. I've known your father for years, Barry. He's a very sound, straightforward man and expects others to be the same. Give them a call."

"Thanks, boss," Barry said. "I will. And I'm sure Sue'll be pleased that the word's out. She says she's never been very good at keeping secrets."

"Well," said O'Reilly, "no time like the present. There she is." He pointed to where Sue was waving at them through the open flap of the refreshments tent. "Now about that drink . . ."

Barry waved back at her. "She's been reading up on Marseilles. I think you know Sue's a bit of a revolutionary at heart so she's been learning all about 'La Marseillaise,' France's national anthem. It means 'the song of Marseille.' That scene in *Casablanca* where everyone in Rick's Bar starts singing it is a favourite of hers and—"

"Interesting," O'Reilly said, "and in the light of your recent marvellous news, Kitty and I are buying today," he clapped Barry on the shoulder, "but, and I think I might be quoting Humphrey Bogart when I say, 'What *does* it take for a man to get a drink in this town?' "

28

Temptations Both in Wine and Women

The lift would only hold two. "Come along, Fingal," Elly Simpkins said. "I'll take you up to the flat and then we'll send the lift back down for John and Michelle."

Fingal followed her into the little wrought-iron cage with its concertina folding door. She shut the door with a clang and as pulleys and cables whirred and creaked, the lift ascended to the third floor of 16B Saad Zaghloul Square, a four-storey house in a north–south-aligned terrace of similar houses.

Fingal became aware of her scent. The nearness of her in the small lift. She and Michelle had showered and changed at the club. Elly was now in a sleeveless, knee-length dress whose plunging neckline was a little on the far side of decorous.

"Here we are," she said, opening the door. "After you."

Fingal got out, then waited until she had sent the little cage back down and joined him. The lift shaft was in the middle of a square landing. Each wall had its own door. "This one," she said, crossing the hall, unlocking and opening a door. "Do come in."

He followed her into another hall and immediately removed his cap. It wasn't done for men to wear their hats indoors except on armed forces property.

"Whirlwind tour," she said, guiding him along the hall and

opening and closing doors to their left as she passed, but merely pointing at doors to their right. "Guest bedroom opposite the servant's quarters." She moved ahead. "Main bedroom." Fingal peered over her shoulder to see a large carpeted room with dressing tables, a couple of chairs, a huge full-length mirror, and an enormous bed. "Chris and I call that the field. Lots of room for romping." She laughed.

Fingal swallowed and took a deep breath.

"The bathroom's between it and the guest bedroom. Kitchen opposite." She pointed to an open doorway from which came a mixture of heady scents. Fingal recognised the sharpness of lime and the pungent aroma of garlic with perhaps a hint of coriander. She called, "We're home, Hanif."

A small, brown man, dwarfed by a mushroom-shaped chef's hat and wearing a white apron, was wiping his hands on a tea towel as he came into the hall. "Welcome home, Mrs. Simpkins. Dinner is coming along splendidly." His English was barely accented.

She said, "*Shukran,* Hanif," which Fingal had learnt meant "thank you." "This is Surgeon Lieutenant O'Reilly."

"I am very pleased to meet you, *effendi.*" He bowed and his hat jiggled as he straightened. "Please let me take your cap."

"Thank you." Fingal handed it over.

The doorbell rang.

"Excuse me," Hanif said, and went to let in John and Michelle Collins.

"You two know your way," Elly said. "John, be a pet and make the drinks. You know what us locals take. Fingal?"

"Do you have an Irish whiskey?"

"Would Paddy do?"

"Lovely," he said. "Neat, please."

She led him through a bead curtain hanging in an archway. The beads rattled as he passed into a spacious living-cum-dining room. Overhead, a long-bladed electric fan whirled noiselessly. To his right an expansive table of polished mahogany surrounded by eight chairs occupied most of that end of the room. The floral centrepiece drew his gaze: a vase filled with flowers of many pointed lilac-coloured petals enclosing a stellar flare of yellow stamens in their centres.

"The flowers are pretty," he said.

"Mmm," she said. "Egyptian lotuses, the country's national flower. Only plant as far as I know that has flowers and fruit at the same time."

"Interesting," he said.

Past the table and set against the wall was an enormous Welsh dresser. To his left two sofas and two armchairs were arranged in a semicircle around a low coffee table. An ornate rug, which he guessed was probably Persian, was hung on the wall. Fingal peered at what he recognised as a water pipe in a corner. "Who uses the hookah?"

She laughed. "I do. Apparently a Persian physician, Abul-Fath Gilani, invented it in the sixteenth century. I smoke a flavoured tobacco called *sheesha*." She looked at him and smiled. "You really have to try it. I'll not mind sharing the mouthpiece if you'll not." She led him across the room to a pair of tall French windows in the far wall.

"Perhaps I will," he said, deliberately leaving it vague about whether he'd smoke with her or would object to sharing the mouthpiece, and returned her smile. Come on, he told himself, a bit of flirting's all right. She's fun to be with.

"Let me show you the view," she said, leaning forward to undo a lower snib on the French windows. Fingal's eye was drawn to her décolletage and he looked quickly away. He followed her onto a balcony. The air was warm on his face, the Alexandrine smells no longer a novelty.

"Below us is Saud Zaghloul Square. The flat faces west."

He looked over a footpath, a row of palm trees, and a narrow grassy park lined with benches, more palms, then a terrace of similar houses on the far side. Although he could still hear the distant hum of traffic, there were only a few pedestrians, no vehicles, and no animals— a peaceful counterpoint to the bustle in other parts of the city.

"Out that way," she pointed north, "you can see the East Harbour on the far side of the Corniche. It's only about six minutes from here to the dockyard. Very convenient for Chris getting to and from his work."

Funny, Fingal thought, how lightly she referred to what her husband did as "his work." As if it was as humdrum as going to an accountant's office. Chris's workplace, like Fingal's, could at any time turn into a raging inferno of bursting high explosives and screaming splinters of steel or a watery tomb.

She turned. "Now," she said, "drinkies. Goodo," and headed back into the room where John and Michelle were standing at the living room end. Each had a glass in both hands.

"Here you are, Elly," Michelle said, handing her hostess a cut-glass tumbler.

"One Paddy whiskey, Fingal," John said. "No water."

"Thanks," Fingal said.

"Let's everybody sit," Elly said.

Fingal lowered himself onto a sofa and was not surprised when Elly sat beside him. There were bowls of figs, dates, and kumquats on the table.

She raised her glass. "To new friends." She looked directly at Fingal, who with the others echoed the toast and drank. "Now," she said, "Michelle and I will be going shopping tomorrow. I imagine you two salty sailor men will be at your work. You're a bachelor, Fingal—"

"Actually, he's engaged," John said.

"Your fiancée here?" Michelle asked.

"'Fraid not," Fingal said. "Deirdre's back in Ireland." And he wished she *were* here. If that was the case, he'd not be finding Elly Simpkins so devilishly attractive.

"If you're alone, then," Elly said, "is there anything you'd like me to get for you, Fingal? It'll be no trouble and now you know where I live I hope you'll not be a stranger."

"That's very kind, Elly," Fingal said, "but just at the moment I can't think of anything I want or need." Liar. He'd been having fleeting erotic images ever since she'd shown him that enormous bed and made the remark about "lots of room for romping." A glowering Presbyterian minister and a line from a childhood hymn flashed into his mind: "Yield not to temptation, for yielding is sin."

"Let me know," she said, "if you change your mind." And he felt her move a little closer.

"I will." He sat back, sipped his whiskey, and was content to listen to the conversation of the three old friends.

Hanif, now hatless but wearing a short white cotton jacket and white gloves, came in. "If you wish, madam, I am ready to start serving the soup. The Gewürtztraminer's chilled and the claret has been decanted."

"Splendid," Elly said. "Please do, and we'll start with the white." She rose. "Please follow me."

Fingal brought up the rear on the short trip to the table.

"We'll not play head-of-the-table games. John and I will sit over on that side in the middle and Michelle and Fingal together on this side."

Fingal sat facing Elly and felt a certain relief to be a little distant from his hostess.

A glass of white wine stood beside each place setting. Elly pointed to the dishes. "Those are plates of pita bread and mint yoghurt. If you'd prefer . . ." she offered a plate to Fingal, "you might like to try some *tehina*. It's sesame paste with lemon juice and garlic."

He scooped some of the *tehina* up with a piece of pita and popped it into his mouth. "That," he said after he'd swallowed, "is very tasty." He sipped his wine.

Hanif appeared with a steaming tureen. "*Molokheyyah*," he said.

"Please serve, Hanif," Elly said, and as the manservant ladled the green liquid into soup plates she explained for Fingal's sake, "*Molokheyyah* is made from stock, mallow leaves, garlic, and coriander. In Alexandria, the chefs add shrimp, but in Cairo rabbit is preferred. I usually start dinner parties with it because if anybody's going to kiss anybody later they'll all have eaten garlic." She laughed.

Fingal nearly choked on his first mouthful of soup.

"Really, Elly," Michelle said, "you'll embarrass Fingal. Pay no attention to her. Elly Simpkins is the greatest tease in Alexandria. And she's daft about Chris and the boys."

"You and Chris have children . . ." Fingal was tempted to say "Mrs. Simpkins" to restore a little formality to the conversation, but instead stuck to "Elly."

"Two perfectly rambunctious sprogs," she said. "Martin's nine and Geoffrey's eight. They both board at a frightfully expensive prep school back in England and spend the hols with my mummy and daddy."

"You must miss them," John said.

"I do, but Chris needs me here and it's always been the fate of us British in foreign parts to send the kids home for schooling. You get used to it." She smiled at Fingal. "Chris's *Touareg*'s at sea quite a lot too. It does rather leave one with time on one's hands, if you know what I mean. One can get a trifle bored." She sipped her wine.

I'm bloody well sure I know what you mean, he thought.

Hanif began setting dishes for the fish course on the table. "I've prepared some *samak makly* fried local fish. The grouper was still alive when I bought it in the *souk* this morning and there is also some *calamari*."

"Thank you, Hanif," Elly said.

Fingal's nose was assailed by the most wondrous aromas.

"Help yourself, everybody," Elly said.

Fingal waited for Michelle to serve herself then took a portion of fish and several pieces of calamari, which he knew to be squid. The flesh of the fried grouper was white and flaky with a delicate flavour and contrasted nicely with the rubbery squid. "This is wonderful," he said.

"Glad you're enjoying it, Fingal," Elly said, "and there's lots more to come."

Little was said as the fish course was devoured.

"Now," said Elly, "would anybody like to smoke before the next course?"

"Funny isn't it?" Michelle said. "The very idea used to be so *in-fra dig,* but ever since we found out Queen Elizabeth does, it's all the rage now."

John offered his Player's.

Fingal shook his head. "Anybody mind a pipe?"

"Go right ahead," Elly said, helping herself to a cigarette and fitting it into an ivory cigarette holder.

"Just like Marlene Dietrich," John said.

"Not a bit," Elly said, and let go a blue puff. "I've never boxed in a Turkish trainer's gym in Germany, and I much prefer men to women." She smiled at Fingal.

"Rumour has it," Michelle said, "she had an affair with James Stewart."

"Now," said Elly, "there's a boy whose slippers I'd not mind finding under 'the field.'"

"You are incorrigible, Elly," Michelle said, and laughed. "Pay no attention to her, Fingal. She'd flirt with her shadow. Everyone knows Elly's a one-man woman."

"I'm glad to hear it," he said, but he wondered, and asked himself, did he really want to find out if it were untrue?

As Fingal sat quietly letting the small talk pass him by, Hanif began bringing in more dishes. Each was covered by a silver dome. He cleared the dirty plates on his return trips to the kitchen and finished by placing a decanter of red wine in the centre of the table beside the vase of Egyptian lotus flowers.

"Shall I pour the claret?" John asked.

"Please do," Elly said. "It should be passable. It's a Chateau Lafite Rothschild."

Typical English understatement, Fingal thought.

"Now," said Elly, stubbing out her smoke, "main course time," and lifted the first dome. "*Kebda Iskandarani*," she said. "Seasoned fried liver."

"It smells delightful," Michelle said.

"And that's deep-fried *falafel*," John said when Elly lifted the lid from a plate piled with brown balls. "Ground chickpeas if you've not had it before, Fingal."

"Pretty much all new to me," Fingal said, smiled, finished his second glass of white, and sipped his red. It was exquisite.

"And those are lamb kebabs," Michelle said. "They should be cooked over charcoal, but Hanif does something magical in the kitchen."

"He's a gem without price," Elly said. "Now, this is your vegetable course," and she uncovered a tureen. "*Mashi*, which is seasoned rice stuffed into aubergines and put in this pot and covered with lemon juice."

Fingal's tummy rumbled. "It certainly beats naval cooking. It's my first real taste of the local cuisine. Thank you, Elly." He swallowed more claret.

She inclined her head to him, smiled, and said, "Now everybody tuck in."

As plates were being filled, John said, "Just be grateful you're having your first taste in a civilised house. A few of us went out into the desert and were entertained by an Abadan sheik."

"Abadan?" Fingal said.

"They're a Bedouin tribe," Elly said.

"I see." Fingal bit into a mouthful of the liver. Wonderful. Perhaps if he got the recipe from Hanif, Mrs. Kincaid would be able to make the dish. Doctor Flanagan's housekeeper in Ballybucklebo was a good cook and Fingal fully intended to return to the practice post-war.

"They invited us to dinner—the Beduoins are renowned for their hospitality," John said. "You all sit in a huge tent on carpets round an enormous circular brass plate piled high with rice. Everybody uses their right hand to indulge themselves in a kind of lucky dip into the rice. It is considered polite to give delicacies to guests and very impolite to refuse." He paused.

Fingal had just pulled a piece of lamb from the kebeb skewer and popped it in his mouth.

"I truly cannot recommend sheep's eyeballs," John said in a deadpan voice. "Not one bit."

For the second time that night, Fingal nearly choked on his food. He looked up to see Elly smiling at him and felt a pressure on his foot, then his ankle. "I'm not sure I'd like eyeballs," she said, "but I do think it is polite for the host or hostess to offer the best the house has to offer."

Perhaps it was the whiskey and three glasses of wine, perhaps it was the faint taste of her perfume, the pressure on his ankle, the invitation in her voice, or a simple physical longing, but before he could stop them the words were out. "I believe, John, you did say it would be considered impolite to refuse." And as he spoke, he lifted his other foot and placed it on top of Elly's.

29

Scare Me with Thy Tears

O'Reilly took the stairs of Number One two at a time. He had come back from Belfast after another meeting with Charlie and Cromie to sort out more last-minute arrangements for the reunion at Dublin's Trinity College and Shelbourne Hotel in September. Barry was on call and downstairs in his quarters, and Jenny out with her young lawyer, Terry Baird.

He charged into the upstairs lounge. "I'm home, love," he said, heading for the decanter of Jameson on the sideboard. "How was your day?"

Kitty had pulled a chair into the bay of one of the bow windows and was sitting with her back to him, apparently enjoying the view over the church steeple, the village, on over Belfast Lough, and beyond. She half-turned to him and said, "It could have been better." Her voice was flat. She turned back to face the window.

He crossed the room, ignoring Lady Macbeth, who was curled up in front of an unlit fire, and stood behind Kitty, hands on her shoulders, gently massaging. "One of those 'Mother said there'd be days like this' days, pet? Nursing can be pretty tough sometimes. I know. Did you lose a patient?"

She looked up and he saw a tear slip down her cheeks as if in a hurry to get away and hide its embarrassment. Her eyes were red so she must have been crying, and that wasn't like Kitty. Whatever was troubling her was a damn sight worse than the way she'd said, "It could have been better."

"Darling, what's wrong?" O'Reilly moved round the chair and hunkered down in front of her as he would have with a frightened child. He clasped one of her hands in both of his and looked straight into her grey eyes.

She said quietly, "Fingal, I got a letter today . . ." Her voice trailed off then she said, "It gave me quite a shock."

"A letter?" O'Reilly frowned. Whatever was in it must have indeed been upsetting, but why had it taken Kitty until now to weep? The post was delivered in the morning.

"It had been addressed to the old Bostock House nurses' home on the grounds of the Royal. I used to live there during and after the war, before the Broadway Towers flats opened a couple of years ago. All mail for the hospital site goes to a central mail room. Someone there had used her head, knew me by sight, guessed who it was for, and brought it to Ward 21 just before I left for home. The letter had a Spanish stamp."

"Spanish? From someone you knew in Tenerife?" O'Reilly frowned.

She swallowed and nodded. "Sort of. I didn't open it until I got home. I'd just finished reading it as you came in."

He could see two light blue sheets of air mail notepaper clutched in her right hand. Perhaps one of her colleagues from the orphanage where she'd worked during the Spanish Civil War or one of the orphans, who would be in their thirties now, was in trouble? "Do you want to tell me what it's about?" he said.

She nodded, pulled a hanky from her sweater's sleeve with her free hand, dried her eyes, blew her nose, and straightened her shoulders. "Yes. Yes, I do. It's about a past that I thought was long forgotten—" She took a deep breath. "—but it's not."

O'Reilly frowned but kept his voice low. "Kitty," he said, "I love you. If something's bothering you I want to know what it is." He squeezed her hand, and waited.

"And I love you, Fingal. I'd not hurt you for the world. It's a long story and I'm not particularly proud of it. But what's done is done."

The backs of O'Reilly's knees were starting to hurt, but he didn't want to stand up. Not yet. Give her time, he told himself.

"When I left you in 1936 I was hurt, angry. I hid in my work. The children needed love, I did too, and looking after them filled my days and my nights when I was on duty. San Blas, where the orphanage was, is on the southeast corner of Tenerife. It was only a tiny place. There wasn't much to do when I was off duty." She looked him in the eye. "There was a fishing village, Los Abrigos, about a mile away. I used to walk there along the coast. It was such a pretty little place with the houses painted in bright colours and the fishing boats all reds and blues. There was a good fish restaurant . . . it was always busy, overlooking the harbour . . ." She managed a smile. "I don't suppose you've ever had *bocarones*?"

He returned her smile. "You'd be right."

"They're filletted anchovies pickled in vinegar, them and a plate of *gueldes*—you'd have had them here as whitebait, deep-fried herring fry straight from the sea—and a glass of local *vino blanco* . . ." She sighed.

O'Reilly wondered where all this was leading, heard one knee creak, but hung on waiting. He sensed that the preamble was how Kitty was readying herself to tell him what she must. She was like a wild duck that had been offered bread, swimming from side to side, drawing up the courage finally to dart forward and take it.

". . . and some of the sunsets over the Atlantic. I've never seen anything like them." She stared at the floor. "I'd been in Tenerife for a year, still missing you, but perhaps not quite as much as at first."

And although that wounded O'Reilly's pride, he recognised that it should not. Their romance had been well and truly over. She had been free to do exactly as she saw fit. He was able to say, "I understand."

"Thank you," she said. "Anyway, I was in Los Abrigos. I'd finished my meal and was having a second glass of wine. I remember it so clearly. The sky was all reds and scarlets shot through with chrome yellow and topped by these little dove-grey clouds. The sky above them was velvety and there was one tiny star alive." She smiled and made a huhing noise before saying, "I know it must sound corny to you, Fingal, but the owner of the restaurant used to sing and play a guitar. That night he was singing a Mexican song, "Granada" . . ."

And something important happened, O'Reilly knew. He knew. People rarely remember any given moment in such minute detail unless, unless there's a damn good reason. And he realised that it must be a man. Had some man written to Kitty? After all these years? To his surprise, the thought rattled O'Reilly.

"A voice said, *'Disculpe Señorita, no hay más asientos, aqui estoy mtired. ¿Puedo sentarme en su mesa?'* I looked up. It was a dark-haired man who had piercing brown eyes and a scar beneath the right one. By then I knew enough Spanish to understand that he was asking if he could sit at my table."

She does remember the exact details, O'Reilly thought, after thirty years, and he sighed.

"He seemed to be terribly out of breath. He was a complete stranger." A smile came and went on her lips fast as the flicker of a candle in a breeze. She took a deep breath.

O'Reilly stood, perhaps because the ache in his knees was becoming unbearable; perhaps, he recognised, he needed to step back emotionally to prepare himself for what might be? No, damn it, what was going to be coming next. And that need was stupid, he told himself. She owed you nothing. Nothing. So why is your hand trembling?

"I said, *'Si señor, pero yo no hablo mucho Español. Soy Irlandés.'* He sat and said, 'Thank you. I speak English, but no Irish.' That made me laugh. He introduced himself, 'Mañuel Garcia y Rivera.' He had a lovely smile and he really was having trouble breathing. I thought he might be asthmatic." She sighed. "It all seemed so innocent." She stood. "Fingal," she said, "I want to tell you everything, but . . ."

He frowned. But what?

"I'd like you to take me for a walk on the beach and I'll try to explain it to you there." She rubbed the back of one hand across her eye. "I got such an immediate jolt about what I read in the letter it made me cry and I still feel . . . I feel hemmed in . . . I need to get some fresh air. Will you give me five minutes, darling, to wash my face then we'll go? I'll tell you all about it then."

"Of course," he said.

She pecked him and fled.

He shook his head. This Garcia y Rivera must have played a pretty important part in her life, and he resented that. He'd no right to, but he did. O'Reilly nodded. He hated to see anyone upset, and Kitty O'Reilly, née O'Hallorhan, wasn't just anybody. He glanced at the sideboard to where a two-thirds-full decanter of Jameson's whiskey stood. He shook his head. His pre-dinner tot was going to have to wait. They were going for a walk. Now don't, he told himself, let your imagination run riot until Kitty's ready to explain. She knew a man in Tenerife years ago. She's had a letter from someone in Spain and the letter has upset her. That's all you know. It might not be from him. And she's not keeping anything from you. Don't go putting two and two together and getting five. There's probably some perfectly innocent explanation and, anyway, you're going to find out the whole truth very soon. So why are you pacing up and down in front of the fireplace not even bothering to light your pipe, disturbing Lady Macbeth?

Grateful for the distraction, he watched as the little cat yawned, stood, arched her back, stretched her front paws out in front of her, lifted her haunches, and stuck her tail straight up in the air before taking a few leisurely paces, jumping onto an armchair, and curling up to fall fast asleep.

"There," Kitty said. She'd put on a head scarf and a light cardigan. "That didn't take long." She managed a small smile.

"You look grand," he said, which wasn't entirely true. Although she had repaired her makeup and brushed her hair, the telltale red lines had not left the whites of her eyes. "Are you ready, and are you sure you'd not rather stay here?"

She nodded.

He kissed her and said, "Come on then," and held the door for her. "I think," he said when they reached the hall and he moved to the front door, "perhaps we should leave Arthur at home." There might be some serious things said and O'Reilly wanted no distractions.

"No, Fingal. He hasn't had his walk today. We should bring him."

He smiled, said, "Fair enough," and thought, You are a considerate woman, Kitty. O'Reilly turned and headed for the back door.

30

Merely Innocent Flirtation...

"Oh, dear," said Elly, regarding the empty decanter as everyone finished their main course, "I do think the claret's *kaput* again. What would everyone like with dessert? Something sweet?"

The pressure of her foot increased on Fingal's ankle. He cleared his throat and told himself, Slow down on the drink, boy. He had a vivid picture of a naval signal flag, quartered in red and white for the letter U. It meant, "You are standing into danger." Even so, it was amusing and indeed arousing to be flirted with by such an attractive woman—provided it went no farther.

"A nice Château d'Yquem Sauternes, perhaps?"

"Sounds lovely," Michelle said.

"Have we one chilled, Hanif?"

"Of course, madam." The manservant vanished, only to reappear with a bottle. He showed the label to Elly, who nodded, waited for Hanif to uncork the bottle, sniffed the cork, and sipped the splash he put into her glass. "Splendid," she said, poured for Michelle, and continued, "Hold out your glass, Fingal."

"Um," he said, "I hope you don't mind, Elly, but to be honest I've never really liked sweet wines." Which was true. He had always thought them sickly.

"Oh dear, Fingal," she said, and the pressure of her foot lessened. She canted her head to one side. "You know, 'Fingal' seems dreadfully formal. I think I'll call you Finn."

Fingal could imagine her in a pet shop admiring a puppy and remarking, "I think I'll call you Fido." "The only one who does is my elder brother," he said with a smile, "but your Eleanor has been shortened to Elly, so why not?"

"Thank you, Finn, and as you don't like sweet wines, is there anything else I can tempt you with?"

The trouble, Fingal thought, with double entendres is that they only ever have one meaning. "I think," he said, "I'll have a little rest"—she took her foot away—"but if we're going to have a nightcap, I'm sure I could manage another Paddy a bit later." He thought about "later" as he watched Hanif filling the others' wineglasses. Elly had pointed out the servant's quarters. If this man lives in, it will be hard for her to get any further than she has already. Not with an in-house chaperone. Fingal patted his tummy and sighed contentedly.

"Splendid," she said. "Pour, please, for me and the others, Hanif, then bring in the desserts."

"I don't suppose you'll have had either of these, Fingal," Michelle said when the plates were set on the table. "That one's *basbousa*, semolina soaked in sugar syrup topped with almonds. The other one's my favourite, *luqmat al-qadi*. They're round doughnuts that are crunchy on the outside, syrupy inside."

"I'm going to have a bit of both," John said. "Perhaps it'll slow me down a bit. Give you a better chance at our next squash game, Fingal."

"I think," said Fingal, "if I'm going to play any more games, I'd better think about trying to get fit."

He felt the pressure on his ankle again as Elly said, "I'm sure we can arrange all kinds of exercise for you, Doctor."

Fingal swallowed and moved into shallower waters. "But for now,

I'm going to keep up with you, John, and try all the desserts." He helped himself. Michelle was right about the *luqmat*. Delicious. He took two more.

"What," said John, "has anybody heard from home since last we met?"

Fingal stopped chewing. Ma's recent letter had been full of her work for a charity for unwed mothers. Lars had brought Fingal up to date with the state of a new orchid that was being cultivated in his greenhouse. Hardly earth-shattering intelligence. He'd had a letter from Deirdre two days ago. It had been dated May 19, before the Dunkirk evacuation. It was the usual much-hungered-for mix of un-censorable chitchat and professions of her love, her yearning for his return next month. And broad hints about how she was going to make things up to him for their forced separation once they were married. He should think of that rather than be welcoming Elly's shin-stroking under the table, but the very thought of making love to Deirdre seemed to make Elly more desirable. He started chewing again, tried to ignore Elly, and paid attention to what was being said.

"Mummy managed to get tickets to see the new flick *Gone With the Wind* in the West End," said Elly. "She said Vivien Leigh was marvellous as Scarlett O'Hara, Leslie Howard was quite dishy as usual, and Clark Gable wonderfully wicked as Rhett Butler."

"I wonder if it'll ever get to Alex?" John said.

"I wonder if Clark Gable will ever get to Alex, more to the point," she said with a chuckle. "Everybody ready for coffee?"

Heads, including Fingal's, nodded.

"Hanif, please," she said, "then when you've tidied up you can run along home." She grinned at Fingal, who sat upright.

"Let's," she said, "take our coffee and liqueurs on the balcony. John, will you see to the drinks? Finn," she said, with emphasis, "would like another Paddy and I'll have a Hennessy XO. You know where everything is." She rose and the others followed suit.

Elly led the way through a second set of French windows into the dark of an Egyptian night. A sliver of waxing moon was beginning to set. This second balcony was furnished with rattan chairs and a circular table. Elly lifted a box of Swan Vesta matches from the tabletop and lit two candles inside glass globes. "Sunset in June," she said, "is about an hour earlier than back home." She plumped down in a chair and said, "Come and keep me company, Finn."

He sat by her side with Michelle on his other flank.

"Where is home for you, Elly?" said Fingal, taking a sip of the whiskey.

"John and I were stationed in Portsmouth before the war, but home for me is Bishop's Stortford in Hertfordshire. Daddy's the vicar, but mummy's family have a bit of cash so I was packed off to Cheltenham Ladies' College when I was thirteen."

"That's a famous girls' school," Fingal said, impressed.

"Raaather," she said, making her already polished accent even more upper class. "Lots of 'Jolly Hockey sticks,' don't'ch know?" She laughed, then said, "More like a bloody prison camp. I got expelled in my last year—for smoking. Daddy was blazing." She laughed and Michele said, "If the navy ever commissions an HMS *Incorrigible*, I think they'll be naming her for you, Elly."

That made Fingal guffaw.

John appeared. "Drinks," he said, set four glasses on the table, and sat beside his wife. "Can't stay much longer, Elly. I have the morning watch tomorrow on *Nile*. Four A.M. to eight. When we go, can we give you a lift to the dockyard steps, Fingal?" John asked.

"I'll look after Finn," Elly said. "You go and get your beauty sleep, John."

Michelle laughed. "If Elly's driving, Fingal, remember to hang on. Chris bought a Peugeot and she thinks she's Dick Seaman."

"I hope not," said Fingal. "He crashed in the Belgian Grand Prix last year and I'm afraid that was the end of him."

"Good heavens. I didn't know that. It just shows you how isolated you get here," said Michelle. "I try to keep up with news from home, but it's not always easy."

"Dick Seaman was driving much too fast on a wet track. Don't worry, I'll take special care of you, Finn," Elly said, and he knew that in the darkness outside the candles' glow, no one could see that she had taken his hand under the table.

Hanif appeared with a tray loaded with four plates. On each was a small cup and saucer on which lay a sweet biscuit. A second saucer supported a small copper container, broader at its base than at its top, with a long wooden handle.

"Elly and Chris—" said John.

An unintended reminder to Fingal that Mrs. Eleanor Simpkins, Elly to her friends, was married to a fellow naval officer.

"—always serve *qahwa ghali,* Egyptian-style coffee." He tipped the contents of his copper container into his cup.

Fingal followed suit and sipped. "It's delightful," he said, savouring the rich, dark brew.

They sat in companionable silence, sipping their coffee and liqueurs, probably all, like Fingal, grateful for a lull in the conversation. He took another mouthful of coffee and let the sights, sounds, and smells of the Egyptian night wash over him: As there were no enemy aircraft within flying distance and wouldn't be unless Italy declared war, the city was not blacked out and its lights shone into the night sky hiding all but the brightest stars. Night insects buzzed and moths attracted by the candles fluttered, one coming too close and crashing on burning wings much as Fingal imagined an enemy bomber might, caught in *Warspite*'s antiaircraft fire. Traffic hummed from the Corniche and although the air was redolent of spices, the inescapable Alexandrine animal dung aroma hung on the night air.

Hanif appeared noiselessly. "Excuse me, madam. If that will be all?"

"Yes, Hanif. Off you trot," Elly said. "I'll see to finishing up." She squeezed Fingal's hand.

"Been a lovely evening, Elly," said John, standing, "but Michelle and I really must be running along."

Michelle rose. "No need to get up, Fingal."

Fingal had started to leave his chair, but Michelle's polite admonition and downward pressure from Elly's hand kept him seated.

"Lovely meeting you," Michelle said. "Now see that Elly behaves herself."

"I will," Fingal said.

"I'll see you out," Elly said, glass in hand. "Excuse me, Finn. I'll be right back."

He took a deep breath. Make your excuse and get out of here, he thought. And yet it had been months since he'd had any close contact with a woman. Her perfume lingered and he heard her laugh as she bade the other guests farewell. He cleared his throat, looked at his half-empty glass. Right. A bit more chitchat, finish this, then home to *Warspite*. And to keep his conscience clear, as soon as he got to his cabin, he'd write a long letter full of love to Deirdre.

"Will you blow out the candles, come inside, and close the windows, Finn?" Elly called.

Fingal dealt with the guttering flames, smelled the wax as the wicks let off black smoke. He stood, mouthing "Smoke Gets in Your Eyes" to himself.

> . . . how I knew
> my true love was true . . .

Then he closed the French windows and turned to see Elly, drink in one hand, cigarette holder in the other, reclining full length on one of the sofas, her legs together, knees slightly flexed. If she had both hands clasped behind her head, she might have been the model for

Goya's two paintings of the Maja; the Clothed and the Naked versions. "It's—it's been a lovely evening," he began.

"Come and sit beside me," she said, drawing her knees up, forcing her skirt to slip well up her thighs.

Fingal swallowed and moved closer. "Elly, I—"

She made a moue. "Don't be such a bashful boy, Finn. Come and sit down. If you're worried about Chris, I love him dearly, but we have an arrangement. He's not actually on *Touareg* tonight, and I don't mind really. Don't you know there's a war on? Old conventions? Pffft." She sipped her brandy. "What time do you have to be back on board?"

Fingal inhaled, noticed the little ripples in the whiskey in his glass, and said, his voice hoarse, "At the dock by ten thirty."

"Well," she said, holding her arms open wide, "it's only twenty past eight. I always arrange my little soirées to accommodate any shipboard officers who might come. We've all the time in the world. Come and sit down."

Fingal looked at her, her striking, smiling eyes, open lips, the rim of her areola showing on the swell of her left breast, and the firmness of her thighs. He found himself picturing her naked like the Maja. And he wanted her. He wanted her very much. Deirdre would never know.

He sat in the hollow of Elly's body, leaning against her, feeling her warmth as she wrapped her arms round his neck, pulling him down. Her lips and her tongue found his and he responded, freely, joyously, longingly.

"Why," she said, "don't we go along to the field." She chuckled. "Have a little romp?" She stood and took his hand, bringing him to his feet.

This is all wrong, Fingal thought. I shouldn't be doing this, but I want this woman. This wanton, lovely, free-spirited woman.

Outside, through the closed French doors, the night was rent by roaring and screeching. What the blazes? Fingal disentangled himself from Elly and stood rooted in his tracks. He recognised the high hooting of destroyers' sirens, the tenor whoops of the cruisers, and the basso profundo rumblings of the battleships. He remembered Richard saying in a gharry on the Rue des Soeurs that in case of emergency, successive blasts on ships' sirens was the signal for immediate recall.

"Elly," he said, "I'm awfully—"

"Don't be silly," she said, readjusting her neckline to a more modest drape and smoothing down her skirts, "I'm a navy wife. I understand. Come on. I'll run you to the boarding steps."

It wasn't until Fingal was getting out of her car at the dockside that he realised—between the erotic tension just before the sirens had sounded and the mixed feelings of dashed desire and relief at being given a foolproof excuse to get away—he'd forgotten to collect his cap.

31

Remembered Kisses After Death

An ever-joyous Arthur Guinness tumbled out of his kennel the minute O'Reilly and Kitty emerged from the kitchen.

"Heel," O'Reilly said, and the big dog tucked in. O'Reilly's mind was racing and his legs followed suit, setting a brisk pace through the village with Kitty in step beside him. Neither of them spoke as they waited briefly beside the Maypole for the traffic light to change. But once across they were thwarted by Helen Hewitt coming out of the tobacconist's.

"Och, Doctor and Mrs. O'Reilly, how are the pair of you?" She bent and patted Arthur, who, well-mannered as he was, sat down when O'Reilly stopped walking.

"Grand altogether," said O'Reilly, feeling the urge to laugh at the polite lie. "How are you getting on?"

"Couldn't be better," Helen said. "I passed my chemistry and zoölogy exams last month so I'll be going into second year in September. I never thought a wee girl from my kind of background could ever get a chance to be a doctor, but here I am. My da's tickled pink. He never quits telling people."

"He has every right to be proud, and we're all very pleased for you, Helen," Kitty said.

"Thank you." Helen smiled and said, "I've time off from that summer job you helped me get as a ward orderly in Newtownards Hospital, Doctor O'Reilly, so I'm staying with my da, and I'm going up to Belfast tomorrow. You mind Doctor Laverty's pal Jack Mills?"

O'Reilly nodded.

"We ran into each other at a hop in the Student's Union a couple of weeks back. Asked me to give him another chance. And he's a very handsome lad." She winked at O'Reilly.

"Good for you, Helen," he said, pleased for her, but eager for the privacy of the beach. "Now we must be running along."

"Good evening to you both." Helen lit a Gallagher's Green and headed off up Main Street.

"Nice girl," Kitty said after a while of walking down Station Road.

"She is, and very bright. I just hope Jack Mills doesn't hurt her a second time." He glanced at Kitty and immediately regretted the remark. Her lips were pursed and she was nodding her head in emphatic agreement. O'Reilly could practically hear her thoughts. Wasn't that what he'd done to her all those years ago? And because it was, she had no reason not to—to do *what* with this Garcia y Rivera?

"Hi on out, Arthur," O'Reilly said as they started to climb a sand dune. The dog loved to run, and perhaps watching him might distract Kitty from O'Reilly's last remark. The breeze whispered in the marram grass and the sand crunched underfoot. It was heavy going and he took Kitty's hand to give her a pull uphill.

"Thank you."

"Look at that," he said as they crested the dune. More sandy ridges lay ahead before the beach proper. The tide was out and the strand glistened nearly as brightly as the sun's golden evening path across the lough. Fork-tailed, black-capped terns wheeled above and oyster catchers flew in line astern giving piping cries.

He continued to hold her hand for the descent to a well-worn route at the foot of the sand hill. Once on it they were in a private place unless someone else out for a walk came along.

Arthur came trotting up, panting, pink tongue lolling, satisfying himself that his people were where they should be before charging off again.

Kitty stopped and said, "I'll explain as we walk along. It'll be easier for me." Then she kissed him, a soft, gentle kiss.

"Fine," he said, not fully understanding why, but willing to accept what she said. He squeezed her hand.

"First, Fingal, I love you with all my heart. I always have, but I heard what you said to Helen."

He bowed his head.

"It hurt me when you put medicine first before me, not once, but twice. A year later it still hurt."

"I'm sorry . . ."

"Sssssh," she said, "what's done is done. And I didn't mention it to bring up old wounds, just to, well, explain, what happened to me in 1937. I was lonely, my Spanish was improving, but it was hard work maintaining a conversation and there were very few people around who spoke English. Agnes Brady, the girl from Dublin I'd come out with, was there, but we weren't always off duty together. Something attracted me to Mañuel from the moment he sat down." She said it in such a matter-of-fact way she might have been describing a long-ago shopping trip to Belfast, but she'd said "Mañuel" not "Mister Garcia y Rivera." The use of his Christian name was telling. "He ordered *caballa ahumada,* smoked mackerel, and asked me if I'd join him in a glass of wine. We chatted. His English was very good. He told me he had seen me there before, but had never had the *valor,* the courage, to speak to me. But that night he did. The sunset died, the café owner was singing some Catalonian love songs, a full moon rose over—"

"Kitty, it's all right. I understand." He wanted her to stop. He didn't want to hear the details. He didn't want to, but he knew he'd have to listen—for her sake.

"No, you don't understand, Fingal. Let me tell you. I need to tell you," she said. "Mañuel had a very sad history. He'd been a lecturer at the Complutense University of Madrid. A historian specializing in the Napoleonic wars. He and his wife and family lived on the campus. That district was heavily shelled by Franco's forces in November 1936 . . ." She stared out to sea before turning back and saying, "His wife was killed . . ."

Now he heard the sadness, but anyone could feel sorry for a recently widowed man. "I'm sorry to hear that," O'Reilly said reflexively, still forcing himself to listen to a story he really didn't want to hear. "I've seen what shelling can do." And his mind flew back to the carnage after Narvik, Calabria, Crete.

"Mañuel lost half a lung, and nearly lost an eye. But his little girl, Consuela, who'd been two then, survived unharmed. When he was well enough, they moved to San Blas to be with his family. Consuela had turned three by then. He wanted nothing to do with the fighting. Even if he had, with only one lung he couldn't enlist."

"It's all right, Kitty," O'Reilly said, but it wasn't. He recognised that he was starting to feel jealous.

"Fingal, I don't know why I feel guilty about this. You and I had parted, you had found a new love, and yet I feel that telling you this, I'm hurting you, even betraying you." She inhaled, held her breath, then let it and her next words out with a rush. "We had an affair. I—I fell in love with him."

Silence hung. So two and two did make four. In the upstairs lounge, he'd been trying not to admit the possibility. O'Reilly tried to understand how he felt. Kitty, who had been in her late twenties, had had no obligation to him. None at all. They had parted. He'd lost his virginity when he'd been in the merchant navy and he'd married Deirdre after he and Kitty had parted. Damn it, he'd even come close to having an affair himself when he was engaged to Deirdre.

"I see," he said. He frowned. He remembered a night in Alex in 1940 at the Cecil Hotel. Patrick Steptoe had mentioned how, on the way out from England, his troopship had stopped at Santa Cruz de Tenerife. And didn't you, when he told you that, O'Reilly, didn't you hope that Kitty O'Hallorhan had found a new love? And didn't you wish it for her many times after that? He was an intelligent man. He should be able to accept that what Kitty had done was none of his bloody business. Then why was he feeling the way he might if an opposing forward had tackled him from the blind side?

He mustn't let Kitty see that he was hurt. This was clearly hard enough for her without saddling her with more guilt. "There was no reason that you should not have." He worked to keep his voice steady. "I told you. I understand . . ." At a purely intellectual level, but my pulse is racing and I'm starting to sweat.

"Thank you for that, Fingal. Thank you so very much."

He heard the catch in her voice.

"He was a very sweet man, eight years older than me."

O'Reilly hesitated before asking the inevitable. "You were young, free, eight years isn't much—why didn't you marry him?"

She shrugged. "Religion . . ."

O'Reilly nodded. He was no stranger to the Catholic-Protestant divide in Ireland.

"Mañuel was Catholic and he became devout after his wife died. Spain was a very Catholic country then, especially in the villages. I was an outsider, a Protestant. His family didn't approve."

"Yes," he said softly. "Yes, I see."

A panting Arthur ran up, satisfied himself, and galloped off again.

They were out of the dunes and onto the strand when Kitty stopped and said, "His daughter Consuela was a lovely little thing. When she could talk she always called me Tia Kitty, Auntie Kitty." She smiled.

O'Reilly smiled in return. Tia Kitty.

"I *needed* them, Fingal. They were the family I never had . . ." She looked him in the eye. "Might have had, but—"

"I'm sorry, Kitty," he said, and he was.

"When the orphanage closed in 1940 I felt I had to leave Tenerife. I knew that part of him wanted to marry me, but his family was not encouraging . . . To be honest, though, neither of us could picture the future together. I knew firsthand those same troubles in Ireland. The World War was raging, he knew he'd have to return to Madrid and try to pick up his life there. And I knew I had to return to Ireland. Those three years had been like a dream away from the reality of the war. We wrote to each other for three more years. By that time I was learning to be a neurosurgical nurse at the Royal Victoria. I was getting on with my life. And yet . . ."

"It must have been very hard for you, Kitty," O'Reilly said. "When Deirdre was killed it cut me for years, but at least I knew where I stood."

She hung her head. "I didn't. I couldn't seem to let go. I couldn't. Life seemed very bleak in Ireland, away from the sun and the warmth. Away from Consuela—she was six going on seven—away from him." Her eyes misted and O'Reilly took her in a huge hug.

"It's all right," he said. "I understand." And he was trying to, feeling her pain at her loss through his own when Deirdre had died.

"I finally did let go. I wrote him one last letter, concentrated on my work, my painting, my life and the memories faded; and then years later you came back into my life, you wonderful man." She kissed him, then said, "Everything seemed so perfect." Her lip was trembling and it seemed she couldn't go on.

O'Reilly waited then and said at last, "And then he wrote to you and you got the letter today? What does he want?" Keep a grip, O'Reilly, he thought. Give her all the help she needs. Even if this man has resurfaced, Kitty and I together can deal with it. Must deal with it.

She shook her head. "It wasn't from Mañuel. He—he died, six weeks ago. His other lung just gave up." She swallowed, her voice quavered, and a tear fell. "That was what was in the letter that I'd read just before you came home this afternoon. He was a dear, kind man and had meant a great deal to me, and now to find out he was dead and gone."

"I'm sorry." He knew that while he would not wish death on anyone, at that very moment he was feeling relieved.

Kitty's words came out in a torrent. "Consuela—she's thirty-three now—was going through her father's papers and found my letters to her father, and to her." Kitty pursed her lips. "She remembered me, her Tia Kitty." She took a deep breath. "She said her father still spoke of me up until he died . . ."

Arthur reappeared and in that way of some dogs must have sensed her unhappiness, and sat at her feet licking her hand.

O'Reilly too, wanted to comfort Kitty, but a young couple were walking by not far away, hand in hand, light of step. He lifted her chin so he could look into her eyes and said, "Kitty, Kitty. It's terrible when you lose someone you've loved. I do know. It's even more terrible when they die far away and you don't know for weeks then the news comes like a bombshell out of the blue."

She nodded against his hand.

"I understand why you have kept this to yourself all these years. It wouldn't have served any purpose telling me. I'd have done the same in your shoes."

"Truth?"

"Truth." He certainly hadn't told her or anyone else about a naval officer's wife called Elly in Alexandria, nor would he ever. He said, "I'm glad you've explained. Bless you. Now, have you told me everything?"

She said, "Not quite."

It hit O'Reilly as lightning strikes a tall tree. My God, did she have his child? Is this Consuela . . . No, no, didn't Kitty say that the child was already two years old when they met?

"Consuela wants to see me, and I'm not quite sure what to do."

O'Reilly sat for a time in silence, trying to work out what the implications of a meeting might be. "Neither," he finally said, "am I."

32

The Voice of a Great Thunder

Fingal climbed up inside *Warspite*'s bridge structure. Tom Laverty had kept the promise he'd made in the Cecil Hotel. Today, Tuesday, June 11, their ship and an important part of the fleet were steaming through the Grand Pass, the swept, mine-free channel outside the harbour, as they left Alex. Part of the sortie's purpose was to test-fire her great guns, and Fingal, thanks to Tom, was going to be able to watch from a special vantage point, see for himself what a fifteen-inch-gun battleship could do when engaged.

He'd experienced the rifles' pounding at Narvik, but only by their God-awful roaring and the ship's shuddering. It was still hard to believe that the recoil from those enormous blasts had done enough damage to *Warspite* herself that she'd needed repairs in Alexandria. It hadn't been until the 24th of May that the Alexandria Dockyard staff had declared her "In all respects fit for sea."

He walked along a corridor on number two "platform"—the name for the decks in the bridge superstructure. Tom's cabin was five levels up from the main deck where Fingal berthed and ordinarily worked, six levels up from the medical distribution centre, which was Fingal's action station and from which he could see nothing except the human wreckage of any battle.

Fingal knocked on Tom's door, heard his distracted "Come in," opened it and stepped over the sill. "Morning, Tom."

Tom looked up from where he sat at a desk, writing. He grinned and said, "Morning, Fingal. Just starting a letter to Carol, but I don't think I'll get much chance to post it for a while."

"Why not?" Letters, Fingal thought, the serviceman's lifeline to home. Deirdre's missives, full of a cheerfulness he knew like his own to be forced, and love, which, like his own, was deep and true, were a comfort—but he remembered their last night in Belfast. Longed to hold her. Make love to her. Tom was probably feeling the same.

"This trip might just get to be exciting," Tom said. "After we've scared the living bejizzis out of any passing seagulls and dolphins by firing our big guns and satisfying ourselves they are A1 at Lloyds, we're going to cruise off northwest Crete. See if we can tempt Benito Mussolini's Regia Marina to come out and play. ABC wants to try to get an early dig at the Eyeties."

"Scuttlebutt has it we've scored one already. Have you heard?" Fingal said.

"I have," Tom said. "One of our destroyers, *Decoy,* attacked a sub last night and there was a two-mile oil slick this morning. The admiral's pretty quick off the mark."

Fingal said, "He certainly is. Il Duce only declared war on France and Great Britain yesterday."

Tom nodded his agreement. "I liked Richard Wilcoxson's *craic* in the wardroom anteroom before dinner last night," Tom said. "'I see old chubby chops is rushing his heroic people to the desperately needed succour of Germany,'" Richard said, "'since it *is* currently the winning side.'"

Fingal laughed.

"Cunningham's right to try to get in the first punch," Tom said. "We were briefed late last night. We'll be carrying out a provocative sweep northwest of Crete. He hopes the Italians will be tempted to come out from their base at Taranto. They have two older battleships, *Conte di Cavour* and *Giulio Cesare,* ready for immediate action and we need to try to lower the odds. Before long, Mussolini will have much more up-to-date ships at sea."

"After Dunkirk it wouldn't hurt to give the folks at home something to cheer them up by way of a victory," Fingal said, shaking his head. "The debacle in France was a bit personal for me . . ."

"What's up?"

He heard the concern in Tom's voice. "I never told you much about my medical student days, but it's probably the same in the navy. You make your best friends when you're young and share the same crises, like exams, losing patients."

Tom nodded. "I still keep in touch with three lads I met when we were midshipmen together."

"I was at Trinity with a chap called Bob Beresford. He was—is—a sound man. Very sound. Useless clinician, but a first-class research worker. He and I grew close. He volunteered, joined the Royal Army Medical Corps, and was posted to a light tank unit. They were in France. I still don't know if he's alive or dead or a POW. I keep hoping I'll get a letter from him. I know it's far too early to expect to hear, but I worry about him."

Tom cocked his head and looked at Fingal. "More than three hundred thousand men were evacuated. They'll still be trying to sort that shambles out. Your pal could be anywhere in England."

Fingal looked up and smiled at his friend, who squeezed Fingal's shoulder and said, "I'm sure Bob—that's his name?"

Fingal nodded.

"I'm sure Bob will be all right."

"Thanks, Tom," Fingal said, knowing full well that Tom had no reason for his confidence but grateful for his friend's words of comfort. "I'm sure I'll hear soon. Now, should we be heading up so we can watch?"

Tom grabbed his cap. "Come on then. Three more platforms up for us. We're going to the open upper bridge and compass platform, practically the highest vantage point aboard." Tom handed Fingal some cotton wool. "I'll tell you when to plug your ears before the fun starts." He headed for the door. "Let's go."

Fingal dutifully followed, but two decks up on the admiral's bridge both he and Tom had to come to attention and salute. The Commander in Chief Mediterranean Fleet, Vice Admiral A. B. Cunningham, C.B., D.S.O., and bar, was heading toward his charthouse, which was sited at the most for'ard part of this deck.

The admiral, a well-set man with silver hair showing under his cap, a round face, large ears, piercing eyes, and a square chin just beginning to double, returned the salute. "Laverty. Brought a friend to see the fun?" He had a soft Scots burr. "And do stand easy."

"Yes, sir," Tom said. "May I present Surgeon Lieutenant O'Reilly?"

"An Irishman, I believe?" His eyes twinkled.

"Ulsterman, sir," Fingal said.

"It was all one country when I was born there in Rathmines in Dublin."

"I used to live in Ballsbridge not too far from Rathmines. My father taught at Trinity and I know your father did too, sir," Fingal said.

"He did, and I hear, because Hippocrates told me, that you are a navy boxing champion, young man, and an Irish rugby international. *Warspite* fields a seven-a-side rugby team during quiet spells in Alex."

"It's a faster game, sir, with only half the number of players per side than I'm used to," Fingal said, amazed that this man, who must have the woes of the world to contend with, could spend time with and be so knowledgeable about a junior officer. "Perhaps I'll give it a try."

"Think about it," the admiral said, "now, if you'll excuse me?" His smile was self-deprecatory. "For better or for worse, I've got a fleet to run. Enjoy the show."

Fingal and Tom came to attention and saluted as the senior officer let himself into his chartroom.

As they headed off, Fingal said, "Kipling would have liked our boss. He certainly can 'walk with kings—nor lose the common touch.'"

"And I have the feeling he can probably 'meet with Triumph and Disaster and treat those two impostors just the same,'" said Tom with a laugh. Clearly Tom Laverty had learned the famous Kipling poem— that paean to Victorian stoicism—in school as well.

"I suspect he'd much prefer triumph," Fingal said.

Tom laughed. "He's very much regarded and tipped for even more senior command. Might even make admiral of the fleet one day, get a peerage."

"And I reckon he'd deserve it," Fingal said as he followed Tom to the upper bridge and compass platform.

Warspite was steaming at twenty knots and the wind of her passage made Fingal's cheeks glow. Behind him, the fifteen-inch control tower reared up the height of two more decks. The crew in there would be using optical instruments to calculate range, speed, course, and bearing of any targets and then passing the information to the transmitting station deep in the ship's bowels where calculating machines would work out the coordinates and pass the aiming details to the big guns. Astern of the tower, flags were being run up the signal halliards of the fore signal yard. On this deck there were two searchlight sights and two target-bearing sights, all manned. Projections from the main part of the deck, platforms with guard rails, jutted out to port and starboard. Each bore twin, single-barreled Oërlikons mounted on one pedestal, manned by a gunner, and pointing up.

The man wore a white asbestos antiflash balaclava, a steel helmet, and long gauntlets. Another helmeted rating armed with high-powered binoculars scanned the blue, cloud-spotted skies for enemy aircraft, ripe crops it was to be hoped, for the antiaircraft gunners' grim reaping. Fingal moved to the port platform astern of the gunner and looked to where the smoke from *Warspite*'s boilers roiled down from the single funnel trunking inside which he knew were four exhaust stacks. The smoke lay in greasy black coils where the white-capped sea was churned to a foaming wake by the ship's propellors. The stink of burnt fuel filled his nostrils.

"That's HMS *Eagle*, half a mile astern," Tom said.

Fingal looked at the seemingly lopsided ship, her bridge structure and funnel offset to the starboard side of a flat flight deck. There, four Swordfish, their spinning propellors flashing in the sun, were at readiness.

"And that's HMS *Malaya*, another of our sisters astern of *Eagle*," Tom said.

All around *Warspite*, a phalanx of cruisers and destroyers kept perfect station, ships in serious light-grey business suits striding purposefully across the sea, intent on showing the world that Britannia still ruled the waves.

"Thanks for fixing this up for me, Tom," Fingal shouted, his ears filling with the wind's keening in the halliards above, the roaring of the turbines below. "It's not just because I think it's going to be fun seeing the guns fired. I think . . . I think it's important for their MO to understand what the crew are experiencing in battle."

"It'll not be quite the same," Tom said. "No one's firing back."

Fingal laughed. "That's the only reason I can even be here. With the fleet not in the presence of any enemy, I can stay on deck unless the call comes to close up for action stations."

"I think," said Tom, "you may be in for a bit of a surprise. Those things really do make a hell of a racket."

"That's all right," Fingal said, and grinned. "I suspect all little boys and a great many grown-up men love things that go 'bang.'"

"They'll be doing that soon enough," Tom said. "Now look." He pointed for'ard at what on a clock face would be ten o'clock. "The target's being towed by a destroyer about five miles off our port bow. See her?"

Fingal nodded.

"The other ships will leave a clear corridor between us and the target. Look, there they go now."

Fingal saw a cruiser and three destroyers turning away, showing their sterns as they took up their new positions.

"Any minute now," Tom said. "We'll only be able to see our shell splashes and we won't be firing live rounds." He glanced down.

Fingal followed his friend's gaze. In unison, the gunhouses of A and B turrets began swinging smoothly, ponderously, to port before steadying on the bearing Tom had indicated. All four gun barrels moved from the horizontal until they were angled up, but not all to the same degree. Their rising and falling, until each had found its assigned elevation, reminded Fingal of the gentle rise and fall of kelp in a rolling sea. A quick glance astern confirmed that X and Y turrets had conformed.

"Ranging shots will be fired in salvoes," Tom explained. "That's one gun of a pair at a time. They'll try to straddle the target by putting one shell over and one shell on this side of it. That gives the directors the information they need to calculate the exact settings to lay the guns accurately on the target. Get out your cotton wool and bung your ears."

Fingal did as he was told.

Even with his ears blocked he was aware of a clanging of bells. Tom had told him that bells were the signal to—Holy Mother of God—

Fingal's world had become an insane maelstrom of light, noise, and stinking smoke. The firing of number-one gun was immediately followed by the number-two gun of A turret. From each barrel, a tongue of orange flame leapt from the muzzles for yards over the sea as four hundred pounds of the explosive cordite was transformed in a millisecond to a ball of superheated gas. Even as the flame persisted before dying, mahogany-coloured smoke poured from each gun, smoke in such quantities that Fingal had not believed could exist, so dense that some of it tumbled to the sea below. Nor had he been prepared for the intensity of the stink as part of the cloud was blown back to where he and Tom stood. Simultaneously he was engulfed by a chest-crushing roar that his body felt as much as heard. It was hard to breathe. And over the thunder came an audible hiss of the departing one-ton shells, which could be hurled to a maximum range of eighteen miles. For sheer spectacle, the sound and fury were as dramatically gripping as anything Fingal had ever witnessed and he wanted to cheer aloud before a more sobering thought struck. When fired in battle, the guns' sole purpose was to wreak death and destruction.

He stared along the line the shells must take to the target. He had been told that an observer standing behind the guns could follow the flight of the massive projectiles as they arced up into the blue sky at a velocity of 2,450 feet per second on their way to their target. He watched them fly and shuddered, thinking about what such engines of destruction would do to flesh and blood in a real fight.

Between the ship and the horizon he saw two towering white splashes near the target as the shells landed.

He clapped his hands over his ears. The barrels, which had slid back onto their recoil mechanisms with a force of four hundred tons, were now returned to firing position. *Warspite*'s sixteen-man gun crews could maintain a rate of fire of two shots per minute from each barrel. But before A turret could fire again, the earlier shattering sequence was repeated exactly when B turret thundered.

How, he wondered, sneaking a look, how did they do it? How did the aircraft spotters and Oërlikon gunners who stood near him, how the hell did they tolerate the din and stink and total assault on the senses every time the ship went into action? All four men seemed to be quite unaware and were concentrating on their duties.

Fingal felt a tugging on his coat sleeve, and in the few moments before X turret spoke, managed half to hear, half to lip-read his friend saying, "Had enough?"

Fingal nodded and together they started to make their way below, neither bothering to speak as the gunnery exercise continued. His body was shaken physically by the sights, sounds, and sensations he'd experienced. He'd seen for himself the only reason that twelve hundred men and all the intricacies of the great ship *Warspite* existed. Everything was in place solely to bring those eight massive engines of destruction, the fifteen-inch rifles, to work against ships and shore installations of an enemy—and an enemy's personnel.

Half of him was proud of his ship, made more secure in the knowledge that his country had such weapons and would one day soon be bringing them to bear on the foe, each blast of the mighty rifles one tiny step closer to victory and the end of this lunacy called war.

But another part of him realized that watching what before he'd only heard and felt had brought back many of the feelings he'd had after Narvik. He had tried to stifle them then. Put them to the very back of his mind.

Now those memories came back of the destroyed German ships, the smell of burnt flesh, the mutilated men. He had vivid mental images of Doctor Fingal O'Reilly, supposedly inured by his training to the pain of others and the sights of injuries, turning his face away, choking back tears, and trying to be strong enough to comfort a sailor who had been a professional soccer player before the war. With only one leg there'd be no more goals for Aston Villa in that young lad's future.

"Impressive, aren't they? The guns," Tom asked when they reached number two platform, where Tom had his cabin.

Fingal nodded, but said nothing.

"You all right?" Tom asked.

Fingal nodded. "Pretty much. I've seen what I wanted to. It's rocked me a bit."

"You mean the physical concussion?"

Fingal shook his head. "No. I was thinking . . . about what our guns did at Narvik. I operated on a young German. I found out his name—Wilhelm Kaufmann. He was from Hamburg."

Tom looked puzzled, but said nothing.

"He did very well for six days." Fingal took a deep breath. "I suppose I should have kept a professional distance." He looked Tom in the eye. "Then he had a relapse and the last thing he said on the seventh postoperative day was '*Mutti*'—Mummy." We buried him at sea that night." Fingal lowered his gaze and said in a low voice, "I should have heeded old Rudyard's advice." He looked up at Tom. "'If all men count with you, but none too much.' Wilhelm was an only son."

"I couldn't do your job, Fingal," Tom said. "And it's easier for me. I don't have to look at our handiwork like you do." He stood close. "If it's any comfort, we didn't start the war, but we have to defend ourselves, and no matter what the cost we must, we must win."

"Thanks, Tom," Fingal said, and managed a small grin. "They don't actually train us in medical school to be dispassionate, but it is subtly encouraged; patients are referred to by their initials, not names; the senior staff all have an air of clinical detachment. With all you see in those years it just happens. Most students have built their own armour plating, just like *Warspite*'s, by the time they've qualified, but I've always found it hard not to get upset. It's such—it's such a bloody awful waste." He squared his shoulders. "Right. I'll be off. Thanks for showing it to me and just . . . thanks."

"I'll see you before dinner," Tom said. "I'm going to finish my letter to Carol, see how the bump's coming on." Since it had been confirmed that Tom's "trying to have a baby" was so far successful, he and his wife referred to the unborn as "the bump."

"Good idea. I'm going to write to Deirdre," Fingal said, and wished, how he wished she were here so he could tell her—tell her what? That he was confused? That his job was to make people better, not to patch up the wreckage that his ship's guns and the enemy's guns were going to cause? That war was an obscenity, but that he must set that aside and do his duty—because he must? "I'll see you in the ante-room later," Fingal said, "and thanks again for letting me watch."

He walked along the same corridor, lips pursed, fists clenched. But, he asked himself, am I the same Fingal O'Reilly who passed along here earlier today excited at the prospect of watching the big guns in action? He shook his head. He simply did not know. But in the months to come he was sure the Italians would put to sea, and in the grappling of the fleets he was going to find out.

33

Requireth Further Comfort or Counsel

The village seemed deserted as the night drew in and the rooks, cawing and flapping overhead, tumbled down the sky and into their rookery in the old elms of the Ballybucklebo Hills.

O'Reilly had not held Kitty's hand nor felt much like talking, and as Kitty had remained silent he'd guessed neither had she. "Consuela wants to meet me and I'm not quite sure what to do," she had said on the beach. The question still hung in the air between them like smoke on a still day.

Now, with Arthur put to bed in his kennel and the back door closed behind them, the normalcy of the everyday was reasserting itself. "Go on up and have your whiskey," said Kitty. "I really don't want a drink tonight. I'll get dinner started. One of Kinky's steak and kidney pies. It'll take about twenty-five minutes to heat and do the spuds and veggies. One of your favourites, love."

"Terrific," he said, trying to sound enthusiastic about the grub. He was relieved to be given the opportunity to think things out alone and suspected Kitty knew that. "I'll be down in twenty-five minutes then."

At the sideboard in the upstairs lounge he poured and then walked, glass in hand, to stand in the bay window. In the gloaming, the steeple stood limned against the darker waters of the lough and the mellow softness of the distant Antrim Hills on its far shore. The three running lights on a freighter heading for the Irish Sea glimmered two white, one green, tiny jewels—diamonds and an emerald—set on the jet silhouette of the ship. It bore them to a rendezvous with the earliest diamante evening stars. Venus, goddess of love and beauty, brighter than all the rest, had risen over the ship's stern.

Venus might be rising, but O'Reilly's heart sank. Damn it all, he told himself, you're a grown man. You had no claim, none whatsoever, on Kitty O'Hallorhan after you parted in '36. That's crystal clear, so why the hell, thirty years later, are you— He realised how tightly he was clasping the Waterford glass and relaxed his grip. Why is it eating at you and why shouldn't this Consuela woman come to Ireland? He sipped his drink. Or, come to think of it, perhaps they could go to her. The Spanish government had since the '50s been developing a stretch of rugged Mediterranean coastline, the Costa Brava, as a cheap tourist destination. Cromie and his wife had gone on a package tour to Lloret de Mar last year and raved about it when they came home. Should he and Kitty meet the woman somewhere like that? Somehow Tenerife, which must have bittersweet memories for Kitty, did not appeal.

Or should they perhaps simply ignore this Consuela? There was a thought. He narrowed his eyes, and sipped. *There* indeed was a thought. She would have no way of knowing if her letter had been delivered. Why not let the past slip away? Pretend it never happened. He made a harrumphing noise in his throat and shook his head. He'd never in his life refused a head-on challenge.

He became dimly aware of the aromas of steak and kidney wafting upstairs. O'Reilly sighed. Even that failed to move him. He sat in an armchair, welcomed Lady Macbeth onto his lap, stroked the little cat's head, sipped his whiskey, and tried not to get irritated with himself for his indecision. He couldn't even be bothered to read a book.

"Did you enjoy that, Fingal?" Kitty asked.

"Very much," he said, and forced a smile, "but no thanks. I couldn't manage a second helping." He saw her frown and could guess she was thinking, That's not like Fingal O'Reilly. Conversation during the meal had been desultory, about as personal as a discussion about the weather between a couple of English strangers on a train.

"Is it bothering you so much, pet?" she said, coming to what they both knew was the crux of the matter. "I'm not apologising for what happened."

"Nor should you."

"I'm just sad that someone who meant a great deal to me at one time has died."

"'. . . any man's death diminishes me'?"

"That's part of it, but he wasn't just any man either. I think you understand that."

O'Reilly nodded. "I do, and I know I'm being unreasonable." He looked straight at her, nodded his head, and said slowly, "It's just going to take a bit of getting used to. You telling me all this came as something of a shock."

She pursed her lips then said, "I'm sorry. Perhaps I should have kept it to myself."

"I don't think so," he said, staring at the tablecloth. "You and I have always told each other the truth. I'm being irrational, I know. I just need a bit more time." He looked up at her. "I love you, Kitty, and I've no reason to be jealous—but damn it all, I am." It helped to say out loud what he'd been trying to avoid recognising. "And I simply don't want to help you to decide what to do about this Consuela woman. Not yet." Despite his earlier resolve, he was leaning toward suggesting that they simply pretend the letter had never been delivered. Forget all about it. "I don't know if it might not be better to let sleeping dogs lie."

"I understand. I'm not sure myself." She smiled at him. "What I am sure is that I love you, Fingal. I know this is ultimately my decision to make, but I don't want to make it on my own. If we do see her, I want us to do it together," she said, and stood. "We'll not talk about it anymore tonight. Give me a hand to clear off and then let's go and watch *Softly, Softly*."

"Right," said O'Reilly, standing. The weekly Saturday night police drama, which the BBC had been broadcasting since January 1966 as live performances, might be just what he needed to get his mind off the conundrum that wasn't going to go away. It might be seen in a clearer light after his brain, having been consciously focussed on something else for a while, and after a night's sleep, might find a way to cast a clearer light on the question.

It had been a broken, sleepless night, and by breakfast time O'Reilly was no closer to knowing what to do. His eyes felt gritty. They'd both feigned cheerfulness at breakfast, avoiding the subject altogether, and now with Jenny on call and Kitty paying back a favour to Sister Jane Hoey with an extra shift at the Royal, O'Reilly had decided to go and see his brother in Portaferry. A quick phone call had confirmed that Lars would be home.

A little after ten O'Reilly put Arthur into the back of the Rover—there'd be time to give him a decent run—and drove up and over the Ballybucklebo Hills, then on toward Newtownards. He was going to drive through Greyabbey, but had an idea and so stopped on the Main Street outside a pebbledashed house next door to the RUC barracks. A man with a neatly clipped grey goatee eventually answered the door.

"Och, Doctor O'Reilly. Sorry to keep you waiting. I was in the studio out back. Great to see you. Come on, on in." He stepped aside.

"Thanks, Bob," O'Reilly said, moving into a small, neatly furnished front parlour. "How's your work going?"

"Have a pew." The man settled himself in a worn wingback chair and started rubbing at a splash of azure-blue paint on his thumb. "Work is going well, thank you. I'm getting a lot more commissions every week, and I'm selling in the gallery next door."

"That's good to hear. I'm happy for you, Bob." When O'Reilly had first met Bob Milliken a couple of years ago on the foreshore of Strangford, both men had been shooting a dawn flight. Later that day, the house painter had brought O'Reilly home and shown him some beautifully rendered watercolours of Strangford and the waterfowl that lived there. Bob had said he was considering painting watercolours full time and O'Reilly, who had been charmed by the man's work, had encouraged him. "So you don't regret taking the chance?"

Bob shook his head. "Best thing I ever did. I'm making a good living as an artist and I'm doing something I love."

"I'm delighted." O'Reilly had worried for several months that his encouragement might have been misplaced.

"Cup of tea?"

O'Reilly shook his head. "I'm on my way to Portaferry to have lunch with my brother and I have to give Arthur his walk at the stream at Lisbane before that. So I should be getting on, but I wondered if you still had that wee picture of the snipe?" O'Reilly and Kitty's most recent outing to Gransha Point had included a stop to see Bob. She'd much admired the piece.

"I do. I'll go and get it."

Bob returned in minutes. "Here." He handed O'Reilly a four-by-eight-inch frame holding a picture of a single cock snipe diving through the air, wings fully spread, long narrow beak pointing ahead, all against a powder blue sky punctuated by the stems of three tufted reeds.

"Lovely," O'Reilly said, remembering how her grey eyes had sparkled when she'd first seen it. "How much?"

Bob smiled. "For you, Doctor? Ten pound ten."

O'Reilly rose, shook Bob's hand, and said, "Done. Will you take a cheque?"

"Aye, certainly."

It took moments to write. "Forgive me for running, Bob."

"Never worry." They took the few steps to the front door together. "Feel free to drop in anytime, and say hello to Mister Lars for me."

"I will. See you soon," O'Reilly said as the painter ushered him out and he headed for the car, the little painting tucked under his arm.

A happily walked Arthur, who had started two snipe from the banks of the stream at Lisbane, was fast asleep in the seat-well of the Rover when O'Reilly parked outside his brother's house. The day wasn't too warm, but O'Reilly rolled down the window, let the big dog snooze on, and clambered out of the car only to be struck, as always, by the sight of Strangford Lough laid out before him.

"Finn."

O'Reilly spun on his heels and turned to face his brother.

"Good to see you, Finn. Come in." Lars led the way to the house and held open the door.

"And you, big brother." O'Reilly stepped into the familiar hall. He noticed a bowl of orchids on a table. Lars and his exotic plants.

"We'll go on into the lounge," Lars said.

O'Reilly turned left into the spacious room with its views across the narrows at the mouth of the lough to Strangford Town on the other side and the great bay of the Castleward Estate east of the town. As always he paused to admire a skyscape in oil of a boiling in the heavens, a gargantuan storm that Ma, God rest her, had painted in '36 as their father had been dying of leukaemia. "Ma was a very good artist, Lars," O'Reilly said, and for an instant remembered Kitty admiring the same scene when he'd taken her to Lansdowne Road for dinner on his graduation night. Ma had glowed when Kitty, no mean painter herself, had admired the work.

"She was that, Finn." Lars indicated an armchair. "Have a pew. Tea? Coffee?"

O'Reilly sat and shook his head. "You're sure you've time for lunch at the Portaferry Hotel?"

"I do. I've made a reservation."

O'Reilly nodded. "Good. Then, no, nothing now."

Lars sat. "How are you, Finn? You've something on your mind, you told me. Or were you out on a call last night too? You look like you didn't get too much sleep."

"I didn't. But not because of a patient," O'Reilly said.

"And you said it's something about Kitty? She's not ill, is she?"

"Nothing like that. It's—it's difficult to explain."

Lars leant forward, folded his right arm across his chest, and cupped his chin with his left hand. "Fire away."

"You remember in the '30s. Kitty and I were an item, then we weren't, then we patched things up for a while until my work got in the way again and then—" O'Reilly stopped, not sure how to continue.

"And she went to Tenerife. I do remember. I thought when you met Deirdre you were quite over Kitty. I certainly didn't expect the pair of you to get wed so late in life, but I'm delighted for you."

O'Reilly detected a faint tinge of sadness in his bachelor brother's voice. "Me too, but . . ." O'Reilly stood, walked to the window, and stared out at the little car ferry heading out from the Strangford shore on its way to Portaferry, battling the strong currents of an ebb tide at its peak. "Och, Lars, there's no point ploughing the same furrow twice. Deirdre's gone. I'm married to Kitty now, I love her dearly"—he'd tell no one else save Lars and her his deepest feelings—"but last evening she told me something that's got me all at sixes and sevens." He paused.

A stronger-than-usual wave hit the little ferry and for moments she was shoved completely off course.

"Go on, Finn," Lars said in a soft voice that had O'Reilly imagining his solicitor brother comforting a recent widow as they discussed the probate of her late husband's will. "Come and sit down."

O'Reilly did, still watching the little vessel from the corner of his eye.

"I know it's difficult for you, Finn. Usually it's the other way round, you sorting out problems for your patients, but I am your brother."

O'Reilly nodded. He took a deep breath. "When I came home last night, I found her in tears. She'd got a letter from Spain. She told me that when she'd been nursing in Tenerife she'd had an affair with a Spaniard." O'Reilly couldn't bring himself to name the man. "He died six weeks ago. Learning of it must have brought back a flood of memories for her. And for me . . . I've always had far too vivid an imagination . . ." It took no effort to see himself in Narvik in 1940, four decks down on *Warspite*, hatches battened down, and under German fire. His mind had run rampant picturing the compartment flooding, thinking he could even smell the oily water. Right up to today he could recall how, when the action was over and Richard Wilcoxson had let his medical staff go on deck for a breath of fresh air, Fingal had felt waves of the blessed relief from his own claustrophobia brought on entirely by letting himself picture too clearly what might go wrong.

"When she told me some general details I should have accepted them simply as cold fact, her confession as if to a priest, me in this case, her need to get it off her chest. I'm well used to handling unpleasant facts without embellishing them on behalf of my patients, but when it came to myself? My bloody mind went beserk. I had all kinds of scenes in my head." He half snorted a laugh. "Scenes in glorious, bloody Technicolor, moving pictures of them walking in the moonlight in a fishing village called Los Abrigos, drinking wine, laughing together, him calling her '*mi corazon*,' kissing her. Lars, don't ask me to tell you exactly how I pictured them making love . . . Just don't." He inhaled.

"I can guess," Lars said. "Not pleasant for you. Not pleasant at all."

"And here's the thing." O'Reilly scratched one ear. "I've no right to be jealous, but . . ." He looked into Lars's dark eyes. "Damn it all, I am. Very jealous."

Lars nodded. "I think," he said, "that's perfectly natural. I'm sure I'd have felt exactly the same had I been in your shoes, Finn."

"Honestly?"

"Mmmm," Lars said, looking down to the floor. "You know, Finn, I still think about the judge's daughter in Dublin. Jean Neely. I can still remember how it felt when she turned down my proposal of marriage on a Christmas Eve. Married some other bloke."

O'Reilly frowned. "I could tell you were hurting back then. I tried to help. I'm sorry if I wasn't much use."

"I was. Hurting sore, but you tried, Finn. You tried your damnedest. That's what brothers are for. That's why I'm trying to understand and help you today."

"And you are. Just by listening you are. Letting me spill it all out." Then a small smile started. "You know," he said, "it is a comfort, Lars." O'Reilly noticed that the ferry was much closer to the Portaferry side now and seemed to be coming back on course. "Thank you." He pursed his lips. "There is one other thing."

"Go on."

"It was the man's daughter who wrote to Kitty. She's a woman in her thirties now. Her name is Consuela." He paused.

Lars frowned. "I hesitate to ask, but are you worried that—"

"Kitty might be the mother?"

Lars inclined his head.

"No. Kitty went there in late '36, started seeing the fellah a year later. At that time his little girl was two going on three."

"That's all right then." Lars smiled. "I think, brother," he said, "once you've confronted the green-eyed monster for a while longer, you'll see you've nothing to worry about."

"Except this Consuela wants to meet Kitty." He hesitated. "I'm convinced the woman's not Kitty's child, she would have told me, but I'm not sure what upsets seeing Consuela might cause for Kitty . . . and for me. I'm not sure I want to know." There, it was out.

Lars pursed his lips, nodded, folded both arms. "I'll bet you know as much about the law as I do about medicine."

"Me? The law?" O'Reilly smiled. "Probably a damn sight less."

"We have a thing called 'disclosure.' It insists that the parties to a dispute—in my kinds of cases that usually involves wills, property, or the occasional divorce—"

O'Reilly frowned. He wasn't sure what Lars was driving at.

"All it means is that, for example, in a divorce suit both parties must honestly put before the court all their assets. Hold nothing back so there are no nasty surprises."

O'Reilly rose again. "And you think it would be better to meet this woman, and find out, than spend forever speculating?"

"Not for me to say." Lars shook his head and said, "That's got to be your decision, Finn, yours and Kitty's, but haven't you always told me the thing patients have the most difficulty dealing with is uncertainty? That they'd prefer to know their diagnosis even if the outlook's grim rather than be left in limbo?"

"Yes." O'Reilly smiled. "Yes, of course. Why the hell couldn't I work that out for myself? I'm not a stupid man."

"No, you're not," said Lars, "But jealousy is—" He stopped. "Jealousy is difficult. I remember reading one of Lawrence Durrell's books about ten years ago. I can't remember which one . . ."

"One of the books in his Alexandria Quartet perhaps? I was bloody well based there." And bloody nearly went off the rails there too, he thought, when I was engaged to Deirdre. If there are any guilty parties, I'm the closest to filling that bill.

"I think it was one of them. Anyway, it was pretty avant garde stuff, not my cup of tea, really. But something stuck with me, something one of the characters said: 'It's not love that's blind, it's jealousy.' It made sense to me. Jealousy makes us blind. It's made you blind and I've just tried to help you to take off the blinkers, that's all. The least I can do for my little brother."

O'Reilly rocked gently on his heels, wondering how his bachelor brother, a village solicitor who spent his days expediting wills and conveyances, had gotten so damned wise. Finally he said, "By God, Lars, you've said a mouthful. And by God, you're right. Thank you."

"Och," said Lars, rising, "I'm sure you'd've worked it out for yourself in time." He glanced at his watch. "Shall we take a quick walk along the shore to give us an appetite, then have our lunch?"

"I'll bring Arthur," O'Reilly said. "He's in the car." The mention of the shore made O'Reilly glance out of the window. The ferry had made safe harbour and was discharging its cars. He turned back to his brother. "Thank you, Lars. Thank you. I'll tell Kitty what you've helped me to see when she gets home tonight and if she agrees then we'll just have to decide whether we want a guest or whether we'd like a holiday on the Costa Brava or somewhere else in Spain."

"And now you have to decide to get a move on. I don't want to be late for our luncheon reservation. Mrs. Maguire takes a very dim view of tardiness," Lars said with a laugh.

As O'Reilly caught up with his brother, he squeezed the man's upper arm. "Thanks for listening, advising," O'Reilly said. "It's good to be here, Lars. And a pint, roast beef, Yorkshire puddings, carrots and roast potatoes will certainly hit the spot." For the first time in almost a day, O'Reilly felt hungry. He passed Ma's turbulent skyscape and was struck by how different it looked. With that ray of sunshine coming in through the window, the painting didn't look so forebodingly ominous as it had when he'd arrived.

34

Tread in the Bus on My Toes

O'Reilly looked up from where he sat at his rolltop desk in the surgery. The sounds of hoovering had stopped and Kinky was greeting someone at the front door of Number One. He was dealing with yet another idiotic request from the ministry for more paperwork. Ever since the introduction of the National Health Service, these benighted forms had seemed to breed like rabbits—and at least he could take his shotgun to those. He peered over the half-moon spectacles perched on the bridge of his nose. "Come in."

"Doctor O'Reilly, sir, I do have Willie Dunleavy and Alan Hewitt here and I think it would be a good idea if yourself would take a look at Willie, so."

"Bring him in, please." Barry was doing home visits this afternoon, and once O'Reilly had finished filling out these damned forms, he and Kitty, who had a half day and was upstairs, were meant to be heading to Bangor to talk to the town's travel agent about package tours to Barcelona. Kitty wanted to visit the Picasso Museum and the Joan Miró Foundation there. But when Kinky thought a patient needed to be seen at once—they needed to be seen at once.

Kinky pushed the door wide to reveal Alan Hewitt supporting Willie Dunleavy as the man hopped in on his left foot.

"Hang on." O'Reilly stood and moved the T-bar under the

examining couch so its top end was tilted at forty-five degrees to the horizontal. "I'll help you put Willie on the couch, Alan," he said.

Between them they gently manoeuvred Willie, who promptly yelled, "Go easy, you clumsy buggers." His head lolled back against the top of the couch. "Ah, God, be careful. Jasus, Alan, but you're a ham-fisted bastard."

For a second O'Reilly was tempted to order Willie to mind his manners. He never had managed to tolerate rude patients. He usually found a way to follow the motto of his old boss: never let a patient get the upper hand. But until he knew what ailed the normally jovial publican, he would say nothing except, "Would you like Alan to leave us alone?"

"Not at all. I don't mind if you stay, Alan."

Alan Hewitt nodded.

"Right," said O'Reilly. "So what seems to be the trouble?" He took Willie's wrist to check his pulse and noted that the skin was hot and clammy, the heartbeat rapid.

"I was doing a wee job in the cellar of the Duck, and Mary come down. Says she til me, she says, 'Alan, could you come up and see what's wrong with my daddy? He's howling his head off and he's madder than a wet hen, and he's just bit the head off a customer.' Right enough when I got upstairs I didn't know what had got in til you, Willie. You gave me a right ould tousling too."

"You'd be just as cross if you'd a stoon in your big toe like the one I got a couple of hours after one of them buck eejits from Guinness ran a delivery trolley over my foot."

Pain coming on some time after trauma rather than immediately, extreme emotional irritability, fever. Already things were starting to add up. "Have you had the pain before?" O'Reilly asked.

Willie shook his head. "If I had, Doctor, you'd've been the first til know. It's ferocious, so it is."

"And do you feel anything else wrong?" O'Reilly said.

Willie shook his head. "The feckin' pain's enough, so it is." He was visibly sweating.

"Mary had til stay," Alan said, "and look after the customers. I thought I'd better bring him here. It's no distance."

"Maybe not for you. I had til hirple like a man on a bloody pogo stick." Willie took a deep breath and moaned.

O'Reilly waited until the moaning stopped, then said, "Could I take a gander?"

"You go dead easy taking off my shoe and sock," Willie said.

"I will," said O'Reilly, "but first I want you to take off your jacket and roll up your sleeves."

"What? Are you daft? It's my feckin' toe, you eejit. Can you not tell my toe from my elbow?"

"I think the usual expression to describe an eejit is someone who can't tell his arse from his elbow," said O'Reilly mildly, and Alan Hewitt let out a sharp laugh.

"Bloody lovely," said Willie, scowling at his friend. "You'd laugh at a man in pain. Right bloody Job's comforter you are, Alan Hewitt."

"Sorry, Willie, I—"

"Give me a hand, will you, Alan?"

"Aye, certainly, Doctor."

Between them they managed to take off Willie's Donegal tweed sports jacket and roll up his shirt sleeves. "Sit you down on one of the chairs, Alan," O'Reilly said, then began to examine Willie's forearms, soon finding what he was looking for, a shiny, painless lump the size of a broad bean over the point of the left elbow, and two similar lesions on the tendons of Willie's right forearm. A quick examination of his ears, nose, and eyelids did not find any similar lumps, the term for which was a tophus. But they were not always present in those other sites. Ignoring Willie's grumbling, O'Reilly said, "I'm going to take a look at your toes now, Willie."

"About bloody well time," Willie said, and as O'Reilly began to unlace the man's left shoe said, "For God's sake it's my other big toe. The other one."

"I know," said O'Reilly, setting the shoe aside and peeling off the sock, "but doctors always examine both sides to make a comparison."

There was nothing out of the ordinary to be found. "Now," he said, "I'll be as gentle as I can," and unlaced the right brogue. He opened the shoe as widely as possible. "Give me a hand, Alan." O'Reilly showed Alan how to hold the leg up, then slowly started to take off the shoe. Willie whimpered, but in short order off had come shoe and sock. "Hang on," O'Reilly said, pulled a pillow from under the couch, set it under Willie's heel and said, "Put his foot on that, please, Alan."

The joint between big toe and foot, the first metatarso-phalangeal joint, was swollen, red, shiny, hot to touch, and no doubt would be exquisitely tender if O'Reilly squeezed or moved it. "I can tell you what I think's wrong, Willie."

"Thank God for that," Willie said. "What is it?"

"I'm almost certain it's gout."

"Away off and feel your head. Gout? That's what lords of the manor like the marquis get drinking port every night and eating all them rich foods like lobster and pheasant under glass. Not ordinary folks like me."

"Not only do ordinary folks get it, one of the things it does is make the victim extremely irritable, and you know, Willie, you've hardly been the spirit of sweetness and light since you got here."

Willie hung his head. "I'm sorry, Doc, but it stings like blue buggery."

"I do know, so never worry about being grumpy," said O'Reilly, "and you give Willie a fool's pardon too, Alan. He can't help being bad-tempered just at the moment. His toe'll feel like a red-hot poker."

"Aye," said Willie, "it does, and in July too, when there's no one ordering mulled wine, so there's not."

Every publican knew that wine was mulled by plunging a red-hot poker into a flagon of spiced wine, and O'Reilly realised that Willie was trying to make a joke. "That's the spirit, Willie. Now I've one more wee thing to do, so just bear with me, and you go away and sit down again, Alan."

O'Reilly went to the instrument cabinet, took out a wrapped, pre-sterilized hypodermic syringe, put it with a bowl of Savlon and some swabs on a trolley, and scrubbed his hands. He pushed the trolley over to Willie. "Be a good lad, Alan," O'Reilly said. "Push the screen over and give us a bit of privacy."

Alan did.

"Right," said O'Reilly. "This will only sting for a sec."

Willie didn't even flinch as O'Reilly took a sample from the tophus on the left elbow.

"I'll be back in a tick," he said, and trotted over to an ancient brass-barrelled microscope. He made a glass slide from a smear of the material in the syringe, put the slide on the stage, peered through the eyepiece, fiddled with the focussing wheel, and with a moment's feeling of satisfaction found what he was looking for. The needle-shaped crystals of sodium biurate seen in samples from gouty tophi were clearly visible.

He went back to Willie. "That confirms it, Willie. You do have gout."

"I'll be damned. You saw it on that there microscope?" said Willie.

"I did."

"And am I going to have to sit in a Bath chair with tons of bandages round my hoof like one of them Colonel Blimps in the cartoons?"

"Only for a wee while," said O'Reilly. "And you'll not be in a wheelchair. You'll be in bed for about a week." He sat at his desk, pushed the hated administrative forms aside, grabbed a prescription pad, and began to scribble. "I'm going to give you colchicine tablets, point five milligrams, and you're to take one every two hours for a maximum of sixteen doses or until you start to get the runs."

"I don't fancy a bout of the skitters, Doctor O'Reilly," Willie said, "but I suppose just about anything'll be better than this here pain."

"I've one more thing up my sleeve," O'Reilly said. "If you do start to have diarrhoea before the pain goes away, I can give you one of the steroids, prednisolone, and . . ." He added more inky spider marks to the prescription. "I've given you a wheen of lint and bandages and some *lotio opii et plumbii,* which is opium-and-lead ointment for putting on the joint." He handed the script and a government form to Willie. "You're going to be off work for a week so I've given you a sick line too, so you can get your benefits."

Willie managed a weak smile. "Right enough, I've been paying my premiums long enough. It's time I got a bit back, so it is."

"When we get you home, Willie, I'll nip round til the chemist's and fill your scrip," Alan said.

"Good man-ma-da," O'Reilly said, "and, Willie, I'll arrange for you to be seen by the dieticians at the Royal."

"Why?"

"Because there are some foods—and drinks—you should avoid. They'll explain that to you."

"Like what?" said Willie suspiciously.

"I'm no dietician, but I think you're probably going to have to cut back on red meats and offal."

"Willie Dunleavy without his liver and onions and steak and kidney pie? No sweetbreads? No tripe? That'll be something to see. You think he's bad-tempered now—" Alan said.

"Houl your wheest, Hewitt," Willie said.

"I'm afraid it gets worse," O'Reilly said. "No beer either."

Willie's face took on the demeanor of a disappointed bloodhound. "Och Jasus, Doc," he said. "It's like thon ould joke when the doctor cuts your man off all the good grub and drink and cigarettes. 'And will I live forever if I do?' says your man. 'No,' says the doc. 'It'll only feel like forever.'" At least he was now trying to force a smile.

"Sorry about that, Willie, but we have to get rid of the pain for you," O'Reilly said. "And I want you to drink five pints of water every day to flush out stuff called urea through your kidneys."

"Water?" said Willie. "And me a publican? What'll my customers think?"

"What they already think, Willie Dunleavy," Alan said. "That you're a sound man and they'll be sorry for your troubles."

O'Reilly nodded. "For the long term, Willie, you'll have to take sodium salicylate three times a day. It's made from wintergreen and is a relative of aspirin, but we'll not get you on that until the pain's over." He smiled. "It'll be no difficulty for me to drop in and see you at home. See how you're getting on."

"And when you do, sir, the pints're on me."

"Fair play," said O'Reilly. "I'm sorry I don't have a wheelchair to get you home."

"Never worry," said Alan, "I'll go and get Lenny Brown. He's in having a jar—the Yard's shut for the Twelfth Fortnight. He offered to help bring Willie over here but I thought mebbe he'd be going straight til hospital so I told him not to bother. But he'll be happy to lend us a hand on the way back."

"I'd not mind having a word with Lenny either," said O'Reilly as a thought struck. "You and Lenny mates, Alan?"

"Aye. We are indeed. We go til the grues together."

O'Reilly had never understood why Ulstermen referred to racing greyhounds as "grues" or "grue dogs." He nodded and said, "And have you told him about how well Helen's doing?"

Alan flushed. "I have that," he said. "All it took was for her til get an education and now look at her."

"Mmm," said O'Reilly. "Mmm. Off you trot, and Willie will be ready to go when the pair of you get back." And if O'Reilly and Connie Brown couldn't persuade Lenny that Colin should sit the Eleven Plus, another word from Alan Hewitt might. It was certainly worth a try.

As Alan left, O'Reilly turned to Willie and said, "Come on then. I'll give you a hand to get dressed."

Willie blew out his cheeks. He bent forward. "I can put on my left sock and shoe if you'd just hand them til me, sir."

As O'Reilly passed them he heard the phone ringing. Kinky would answer it. "I'm sorry," he said to Willie, "that medical science can't cure gout completely, but with a bit of luck we'll be able to keep you pretty much pain-free, and when Alan's at the chemist's get him to pick up some Panadol as well. You'll not need a scrip, but it'll make you a bit more comfy until the colchicine starts to work."

"I appreciate that, sir—" was as far as Willie got.

Kinky rushed in. Her face was flushed. "That's Miss Hagerty, the midwife, on the phone, sir. Says it's urgent."

"Right," said O'Reilly, running to the phone in the hall.

"O'Reilly here. Yes, Miss Hagerty. I see . . . Yes, all right, I understand. You can hardly be in two places at once. I'll see to it. Goodbye." He hung up and roared upstairs, "Kitty, come on down here. I've to go out to the district to do a delivery and I could use a trained midwife's help."

He barely heard her agreement as he dashed into the surgery and grabbed the midwifery bags. "Sorry, Willie. Got to go." He ran into the hall to meet Kitty coming downstairs. "Doreen Duggan's having contractions every three minutes and Miss Hagerty is tied up with another delivery. Are you ready to bring a wee one in the world with me, Mrs. O'Reilly?"

Kitty smiled, took one of the midwifery bags from him, and headed for the door. "I can't think of a better way to spend my Thursday half day, Fingal O'Reilly, so get a move on."

35

The Rockets' Red Glare,
the Bombs Bursting in Air

Sailed late this evening, Sunday, July 7, 1940, for Malta to escort two convoys from there back to Alex. Warspite in company with two slower battleships, Malaya and Royal Sovereign, as well as HMS Eagle and her seventeen torpedo bombers, five light cruisers, and seventeen destroyers.

Fingal blotted the ink and, still holding his war diary, pushed his chair back from the table in his cabin. How, he wondered, would this present sortie differ from their earlier, relatively uneventful one when he'd seen the great guns being fired? There'd been no serious action since *Warspite* had come to Alex, but things were very different now.

Italy had declared war on June 10. The British could now expect hostile attention from some fifty Italian U-boats said to be at sea, Italy's naval surface vessels, including two modernised battleships, and Alex was in range of airfields in Italian Libya and their Regia Aeronautica bombers.

Matters had moved apace since the gunnery practice cruise a month ago, but—he smiled to himself—only on the war front. He'd assiduously avoided the Sporting Club since that evening with Elly Simpkins. He could smile at it—now—but it had been a near-run thing. Now he could enjoy the erotic frisson without the need to feel guilt. Well, not much guilt. And somewhere out there among the destroyers of the screen was HMS *Touareg,* Chris Simpkins's ship. Not for the first time Fingal wondered how long the Simpkinses' apparently "open marriage" could last.

He flipped back a few entries in his diary. There had been more dramatic developments, few of them good, in Europe and all over the Med.

> *June 12.* Cruiser Calypso *sunk west of Crete.* June 15. *Malta maintaining antisubmarine patrols with destroyers and Sunderland flying boats.*

The ungainly-looking four-propeller planes were made, he knew, by Shorts Brothers, whose headquarters was in Belfast. He sighed, felt the familiar leap in his heart at the thought of home and Dierdre, and continued reading.

> *Malta is under constant air attack. Fourteen obsolete biplanes, Sea Gloster Gladiators, are the only available air defence. Being sent up in flights of three.*

He lit his pipe.

> *Night of* June 20th, 21st. *Combined Anglo-French fleet successfully bombards Italian fortress at Bardia in Italian Libya.* June 24. *Terrible news. France signed an armistice with Germany two days ago. The war in Continental Europe is over. Britain and the Empire are all that now oppose Hitler and Mussolini. Crew paradoxically seem to be relieved because we are on our own without any hindrance, as they perceive it, from foreign allies. Can't say I feel the same.*

He let go a puff of smoke. The thought of Europe completely in the hands of the Nazis was sobering. For many reasons, not the least of which was his own personal—and selfish—concern. Would this mean I'll not be able to get home to Haslar and to Deirdre? He glanced at her framed photo beside his cot. I miss you, girl. Richard Wilcoxson hadn't been sure about Fingal's chances of going and the best he'd been able to do was suggest that Fingal try to be patient. It wasn't easy. Not one bit when his gentle, laughing girl with the soft deep eyes and warm lips was three thousand miles away and having to be patient too.

He read on.

June 28. Three enemy subs reported sunk. Boost to morale. About time.

A new page.

July 1. Much going and coming by our Admiral Cunningham and his staff and the French Admiral Godfroy in charge of the Alex-based French ships. July 4. All the negotiations have culminated in an agreement for peaceful decommissioning of the French vessels. We were lucky. Tom Laverty says it could have been ugly. We might have been forced to open fire in the harbour here on our recent allies the way HMS Hood *and her accompanying ships had to bombard the French fleet in Mers-el-Kebir (Oran), Algeria, on July 3 to stop their warships falling into German hands.*

He closed the book and put it back in a drawer, trying to block out what must have been a horrific scene, but as usual his vivid imagination kicked in and he shuddered. He put his pipe down and lay on his bed fully clothed, staring at the ceiling. He had the morning watch, from four A.M. to eight, and knew he should grab a quick zizz before heading to the sick bay. He closed his eyes and tried to relax. Who knew what the day might bring?

⊡

"Morning, Fingal. Paddy." Richard Wilcoxson, precisely on time as always, stuck his head into the space in the sick bay that served as the office.

"Och," Paddy O'Rourke said in his best stage Irish, "top of the morning to ye, sir."

"And," said Richard, "I believe the correct response to a bogtrotter like you would be, 'And the rest of the day to yourself,' CPO O'Rourke."

Paddy chuckled and said, "Saving your presence, your honour, but you're the only man on the ship I'd let call me that."

"Morning, Richard," Fingal said, laughing at his colleagues' good-natured teasing. "Not much to report. The watch has been pretty quiet and the sick bay's empty. No customers." Which wasn't surprising. Standard in-harbour routine in Alex was to transfer any serious cases to the base hospital. Only two days ago Fingal had had to arrange the admission of a chief petty officer with a suspected ruptured amoebic liver abscess. It had taken quite a struggle to persuade the senior sister at Queen Alexandria's Royal Navy Nursing Service to disturb a senior medical officer taking his ease in the mess. Fingal smiled. That was one personal battle he'd enjoyed winning, particularly as the patient was now doing well.

"Not much doing on deck either," Richard said. "With a bit of luck we may have—"

The Tannoy's tinny tones squawked: "We have just had a sighting report from one of our submarines, HMS *Phoenix*. Two enemy battleships and four destroyers two hundred miles east of Malta are steering south, possibly covering a convoy to Libya. They will be shadowed by

Sunderland flying boats out of Malta. Our fleet will steer northwestward at twenty knots and try to intercept. That is all." Click.

The three men looked at each other in silence until finally Richard said, "So, you're *not* going to get the rest of the day to yourselves, gentlemen. There is just a possibility that things might get interesting a little later and we could be very busy. So you two nip off and get a bite." He stuck his head round the curtain and yelled, "You there, Ronnie?"

A Cockney voice answered, "Aye, aye, sir."

"Barker's just come on watch. He and I will keep an eye on things here. Take sick parade in the dispensary as usual. No need to go to our action stations yet so off you trot."

Paddy headed for'ard to the CPO's mess and Fingal aft to the wardroom.

He was almost there when the air-raid warning gongs clanged, followed by the bugle call to action stations. He knew he should hurry back to his post in the ship's bowels, but was within feet of the doorway to the open upper deck. He could feel the compelling pull of curiosity mixed with apprehension tugging at his insides. They'd not miss him below for ten minutes. He let himself out, dogged the watertight door shut, then stood beside the gunhouse of X turret. It was a glorious Mediterranean summer day. Except where it was being churned by the wakes of the great ships in the central column and their escorts steaming on all sides, the sea was that enamel-blue, barely rippled by a light breeze that was less than the wind of their twenty-knot passage.

Overhead a few high wispy clouds drifted, and near the sea the smoke from the funnels of the fleet made dirty dark smudges. Land had dropped astern and the air was so clear that when Fingal looked to the horizon he had no difficulty seeing the curvature of the earth.

It was a nearly perfect day for cruising, but sadly a truly perfect day for enemy aerial observation. There were no rain squalls or fog banks for the fleet to hide in.

The smell of fuel, the roaring of the ship's turbines, and the thundering of her propellors assailed his senses. Holy Mother of God. Involuntarily he ducked as he spotted, coming in from ahead, a series of regularly spaced dark dots. Around them the air was becoming pockmarked with black puffs that materialized from nowhere, drifted, and were dispersed by the slipstreams of the oncoming aircraft. Now he could hear the continuous drum rolls of the antiaircraft fire from the escorting vessels, the thrum of aero-engines.

One of the dots, closer now so he could recognise it as a twin-engined monoplane, staggered, dropped a wing, and recovered for a moment. Fingal barely recognised that he was holding his breath. A fiery tail was dragged from one engine, and the nose of the Italian plane dipped, steeply, more steeply, then the whole machine began to spin and gather speed. He could hear the crescendo of the scream of its dive until one wing was ripped away and the rest hit the sea in a welter of high-thrown spray. The wreck and even the ripples of the splash had soon vanished into an unmarked watery sarcophagus. Fingal exhaled. He'd not seen any parachutes. Poor young bastards. He took no consolation from recognising that their end would have been quick.

Now the enemy bombers were nearly overhead and *Warspite* began her own defence. He could see the aftermost Oërlikon gunner, his weapon's barrel pointing nearly vertically, blazing away in an almost continuous stream of fire that flashed from the muzzle. From all over the ship came the single barks of her four-inch, high-angle weapons, the continuous pom-pom-pom-pom from her eight-barrelled two-pounder "Chicago pianos," and the chattering of other singly and doubly mounted Oërlikons. Clapping his hands over his ears barely lessened the row, and nothing could prevent his nose from being filled with the acrid stench of burnt cordite.

The explosives and lethal metal shards would cut through flesh and bone, arteries and nerves as mindlessly as they would chew into the thin metal skins of the bombers. And all the rounds that were being poured in torrents from *Warspite* were also being hurled in an equal or lesser degree by every ship in the fleet as soon as enemy aircraft came within range. The sky was darkened by the smoke of exploding shells.

He continued to watch the oncoming flight of the enemy squadrons, now reduced by two more aircraft that had hurtled down leaving smoke trails in the sky. Another, he guessed, must have suffered a direct hit to its bomb bay because it flared like a bright sun and then simply vanished. Those unlucky bombers had been insects swatted down by the behemoths below, enraged by the pests' attempts to sting. Yet not another plane had deviated from its alotted bomb run. How did the aircrew find the courage to press on when every atom of self-preservation must be screaming, "Get the hell out of here!" Their cockpits must reek of the smell of fear, but still the planes came on.

He glanced at the lone, unflinching Oërlikon gunner aft. And was that man's courage any more or any less, standing there nakedly unprotected from machine gun strafing and bursting bombs?

What men did for "duty's sake" amazed Fingal, humbled him, and never on this great ship had he ever heard from any officer or man sentimental drivel about "For love of King and Country." He could hear the voice of his father, the late professor of Classics and English Literature, quoting Wilfred Owen's *"Dulce et decorum est pro patria mori,"* "How sweet and right it is to die for one's country." The hell it was, although Professor Connan O'Reilly could perhaps be forgiven for being sentimental about warfare. He'd tried to volunteer in 1915, but had been judged to be too old. He'd never seen firsthand the carnage in the trenches, and for what? So the heroes' sons could fight a second round with Germany and her allies? Madness, insanity, and Fingal imagined the Italian airmen, stolid and practical, stifling their fears and getting on with their jobs. It was, as far as Fingal O'Reilly was concerned, bravery of the highest degree. He admired both sides, just as he would treat the wounded without concern for nationality.

He saw a neatly spaced line of bombs exploding in the sea close to a cruiser. The water, filthy from the stain of the explosives, rose in towering columns high, high, above the bridge of the targeted vessel before crashing back into the tumbled ocean and over the decks of the ship under attack.

Warspite shuddered stem to stern from the recoil of her own weapons and the underwater shock waves spreading out from the exploding bombs. She heeled to port. Her captain must have ordered a defensive change of course.

He felt someone tugging at his sleeve. He turned and saw AB Henson. No, there was a killick badge sewn on his sleeve. Leading Seaman Henson must have achieved his much-desired promotion. He was having to yell over the racket. "Begging your pardon, sir," he proffered a steel helmet, "but Mister Wallace, my officer, sent me. He said, and I'm quoting him, sir, honest, 'Tell that silly bugger of an MO to get under cover. Make him understand that falling shrapnel from our own guns can kill. And if—' his words, sir, not mine, honest, 'the daft sod won't, at least get him to wear a tin hat.'" He offered the helmet once again.

There was an explosion louder than the rest and Fingal turned and stared at the cruiser abeam and to port. He thought it might be HMS *Gloucester*. There was a row of near-miss bomb splashes tumbling back off her far side, but her bridge was a flaming shambles. One bomb at least had hit and he doubted very much if steel helmets would have been much protection for the poor sods on duty there. Farther away a destroyer had hauled out of line and smoke was pouring from her foredeck.

He took a deep breath. He had been thoughtless, even reckless, in satisfying his curiosity instead of reporting to his station, and if a bomb hit *Warspite* all the medical staff would be very busy.

"Thank you, Henson, I appreciate Mister Wallace's concern, but I won't need it. I'm going below now," Fingal said. "I've seen enough."

36

Dear Nurse of Arts . . . and Noble Births

"Thank God you're here and thanks for coming, Doctor O'Reilly." Dougie Duggan, the sleeves of his collarless shirt rolled up, held open the door of his terrace house in the council estate. "Doreen's upstairs. Her sister Mabel's with her, so she is, and wee Daphne, our daughter, is at her granny's."

Fingal carried his two maternity bags into a narrow hall with a staircase at one side. Kitty followed.

A quavering moan, which rose in intensity before fading, drifted from above, and the smells of fried bacon and boiled cabbage wafted through the half-open door to the kitchen at the end of the hall.

"You know Mrs. O'Reilly," O'Reilly said. "She's a trained midwife."

Dougie Duggan nodded. "I'm very glad you've come, missus." He rolled down his sleeves. "It's no place for a man when his wife's having a wean, but I reckoned I should wait til someone got here, seeing Miss Hagarty's tied up with another delivery."

Kitty smiled. "I'd have thought it wouldn't be a bad idea if a husband was nearby to give a bit of support."

Dougie Duggan tipped his head to one side. "No harm til you, Missus O'Reilly—"

The inevitable Ulster preamble, O'Reilly thought, to a flat-out contradiction.

"No harm, and mebbe things is different in Dublin where you come from, but up here—"

This time the moan was louder. More intense.

Dougie Duggan stared up at the ceiling, shook his head, and grabbed a sports jacket from a peg on the wall. "Up here, men get off-side when women is in labour. Always have done. It's only natural. Having wee ones is women's work." He took a pace through the open door. "Mabel'll know where til get me when it's all over, so she will. Away you on upstairs, Doctor and Missus O'Reilly." And with that—he fled.

"Things are not different in Dublin where I come from." Kitty shook her head. "Natural, he calls it."

"Come on," O'Reilly said, and started to climb the stairs. "Dougie's right, of course. Whether it's natural or not, it is the tradition. Women do the labouring—and they don't call it that because it's easy—and the men, well, the men disappear—"

"Down the boozer with their pals," Kitty said. "I know. The Duck may be in for a busy afternoon."

O'Reilly stopped on the landing. "Mary Dunleavy may be. Her dad's going to be in bed for a week. I'll tell you about it later. Right now," he pushed open a bedroom door, "we've a job to do."

He bent and set both bags on a carpeted floor and immediately was aware of the smell of amniotic fluid. The membranes must have burst already. Miss Hagerty had told him that Doreen Duggan's last labour had lasted only seven hours and the contractions of this one were now coming three minutes apart.

The bedroom was big enough for a double bed, two chairs, and a dressing table. Chintz curtains were pulled back, and bright sunlight spilled into the room. "Hello there, Doreen, Mabel. Wee one's on its way?" O'Reilly said.

"It is, Doctor." Mabel, a beefy brunette woman in her late twenties, was sitting on the side of the bed holding Doreen's hand. "Poor wee Doreen's getting ferocious pains, so she is. I'm very glad youse could come. I'd've done my best if I had til," she lowered her voice and whispered, "but see that there Dougie? See him? About as much use as teats on a bull."

O'Reilly hid a grin, but he heard Kitty chuckle. "I'd better get to work and take a quick look. If you'd excuse me?" He wasted no time introducing Kitty. She'd take care of that herself.

As soon as Mabel had moved away from the bed, O'Reilly took her place. "The baby's only two weeks early, Doreen, and the pregnancy has gone very smoothly. Miss Hagarty would be handling your delivery as usual if she wasn't already at another confinement. So there's no need to worry," he said. "And it sounds like you're moving along so I need to get a look at your tummy." He turned back the bedclothes and hoisted her flannel nightie.

"Go right ahead," she said, "and I'm dead glad you're here, sir." She managed a weak smile that crinkled the corners of her blue eyes.

Before he could do more than lay one hand on the great swollen belly with its silver *striae gravidarum,* stretch marks, Doreen grabbed his free hand and started to squeeze. Again she moaned through clenched teeth. Under his examining hand he felt the uterus, which in labour is simply a huge, muscular piston, contract until at the peak of the labour pain it was as hard as an anvil. His left hand felt as if she was crushing it to a pulp.

He glanced at his watch so when the next contraction came he could assess the duration of this one and the interval between the two. And this wasn't an early labour contraction either. The birth would be soon, he was sure. As he waited for the wave of muscular spasm to pass, he heard Kitty saying, "I'm Kitty O'Reilly. I'm a nurse and a midwife. I'm here to help Doctor O'Reilly." He smiled. Exactly. The fact that they were man and wife was irrelevant at that moment; that they were trained professionals was important.

Kitty said, "We need your help too, Mabel."

"Aye, certainly. What'll I do?"

"Can you bring up a good wheen of old newspapers?"

"Aye. I can. There's a brave clatter under the stairs."

"Then off you trot."

"Do you not want any hot water, Mrs. O'Reilly? Everytime a woman has a baby on the telly, like in that there *Doctor Kildare* or in the fillums, the doctor always tells someone to boil lots of water, so he does."

Kitty laughed. "I never know what for unless they all drank gallons of tea."

"Oh, I see, that's all right then," said Mabel. "I'll go and get the papers."

O'Reilly glanced at Kitty. Without any bidding, she was starting to open the maternity bags and prepare the instruments.

Doreen stopped moaning and both the pressure under O'Reilly's right hand and Doreen's iron grip of his left eased.

"Good lass," said O'Reilly. "When did the pains start?"

Doreen used the back of her right forearm to push back locks of auburn hair that had fallen over her sweaty forehead. "About three hours ago, Doctor, and my waters broke about fifteen minutes back." His nose had not been wrong.

"All right." And her last labour hadn't been very long. He told himself to get a move on. It took a very few minutes to complete an abdominal examination and report to Kitty with a running explanation for Doreen, "One baby, right dorso-anterior, that's with its back to the front and to your right, Doreen, and that's as it should be, a vertex presentation right occipito-anterior. The baby's head is coming first with the back of its head to the front and to the right. The head is nearly engaged, and that tells me the widest part of the baby's head is where it should be on its way into your pelvis. You're cracking along."

"Doctor O'Reilly?" Kitty handed him an aluminium Pinard foetal stethoscope with its circular flat earpiece and its wide trumpet of a mouth.

He took it and with his back turned to Doreen he winked at Kitty and was rewarded with a lovely smile. "Just going to check the babby's heart rate, Doreen." He put the wide mouth on the abdominal wall, leant with his ear to the earpiece, listened, and counted. "It's going like a liltie at a hundred and forty-four beats a minute, regular as clockwork. Perfectly normal." He grinned at Doreen and she smiled back in return, but it vanished as she gritted her teeth. "You went to antenatal classes," O'Reilly said, "and they taught you how to breathe, just like your last delivery. So pant, Doreen, when a pain comes. We don't want you pushing yet. Pant. Big breaths. Biiiiiig breaths."

The puffing, panting mother-to-be got through another contraction.

"I think this might help, Doctor," Kitty said, playing the part of the midwife to perfection. She handed him a face mask attached to a small cylinder by a valve and piece of polythene tubing. The initials "BOC" for British Oxygen Company and the word ENTONOX were printed on the cylinder.

"Great idea," O'Reilly said. "Thank you." He took the equipment and for a moment had a mental image of himself learning to give anaesthetics in 1940 at the Haslar Naval Hospital near Plymouth. "This is a fifty-fifty mixture of laughing gas and oxygen, Doreen," he said, laying the cylinder on the bed beside her and handing her the mask. "The second you feel a contraction starting, clap the mask over your nose and mouth—" He showed her how. "—and take deep breaths. It'll cut the pain, but it won't knock you out and it won't hurt your baby. Nurse O'Reilly will help you while I go and wash my hands."

As he was leaving, Mabel returned with an armful of old newspapers. "We're going to spread these on the mattress under you," Kitty was saying, "and put a rubber sheet on top of them to protect your bedclothes. Can you roll onto your left, Doreen?" Supremely confident that the midwife training Kitty had received at the Rotunda Hospital in Dublin had not deserted her, O'Reilly headed along the landing looking for a bathroom where he could wash his hands.

Half an hour had passed since O'Reilly had put on rubber gloves and carried out a pelvic examination. He had determined that the neck of the uterus, the cervix, had become paper-thin and dilated to eight centimetres—only two more to go before the birth canal was free from obstruction. The leading part of the baby's head had descended well into the pelvis, and the landmarks on the tiny creature's head had allowed him to determine that although the head was lying with its widest part in line with the widest axis of its mother's bony pelvis, as it descended farther toward the outside world the head would rotate until it was lying, he smiled at his nautical usage, exactly fore and aft in relationship with the middle of the mother's pubic symphysis in front and her coccyx, her tailbone, astern.

During those thirty minutes Kitty had kept a regular watch on the mother's blood pressure and both her and the unborn's heart rates. All had remained normal, and judging by how little she now moaned, the Entonox had certainly helped reduce her ability to feel the contractions.

He was now jacketless with his shirt sleeves rolled up, wearing a floor-length red rubber apron, face mask, and rubber gloves. He stood on the right side of the bed. Kitty, also bare-armed, gloved, and masked, was on the left. Mabel had withdrawn with a promise that she would "put the kettle on anyroad, because even if nobody else wanted one, she was sure Doreen would like a wee cup of tea in her hand once the baby was born, like."

"Won't be long now," he said to a drowsy Doreen, who at that moment was gasping into her mask as a contraction hit. As he had been taught as a student all those years ago at the Rotunda, the toughest part of midwifery was the waiting, but the waiting was nearly over. At the peak of this contraction, a black circle appeared, about the size of one of those American silver dollars he'd seen during the war. "She's fully dilated," he told Kitty, "and the head's nearly crowned." It would be fully crowned when the widest diameter of the baby's head had entered the world.

"Time to get her pushing," Kitty said.

"Aye," said O'Reilly, "you've not forgotten your old trade."

"No, but I had almost forgotten how exciting it is to help bring a new wee one into the world," she said. "The last time we did this was more than a year ago now, before we were married." She puckered at him then asked, "Dorsal or left lateral?"

"Dorsal," O'Reilly said. "I think she'll be able to push better and be a bit more comfortable. In fact . . ." And why not? "You're on her left side. Why don't you deliver her and I'll help?"

"May I?"

"Don't see why not. You're fully trained and it's like riding a bicycle. You don't forget how. It all came back to me after the war." And not giving Kitty the chance to back out, O'Reilly said, "Doreen?"

"Uhhh?"

"I want you to lie on your back and draw your knees up. The baby's coming. You're going to have to push now."

Doreen nodded.

Kitty turned and leaned over Doreen's left thigh, facing the foot of the bed, while O'Reilly supported the labouring woman's shoulders.

Doreen started to make a growling noise in her throat. Another contraction was starting.

O'Reilly put one arm round her shoulders and helped her to bend so she was squatting more vertically. "Push, Doreen. Push."

The veins stood out on her forehead. She clenched her teeth and O'Reilly could feel the effort as Doreen contracted her belly muscles to add downward pressure to that being exerted by the uterus.

"Push."

"Head's crowned," Kitty said. "Starting to extend. No more pushing."

"Big breath, Doreen. Pant." O'Reilly knew that now the widest part of the baby was through the pelvic canal, the back of the head, the occiput, would pivot on the symphysis and it would be Kitty's job to guide and control it so that there was no tearing of the mother's tissues by the baby's face and chin. Her task would be easier if the forces bearing on the baby were lessened.

Doreen's breathing became more shallow. The uterine contraction had passed.

He looked to where Kitty was busying herself with a mucus-trap suction device, using her own mouth to suck on one end while at the other a narrow plastic tube cleared the baby's mouth and nose of mucus that would drop into a plastic bottle between the two tubes.

"I have to push again, I have to."

"All right, Kitty?"

"Go ahead. The shoulders will be here in no time." Kitty sounded as if she was out for a gentle ramble on a beach. No fuss. No bother.

To the manner born, O'Reilly thought. She'd come a long way from the student nurse who, back on a ward at Sir Patrick Dun's Hospital in the '30s, had collected up all the old men's false teeth and washed them in one basin—with predictable results when she'd tried to match each set of dentures with each set of toothless gums. Kitty really was a consummate professional now and he admired that greatly.

"All right, puuush." O'Reilly supported Doreen's shoulders and watched Kitty as she guided the newly emerged baby's head, then its shoulders and its trunk from the birth canal. He could see the umbilical cord—the spirally, twisted pair of arteries and one vein surrounded by protective jelly.

"It's a boy," Kitty said with satisfaction.

Doreen's reply was drowned by a powerful screech.

"And he's a boy with healthy lungs," O'Reilly said as Kitty gently laid the baby on the rubber sheet and clamped and cut the umbilical cord.

O'Reilly lowered Doreen onto her pillows. "Just be a tick," he said, and moved to the foot of the bed. "All right?"

"Fine," Kitty said. "No tears and I've just to wait for the afterbirth. You carry on."

"Right." He inclined his head. "There's ergometrine already drawn up in a syringe for when you're sure the placenta's out in one piece. I'll see to the wean." He had a towel ready and picked up the chissler, gently wiping away the greasy, whitish *vernix caseosa,* the waterproof material that still clung to the baby's skin. As he worked, he calculated the Apgar score, named for the American anaesthetist Virginia Apgar, who in 1952 invented a ready reckoner for assessing the health of newborns. Her own name was the mnemonic for the criteria by which the baby was graded. Appearance. Pulse. Grimace. Activity. Respiration. On a scale of nought to ten, O'Reilly gave young Duggan a nine. First rate. Then he quickly made sure that the baby boy had a full set of fingers and toes. Finally he fished in his trousers pocket and brought out a small bottle of silver nitrate. A few drops in each eye would protect the baby from gonorrhoeal eye infection contracted during passage along the birth canal, and subsequent blindness. While it was unlikely that this infant was at any real risk, it was always better to be safe than to be sorry.

He picked up the bundle. He had wrapped the newborn in his blanket so that a hood was formed around its head—babies could lose a lot of body heat through their heads. "Here you are, Mammy," he said as he presented her with her new son. "One healthy wee boy complete with all his bits and pieces."

She smiled and took the bundle. "Thank you," she whispered, peeping in under the hood and pointing with an outstretched finger. "Och," she said, "och, Doctor O'Reilly, he's beautiful. Thank you. And thank you, Mrs. O'Reilly." Two tears ran down Doreen Duggan's cheeks. As she smiled and spoke gentle nonsense words to the babe, a tiny hand reached out and clasped his mummy's finger.

And Fingal Flahertie O'Reilly, tough as nails, felt a lump in his throat but managed to keep his voice level as he said, "Och sure, and doesn't a baby bring his own welcome? Well done, Doreen." He swallowed, took a deep breath, and looked down to where Kitty had put the placenta in a dish and was finishing washing Doreen's nether regions. "And well done, Nurse Kitty O'Reilly." He grinned and blew her a kiss. "Do you know," he said, "if you didn't already have a job looking after me I'd offer you one."

O'Reilly looked hard at the woman he loved. He'd been absolutely right trusting in her professional skills to manage the delivery, just as, he shook his head, he'd been a bloody eejit mistrusting her about this business with the Spaniard before the war.

He laughed and said, "I'll tell you what I think, Kitty O'Reilly. As Donal might say, 'You done good,' and to celebrate let's not bother going to Bangor today. We'll go home and have a jar."

"I'd like that," she said, and smiled at him.

Kinky would be home with Archie, Barry was heading directly to Holywood to see Sue after his calls, and after a jar or two Fingal O'Reilly was going to show Kitty O'Reilly exactly how much he loved and trusted her.

37

Those in Peril on the Sea

Fingal clutched the rope harness that suspended him between *Warspite* and HMS *Touareg*. This is bloody well terrifying, he thought as he was transported between the two vessels in a bizarre contraption called a breeches buoy. Even his vivid imagination had not envisioned this when he had risen before dawn for the morning watch. He felt like a spider crossing its web and looked up at the thick rope running between the two ships. His seat, a circular life ring with attached canvas short trousers, hung from a block trundling along the hawser from *Warspite* to the destroyer. The line being used to haul him across the sea, tossing and churning between the two vessels, swung, swayed, and, oh Jesus, dipped then tautened again, but at least he was making progress. He could hear the tumbled waves displaced by the passage of the two vessels slapping against their hulls. As ever, the roar of *Warspite*'s propellors thundered on. It was a feat of seamanship keeping the two ships running at exactly the same speed and maintaining the same distance between them. Fingal offered up a silent prayer that both helmsmen were really on their toes. His imagination had no difficulty conjuring up pictures of what would happen if the ships hit broadside to broadside with him, the mustard in the sandwich, or swung away from each other, pulling apart the rope and dumping him into the water. Being swept into *Warspite*'s four huge propellors was an image never far from his mind. He stared at the destroyer's deck and willed the crew there hauling him in to hurry up. Hurry. Up.

Everything had happened so quickly he'd barely had time to anticipate the precariousness of his current position, but he was making up for it now.

When Fingal had reached his action station less than an hour ago, there had been no more sounds of the air raid, and the antiaircraft guns had fallen silent, so he'd assumed the surviving Italian bombers had gone home.

Richard Wilcoxson had risen from his chair in the for'ard medical distribution centre. "It's all right, Fingal," he said. "We know you stopped to watch the air raid—"

"I'm sorry—"

"No need to be. We've all done it. Curiosity's a natural human response. So is a fear of heights. I hope you're immune."

Fingal had frowned and said, "I'm sorry. I don't understand." He wondered why CPO Paddy O'Rourke and PO Fletcher were both looking at him as if he were a child about to be taken to the dentist instead of for an anticipated treat. "We're four decks down here."

"I'm afraid you're going to be up in the air soon." Richard clapped Fingal on the shoulder. "You can refuse if you like, but you're the best officer I have for the job."

"What job?" What the hell was going on?

"Did you see any of our ships hit?"

"A destroyer."

"That was *Vixen,* an old V-and-W-class destroyer. She has damage for'ard but her engine and steering's fine so ABC's sent her home to Alex."

"And I saw an explosion on *Gloucester*'s bridge."

"It killed her skipper and seventeen others. She and *Touareg* both took a couple of very near misses. Lots of bomb splinters. Both ships are still able to keep up with the fleet and fight, but *Touareg*'s got three dead and a number of casualties, one or two serious. Their MO was one of those killed. ABC's asked me to send over a replacement."

Realisation dawned. "And you want me to . . . ? Oh shite . . ." And he'd known he couldn't refuse, not if he ever wanted to look Richard or the SBAs in the eyes again.

"The breeches buoy is being rigged as we speak."

And here he was now dangling over the guard rails of the much smaller ship. Hands grabbed the contraption, dragged him inboard, and helped him to struggle free of the harness. Fingal, had he been on his own, would have dropped to his knees and kissed the iron deck.

"Welcome aboard, sir," a petty officer said. "Hope you'd a pleasant trip, now hang on a jiffy, please." He turned his back for a moment. "Right, you lot, breeches buoy crew, you know the drill. Get at it. Handsomely. You're in charge, Ronson. Don't drag that little battleship under if you can help it."

"Aye, aye," said the leading seaman called Ronson, and the assembled men laughed and bent to their tasks.

The PO turned back to Fingal. "Skipper says to take you straight to the sick bay, sir. No need to report on board to the officer of the deck. Better you get on with your job, sir. So if you'll follow me?"

Fingal fell in step with the man. The destroyer, tiny in comparison to the great grey behemoth steaming alongside, was certainly more lively. The deck pitched and rolled, which didn't seem to faze the CPO. But twice Fingal had to grab at a rail for support. On his way he saw the evidence of splinter damage on the starboard side, bright scores in the steel of the upper deck, jagged holes in a gun shield and, high up, dents and a gap where smoke was leaking from a rent in the foremost of her two funnels. One ship's boat was hanging drunkenly in twisted davits and had been smashed to matchwood. Damage-control parties were hard at work. One sailor, stripped to the waist, was swinging a sledgehammer against a lump of twisted metal and singing to himself to the tune of "The Girl I Left Behind Me."

> Oh, I don't give a fuck
> for the killick of the watch. *Clanggg*.
> or the chief of the working party. *Clanggg*.
> I'm watch ashore at half past four
> I'm Jack, me fucking hearty. *Clanggg*.

He grinned and said, "Roll on my Blighty leave," *Clanggg*.

If this man was anything to judge by, the morale here was as high as it always had been on *Warspite*, Fingal thought as he was led to the sick bay.

"The wounded are in here, sir. This is one of the SBAs, Leading Hand Johnston. He'll show you the ropes and if you'll excuse me, sir, I'll be off." The chief petty officer left.

"So, you're going to show me the ropes, are you, Johnston? Seems to me I've already been shown the damn things getting here," said Fingal with a smile.

The SBA, a man of about twenty-five, blonde, tall, and stringy, with "Mother" tattooed on his forearm, came to attention, stifled a laugh, and said in a thick Liverpool accent, "Yes, sir. Glad to have you aboard, sir."

"Surgeon Lieutenant O'Reilly. Stand easy, Johnston," Fingal said. "How big is the staff of the medical department?"

"The MO's . . . well, you know about that, sir. Bloody sad if you ask me. He was a good bloke. It's just me and my oppo now, sir, Leading SBA MacRae. He's in the captain's day cabin setting up. We use it for an operating theatre, and we're going to need it. You'll be happy to know Mac's a bloody good anaesthetist."

"I am relieved," Fingal said. Very relieved, he thought. He began to sweat, suddenly aware that the place was vibrating and noisy. The smell of disinfectant overpowered the smell of fuel oil. "God," he said, "but it's hot in here."

"Can't be helped, sir. We're over the gear room, and there are steam pipes all over the shop." The man lifted his cap and rubbed a forearm over his forehead. "Still," he said, "we've room for eleven cot patients and two bunks." He pointed into the room. Two sailors, Fingal assumed they were part of the ship's first-aid party, were moving between two rows of sitting and lying men, many sporting bandages and slings. One man, a first-aider bending over him, kept repeating, "Bloody hell I'm cut. Bloody hell I'm cut." He was probably suffering from shell shock too. Both bunks were occupied.

"And how many wounded need immediate attention?"

"We've two men in bunks. One's a pom-pom gunner who got a thump on the head. He's out like a light. Before he went on deck, Surgeon Lieutenant Fenwick reckoned the lad had got blood in his skull."

"What the hell was the MO doing on deck in the middle of an air raid?"

"First-aider found a bloke trapped under that smashed boat you probably saw. He was in awful pain—back injury, and too badly hurt to move without immobilizing him. Asked the MO to come and take a look. Give the lad morphine before they tried to shift him." He pursed his lips. "Poor old Fenny was like that. Never could say no to a sick or injured man. We'll miss him, sir."

O'Reilly nodded and hoped if a similar situation arose for him he'd have the guts to do what Surgeon Lieutenant Fenwick had.

"Another near miss did for the trapped man and our MO before they could get down here."

"I see." O'Reilly shook his head. Tragic, but his job now was not to mourn. It was to deal with the living. He'd think about his late young colleague when the wounded were seen to. "You said you'd two bunk cases?"

"Aye. T'other lad copped it in his arm. We've a tourniquet on it, but . . ." He shook his head.

Another amputation.

Almost the same as the first two cases that Fingal and Richard had worked on after Narvik, but here there'd be no Richard Wilcoxson to ask for advice. "And the rest?"

Johnston grinned. "Nine others. Bumps, bruises, couple of cuts'll need stitching. We can do that here, and as best as I can tell we'll be setting one wrist and one broken forearm. We have them in splints, but they'll need to be put to sleep too, so you can reduce the fractures, sir."

Fingal slipped off his cap and battle dress blouse jacket. "Is there anyone of the walking wounded I need to examine before we start operating?" He was well used to the diagnostic skills of the SBAs on the battleship and was equally willing to trust these men.

"Don't think so, sir."

"Right," said Fingal. "I'd better take a look at the head injury first." No time, he thought, for names. Fix them fast, then move on to the next. Not his kind of medicine at all.

One successful burr hole to release the blood in the gunner's head, one left mid-upper arm amputation, two reduced and plastered fractures, and four lacerations sutured and dressed later, Fingal was reexamining the recovering head injury. He'd found operating more of a challenge here than on *Warspite*. The little ship never seemed to be still, particularly when she heeled as she weaved, raced ahead, or altered course during three more air raids that, praise be, had stopped at sunset about four hours ago. The ending of the clamour of exploding bombs and the hammering of antiaircraft fire was a blessed relief.

The only sounds now were those of the ship's machinery, air fans, and the snores of some of the patients.

He became aware of both the SBAs coming to attention, looked up, and in the dim lights of the sick bay saw a man in shorts and white shirt with straight gold bars on his shoulder boards. A Lieutenant-Commander, Royal Navy, who must be the skipper.

A well-modulated voice said, "Please don't let me disturb you, Doctor, until you've finished."

Fingal took the man at his word and satisfied himself that his patient was breathing normally, his pulse and blood pressure were normal, his pupils were equal and reacted to light, and his reflexes were normal. Fingal stood. "Sir," he said and, remembering Richard Wilcoxson's words, didn't salute because neither he nor the captain were wearing their caps. "Surgeon Lieutenant Fingal O'Reilly, late of HMS *Warspite,* reporting on board."

"Glad to have you, O'Reilly. Welcome aboard." He grinned. "I watched your ride over here. If you enjoyed it, you must be the only man in the navy who would have. Thank you for coming. I'm the owner—"

Which by now Fingal knew was navalese for captain.

"—Bill Huston-Phelps." He offered a hand, which Fingal shook.

"I'm not ashamed to tell you that I did not enjoy it . . ." Fingal said.

The captain laughed.

"But I am pleased to report that of the injured, sir, we are confident that all the walking wounded should make full recoveries. The man with the head injury and the one whose arm I had to amputate should be put ashore at the base hospital once we return to Alex."

"I understand. Seems to me you've done an outstanding job."

"With the captain's permission, I couldn't have without the professional skills of both leading SBAs. I feel they should be recognised."

"Mmm," said the captain. He turned to the two. "Very well, Johnston, MacRae. Well done. Stand easy. I'll take Lieutenant O'Reilly's recommendation under advisement." He turned to Fingal. "Naturally, being the navy I'll need your report in writing—" He must have seen Fingal's eyes raised to the heavens. "I know," the captain said. "Sometimes I think our service runs on paper, not fuel oil. Put it down and I'll try for a 'Mentioned in Despatches' for them."

Fingal saw one grin at the other.

"Now," the captain said, "you all must be famished. I've arranged for a cook to see to you SBAs, one at a time in the galley, and, Doctor, if you feel you can leave your charges for a while?"

"I think so, sir. They'll be in good hands."

"My steward will rustle something up for you if you'll come with me."

"Certainly, sir." O'Reilly grabbed his battle dress blouse and cap and followed the captain.

"MacRae, if you need Lieutenant O'Reilly, he'll be in the wardroom or—" He turned to Fingal. "I'm sorry, but it's the best we can do, the late Surgeon Lieutenant Fenwick's cabin. You must get some sleep."

"Thank you, sir."

The captain stepped over the sill of the hatch and together they walked for'ard on the open deck between the burning stars above and the glow of the bioluminescence of the waters beneath.

"Pity about Peter Fenwick," the captain said. "He was a good man. A good MO." He stared ahead. "I hope we can get a replacement in Alex."

The captain wasn't being heartless. Already Fingal had learnt in war that as death was a constant the survivors tended to be very matter-of-fact about fallen friends, if only for mental self-preservation. He hadn't known Fenwick, and yet Fingal's heart ached. He almost missed the captain saying, "Lieutenant Simpkins was a good officer too."

"Who?" Fingal stopped in his tracks. "Chris Simpkins?"

"I'm afraid so."

"Good God."

"You knew him."

"No. No, I didn't," Fingal said. "But I've met his wife, Elly."

Huston-Phelps gave Fingal an appraising glance.

"What the hell am I going to say to comfort her when we get back to port?"

"She'll have heard the news long before we're back in Alex. When ABC sent *Vixen* home this morning he'll have made arrangements for the next of kin of our fallen to be notified as soon as possible after she docks. Mrs. Simpkins will be visited by someone from the fleet chaplain's office, and navy wives stick together. She'll not be short of sympathetic company, O'Reilly, you can be sure of that."

"I see," said Fingal. He knew the captain was right. All the familes of the *Touareg*'s and *Gloucester*'s dead would have the support of the navy behind them, that was true. And while he felt for them, this was different. He knew Elly personally, had sat at her dinner table, sipped her wine, eaten her food, laughed and joked with her at that marvellous meal. It hurt him to think of her sad, lost, and grieving. What would he say to her once he was back in Alex?

38

It Is the Generous Spirit

"Will I go over til the Duck and tell Dougie til come home and see his new son?" Mabel asked. "He's a right wee dote, so he is." She fussed about fluffing Doreen's pillows and making sure her sister's cup of tea was full.

"Wait a minute, Mabel," O'Reilly said. He had finished a more thorough and perfectly satisfactory examination of the newborn, who was snugly asleep under a blanket in a drawer that served as a cot. O'Reilly untied his rubber apron and handed it to Kitty. "Have we a lot of tidying up to do?"

She shook her head. "I didn't use much from the midwifery bags other than a couple of clamps and scissors for the cord, and a basin for the afterbirth. The rubber sheet and a couple of towels need washing, but that's about it, and it's the midwife's job to see to it. Won't take me long."

"In that case, Mabel, you stay and keep Doreen and the chissler company, and if you'd not mind, Kitty, I'll go over to the Duck." He saw her frown and one eyebrow go up. "I know I said we'd go home to have a celebratory jar, and we will the minute I've finished there. It's not what you think. I want to see Dougie, but there's a man at the Duck I want to talk to in front of his friends."

"Oh," she said. "I thought you wanted to see the proverbial man about a fictional dog."

O'Reilly laughed. "Seeing a man about a dog" was a catch-all excuse for a departure and covered everything from needing a pee to nipping over to the pub.

She smiled. "You run on and if you want to wet the babby's head while you're there, go right ahead." She frowned. "But what'll I do with the midder bags? They're heavy."

"Leave them here with the Duggans and take the Rover home. I'll walk to the Duck and home's no distance after that, then I'll get the car, and come back for the bags."

"Then we'll toast the new arrival." She smiled. "It's a very satisfying thing bringing a new life into the world. Thank you, Doreen, for letting me help."

"Thank you, Mrs. O'Reilly," an obviously tired Doreen said, "and you, sir too, and tell my man not til be too long. We need to give—" She smiled over to where the youngest Duggan was gurgling in his drawer. "The babby a name and . . ." She hesitated. "I know Dougie has a thing for the letter D and is thinking on David, but, Mrs. O'Reilly, would you mind if we gave him the second name Kit, like?"

"David Kit Duggan. That's a lovely name and I'd be extremely flattered," Kitty said, and the colour in her cheeks heightened.

"And I'll be off," O'Reilly said. "See you at home soon, Mrs. O'Reilly."

At four thirty on a Thursday afternoon the Duck was relatively empty. Mary Dunleavy, newly washed glass in one hand, tea towel in the other, stood behind a deserted bar counter. The usually thick tobacco fug was more of a mist than a pea souper, and the hum of conversation was muted. It was still early in the day and the Duck didn't usually start filling up until about five thirty. Besides, the workingmen who were the pub's regulars would be enjoying their holidays, for this was the Twelfth Fortnight and many would have gone to places like Bangor and Newcastle in County Down, Portrush in County Antrim, and Portstewart in County Derry. A few might even be giving the Costa Brava a go. Donal Donnelly had become a less frequent Duck attender since the birth of his daughter and anyway it was early for Donal too. And since his heart attack Bertie Bishop, good Lord, O'Reilly thought, as his eyes became accustomed to the room's dim lighting, there Bertie was, bold as brass sitting with Alan Hewitt, Dougie Duggan, and, the man O'Reilly was after, Lenny Brown. Each of the four had a nearly full pint in front of him.

"Good afternoon to this house," O'Reilly said. "Pint, please, Mary. Your dad get home all right?" He replied to the "Afternoon, Doctor," and "How's about ye, sir?" coming from the occupied table with "I'll be with you in a minute."

"Aye, sir," Mary said. "I've him tucked up in bed with a couple of pillows on each side of his sore foot til keep the bedclothes off, so I have." She poured one-third of a glassful, letting the stout run down the inclined inside of the straight glass. "He says that's more comfy for his poor ould toe."

"Good lass," said O'Reilly. "He'll start getting better soon. Keep making him drink water and take his pills. If you're worried you'll let me know?"

"I will, sir." She set the glass on its base to let the foamy beer settle. "If you're going to join the other men, I'll bring it over when it's poured," she said.

"Grand," said O'Reilly, left half a crown on the counter, and wandered over to the table. "Gentlemen."

"Have a pew, Doc." Alan Hewitt vacated his and pulled over a straight-backed wooden chair from another table.

O'Reilly planted himself on the new chair and started fishing round for his briar.

"And?" big, open-faced Dougie asked. "And? Is it a boy or a child?"

"It's a wee brother for Daphne. And before you ask, Dougie, he's got all his fingers and toes and the girls of the village will be looking worried in about sixteen years."

"Younger than that if he's anything like his daddy was," Alan said.

Dougie grinned, grabbed O'Reilly's paw, and began pumping it like someone drawing water from a hundred-foot well. "Och, thanks, Doc. A wee boy? That's grand. Thanks a million. Let me buy you a pint. I'm a daddy again and I have a wee boy." He clasped his hands above his head like a victorious prizefighter.

"Thanks"—O'Reilly shook his head—"but I'm just in for the one and it's on the pour and paid for."

"Good for you, Dougie," Alan said, raising his glass and clapping the proud papa on the back. "Any ould tinker can put a hole in the bottom of a bucket . . ."

In unison four voices supplied the follow-up line, ". . . but it takes a craftsman to put a spout on a teapot."

There was general laughter, amid which Mary delivered O'Reilly's pint and quietly retired.

"Well done you, Dougie," Lenny Brown said. "And you rear him right. Get him apprenticed to a good trade." He caught O'Reilly's eye and inclined his head.

So that's the way the land lies about Colin, O'Reilly thought. Now what can I do? He raised his glass. *"Sláinte."*

There was a chorus of "Cheers," then Dougie said, "Maybe you're right, Lenny, but never mind his job. That's years away. When he's only a bit grown, him and me can kick a soccer ball about and I'll have him supporting Glentoran."

Clearly a career for the newest Duggan was miles from Dougie's thoughts.

"And tell him about the Orange Order," Bertie said. "We're always on the lookout for new—" He stopped. "Alan, I'm sorry. I'd forgotten you dig with the left foot."

"Never you worry, Mister Bishop," Alan said. "Us Catholics don't mind the local Orangemen. There's never been no trouble in Ballybucklebo, and it's just a parade you have, and it'll be next Tuesday. Sure it's always great *craic*. The kiddies love the bands. You mind a couple of years back Donal Donnelly's kilt fell down and—?"

"And Seamus Galvin put a tenor drumstick right through my front window?" O'Reilly said, and laughed.

"And me dressed as King Billy and all, and the bloody horse threw me. The whole thing was a quare gag that year."

It had been a cause for great hilarity, but for Bertie Bishop to laugh at himself—and in public? *Mirabile dictu,* O'Reilly thought. Would wonders never cease? Perhaps Bertie really is a changed man since his heart attack last Halloween.

"Now never mind parades. See you rear that wee lad up right, Dougie Duggan." Bertie wagged a finger at Dougie and said, "Flo and me never had none." He sounded sad. "Wee boys need to be brought along. When they grow up, they'll be the men of the house."

O'Reilly took a pull on his pint and kept an eye on Lenny Brown, who, up till now, had been silent except to offer his congratulations and imply that Colin was not going to get his chance at the Eleven Plus. Let's see what Bertie's opinion on another subject is, and let's see if it leads anywhere. "Do you think wee girls need bringing along too, Bertie?" O'Reilly was pretty sure he knew what Bertie's answer would be to that.

"Wee girls isn't the same," Bertie said, shaking his head and slipping one thumb under the lapel of his blue serge suit jacket.

He is now calling this meeting to order, O'Reilly thought. Bertie is going into his public speaking mode. "And why are they not the same?"

"Because most wee girls' jobs is til find a good husband. I used til think we spent a lot of taxpayers' money on giving them too much learning, so I did."

Time to give the pot a little stir, O'Reilly thought, still watching Lenny. "Do you agree with that, Alan? You've a wee girl."

"Helen's not so wee." He took a pull on his pint. "And saving your presence, Councillor, no harm til ye, but I think your head's full of hobby horse shite, so it is."

O'Reilly hid his grin. Bully, he thought, for the Irish pub where any one man's opinion was as good as the next.

"Why do you say that?" Lenny asked.

"Because if Mister Bishop thinks it's a waste of money, he's dead wrong. My wee girl got her Eleven Plus. I wanted all of mine educated. I didn't want any of my kids, boys or girls, ending up like me . . . only a builder's labourer."

"And a bloody good one," Bertie Bishop said, and drank.

"Thank you," Alan said. "But—"

"I think," said Lenny, "a wee lad should go intil his daddy's trade."

"You mean like Jesus?" Dougie asked. "He was a carpenter like his daddy." Dougie was starting to sound slurred, which was permissible for a brand-new father, but it was hardly going to make him a stellar debater.

"Carpentry's an honourable trade," O'Reilly said, nudging the conversation along. He took a long pull on his stout and lit his pipe.

"You see, Doctor, that's what I was trying to tell the missus, and you, and Miss Nolan."

"Tell them what?" Alan asked.

Lenny took a deep breath. "They want my Colin to sit the Eleven Plus."

For a moment nobody spoke, then Alan Hewitt said quietly, "My

Helen got it, Lenny. My Helen went on til grammar school." He raised his voice and pointed at his own chest. "And me a labourer, but see her? See my Helen?" His eyes shone and his voice took on the tones of a man who had won a gold medal. "My Helen's going for til be a doctor. Nobody wasted any money on her, so they didn't. I reckon if you're looking for value for money you just take a quick gander at my Helen." He frowned and shook his head at Lenny. "Give your wee lad a chance too, Lenny. It'll not cost you nothing. Nothing."

"My wee lad's going til be a plater like his daddy."

Bertie Bishop said, "You're daft, Lenny."

O'Reilly spun to see Bertie Bishop scowling and shaking his head. "I never got no proper education, but I bettered myself."

"So can Colin. He doesn't need no fancy exams."

To O'Reilly, Lenny was now like a boxer being backed into a corner. Still defending himself but losing confidence.

Bertie's nostrils flared. He was not a man who suffered fools gladly. "Look," he said, "I was fourteen when I had til leave school." He looked pensive. "I wanted til be an engineer, but the family needed the money." He shrugged.

Lenny frowned. "But you've done very good, Mister Bishop, with your construction company and all."

"Aye," said Bishop. "I've had til work sixteen-hour days, be a mean man with a penny, work the likes of you, Alan, bloody hard." He spread his arms wide. "And where did it get me? I bloody near died last year and I've had time til think since then. I made money. I made a name for myself here." O'Reilly heard the man's wistful tones. "But I never got for til be an engineer and *that's* what I wanted. I wanted to build more than houses. I wanted to build bridges and factories, maybe even one of them glass-and-steel skyscrapers. Think on that, Lenny Brown. You think bloody hard."

O'Reilly realised his mouth was hanging open. Bertie had confessed to that? "That's a big mouthful, Bertie," he said. "Took a lot of guts to say it. I'm proud of you." He put his pipe mouthpiece back between his teeth and inhaled.

"Aye. Well," Bertie said. "And maybe I'm wrong about girls too, Alan. More power to your Helen and other lasses like her. It was that wee lady doctor Bradley that saved my life, so it was."

"You've me convinced anyroad, Mister Bishop," Dougie said. "My wee David, that's what we'll call him, my wee David can grow up til be what he likes, so he can." He pointed an unsteady finger at Lenny. "Your Colin deserves a chance too."

"Hear, hear," said Alan Hewitt. "This is 1966. There's no reason why anybody can't rise above their station . . . if they get themselves learned right."

"You've been very quiet, Doctor," Bertie said.

"And it's not like himself," Dougie said, clearly fortified by the drink.

"What's your opinion, Doctor?" Bertie wanted to know.

O'Reilly thought about the evening he and Kitty had spent mackerel fishing, when he wondered what bait might lure Lenny Brown into changing his mind. Had the opinion of his two friends here and the confession of Councillor Bishop done the trick? "Lenny knows my opinion . . ."

"Aye. I do, so I do."

Lenny Brown's voice was even less resolute, and yet he was a stubborn man and if O'Reilly didn't bring the point home, this might all come to nothing. Come on, he said to himself, find something more. He smiled. Lenny and Alan liked the grues. "I'll give you two-to-one on a five-pound note that if you let Colin sit he'll pass."

"Doctor O'Reilly, sir. I may not want him to sit the exam, but if you think I'm going to bet against my own son—"

"O'Reilly, go away and feel your head. Lenny, I can do better than that," Bertie Bishop said. "You don't need to bet nothing if you admit it's the best thing for Colin, like it would have been for me, til get properly learned and give him a better chance? Are you a big enough man to do that?'"

Lenny sighed, hung his head, and looked up. Then he clasped his hands, glanced from eye to eye, and took a deep breath. "Well, I . . . I mean . . ." The words came in a rush. "Maybe . . . maybe I've been thinking more of myself, not wanting til have a clever son looking down on me, seeing the family tradition of us at the shipyards dying, but," he stretched out a hand to Bertie, which was taken and shaken, "thank youse all for getting me for til see what I've to do for my son. He can sit the bloody thing and if he passes, I'll drive him til Bangor Grammar School myself."

The other four men applauded.

Lenny finished his pint in one swallow and for the first time since O'Reilly had come in, Lenny Brown grinned then laughed out loud and said, "D'you know, Alan, I hope one day I'll be as proud of my wee divil Colin as you are of your Helen."

"Well done, Lenny," Bertie said, "and well stated. Now you never let me finish what I was going to propose."

"Go right ahead, sir," Lenny said.

"I'm a wealthy man. I've no one til leave my money til." He turned to O'Reilly. "Would fifty pounds a year til he's finished help a young lad through university if that's what he wants four or five years from now?"

For the second time, O'Reilly realised he must be looking like a stunned mullet with his mouth wide open. "By God, it would, Bertie," he said.

"All right then, Lenny. You call round at my office tomorrow and we'll have my solicitor draw up the papers. And before you give me any bull about not wanting to take charity, this is not charity. This is an investment, an investment in a young lad's future and in my future. Let me do this for him."

"I don't know what til say, Mister Bishop," Lenny said.

"I do," said Alan, who was renowned for his voice.

"Me too," said Dougie, and despite the law prohibiting singing in Ulster pubs they started, "For he's a jolly good fellow, for he's a jolly good fellow . . ."

And Lenny—and Fingal O'Reilly, who wondered if he hadn't witnessed the nearest thing to a miracle that was ever going to happen in Ballybuckebo—joined in.

39

Full Fathom Five

"We therefore commit their bodies to the deep, looking for the general resurrection in the last day, and the life of the world to come, through our Lord Jesus Christ; at whose second coming in glorious majesty to judge the world, the sea shall give up her dead . . ."

Fingal stood with his head uncovered in a light northwesterly wind under the nearly midday sun as the captain intoned the final prayer for Surgeon Lieutenant Peter Fenwick, Lieutenant Chris Simpkins, and Able Seaman Brinsden. The bodies, each sewn into a sad canvas bundle weighted with a 4.7-inch shell, lay under Union Flags and on top of planks at the edge of the ship's afterdeck. He wondered if, as had been the custom in Nelson's day, a final stitch had been taken through each dead man's nose. When the captain finished the prayer, he and the other officers put on their caps and saluted, the burial party upended the planks, the bosun's whistles shrilled. Fingal heard three splashes. *Sic transit gloria mundi,* he thought. Poor buggers. By now the wounded *Vixen* would be well on her way to Alex, bearing the news to the next of kin.

"Burial party, on hats. Dismiss," the CPO in charge of the detail ordered, and that was that. Typical naval efficiency, a drill for every conceivable occasion.

Touareg had for the duration of the ceremony flown her ensigns at half-mast but had made no effort to heave to or deviate from her course. There was a good reason.

At breakfast one of the destroyer's officers had informed Fingal that the British fleet was southwest of Greece and that the enemy fleet was about 150 miles away, fifty miles from the toe of Italy. It was Admiral Cunningham's intention to place his ships between the Italians and their base at Taranto in Italy's heel to force a battle.

When Fingal arrived on the bridge at noon, there had been a flurry of signalling between *Warspite* and the rest of the fleet. Flags soared up halliards; Aldis lamps clacked and flashed. Radio silence was the order of the day. *Touareg* was one of five destroyers attached to the flagship's close escort and was steaming off the battleship's starboard beam about four cables, or two-fifths of a mile, away.

"This," said Captain Huston-Phelps, reading a message he'd been handed by the signals yeoman, "promises to be interesting, Doctor. I'm glad you've taken up my invitation of last night. You're welcome to stay on the bridge unless we have more casualties for you to attend to. We're within ninety miles of the enemy now and they are heading this way." Before Fingal could answer, the skipper said to the first lieutenant, "Course two seven oh. Speed twenty knots, number one. Conform to *Warspite*'s movements."

"Aye, aye, sir." The ship's first lieutenant repeated his instructions to ensure there had been no misunderstanding, then passed the necessary orders to the cox'n who stood at the ship's wheel, eyes fixed on the compass and said, "Course two seven oh degrees, sir. Wheel's amidships. Steady as she goes."

They were not yet at action stations, but once they were, the cox'n would go to the armoured steering position below the bridge.

"Very good." The first lieutenant focussed his field glasses and stared ahead.

Ninety miles? Fingal was no navigator, but that seemed pretty close. It might not be long before the fleets were in sight of each other and, he swallowed, in range too. From this vantage point he'd be able to see the battle. How had he thought of it after witnessing the gunnery practice? The grappling of the fleets? He'd wondered then, as he wondered now, how he'd feel. He was certainly still a bit rocky after being dangled like a puppet on a string over a roiling ocean, performing surgery on a moving deck, and burying the husband of a woman he'd almost slept with.

Fingal looked up to a sky dappled with high thin clouds and for the moment enemy bomber free. The twenty-knot wind of their passage ruffled his hair where it stuck out from under a steel helmet. All the other bridge personnel wore similar protection. "Thank you, sir. I'd be four decks down on *Warspite*. I'd have no idea what was going on."

"Four decks down behind God knows how many tons of armour," the captain said. "Destroyers are different." He grinned. "Nowhere much to hide really."

As poor Chris Simpkins had discovered.

"You're probably as safe here as anywhere if the only ships firing are battleships at long range. The Eyeties will be too busy trying to hit our battlewagons to bother with shrimps like us—unless we are trying to torpedo them, then they'll give us everything they've got."

There was some comfort in that. In Fingal's mind, there'd not be much left of a 1,850-ton ship like *Touareg* if she were to suffer a direct hit from a battleship's main armament.

"I'll have to chase you if we are going into close action, but until then, you will have time on your hands, so you may as well watch the action if you wish." He handed Fingal a spare set of binoculars. "Here, you'll see better with these."

"Thank you, sir."

"I think you'll find it illuminating. A flying boat out of Malta has identified most of the enemy fleet. There's a pair of *Cavour*-class battleships each with ten twelve-inch guns. They're capable of twenty-eight knots. One's the fleet flagship, *Giulio Cesare*, with Admiral

Riccardi on board. The other's *Conte di Cavour*. They've both undergone recent extensive refits and will be tough nuts to crack. They also have sixteen eight- and six-inch gun cruisers, and more than thirty destroyers. I'm afraid we're outnumbered, and outgunned in the cruiser department, and *Malaya* and *Royal Sovereign* aren't very fast. We may leave them both behind if we end up trying to catch the Eyeties."

Fingal whistled. *Warspite* would have to take on their battlewagons unsupported by any other heavily gunned ships. Not good odds.

"Look," said Huston-Phelps, and pointed astern. "*Eagle*'s coming head to wind."

Fingal put the glasses to his eyes, focussed, and watched as the ponderous aircraft carrier and her escort, including the battered *Gloucester,* swung onto a northwesterly course to give the aircraft the best lift under their wings. Looking to Fingal like little moths, the flimsy "stringbags" took off, formed into V-shaped groups of three, and droned away, each carrying a Mark XII torpedo that they hoped might hit an enemy warship and at least slow her down if it failed to sink her. Their main targets would be the Italian battlewagons.

"You have to admire the Fleet Air Arm laddies," Huston-Phelps said. "You'd not get me up in one of those Swordfish biplanes on a flat-calm day, never mind being shot at too."

Fingal lowered his glasses. "Nor me," he said.

"Flagship's signalling, sir," the yeoman of signals said, and began to read the flickering morse. "Seventh Cruiser Flotilla proceed at best speed."

"That's thirty knots," Captain Huston-Phelps said. "Vice Admiral Tovey's cruisers are going to get among the enemy before us."

Fingal looked through his glasses as the four sleek vessels already ahead of the rest of the fleet began to put on speed. He wondered how their six-inch guns would fare against the Italian cruisers with their eight-inch armaments. And yet airman and sailor alike, facing horrid odds, seemed to go about their business as if it was simply a routine day. Were they inured to fear, too young to be afraid, heroes who were heroes because, although terrified, they carried on nevertheless? He shook his head. He couldn't speak for them, but he was scared. And he wasn't afraid to admit it, at least to himself. Last night, just as he had after Narvik, he'd seen what bomb fragments could do to metal and to flesh. Fragments. What effect a twelve-inch shell would have he'd try not to imagine. His smile was grim. If nothing else, it would be over quickly for many.

The signals yeoman said, "To *Warspite*'s five escorting destroyers, make revolutions for twenty-four knots and maintain screening positions on *Warspite*."

"Very good. Acknowledge."

"Aye, aye, sir."

The skipper bent to a voice pipe, which presumably communicated with the engine room. "Engine room, bridge. Engine room, bridge." He paused, listening to the chief engineer's acknowledgement before saying, "Revolutions for twenty-four knots please, Chiefy."

Fingal heard the jangling of the engine room telegraphs. At times such as these the engineering chief petty officer, Chiefy, would be on the engine control platform. Fingal felt the deck move under his feet as the ship gathered speed. Astern she now was throwing up a high rooster tail of wake. The wind on his cheeks freshened and the funnel smoke streaming astern thickened.

"Tallyho," said the captain. "Our admiral is a pretty aggressive man. He's sending his light forces on ahead to try to slow down the enemy, pushing the hell out of *Warspite*. Look at her go. *Malay* and *Royal Sovereign* will be left behind."

Fingal watched his ship, picturing his friend Tom Laverty busy at his chart table keeping the plot up to date. For the time being her great rifles were trained fore and aft, but as soon as they were in range they would start swinging, elevating, blasting.

Her funnel smoke belched thick, her bow wave creamed away from her sides, flung spray over the forepeak, and the wake boiled above her stern. Even here, four cables away, he could hear the roar of the turbines, the crackling of her battle ensigns streaming out from the fore and main tops.

"ABC's pushing on so he can support the cruisers as soon as possible," the captain said, "but that'll leave the other battlewagons lagging behind. Once we get in range, we'll have ten ships and only one that outguns the Eyeties—*Warspite*. And they'll have, if I've done my sums correctly, thirty-three ships." He grinned. "Real death-or-glory stuff."

"Motto of the Seventeen, Twenty-first Lancers," Fingal said. He was still picturing what a battleship's guns might do to *Touareg,* but he also found himself being infected by the captain's excited enthusiasm.

"I think," said Huston-Phelps, keeping his voice flat, his expression deadpan, "ABC's plan is to surround the enemy." He chuckled.

And Fingal, whether from genuine amusement or simple release of tension, laughed until the combined twenty-four-knot wind and his laughter brought tears to his eyes.

By three o'clock, *Eagle* had flown off a second unsuccessful air strike. Not a torpedo had hit, but all the planes had eventually returned safely to land on the carrier's flight deck, much to Fingal's relief.

"It's been nearly three hours since ABC sent the cruisers in pursuit," the captain was saying. "Visibility is about fifteen miles. The cruisers are ten miles ahead of us and the rest of the fleet ten miles behind."

Fingal glanced astern and had no difficulty making out the bulk of the two battleships. The carrier was off to the east of *Warspite*. Ten miles ahead, the four fast British ships were easy to make out.

"Aha," said the captain, "*Neptune,* one of the cruisers, has just signalled, 'Enemy battle fleet in sight.' " He grinned. "The last time that signal was made in the Med, Nelson was in command."

Moments later, a Swordfish biplane was catapulted off *Warspite*'s deck and headed in the direction of the enemy.

"The plane will spot the fall of *Warspite*'s shells when she opens up and radio back corrections," the captain said. "We'll listen in." He gave instructions for a repeater speaker to be switched on on the bridge. "It'll be in Morse code, but our yeoman will give us a running commentary."

The cruisers had opened fire, and even at this distance Fingal could hear the sounds of gunfire and see the flashes from the British cruisers' guns and beyond them the flickering of guns being fired by the enemy forces. Waterspouts, white and discoloured by the shells' explosives, towered above the distant ships. Fingal was sure it must be only a matter of time before one or more of the outnumbered British cruisers were hit, but he'd not seen any telltale towering gouts of flame from any of their hulls. He recalled a phrase his father had once used and had attributed to a Prussian, von Clauzewitz, "The fog of war." Certainly up ahead, as funnel smoke and the cordite fumes of many guns hung low over the water, it was difficult to be sure exactly what was happening.

"Amazing," the captain said. "Admiral Tovey's handling his force like a destroyer flotilla commander, dashing here and there, unsighting the enemy gunners and—"

Fingal was deafened. *Warspite* had let go a salvo from A turret, immediately followed by one from B. He ducked instinctively. The last time he'd seen her fire her great guns he'd been watching from directly above. Now he had a different perspective on the sheets of flames pouring from each muzzle and the dense mahogany-coloured smoke. The cruiser sailors would be heartened by the arrival of *Warspite*'s one-ton shells among the enemy. It must be, Fingal thought, like the intervention of a big brother in a playground squabble between rival kiddies' gangs—but a potentially lethal intervention.

Shortly after, Fingal became aware that his view of the enemy squadrons was becoming even more obscured. "What's going on, sir?"

"It seems our Italian friends don't want to play anymore. They're laying a smokescreen and turning away, and . . . hang on."

"Signal from Flagship, sir. Time three thirty," the signals yeoman said. "*Warspite* and destroyers will steam in a circle to permit *Malaya* to catch up."

The skipper gave the necessary helm orders, and *Touareg* heeled into a turn to starboard and completed a 360-degree manoeuver before steering northwest again with *Malaya* in company. *Royal Sovereign* was still lagging behind.

"Here comes trouble," Captain Huston-Phelps said, and ahead, appearing from the man-made fog bank, Fingal could begin to make out the ghostly shapes of two huge Italian ships. The leading ship carried five of her great guns in two turrets on the foredeck. The three in the lower turret spoke.

"We're almost on parallel courses," the captain said, "so both sides will soon start firing broadsides, but *Warspite* will range with salvoes."

"I watched her doing that on a gunnery exercise," Fingal said. "Each gun of a pair fires, then they correct the range." He didn't get a chance to say any more because with a roar like that of an approaching train, three Italian shells arrived and their deafening explosion and waterspouts bracketed *Warspite*.

Nearly simultaneously, *Warspite* fired at the Italians' leading battleship. Once more the roar, the flames, the smoke.

Fingal watched as the waterspouts rose close by the closest Italian ship. "Pretty impressive," the captain said. "The range is twenty-six thousand yards."

"Short by six hundred yards," the signals yeoman said, interpreting the spotter aircraft's message.

Fingal saw the muzzles of the guns of *Warspite*'s two for'ard turrets lift to increase their elevation. Then the rifles bellowed their defiance.

He lost count of the number of times the great guns spoke, but at four o'clock he saw clearly through his binoculars a column of fire arising from near the funnels of the leading Italian ship. The blaze was followed by a huge upheaval of smoke.

Captain Huston-Phelps clapped his hands. "Got the bastard."

The yeoman announced, "Direct hit. Midships. *Giulio Cesare*. Large fire. Heavy smoke. Much steam. Possible damage to boiler room."

"And," the captain said, "at a range of thirteen miles. No one has had a hit on a moving target at that range before. Well done, *Warspite*."

It was well done, Fingal acknowledged, but how many men had ceased to exist? How many were in agony, lying still or flopping like landed fish? A hit in the boiler room? The superheated steam would flay members of the engineering crew alive.

"Look at the buggers run," the captain said.

Already the Italian battleships were turning back into the smoke.

"Orders from flagship, sir," the yeoman said. "All destroyers to counterattack in concert with the cruisers under cover of smoke."

"Sorry, O'Reilly," the captain said, "but we'll be dodging fire from the whole Eyetie fleet now. I'm afraid I'm going to have to ask you to go below to your sick bay."

"Aye, aye, sir." He wasn't sorry. He'd seen enough carnage. As Fingal made his way down the companion ladder, he paused and watched as the two Italian battleships turned tail into an ever-increasing pall of man-made smoke while shells from *Warspite* and

Malaya were hurled into the darkness, doing what damage not even the spotter plane could see.

Fingal sat at the little desk in his borrowed cabin. It was 9 P.M. and *Touareg*'s men had been stood down from action stations some time ago. He'd made one last round of the sick bay and retired to make notes from the conversations he'd had with some of the ship's officers in the wardroom over dinner.

He read his entries.

July 9, 1940. 4 P.M. Destroyer and cruiser attack in smoke. Heavy fire from enemy cruisers, but no British vessels damaged. Warspite's spotter plane reported: "Italian fleet in disarray." Italian aircraft had appeared and in the confusion had mistakenly bombed their own ships instead of the British. Fortunately for the enemy not a bomb had scored a hit. Pity. Could have saved us the trouble. Eventually it was reported that the Italian fleet had got itself back into some semblance of order and was steering west and southwest at high speed for Straits of Messina.

5:35 P.M. British fleet twenty-five miles south of coast of Calabria. No hope of catching Italians but we are under heavy aerial attack. ABC ordered course set for Malta.

Bombing stopped at 7:30 P.M. No serious damage to fleet. One of Warspite's spotter planes set on fire in hangar by her own guns' muzzle flashes. Ditched overboard.

My first and, I hope my last, fleet action. I am a little proud that although scared most of the time, I was able to master my fear. I am amazed that for all the sound and fury, the number of ships and air-craft involved, that so little was achieved by either side and by how one hit from one of Warspite's *big guns could make an Italian fleet turn tail and run.*

He rose. Was it, he wondered, a British victory? Hard to say. British casualities had been minimal when you considered that *Warspite,* with her complement of more than a thousand men, could have been sunk with dreadful loss of life. Even a Tribal-class destroyer carried 190, but no British ships had been seriously hit. Even so, eighteen men had been killed on *Gloucester* and three men had died on *Touareg.* Nothing but a stupid waste.

One of those men was Chris Simpkins, and Elly would be sitting in Alex about to learn that she was a widow and her boys in England were fatherless. In the shock of hearing of Simpkins's death last night, Fingal had blurted out to the captain something about comforting Elly. Now he wondered. After all, he hadn't been Chris's MO and had only met Elly once. Did Fingal have any responsibility to see her at all? He shook his head. He'd not decide now but think on it during the journey back to Alex. Perhaps it might be better to let that hare sit. She'd have a wide circle of old friends and was there much Fingal could add? Probably not.

Besides, he was supposed to be leaving on a troopship for England soon. He fingered Deirdre's green scarf, tucked into the pocket of his shorts. But would any of that still be on? Might he find he was being posted to *Touareg* permanently instead? Already the fleet was one MO short. Fingal had watched them commit his body to the sea this morning. There, never mind a new posting, there but by the grace of God go any of us, including officially noncombatant MOs like Peter Fenwick. He picked up his diary and closed it with a snap.

40

Vast Sorrow Was There

Fingal sat at his desk on *Warspite* and looked around the little cabin. It had been his home for nearly eight months, but tomorrow, glory be, he'd be taking a train to Port Said to join a convoy that would be Liverpool-bound on its return trip. One of the troopships had brought out his replacement, a new MO who would join *Warspite* tomorrow.

When he'd left *Touareg* four days ago, the first thing he'd done after reporting back on board was to seek out Richard Wilcoxson.

"Fingal, you're back. Well done." The man had jumped up from his desk and extended his hand, just as he had done last November at their first meeting. "By all reports you did an excellent job." And Fingal had warmed to the older man's praise. "It's all confirmed, nothing has changed. You start the course at Haslar Hospital early October and I want you back on *Warspite* once you've completed your training."

And there'd been a letter from Deirdre, full of inconsequential gossip and underscored with love and longing. He'd devoured it and immediately written back telling her the wonderful news that the wedding was definitely on and that soon they would be together. He had hers tucked into the breast pocket of his white shirt to read again when he went ashore later this morning. He planned to visit the base hospital and see the two major cases he'd operated on eight days ago on *Touareg*.

His war diary lay on the desk and he idly flipped it open. Some-one had once described war as long periods of boredom punctuated by moments of sheer terror. As usual he had some time to kill before the pinnace took him to shore. He would reread the last entries before putting it into his half-packed suitcase.

July 9th, 5:30 P.M. *Still on* Touareg. *Battle seems to be over. Fleet twenty-five miles off coast of Calabria. Too close to Italian aero-dromes. ABC has ordered course set for south of Malta.*

July 11th. We're been cruising these waters for two days. ABC had to get to high-level conference in Cairo so Warspite *and her destroyers are now headed for Alex. Rest of fleet to Malta to escort convoy. Ital-ian bombing barely ceased during daylight.* Touareg *skipper said the planes came from bases in Libya. Our flotilla attacked thirty-four times. More than 400 bombs were dropped, but not a single ship seriously hit.*

July 12th. Worst attack so far. Cruisers Liverpool *and* Sydney *have joined us. I took the name* Liverpool *to be an omen that I might soon be headed there on my way to Portsmouth. Several casualties in* Liverpool *from a near-miss. Does that mean I'm not going to get away?*

Fingal could laugh now he knew he'd be going home tomorrow, but when he'd made the entry he'd been as superstitious as an old Ro-man consulting the augurs, hoping for favourable omens. He read on.

I was sure Warspite *had had it. From the deck of* Touareg *I could see her disappearing behind the splashes. Counted twenty-four bombs to port, twelve to starboard, all within two hundred yards of her. The whole lot missed. She's a lucky ship.*

Berthed in Alex July 13th. Happy to be back in home port.

He picked up his pen and made a final entry:

July 16. And happy to be back on Warspite. *All quiet in Alex—for now.*

He was glad he had taken the trouble to keep the diary up to date. The roar of the guns, the blasts of the bombs, the deaths and burials of the *Touareg* men—it had all conspired, through some trick of his mind that he didn't understand, to obliterate the memories even though the Italians had been happy to provide *aides memoires* by bombing the dockyard and anchorage on a regular basis. He closed the book, put it in the suitcase, grabbed his cap, and left the room.

"Hello, Fingal," said a familiar voice.

He turned on the steps of the hospital, having just satisfied himself that both of his patients were doing well. John Collins, his squash partner of last month, stood smiling behind him. "Hello, John. What brings you here?" He had given up on the notion of paying a courtesy call to Elly Simpkins, deciding it was better they simply remained ships that had passed on a warm and fragrant night in Alexandria. Now, presented with this very real reminder of her loss, Fingal felt guilty.

"My boss in signals has been in with a nasty case of piles. I brought him some grapes. Thought they might cheer him up. You?"

"Couple of patients to see. I'd been sent to *Touareg* because their MO had been killed before Calabria."

John glanced down. "So I heard." He shook his head. "Bad about Chris Simpkins too."

"Yes, very bad. Have you seen Elly?"

"Mmmm, several times. It came as a hell of a shock when the God wallah appeared and broke the news—a week ago today in fact. But she seems to have pulled herself together and is handling it well," John said. "Perhaps 'well' isn't the best word. Let's just say she's bearing up. Grateful for her friends." He pursed his lips before saying, "I hesitate to ask, Fingal, I'm sure you do enough comforting in your trade, but she knows you were on *Touareg* at the time. 'If you see Finn,' she said to me, 'see if he'll pop in. I only met him once, but he made me laugh.'"

Bloody nearly did a damn sight more. He looked down. Damn it, he'd time enough before he had to be back on board. It would be the right thing to do. That was all. "It's only about a mile to Saad Zaghloul Square from here. Do you think she's home?"

John looked at his watch and nodded. "She and Michelle had an early lunch at the club but she'll be home by now. Decent of you, old boy," John said. "I have a car if you'd like. I can't come in but I'll drop you there."

"Thank you," Fingal said.

The lift with its wrought-iron cage stopped on the third floor of 16B Saad Zaghloul Square. Fingal opened the concertina gate, crossed the landing, and pushed the doorbell. He heard it jingling and expected the manservant Hanif to answer.

The door opened. "Finn. Oh, Finn. You came." Elly Simpkins was certainly not wearing widow's weeds. Her low V-necked, knee-length frock was a fashionable floral print, her hair was neatly coiffed, and he couldn't help but notice the scarlet nail polish that matched her lipstick. "Thank you so very much. Do come in. You know your way."

She closed the door behind him and followed as he walked along the hall, through the bead curtain, and into the big living/dining room. The air smelt of tobacco smoke and he noticed an ashtray on the coffee table. It was overflowing with half-smoked butts. The curtains and the French windows were open and he could hear the traffic.

He removed his cap and put it on an armchair, and as he waited for her to take a seat he saw how carefully she had put on her eye makeup but hadn't quite succeeded in hiding the dark circles under her eyes.

"I'll make us some coffee," she said. "Hanif's at the bazaar. He'll be gone for ages."

"It's all right," Fingal said.

"A drink then?" She nodded at the Welsh dresser where the bottles sat.

"No, thank you, Elly. I just popped in to offer my condolences. John Collins said you'd asked for me. I'm dreadfully sorry about what happened . . ."

"Yes," she said, and her voice was level. "It came as quite a shock, although God only knows why. There is a war on." She shook her head and her laugh was brittle. "I went into a tailspin for days, lay about in my dressing gown chain-smoking." She sat on the sofa and Fingal took the chair opposite.

"I can imagine," he said.

"But yesterday I woke up and I couldn't face it, couldn't face myself. So I told myself to pull my finger out, washed my face, went and had a hairdo and manicure, and treated myself to this new dress, new shoes"—he noticed her high heels—"and some deliciously sheer stockings." She picked up a packet of Player's from the tabletop, took one out, and lit up, greedily inhaling the smoke then coughing. "I really should try to stop smoking," she said.

"I think you're being very brave," he said, remembering what she'd told him about how she and Chris had been perfectly happy for each to see other people. He wondered if her gaiety was in fact a cover for indifference to his death or a stiff-upper-lip façade hiding real grief. "And I'm so dreadfully sorry. If it helps for you to know, I was at his burial at sea. It was very dignified, with full military honours. The captain told me Chris died instantly. Didn't suffer. We should be grateful for that at least."

"I know," she said. "I'd a nice letter from Captain Huston-Phelps." She took a deep drag on her cigarette and blew out smoke. "Apparently I'll be getting a widow's pension."

"That's good." Fingal knew he was struggling for words. He'd come expecting to be offering comfort to a grieving widow. Instead he was talking to a woman who seemingly was taking everything practically. "Um . . . have you told your sons yet?"

She nodded. "I sent Daddy a telegram. He is very sweet. He'll have taken Mummy and gone and broken the news to them at school. And I'm . . ." She looked round the flat. ". . . getting to hell out of here and back home as soon as I can get a berth on a ship."

"I think that's wise. The boys will need their mother."

Her smile and her façade cracked as did her voice when she said, "They do. And I need my man. I can't believe he's not coming back. Ever." She dashed away tears and said, "I—I know this is going to sound crazy but are they absolutely sure he's dead? I mean, I just can't believe it. It seems unreal. As if there's something I could do to bring him back if only I knew what it was."

The doctor in him told him it was normal for people to try to deny the truth, want to do something, anything. "I'm afraid there's nothing you can do, Elly."

She smashed out her cigarette, seemingly unconscious of what she was doing. "Damn it all," she said, "it's not fair. I'm only twenty-nine." She looked up at Fingal. "It's just not bloody well fair. I'm far too young to be a flaming widow."

Anger was all part of grieving and he knew that what Elly Simpkins needed most was someone who would listen and offer her a human touch. "It's desperately unfair, Elly," he said, and moved to the edge of the couch beside her, taking her hand in both of his. "I don't have an answer. I'm truly sorry." She was crying again, the anger forgotten, it seemed, as the tears came. He put an arm round her shoulders and, as he would have with an injured child, gently brought her head down onto his chest, and with his other hand stroked her hair. "It's all right. It's all right." He felt her shuddering and her sobs. She turned her face up to him, and said, "Please, keep holding me, Finn," she said. "Just hold me. Just for a minute."

He shouldn't. He knew he shouldn't, but she needed to be hugged, he told himself, and it would be inhuman not to. His other arm went round her and she put her head on his shoulder. He felt the softness of her against him. A warm tear fell on his neck and he inhaled the woman's scent of her and knew, despite her being the widow of a fellow officer, that he was becoming excited by her nearness.

She pushed herself away, dashed a forearm across her eyes, straightened her back. "I'm sorry," she said and took a deep breath, and with an edge to her voice said, "This is nonsense. I'm over tears. I've cried enough for Chris."

"Perhaps," he said gently, "you need to cry a little for Elly?"

"Why? For the poor grieving widow?" She pursed her lips. "I've done the public show. I didn't say a moment ago I needed Chris. I said I needed my man. I'm a woman. I have a woman's needs and since he took up with that creature . . ." She shook her head and put it back on his shoulder, her arms round his neck, her lips to his. He resisted, knowing he must continue resisting, yet wanting her and to hell with her being recently widowed. He began to respond, but she moved her lips away and looked at him, her gaze never leaving his eyes. "Look at me, Finn. Want me, Finn. Make love to me." He sat, staring, lusting for the woman. He was honest enough to strangle the thoughts that she needed to be comforted, that it was his duty as a human being. Comfort be damned. Duty be damned. He'd been celibate for months. He wanted Elly Simpkins and it was no good deed he'd be doing. His conscience could wrestle with the facts later. His breath came in short bursts and he knew his pulse was racing.

"Your fiancée is thousands of miles away. No one need ever know . . ."

Deirdre, whose letter was in his pocket, between Fingal and Elly's soft breast. As he moved toward her knowing what must happen, he heard a voice, Deirdre's voice in a hotel room in Belfast saying, "I want you to make love to me, Fingal . . . I want to own you and you to own me." And Fingal O'Reilly swallowed, sat stock-still, disentangled Elly's arms, then stood and took a pace back. "I want to own you." Soft, gentle, loving Deirdre. "And I want you to own me," and it had been a shining gift she had given, a benificence too radiant to tarnish with the satisfaction of a few moments' craving. "Elly," he said, keeping his voice low, neutral, "you are a very beautiful woman. A very desirable woman . . ."

"Then take me." She moved toward him, but he said, "I can't." And the heat in him had cooled. "I can't, Elly, and I mustn't."

"Damn you," she yelled. "Damn you to hell." Her eyes blazed. "Damn you, Fingal O'Reilly," but now her words were softening and her tears flowed, and his heart ached in him for her. "I'm sorry," she said and he barely heard her whisper. "I'm sorry. I'm just so tired, so desperately tired."

"Come on," he said, taking her hand, "you need to sleep."

She followed him into the bedroom, making no demur when he turned back the bedclothes, removed her shoes, and tucked her in still fully dressed. "Thank you, Finn," she managed before she rolled on her side and grabbed a stuffed teddy bear that had been lying on the pillow. "I'm sorry. I don't know what came over me. Please don't think badly of me, Finn."

"I don't," he said softly. How he felt about himself was a different matter. He waited until her sobbing stopped and he was certain she was sleeping soundly, then bent, dropped a tiny kiss on her hair, and said, "Sleep well, you poor thing. Sleep well."

Fingal walked softly from the room, his doctor's training taking over. She mustn't be left alone, but he had to get back to *Warspite*.

In a very short time he had phoned HMS *Nile*, spoken to John Collins, and arranged for him to have Michelle interrupt whatever she was doing. He'd wait until she arrived, then head back to *Warspite*. He glanced round the big room and saw something on an armchair. He picked it up from the cushion. This time he'd not forget his cap.

41

The Bomber Will Always Get Through

"You, O'Reilly," said Tom Laverty, "look like the cat that got the cream. Can't say I blame you. Have a good time in Portsmouth, and we'll try to keep the old girl afloat without you."

The anteroom was not busy at two thirty on a Wednesday afternoon. Richard and Tom, who were remaining on *Warspite,* were standing farewell drinks for Fingal and Wilson Wallace, who were not. The former lieutenant had been promoted lieutenant-commander into HMS *Neptune,* a *Leander*-class light cruiser and would be joining her in a week. To replace Wilson, a junior gunnery officer, apparently another Ulsterman called Phillip Nolan, had been promoted from HMS *Liverpool* and he and the new MO would be coming out on the liberty boat to join *Warspite.*

"I wonder what you'll find when you get back to Blighty," Wilson said. "What news we've got by BBC relay says some air attacks are starting."

Tom Laverty's brow furrowed and he sat back in his seat. His imitation of the prime minister's delivery was near perfect. "'The Battle of France is over. I expect the Battle of Britain is about to begin. Upon this battle depends the survival of Christian civilisation.' That's what Mr. Churchill said in his address to the House of Commons last month. Sounds pretty grim to me."

"He might just be right," Richard said, "and for the last four days there have been reports of the Luftwaffe attacking our convoys in the English Channel and our side sending up Spitfires and Hurricanes to shoot down the attackers."

Fingal thought of Ma and Lady Laura, the Marchioness of Bally-bucklebo, with their posters of an airman, a Spitfire fighter, and the slogan, "I'll fly it if you'll buy it." The accompanying collection boxes were all over County Down, and the two women's Spitfire fund, one of many throughout the United Kingdom, had raised the necessary five thousand pounds. He wondered where the fast and lethal fighter was stationed now. He hoped it was where it and its fellows could wreak the greatest havoc amongst the attacking German bombers.

Richard looked at his glass. "Time will tell, but the English Channel is a pretty effective antitank ditch and if the Germans have any plans to invade they'll have the chief of Fighter Command, 'Stuffy' Dowding's Fighters, and the Home Fleet to contend with."

Fingal heard the pride in the man's voice, a pride that he, Fingal, echoed.

Richard clapped Fingal on the knee. "Let's hope you have a safe trip home and that you're not going from the frying pan into the fire. The Luftwaffe had a go at Portsmouth on the eleventh of July when we were still at sea. Aimed for the dockyard, but some overshot. My favourite pub, The Blue Anchor at Kingston Cross, was hit. I know because I heard it on a BBC bulletin. Still, the missus should have been all right. She lives at Fareham, about six miles from where you'll be working. If you're interested, when he was a boy ABC spent three years as a pupil at Foster's School there preparing for Dartmouth Naval College. Anyway, I think she's pretty safe from air raids, but it's a concern."

"Six miles doesn't seem very far," Fingal said. "I'd have thought somewhere deeper in the country would be better and safer." And he wondered with a start if it would be wise to bring Deirdre to live near

Portsmouth. The vital naval facilities were bound to be the targets of many attacks.

Richard grinned and said, "Marjorie's a tough old bat."

Fingal heard the wistfulness and understood how Richard Wilcoxson was feeling. He also recognised the stiff-upper-lip English reticence that forbade any public shows of emotion.

"Fareham's deep enough in the wilds for her. She's working in the Women's Land Army there . . ."

"Is that what they're calling the group of women who've volunteered to work on farms because the men are at war?" Wallace asked.

"It is," Richard said. "The programme was started in the last war. Apparently today one thousand alone of them work as rat catchers. If you could see my Marjorie when she's riled. Mister Hitler should be grateful she'll be working at home and not going to be in the front line once we get one reestablished." He laughed. "She volunteered on September the fourth, '39." He laughed. "I thought us sailors had some pretty ripe expressions. What she said about the Nazis as she went off to volunteer made me blush."

All the men laughed.

"And . . ." His tones conveyed an admixture of pride and concern. "She wants to be near our only son, Tony . . ."

It was the first time Richard had discussed his family in such detail. Perhaps Fingal and Wilson's leavetaking was having the same effect as when Fingal's boarding school broke up for the summer holidays and friends began confiding secrets they'd kept to themselves all term. Why that had always happened he'd no idea, but it had. He listened.

"He's like you, Wilson. Career Royal Navy."

"A chip off the old block," Tom said.

Richard nodded. "I'm very proud of him. He's just got his first command. A destroyer. Her home port is Portsmouth so when she's in, Marjorie can see as much as possible of him." A frown creased Richard's open brow. "I just wish he wasn't on North Atlantic convoys. The U-boats are starting to take a much greater toll than when *Warspite* was on that run."

"It was mainly the weather we had to fight with," Fingal said.

"I'm sure he'll be fine, Richard," Tom Laverty said. "And, well, I didn't want to take attention away from Fingal and Wilson, but speaking of sons . . ." His grin was vast. He reached into a pocket and pulled out a crumpled telegram. "'Last night'—that was two nights ago—'bouncing baby boy. Stop. Mother child doing well. Stop. Love Carol. End.'"

Three voices in unison said, "Congratulations, Tom."

Tom Laverty grinned. "We're going to call him Barry, after my dad, and I've had a word with the skipper. He's going to ask ABC if there's any chance I might get some compassionate leave."

"We hope you do, Tom," Wilson said.

"Bugger the farewell drinks," Fingal said. "Steward, same again, please. We need to wet the baby's head."

"Aye, aye, sir."

"Barry, " Fingal said. "From the Gaelic. Means fair-haired or sharp like a spear. Has a good ring to it. I'll give Carol a phone call in Bangor, Tom. Congratulate her properly." Fingal tapped his left chest. "Phone number's in my diary."

"Thanks, Fingal."

"And I'll look Mrs. Wilcoxson up as promised," he said. He nodded at his suitcase. "I've got your gift for her in there, Richard."

"Thank you, Fingal. Tell her I miss her . . ."

Fingal had seen the simple, elegant, gold and amethyst necklace Richard had selected for his wife and thought Marjorie Wilcoxson was a lucky woman. His boss might have been reticent about showing his feelings, but his choice of gifts spoke of his love and devotion.

Richard glanced down. "And have a decent pint of bitter for me, will you, and a Melton Mowbray pie if you can get one?"

Fingal laughed. "Consider it done. I might even have two pints."

"And you'll call my folks in Portstewart," Wilson Wallace said.

"Happy to, Wilson—"

Alarm gongs clanged, their brazen voices harsh and strident.

"Christ," said Richard, "another bloody air raid. Come on, everybody."

Bugles blared from the Tannoy.

"Action stations."

All the other officers and the mess stewards took off for their assigned posts. The four friends rose. While Tom headed for the bridge and Wilson for the starboard six-inch battery, Richard looked at Fingal. "The raids usually only last about fifteen minutes. It'll take nearly that long to get to the for'ard medical distribution centre. Hardly worth your while. If you want to chance staying here, the risk of a direct hit is pretty remote and you've got about an inch of armour plate over your head that'll keep you safe from shell splinters."

"Thanks. I'll chance it."

Richard offered his hand and Fingal shook it. "I'll see you next year," he said.

"*Deus Volente,*" Richard said, "God willing," and took off at a trot.

"Excuse me, sir," the mess steward said, "sorry about your last round. If you're staying, will you dog the hatch shut after me, please?"

Fingal nodded, and as soon as the man had left slammed the great clamps shut so that watertight integrity was secured.

He moved to a porthole as the ship began shaking when her anti-aircraft weapons let go. He could see a small portion of the sky pockmarked with shell bursts and two aircraft that hardly seemed to be moving. From here he had no idea of the size of the raid.

The row was overpowering. *Warspite*'s multiple pompoms were yammering away, a staccato tenor section, and the four-inch, high-angle guns boomed in basso counterpoint. Every other ship in the harbour would be firing, doing their best to fill the sky overhead with an umbrella of red-hot steel. It amazed Fingal how any aircraft could survive, but they did.

And given how infrequently ships had been hit on the last cruise, it did seem that perhaps the Italians weren't very good bombers. In his months on *Warspite* he'd probably been in his greatest peril from the Atlantic gales.

The detonation of a load of bombs about six hundred yards away deafened him. He watched the by-now-familiar waterspouts leap up and cascade back as the battleship shook. His first selfish thought was, Please don't let the liberty boat get hit. He was so close to taking the first steps on his journey home he couldn't bear the idea of having something delay his departure. God alone knew when the next convoy would leave for home if he missed this one and he so wanted to see Deirdre.

He remembered sitting with her in a field on Strangford's peaceful shore during his last long leave. The bitter January rains had stopped the previous night and a weak sun was struggling to warm the damp grass and produce some faint signs of evaporation. The smell of its drying was heavy in his nostrils. He'd spread his duffle coat on a mound under a great leafless oak and she'd joined him there, leaning against him, head on his shoulder.

She'd kissed him and said, "You don't have to if you don't want to, but I've read in the papers about the convoys and I know your ship is an escort. Can you tell me what it's like? I want to try to understand."

He'd taken a deep breath and had no difficulty remembering. None whatsoever. "It is cold, horribly cold. We've never experienced anything like it here in Ireland. The last couple of days here were raw, but nothing, nothing like day after day at thirty below. Flesh sticks to metal and sheets of ice form on the decks where spray freezes. The poor bloody sailors spend hours chipping it away because if too much forms I think even a battleship could capsize." He shuddered and she hugged him. "I wish I could have been there to keep you warm," she said, and smiled.

"Christ," he said. "I'd not have wanted you there, much as I love you, but a force-nine gale is a monster. No place for man or beast. Can you imagine the wind and waves battering my great ship? Tossing her about? Combers smashing over the bow and sending spume high into the air? And *Warspite* is huge.

"One evening I'd been on my way to the mess. There were life lines rigged on the outer decks and I had to cross a short open space clinging on for dear life." He nodded at his coat beneath them. "That thing was about as windproof as a sheet of tissue paper. I wanted to get into shelter quick, but I saw something and it stopped me in my tracks.

"A little Flower-class corvette was steaming along beside us, not far away, bashing into the seas. I could hear the crash every time she smashed over the crest of a wave. My heart went out to the poor devils on her, a little ship that displaced less than a thousand tons. She was climbing up one of the biggest rollers I've ever seen . . ."

She closed her eyes and he knew she was concentrating as he struggled to paint a picture with words.

"I clung on to the life line, and I couldn't breathe I was so certain she was going to founder. I had to watch. Then I lost sight of her when my ship and the little escort slipped into separate troughs and she vanished from view. I was certain she was gone."

He shook his head and relived the moment.

"I don't know how long it took, but the corvette reappeared climbing gamely up another wave front and over the crest. Her mast and port-side Carley floats had gone overboard, but like a battered boxer she'd shaken her head, staggered to her feet, and stood again to take all her opponent could throw."

He swallowed. "You'll think I was silly, but I found myself cheering like a madman. God bless our skipper or the admiral or whoever gave the order, but *Warspite* started pumping fuel oil onto the seas to quell the waves. I'm still not sure if the corvette would have survived if we hadn't."

Deirdre, who had been holding her breath, blew it out.

"The courage of the sailors who manned her and the unsung heroes, the merchant sailors. They all deserve medals."

And she'd opened her eyes and kissed him and said, "My poor, poor darling, and those poor men."

He could still taste that kiss, but was torn back to the present by more bombs arriving. He saw them quite clearly in the moments before they hit the water. The surface was a boiling maelstrom thrashed to dirty foam by the explosions and rechurned as the new ones thundered in self-immolation. From where he peered through the glass he could see two dirty smudges that had crawled down the sky's blue canvas like two wavering strokes of an abstract artist's charcoal stick. A single parachute drifted slowly down. At least one poor devil had got out.

The enemy were human too. Fingal knew now he'd never get used to having a patient die, from either side, and wondered, not for the first time, how the parents in Hamburg of a young German sailor called Wilhelm Kauffman had taken the news of his death.

Since Narvik, Fingal had known what it felt like to be fired at, knew how scared he was, of dying, yes, of never seeing her again, or being crippled, and perhaps even more terrifying, of not being able to cope as a naval surgeon.

As he moved away from the porthole there was a ferocious blast and *Warspite*, all 33,670 tons of her, heeled sharply to starboard. He grabbed a table for support as badly stowed cutlery, plates, and glasses clattered and shattered on the sole. He heard the thundering on her upper decks of the water crashing down after the bomb burst. That had been a very "near miss" and again Fingal agonized about the wisdom of having Deirdre meet him in Portsmouth.

He'd seen only too clearly what high explosives and shrapnel could do, and the thought of losing her was unbearable. On the other hand, Richard's wife lived in a village several miles from the docks. Might that be a solution? Find a place for them in the country, because married officers could live off base, ashore as the navy called it, unless they were on duty. Although he'd written to her three days ago, this might be his last chance to get off another letter. Trying to ignore the racket, he sat at the table where he'd left his suitcase, opened it, took out his writing kit and a Waterman's fountain pen. He unscrewed its cap and began to write.

My darling Deirdre girl,

I leave today and before long will be able to hold you and kiss you and tell you how very much I love you. Be patient and the days will pass.

There's something very important that I want to discuss with you. On our last trip to sea, and since we have come back to harbour, the ship has been subjected to shelling and many air raids. I have come through them all unscathed so don't worry, but, and this is what I want to ask you, I just heard that the Jerries have been bombing the place where we are to meet and marry, and my guess is they won't be stopping soon.

Darling, I don't want to risk losing you. I want you to think long and hard before you make up your mind, but as soon as I arrive I will ask you to help me decide what is for the best. Perhaps you would be safer back in Ireland?

I don't know when I'll be able to write again, but until I do I have your photo and your green scarf to remind me every day of

*the most wonderful girl in the world, my Deirdre who I love with
all my heart and all my soul.*

Until we meet again be it in Ulster or England—surely the
censor would let that pass—*I love you Deirdre now and I will
forever,*

Fingal.

He looked up. The all-clear was sounding, the air raid over.

He addressed an envelope, slipped the letter inside, and put it
into his pocket, stowing his writing kit in his suitcase beside his war
diary. He would go and wait near the after-port accommodation ladder for the boat. Smoke his pipe. Stare around the harbour and hope
not to see any sunken ships.

He undogged the hatch and stepped out into bright sunshine,
which already was making the quarterdeck steam as the water
hurled aboard began to evaporate. He thought again of drying grass
under an oak tree on Strangford's shore on a January day . . . and
Deirdre.

A working party under the direction of a petty officer was clearing up seaweed and dead fish. The smell of high explosives and
cordite still fouled the air.

Not far away, he saw a ship's whaler being rowed toward the shore
with a bedraggled-looking figure sitting in the sternsheets clutching
a soaking heap of silk. The bloke on the parachute had survived and
been rescued. Good.

Surgeon Lieutenant Fingal O'Reilly leant on the guard rail puffing happily and watched the liberty boat putting out from the dock.

"Excuse me, sir."

He looked round to see Leading Seaman Henson holding his kit
bag. "Just thought I'd let you know, seeing as how you was interested, like, I'm going on that course on Whale Island. I'm going to

be a gunner." His face was radiant, the gap in his teeth obvious when he smiled.

"Congratulations, Henson," Fingal said. This was great news and any guilt he might have felt for not having had a quiet word with Wilson Wallace to see if he could move things along for Henson was banished. "I'm absolutely delighted. I'm going on a course in Gosport myself."

A short silence hung in the air between them. Under ordinary circumstances two men who had shared the same hardships for nine months would be saying something like, "Maybe we could get together for a pint." But in the Royal Navy, the upper and lower decks did not fraternise. Bloody class system was even more pronounced in the navy. There'd be no chance of making friends with Henson the way Fingal had with a Dublin tugger called Lorcan O'Lunney or a cooper with a bust ankle. Fingal glanced inshore and saw that the liberty boat was halfway to the battleship. "I wish you the very best of luck. I hope it won't be long until you're a petty officer."

"I hope so too, sir, and . . ." The man blushed and lowered his voice. "And then after enough time in rank maybe I could be a warrant gunner, even . . . even one day get a commission like you, sir."

Fingal was touched by the younger man's obvious enthusiasm. "I hope you do, Henson. I hope you do."

"I'll be off then, sir," Henson said, and left.

Good luck to you indeed, Fingal thought, leaning on the rail again and puffing away. Twice in nine months he had gone to war. Now he was going from the war to God knew what in England. But come hell or high water, he'd at least see Deirdre. He knew he was a very different Surgeon Lieutenant O'Reilly than the one who'd put Deirdre into a McCausland taxi outside the Midland Hotel in Belfast on a grey November day last year. How different again would he be after he returned to this ship next year? Time, he was sure, would tell.

42

Laughter and the Love of Friends

O'Reilly stood aside to let Kitty and Sue precede him through the arched doorway and into the hall of the Royal Ulster Yacht Club. Barry, who was a member and knew his way around, was leading the little party.

The hum of conversation rose as they approached the bar, and O'Reilly noticed the oil paintings and black-and-white photos on the hall's oak-panelled walls, most of them massive yachts, each crowned with clouds of white sails. One portrait, of a middle-aged bald-headed man with a vast walrus moustache, caught Fingal's eye. There was something arresting about the man, in his high collar and enormous floppy bow tie so favoured by the Edwardians. His eyes were alive with life and they crinkled at the corners from squinting into the sun and the wind.

"That's Sir Thomas Lipton and those are some of his *Shamrocks,*" said a voice from behind him. "He made five challenges for the America's Cup over a thirty-one-year period but never won. He was a member here."

O'Reilly turned to see John MacNeill, Marquis of Ballybucklebo. "Hello, John," O'Reilly said.

The marquis smiled. "Evening, Fingal. Good to see you. I was sorry you and Kitty couldn't come for the grouse last week."

"We were too, but it couldn't be helped," O'Reilly said. "Duty called, but there's always next year."

"True," the marquis said. "I'd love to chat, but as usual I'm late for a committee meeting. Why don't you and Kitty pop over on Sunday for dinner? Myrna will be home and we're having an up-and-coming young actor from Bangor, Colin Blakely, and his wife, Margaret, and an old school friend of mine who's visiting from England. Six thirty for seven?"

"I'll have to let you know. I'm not sure who's on call, but if Kitty and I are both free we'd love to."

"Grand. Give me a ring. I've got to trot now," and with that the marquis headed up a staircase.

He was never still, the marquis. Rugby committees, yacht club committees, Hospitals' Authority, justice of the peace, encouraging up-and-coming talent like the actor, running his estate. Whoever coined the term "the idle rich" had clearly never met John MacNeill.

O'Reilly went into the bar, where Barry had taken a table for six beside a tall, narrow window with mullioned squares in its upper quarter. Kitty was already seated, taking in the splendid view over the club's rolling lawns, across Seacliff Road and out to the mid-August sun-dappled, dancing waters of Belfast Lough. Gulls wheeled over a herring boat heading up the lough for Ballybucklebo pier. She turned to him, her eyes lively with the delight of the scene before her, and patted the chair beside her. He took her hand and sat.

"Isn't that Jimmy Scott and Hall Campbell's boat, the one we went on when we were mackerel fishing in June?" she said.

"I believe it is." He looked more closely. "Yes, it is. That was a good evening."

The mackerel always ran in June, just as the garden fête and horse show were always in July and the opening day of grouse shooting was always August the twelfth. The seasons in their sequence rolled through Ulster. Next month would see the start of wildfowling, and he and Arthur would get a day at Strangford. O'Reilly loved the reliability of it all.

"Right," said Barry, "my shout. Kitty? Sue? I'm sure you'll be having a pint, Fingal."

"And you'd be right."

Barry took the women's orders and headed for the bar.

"You're looking lovely tonight, Sue," Kitty said.

"Thank you, Kitty," Sue said. Her smile was radiant and her hair in a single long plait shone like burnished copper in the light of the sun that was now moving westward over the Cave Hill behind Belfast. Her engagement ring sparkled on her left ring finger. "This is an important evening and I owe it to Barry to look my best tonight."

"And you've succeeded very well," O'Reilly said. "If I was twenty years younger and wasn't married to the best-looking woman in Ulster . . ." He saw the smile in Kitty's grey eyes and simply let the sentence hang.

"Thank you for the compliment," Sue said, cocked her head, gave a wry grin, and continued, "and if I wasn't madly in love with Barry . . ." She too, let the sentence hang.

"Why, Doctor O'Reilly," Kitty said, "I do believe you're blushing."

O'Reilly harrumphed, pulled out his pipe, and made a business of making sure the tobacco was tamped in before lighting up.

"Here we are," Barry said, "Kitty, G and T; Sue, vodka orange; and two pints." He nipped back to the bar to return a tray then took his seat beside Sue.

"*Sláinte,*" O'Reilly said, took a healthy pull—and almost choked. A young woman was approaching the table. She had black hair with a sheen like a healthy animal's pelt. Her face was strong, with a firm chin and full lips. Slavic cheekbones. Dark eyes with an upward tilt and a glow like the warmth of well-polished mahogany. And she walked with a limp. O'Reilly glanced at Barry, who had his back to the woman—a woman called Patricia Spence.

She stopped and said in a soft contralto, "Excuse me. I hope I'm not intruding . . ."

O'Reilly, as befitted a gentleman, rose. As he did, he saw both Kitty and Sue frown and Barry rocket to his feet as if an electric current had been passed through his chair. His eyes were wide, his mouth open, his face pallid. "Pat—" he finally said. "Patricia?"

"Hello, Barry," she said. "I'm sorry to break in on your party but I was . . ." She gestured vaguely to the room.

O'Reilly's mind went back to Kinky's wedding and he saw himself waiting while Kinky and Archie signed the register. He'd been admiring Sue Nolan and thinking how easily she had filled the void left in Barry's life by a certain Patricia Spence. His gaze went from the self-assured woman standing beside their table to Barry, who was looking decidedly uncomfortable.

Barry composed his features, managed a small smile, and said, "Patricia. Nice to see you. It's been a while." His voice was level. "And you're not intruding." He half-turned from her and nodded to his table. "You've met Doctor and Mrs. O'Reilly, of course."

She nodded. "Of course. I'd heard that you'd been married. County Down's a small place. I wish you every happiness."

"Thank you, Patricia," they said, almost in unison.

"And please," Patricia said, "do sit down, Doctor O'Reilly. Barry."

O'Reilly sat, and wondered what Kitty was feeling behind that polite smile. It had been Patricia's overheard confession to Kitty at a New Year's Eve party last year that had inadvertently informed Barry that his romance was finished.

Barry, who had remained standing, said, "And this is my fiancée, Susan Nolan. Susan, Patricia Spence."

Both said, "How do you do," but whereas Sue's smile was open

Patricia's sat only on her lips. Her dark eyes suddenly looked dull, spiritless.

O'Reilly wondered if she was regretting having left Barry and was still carrying a torch. Did that expression apply when she was the one who had broken things off? He knew he'd always had an overactive imagination, but was it possible she was hoping to resurrect something?

"Patricia's an engineering student at Cambridge," Barry said. "She and I are old friends."

Patricia laughed. "Not really, Barry," she said, not unkindly. "It's only been two years since we first met. Perhaps it just seems longer."

"Yes, I suppose you're right." O'Reilly thought he heard a certain wistfulness in Barry's voice, but no ache. No yearning. "Anyway, are you home for the holidays?" he asked.

She nodded. "Michaelmas term doesn't start until October. I had been planning to work in England over the summer but I found myself homesick by May so I'm back and working in Belfast for the summer."

Patricia paused and O'Reilly could not help his overactive imagination from going into overdrive. "I have an old friend in Newry. And he truly is an old friend, Barry." She laughed. "I've known him since he was in short pants. He keeps his boat on Carlingford Lough and we sailed her up here yesterday." She inclined her head to the bar, where a ginger-haired lad wearing a Donegal tweed sports jacket and a Queen's University tie leant and supped a pint. He glanced over, as if detecting the attention, and waved a hand. "I suppose I'd better be getting back to him." She looked at the two empty chairs.

"I'd like to invite you to join us," Barry said, "but we've got other guests coming."

"I understand," Patricia said. "Nice to see you again, Doctor O'Reilly, Kitty." She looked hard at Sue. "Susan Nolan," she said, "you're a lucky woman. Take good care of him. Good-bye, Barry." And with that she turned and limped back to the bar and her friend.

O'Reilly waited.

"She is as pretty as you told me, Barry," Sue said.

"Did I?"

"Did you what? Tell me that she was pretty? Yes, you did," she said. She was trying to look stern but there was laughter in her eyes. She put one hand on his. "Must have given you quite a shock seeing her."

Barry nodded. The colour was gradually returning to his face.

"It's all right," Sue said, "Barry has told me all about her. We've no secrets, have we, love?"

"Not the one," Barry said. And for the briefest of moments O'Reilly heard Elly Simpkins saying, "I think I'll call you Finn." Some sleeping dogs were better let lie.

"I thought she was looking well. I'm surprised to see her here, in Ireland, I mean. I hope her life is unfolding as she'd like," Barry said. He stared into Sue's eyes. "Mine certainly is."

And she puckered and gave him a mock kiss.

Och, to be young, O'Reilly thought. He looked at Kitty, saw her smile back, and realised that while youth had its attractions you didn't have to be twenty-five to be head over heels. He lifted his pint, looked round the little group, and said, "Here's to us. Who's like us? Damn few—and they're mostly dead."

Everyone drank and laughed. The irreverent old Scottish toast had done what O'Reilly had intended, broken the tension that had been hanging over the table since Patricia's appearance.

A man's familiar voice said, "And I'd've thought it being a Thursday you'd be drinking to 'A bloody war or a sickly season,' Surgeon Commander O'Reilly. You know all the daily naval toasts."

"Dad," Barry said, "Mum." Barry stood up, taking his mother's hand. "Come and sit down."

Tom Laverty, still with a full head of hair, the same blue eyes, and an Australian suntan to match the one he'd acquired in the Med in 1940, pulled out one of the vacant chairs and seated his wife before sitting himself.

"You've met Sue, but not Kitty. Mrs. Kitty O'Reilly, my folks, um . . ."

O'Reilly understood why he was hesitating. Barry had probably never used his parents' Christian names but knew that Mister and Mrs. was too formal.

His father resolved the dilemma. "Tom and Carol," he said. "Good to meet you, Kitty, and if a wealthy young doctor I know is buying, mine's a pink gin." He looked at Fingal. "Old habits die hard and your mother, Barry, will have a gin fizz as usual."

"I got into the habit before the war," Carol Laverty said, "when Tom and I were first married and stationed in Valletta, Malta."

"A brave wheen of years ago now," Tom said. He looked appraisingly at Kitty, whom he was meeting for the first time. "Is that old reprobate being good to you, Kitty?"

"Tom," Carol said, "behave," but she grinned as she spoke. She was tanned like her husband, and her thick blonde hair was streaked with silver. Barry had explained to O'Reilly that because his dad hadn't seen his mother for four years during the war they had decided that the gap between Barry and a brother or sister would be too great. He was an only child. His mother, once he had started school, had turned her not inconsiderable muscial talents into a busy schedule teaching piano.

"Is Fingal good to me, Tom? Very," said Kitty, "and he takes good care of his medical partner too, you'll be glad to hear."

Carol smiled and Tom said, "And I hope that son of ours is looking after you, Sue Nolan."

"Oh, he is," Sue said. "He doesn't always approve of my politics, but otherwise he's a pet."

"I'm very glad to hear it," Carol said. "I always worried about Barry when he was little when Tom was away at sea. Trying to be both mother and father to him."

"You did a great job, Carol. I couldn't ask for a better partner," O'Reilly said, "although Doctor Bradley, who runs a well-woman clinic and helps us out with call, is pretty damn good too."

"Sounds like you're well set up, Fingal," Tom said.

O'Reilly nodded. "I am, Tom."

Barry appeared, bringing the drinks. "I've asked the waitress to bring menus. We can order here and then go through to the dining room when the meals are ready."

"Good idea," said O'Reilly, and his tummy rumbled. "Now," he said, "tell us all about Australia."

Barry said, "It must be so pretty with all of the dear little kangaroos flying about."

"Act one—"

"Just a minute, Fingal," said Carol, holding up her hand. "Barry and I used to play that game when he was a boy. He was always reading. It was the Duchess of Berwick in *Lady Windermere's Fan*, by none other than Oscar Fingal O'Flahertie Wills Wilde, for whom you were named, I do believe."

"Right enough," Fingal said, taking a pull on his pint. He laughed.

"Actually," Carol said, "kangaroos are quite a good size and I've never seen one fly. It's the heat that made the biggest impression on me. And the seasons all upside down. It seemed really odd wearing our swimmies and having Christmas dinner on the beach."

"Swimmies?" Kitty said.

"The Aussies add 'ie' to everything," Tom said. "Beer comes in tinnies, not tins, swimsuits are swimmies, and they do this wonderful outdoor cooking on a thing called a barbeque, but they call it a barbie. Grand people. We really enjoyed ourselves."

"Excuse me, sir," a waitress said, "menus, and who'll look at the wine list?"

"Kitty's amazingly good with wines," O'Reilly said. "If you don't mind, Tom, let her pick."

"Fine by us," Tom said. "It's been a while since you and I dined together, Fingal."

"I'll be back for your orders," the waitress said, and left.

"It has, but I still remember those dinners at the Cecil in Alexandria during the war so clearly." O'Reilly turned to Sue. "You know I just missed serving with your dad on *Warspite*. He was arriving just as I was leaving the ship in 1940 and he'd moved on by the time I got back to her in '41."

"Fingal was heading back to Blighty on a troopship to learn to be an anaesthetist . . ."

O'Reilly hoped that Tom would be tactful enough not to say, "and to get married." Kitty was well aware of that part of O'Reilly's past, but there was no need to plough the same furrow twice.

"I knew your dad, Sue," Tom said, "but he was only on *Warspite* for a few months and we weren't close. What's he up to now?"

"Back running the farm near Broughshane. We'll have to have you and Mrs. Laverty over for dinner," Sue said.

"We'd love to come," Tom said, "now we're back from Australia and getting used to being home again."

Carol said, "We came back from Australia on the *Canberra*—"

"Built here in Belfast," Sue said.

"So was the *Titanic*," Barry said, and everybody laughed. Ulsterfolk were noted for their black humour.

"—and I'll bet you much more quickly than you did from Egypt in wartime, Fingal."

"*Canberra* makes nearly thirty knots," Tom said.

"So did our cruisers at Calabria," Fingal said, for a second seeing the flash and flame as *Warspite*'s shell hit the Italian battlewagon *Giulio Cesare*.

"They did," Tom said, "but they weren't able to keep that up for long. We got from Australia to the U.K. in twenty-four days nonstop."

"I think," said Sue, "that's pretty impressive, but I reckon these new jet airliners will put the liners out of business soon."

"Kitty and I are going to be taking flights from Belfast airport to Heathrow and on to Barcelona next month, but we'll be flying with British European Airways on a turboprop Vickers Viscount," O'Reilly said.

"And Jenny and I will look after the shop," Barry said. "You two have a good time."

"We will," said O'Reilly, catching Kitty's eye. "We're going to stroll down the Ramblas, eat *boquerones* and *gueldes* in a seaside restaurant called *El Crajeco Loco*, The Crazy Crab, and see an old friend of Kitty's who lives near there."

"We are," she said, "and I'm really looking forward to it. I haven't seen her for thirty years."

"And it'll take no time to get there by air," said O'Reilly, not wishing to go into details about Kitty's old friend. "I wish there'd been an airline from Egypt to back home in 1940. It took my troopship in convoy more than two months just to go from Port Said through the Canal, and on to Liverpool."

"And if we don't order soon," Barry said, "it'll take nearly as long to get our dinner. They're busy tonight." He looked directly at O'Reilly. "And my principal can get a tad tetchy if we don't feed him regularly."

"Less of your lip, Laverty," O'Reilly said with a grin, and along with the others began to read his menu. He made his choice, took a pull on his pint, and let his thoughts roam. It certainly had been an interesting voyage home, his three months in Portsmouth were well spent learning more of the trade of a seagoing doctor in wartime. And Deirdre. Soft, lovely Deirdre. He sighed. One day that whole story must be told, but, his tummy rumbled again, not tonight. He was in good company, grand surroundings—and although he could eat a horse, the Chateaubriand on the menu looked more appetising, done medium rare with corn on the cob and chips.

Doctor Fingal Flahertie O'Reilly looked round at Kitty and his friends, the two new ones, and a reunion of sorts with two old ones. Next month he had a full-scale reunion to look forward to with his old classmates of 1931–36 from the School of Physic at Trinity College Dublin.

He puffed his pipe, took another pull on his pint, and grinned to himself. Tonight he was as content a man as any man could be.

Afterword

by Mrs. Maureen "Kinky" Auchinleck,
until lately Kincaid, née O'Hanlon

Welcome back, and now it's not to my kitchen at Number One, Main Street, but to my cosy parlour in my own home. Archie's out with his son, Rory, who's all better now from that tropical disease, so, and I'm doing what I promised I'd do for Doctor O'Reilly. Here are five more of my recipes.

I'm starting with one for marmalade because you'll need it to make both my marmalade pudding and my very easy boiled fruitcake.

I did miss marmalade so during the war, but we had the rationing here in Ulster just like they did in Britain. You could only have so much sugar, tea, jam, biscuits, and a whole host of other things and you did need a coupon book to get them. And you couldn't get oranges for love nor money and I did always make my own marmalade. Doctor O'Reilly wants his Frank Cooper's, but och, shouldn't he have one or two little weaknesses?

And some of the stuff you'd to make do with in wartime? Powdered eggs that tasted like yellow sawdust and that awful tinned corned beef that came from some country in South America. And I'll say no more about Spam, so.

It was a very good thing that Ballybucklebo was in the country. Sure couldn't I always get fresh vegetables and eggs and chickens for

Doctor Flanagan? I've put a recipe in here for chicken breasts that I hope you'll try.

And there's one thing that will surprise you. I never thought a good Cork woman would be making one of those curries, but himself learned about one from some foreign troops in Egypt. He persuaded me to try making it after he came back here when the war was over. It came as a surprise, but I found it tasty and you'll never believe what's in it. Corned beef out of a can, so. Still as my ma, God rest her, used to say, "You'll never know if a strange thing's any good unless you do try it," and do you know? She was right.

So here you are, five more recipes. I do hope you enjoy them all.

ORANGE MARMALADE

900 g / 2 lbs Seville oranges

1 lemon

2¼ L / 4 pints water

1.8 kg / 4 lbs sugar

A knob of butter

8 x 250 mL preserving jars and a large, heavy-bottomed preserving pan (not aluminum)

A muslin or cheesecloth jelly bag

Cut the oranges and lemon in half and squeeze the juice into the pan with the water.

Put any pips and pith from the orange halves into the jelly bag and set aside for the moment in a small dish. Cut the oranges into thin shreds and add any pith that comes away to the jelly bag. (The pips and pith contain pectin, which helps the jam to set.)

Add the cut oranges to the water, tie up the jelly bag, and add to the water-and-orange mixture.

Simmer gently, uncovered, for about two hours until the orange peel has softened. Remove the jelly bag and squeeze it into the pan, leaving the pips behind in the bag.

Now add the sugar gradually, stirring as you go, until the sugar has dissolved. If you add a knob of butter at this stage it will stop the marmalade foaming. Now bring it to the boil and cook for about fifteen minutes. If you have a sugar thermometer, the temperature should read 220°F. This is the setting point for jams. Or you can test for setting by dropping a small blob on a cold plate, letting it cool, and seeing if the jam will wrinkle when you push it with your finger. If it does not, then just boil for a little longer and try again.

Heat the washed jars in a hot oven to sterilise them, and leave the marmalade to cool before pouring it into the hot jars. Letting the marmalade cool allows the fruit to be more evenly distributed throughout the jar and not remain at the top. Put covers on as soon as you can handle the jars without burning yourself.

Very Easy Boiled Fruitcake

450 g / 1 lb. dried fruit (raisins, sultanas, etc.)
225 g / 8 oz. sugar
240 mL / ½ pint of warm tea
1 egg
2 tablespoons marmalade
220 g / 8 oz. plain flour
220 g / 8 oz. wheatmeal flour
4 level teaspoons baking powder

Put fruit, sugar, and tea in a bowl and leave to soak overnight.

Next day prepare two 1 lb. baking tins by greasing and flouring them. Turn the oven to 325°F / 160°C.

Stir the egg and marmalade into the fruit mixture, then the flour and baking powder, and divide the mixture between the two tins. Bake in the oven for 1½ hours, until well risen. Test by pressing gently with a finger. If cooked, the cake should spring back and have begun to shrink from the sides of the tin. Cool on a wire rack and serve sliced with butter.

These keep well in an airtight tin for up to four weeks, or they would if Aggie Arbuthnot did not have such an acute sense of smell and know when I had just baked them. Still it's nice to sit down and have a good yarn and a cup of tea with friends, so.

MARMALADE PUDDING

250 g / 9 oz. butter or good-quality margarine
75 g / 2½ oz. fine white sugar
75 g / 2½ oz. brown sugar
150 g / 5 oz. marmalade
225 g / 8 oz. plain flour
½ teaspoon bicarbonate of soda
1 teaspoon baking powder
4 eggs
juice and rind from one orange

Preheat the oven to 180°C / 350°F and butter an ovenproof dish about 10" × 10".

Cream the butter and sugar and beat in the marmalade. Add the dry ingredients and the eggs followed by half the orange juice and grated rind. (Save a little to glaze the pudding top when cooked). Put the mixture into the buttered dish and smooth the top.

Bake in the oven until top is light brown and pudding has risen. This takes about 40 minutes but keep a careful eye on it.

When the pudding is ready brush the top with the remaining juice mixture and serve with custard or cream.

IRISH COUNTRY CHICKEN BREASTS

4 chicken breasts
30 g / 1 oz. butter
1 cup white bread crumbs
5 tablespoons / ⅓ cup white wine
juice of half a lemon
240 mL /1 cup cream
3 egg yolks
75 g / 2½ oz. grated cheddar cheese
salt and pepper

Salt the chicken breasts and cook them in butter in a skillet or fry pan over a medium heat until just lightly coloured on both sides. This takes about 20 minutes. Put them, arranged side by side, in a greased, ovenproof dish. In the butter remaining in the pan cook the bread crumbs until they are golden but not too brown. Set to one side and deglaze the pan with the white wine and the lemon juice until it has reduced to about half its volume. Leave in the pan until you are ready to use it.

Now beat the cream, egg yolks, cheese, and seasonings. Add the cheese and the deglazing liquid from the pan and pour over the chicken breasts and finish by sprinkling the crumbs over the top.

Bake at 400°F / 200°C for about 25 minutes until the top is brown and the egg mixture is firm.

Serve with new potatoes and green peas or beans.

CORNED BEEF CURRY

1 tablespoon vegetable or olive oil

1 onion

2 carrots, chopped small

1 potato or small turnip, cubed

4 garlic cloves, crushed

1 piece of fresh ginger, grated (size about 1")

1 red chili, chopped, with seeds removed

½ small green chili, chopped, with seeds removed

1 teaspoon ground coriander

1 teaspoon ground cumin

1 teaspoon garam masala

freshly milled black pepper

500 mL vegetable stock

1 400 mL tin chopped tomatoes

½ cup raisins

1 can Fray Bentos corned beef

1 cup pineapple

1 small bunch fresh coriander, chopped (about 2 tablespoonfuls)

½ cup / 4 oz. sour cream

Heat the oil in a large pan. Gently sweat the prepared vegetables in the hot oil for five minutes. Add the garlic, ginger, chilis, and spices, then the stock, tomatoes, and raisins. Cook for about 20 minutes and add the cubed corned beef, pineapple, and chopped fresh coriander. Cook through to heat the corned beef and finish by stirring in the sour cream.

Serve with cooked rice.

Author's Note

This is book nine in the series, which started with *An Irish Country Doctor*, a work set in Ulster in the 1960s. In book six, a *Dublin Student Doctor*, I began to tell the story of Doctor Fingal Flahertie O'Reilly, one of the central characters, as a young man while still following his current adventures as an established GP. Two storylines move back and forth over thirty years between the quiet village of Ballybucklebo in the 1960s and the bustle of Dublin in the 1930s. I had hoped in that work to take him from medical school to the end of the Second World War. However, I ran out of space shortly after young Doctor O'Reilly qualified from Trinity College Dublin in 1936.

Fingal O'Reilly, Irish Doctor, the eighth book in the series, once more moved between the '30s and '60s. That structure was chosen because readers had taken Ballybucklebo to heart and wanted to follow the goings-on there. They were also adamant that they needed to find out what further befell Doctor Fingal Flahertie O'Reilly as a young man. Once again, I was only able to pursue his earlier adventures as a GP for one year after his qualification.

Many, many readers wanted to know about O'Reilly's first marriage in 1940 to Nurse Deirdre Mawhinney and about his war service on a remarkable British battleship, HMS *Warspite*. Naturally, the ongoing developments in the Ballybucklebo of the 1960s needed to be followed as well, so here you have *An Irish Doctor in Peace and at War,* following the time-jumping form of its predecessors. I hope you have enjoyed it.

Like its forebears it needs a little explaining. This note aims to do four things: tell you about my interest in *Warspite,* thank people for their enormous help in developing that story, apologise for an omission from the tale, and make you all a solemn promise.

So here we go.

I was born in 1941 shortly after Hitler invaded Russia, and Britain and her empire no longer stood alone in the midst of World War II. My father, Doctor James "Jimmy" Taylor, was an Ulsterman and hence not liable for call-up. He had nevertheless, in 1939, volunteered for the Royal Air Force Volunteer Reserve and was initially stationed in England before my birth. He later served overseas in, among other places, Egypt, which is germane to some of this book. He was demobilised with the rank of Squadron Leader (Medical) in 1946. He had been mentioned in despatches. He maintained an abiding interest in the history of World War II.

We lived in a small house by the Bangor seaside (see etching by Dorothy Tinman in *Country Wedding*). My father stored his books in my bedroom. It is one of the reasons I am a writer. I devoured them all. It is no accident that my first published fiction was a collection of short stories, *Only Wounded: Ulster Stories,* to be republished in June 2015. After falling in love with the collected works of W. Somerset Maugham and Anton Chekov's short stories, how could I not try to emulate the masters?

A Sailor's Odyssey by Admiral of the Fleet Viscount Cunningham of Hyndhope was one tome among many that I discovered in my teens. It was in this book that I first read of the admiral's flagship in the Mediterranean, HMS *Warspite.* I read the work when I was a member of the naval section of my school's combined cadet force, a kind of ROTC for schoolboys, and was considering a naval career.

Although I can still tie a sheepshank and a bowline and signal with semaphore flags, I confess that since the invention of GPS my skills with a sextant are now rusty. My reading about *Warspite* served to reawaken my interest in battleships, which had first been stimulated by my father's hands-on approach for an even younger me.

Royal Naval vessels in the pre- and postwar periods often anchored in Bangor Bay, and opened themselves to the public. It was a proud boast of my father's that he had, as a youth, explored the mighty battlecruiser HMS *Hood*. In 1951, I held Dad's hand when we were taken out in Jimmy Scott's fishing boat to visit the great ship HMS *King George V*. She was one of the warships that in May 1941 sank the German *Bismarck*, which three days earlier had destroyed the *Hood*. I was born three months later in that very year.

My father, for a souvenir of my visit to *KGV*, as she was fondly called, bought me a blue triangular pennant with KGV and her crest and motto on it. Until we moved house in the year of my twenty-first birthday, the flag hung proudly on my bedroom wall.

So are seeds sown.

After qualifying as a physician and beginning specialty training, I supplemented my salary by moonlighting for country GPs, one of whom was Doctor Ken Kennedy. He had two charming daughters, Phillippa and Julia, and a son, Kenneth William Kennedy, a famous Irish rugby football international. The son, KW, had been a classmate of mine at both grammar school and medical school.

When I started writing humour columns about Doctor Fingal Flahertie O'Reilly (published earlier this year in a collected volume, *The Wily O'Reilly*), the seeds that had been planted in my boyhood germinated. By chance, like my father and my father's contemporary and friend Doctor Ken Kennedy, Fingal O'Reilly had seen wartime service. The father had been a surgeon lieutenant on—where else, but on the ship Admiral Cunningham had called "The Grand Old Lady?"—*Warspite*. Her photograph hung in Doctor Kennedy's home, as a similar one would come to hang at Number One, Main Street, Ballybucklebo.

Now, if O'Reilly's story of his time on her was going to be told, it was incumbent upon me to tell it accurately. To that end on matters naval I consulted the following volumes:

A Sailor's Odyssey by Admiral of the Fleet Viscount Cunningham of Hyndhope. As an aside, although it removes a certain amount of authenticity, for more easy understanding of time I have used the convention Lord Hyndhope used in his work. Time is expressed in civilian terms as, for example, six P.M., not eighteen hundred hours. I hope this makes it simpler for those unfamiliar with the twenty-four-hour clock.

Warspite by Iain Ballantyne.

Battleship Sailors by Harry Plevy.

Battleship Warspite by V. E. Tarant.

The Battleship Warspite by Ross Watton, which contains her marine architectural drawings. Her sick bay really was on the main deck and the wardroom on the upper deck aft on the port side.

In addition, I was delighted to be presented with an accurate scale model of the great ship by my longstanding friends Doctors David and Sharon Mortimer. By the courtesy of Doctor Roger Maltby, I was put in touch with Surgeon Lieutenant-Commander Mike Inman, RD, RNR, who read and corrected my naval descriptions. The accuracy is his, the mistakes mine.

While on the subject of accuracy, Fingal wonders, in July 1940, about the location of the Spitfire that his mother and Lady Ballybucklebo's fund had presented to 602 Squadron. Clearly that specific aircraft is fictional, but 602 (City of Glasgow) Squadron, Royal Auxiliary Air Force, was very real. Under the command of Squadron Leader "Sandy" Johnstone, they were with 13 Group in Scotland at Drem Airfield. In August 1940, 602 moved south to Westhampnett, a field in the tactical area controlled by 11 Group, which bore the brunt of the aerial combat. The City of Glasgow Spitfires fought with distinction throughout the thick of the Battle of Britain.

On matters naval I have, when necessary, referred to some real-life figures by name. It is correct that Captain D. B. Fisher CBE relieved Captain Victor Crutchley VC as *Warspite*'s commanding officer on April 27, 1940. Her medical branch and many of her other officers and men are all figments of my imagination, with one remarkable exception from another actual ship.

Doctor Patrick Steptoe was in fact a real person and *was* the medical officer of HMS *Hereward* in 1940–41. After the war, he became a pioneer in gynaecological laparoscopy. In concert with the late Professor Sir Robert Edwards, Nobel Laureate, he was half of the team that produced the world's first "test tube" baby in 1978. In 2010, Sir Robert was awarded the Nobel Prize for his work. Regrettably, the honour is not awarded posthumously. Patrick Steptoe died in 1988 and therefore was not eligible for consideration. Patrick taught me laparoscopy in 1969 and I was proud to consider him both valued colleague and dear friend. In 1987–89 I worked with him and Bob Edwards at Bourn Hall Clinic near Cambridge, England. He was a truly great man and my including him here is in tribute to his memory.

I have taken two other liberties. HMS *Touareg,* nominally one of the Tribal class of twenty-six destroyers, never existed. She too, has been conjured up for dramatic purposes. Her description conforms to that of her real sisters, one of which, HMCS *Haida,* is still afloat in Hamilton, Ontario, as a naval museum. HMS *Vixen,* an old 1918 V-and-W-class destroyer, is also a figment of my imagination.

I have striven for geographical accuracy. Describing settings in Ireland was not difficult. I lived there for thirty years and went back from 2007–10. My knowledge of Greenock and the River Clyde and the anchorage Tail of the Bank, and Glasgow area hospitals is also drawn from my own memory. As a very young doctor, I took six months training at a maternity hospital in nearby Paisley. The unit was affiliated with the Royal Alexandra Infirmary.

Scenes set ashore in Alexandria, Egypt, owe a great deal to an old photograph album of my father's containing pictures he took with a Kodak Brownie during his service in Egypt. Further details were gleaned from *A Midshipman's War: A Young Man in the Mediterranean Naval War 1941–43* by Frank Wade, a fellow Canadian. But for the efforts of our Saltspring librarian, Karen Hudson, I would not have been aware of this invaluable source. She was indefatigable in contacting her friend Lieutenant-Commander Mark Cunningham, RCN. He in turn sought the advice of Sheryl Irwin, librarian at the naval base at Esquimault, British Columbia. Thank you all three.

I hope that explains my interest in *Warspite* and how, to the best of my ability, the authenticity of that part of the book was established.

I also said I had to make an apology. I have received numerous letters asking for information about O'Reilly's first marriage and how he came to be widowed. Honestly, this book was supposed to answer both of those questions, but . . .

But, the road to hell is paved with good intentions, at least so I am told by no lesser authorities than Saint Bernard of Clairvaux (c. 1150), Samuel Johnson, Samuel Taylor Coleridge, Samuel Beckett, Søren Kierkegaard, and Karl Marx. Once more I found myself becoming intrigued with the things O'Reilly and company were getting up to—and ran out of space. Sorry. But—and it's another big but—I also said I will make you all a solemn promise.

The author's note is always the last thing written when a novel is finished, and at the end of this paragraph (after proofreading, of course) the manuscript will be going off to my agent. I will be going off on holiday, but the day after I return, I will start work on book ten, as yet untitled, and in it the story of Fingal O'Reilly and Deirdre Mawhinney will be concluded. Honest to God, it will, so it will— and from an Ulsterman there is no more binding oath.

Until then my very best wishes.

PATRICK TAYLOR
Saltspring Island
Canada
August 2013

GLOSSARY

I have in all the previous Irish Country novels provided a glossary to help the reader who is unfamiliar with the vagaries of the Queen's English as it may be spoken by the majority of people in Ulster. This is a regional dialect akin to English as spoken in Yorkshire or on Tyneside. It is not Ulster-Scots, which is claimed to be a distinct language in its own right. I confess I am not a speaker.

Today in Ulster (but not in 1939–40 and 1966 when this book is set) official signs are written in English, Irish, and Ulster-Scots. The washroom sign would read Toilets, *Leithris*, and *Cludgies*.

I hope what follows here will enhance your enjoyment of the work, although, I am afraid, it will not improve your command of Ulster-Scots.

acting the lig: Behaving like an idiot.
aluminium: Aluminum.
amadán: *Irish.* Pronounced "omadawn." Idiot.
anyroad: Anyway.
arse: Backside. (Impolite.)
at himself/not at himself: He's feeling well/not feeling well.
away off (and feel your head/and chase yourself): Don't be stupid.
aye certainly: Of course, or naturally.

back to porridge: Returning from something extraordinary to the humdrum daily round.

bang his/her drum about: Go on at length about a pet subject.

banjaxed: Ruined or smashed.

barmbrack: Speckled bread. (See Mrs. Kinkaid's recipe, *An Irish Country Doctor.*)

been here before: Your wisdom is attributable to the fact that you have already lived a full life and have been reincarnated.

beezer: First-rate.

bettered myself: I rose in the world by my own exertions.

biscakes: Biscuits (cookies).

bisticks: Biscuits (cookies).

bit the head off: Gave someone a severe verbal chastisement.

blether/och, blether: Talk, often inconsequential/expression of annoyance or disgust.

bletherskite: One who continually talks trivial rubbish.

blue buggery: Very, very badly.

bollix: Testicles. (Impolite.)

bollixed: Wrecked.

bonnet: Hood of a car.

boot: Trunk of a car.

bottle: *Naval.* Reprimand.

boys-a-dear or boys-a-boy: Expression of amazement.

brave: Very.

British Legion: Fraternal organisation for ex-servicemen (veterans).

brogue: a) A kind of low-heeled shoe (from the Irish *bróg*) with decorative perforations on the uppers, originally to allow water to drain out. b) The musical inflection given to English when spoken by an Irish person.

bull in a china shop/at a gate: Thrashing about violently without forethought and causing damage/charging headlong at something.

bully beef: Salted, preserved, and canned beef. Also known as corned beef (the salt came in units called "corns"). That used by the navy was usually produced by Fray Bentos of Uruguay. My mother made a marvellous corned beef curry that my father (RAF) had learned from Indian soldiers in World War II. It is not the recipe given by Kinky here.

camogie: A stick-and-ball team game akin to hurling, but played by women.

candy apples: Apples dipped in caramel glaze.

candy floss: Cotton candy.

can't for toffee: Is totally inept.

chemist: Pharamacist.

chips: French fries.

chissler: Child.

clap: Cow shit.

clatter: Indeterminate number. See also **wheen**. The size of the number can be enhanced by adding **brave** or **powerful** as a precedent to either. As an excercise, try to imagine the numerical difference between a **brave clatter** and a **powerful wheen** of **spuds**.

cod/codding: To fool/fooling.

Colonel Blimp: David Low's British cartoon character with pompous, irrational, jingoistic attitudes, named for the barrage balloon officially described as "Balloon B-limp."

come on, on in: The second "on" is deliberate, not a typographical error.

corker: Very special.

course: From the ancient sport of coursing, where game is started by dogs and pursued by the hunters who run after the dogs.

cracker: Exceptional.

crayture: Creature, critter.

crick: Sprain.

cross (as two sticks): Angry (very angry).

cruibín: Pickled pig's trotter eaten cold with vinegar.

cup of tea/scald in your hand: An informal cup of tea, as opposed to tea that was synonymous with the main evening meal (dinner).

currency: In 1965, prior to decimalization, sterling was the currency of the United Kingdom, of which Northern Ireland was a part. The unit was the **pound** (quid), which contained twenty **shillings** (bob), each made of twelve **pennies** (pence), thus there were 240 pennies in a pound. Coins and notes of combined or lesser or greater denominations were in circulation, often referred to by slang or archaic terms: **farthing** (four to the penny), **halfpenny** (two to the penny), **threepenny** piece (thruppeny bit), **sixpenny** piece (tanner), **two shillings** piece (florin), **two shillings and sixpence piece** (half a crown), **ten-shilling note** (ten-bob note), **guinea** coin worth one pound and one shilling, **five-pound** note (fiver). In 1965 one pound bought nearly three U.S. dollars.

dander: Short walk, or literally, horse dandruff.

dar dar: Noise made by little Ulster boys in imitation of revolver fire.

dead/dead on: Very/absolutely right or perfectly.

desperate: Terrible.

dig with the left (foot): A pejorative remark made about Catholics by Protestants.

do-re-mi: Tonic sol-fa scale, but meaning "dough" as in money.

dote: (v.) To adore. (n.) Something adorable.

dozer/no dozer: Stupid person/clever person.

drumlin: From the Irish *dromín* (little ridge). Small rounded hills caused by the last ice age. There are so many in County Down that the place has been described as looking like a basket of green eggs.

dulse: A seaweed that when dried is used like chewing gum.

duncher: Cloth cap, usually tweed.

eejit/buck eejit: Idiot/complete idiot.

fair play: Good for you.

feck (and variations): Corruption of "fuck." For a full discussion of its usage see author's note in *A Dublin Student Doctor*. It is not so much sprinkled into Dublin conversations as shovelled in wholesale, and also used in Ulster. Its scatalogical shock value is now so debased that it is no more offensive than "like" larded into teenagers' chat. Now available at reputable bookstores is the *Feckin' Book of Irish*—a series of ten books by Murphy and O'Dea.

ferocious: Extreme.

fight my own corner: Defend (usually verbally) my position.

fillums: Ordinarily I avoid using phonetic spelling, but there is no way round it if I am to render the Ulster propensity for inserting the extra syllable "um" into films, movies.

flex: Electrical plug-in cord.

footer: Fiddle about with.

foundered: Frozen.

gag: Joke or funny situation. Applied to a person, humourist.

gander: Look-see.

glipe/great glipe: Stupid/very stupid person.

go away with you: Don't be silly.

gobshite: Literally, dried nasal mucus. Used pejoratively about a person.

good man-ma-da: Literally, "good man my father." Good for you, a term of approval.

grilled: Broiled.

gurning: Whingeing.

gurrier: Street urchin, but often used pejoratively about anyone.

ham-fisted: Clumsy.

hammer and tongs: Fighting fiercely.

heart of corn: Very good-natured.

headsplitter: Hangover.

heifer: Young cow before her first breeding.

hirple: Stagger.

HMS: His Majesty's Ship.

hobbyhorse shite: Literally, sawdust. To have a head full is to be extremely obtuse.

hoovering: Generic use of the name of a brand of vacuum cleaner, to denote using any vacuum cleaner.

houl' your wheest: Hold your tongue.

how's about you?: How are you?

humdinger: Something exceptional.

I doubt: I believe, if accompanied by a negative. "I doubt we'll no see him the night" means I believe we'll not see him. Otherwise, standard English meaning.

I'm yer man: I agree and will cooperate fully.

in the stable: Of a drink in a pub, paid for but not yet poured.

Jezebel: A scheming, promiscuous, fallen woman, named after the biblical (II Kings) wife of Ahab.

Job's comforter: *Biblical.* Someone whose well-meaning advice in time of adversity makes matters worse.

juked: Dodged.

kilter: Alignment.

learned: Ulsterese is peculiar in often reversing the meanings of words. "The teacher learned the child," or "She borrowed [meaning loaned] me a cup of sugar." "Reach [meaning pass] me **thon yoke**."

lip: Cheekiness.

laugh like a drain: Be consumed with mirth.

length and breadth of it: All the details.

let the hare sit: Leave the matter alone.

liltie: Irish whirling dervish.

Lios na gCon: *Irish.* Pronounced "lish na gun." Hill fort of the hound.

lucht siuil: *Irish.* Pronounced "luck shul." Literally "the walking people." Gypsies, also known as travelling people or travellers.

Lughnasadh: *Irish*. Pronounced "loonasa." Harvest festival celebrated on the Sunday closest to August 1 to honour one of the old
gods, Lugh ("loo") of the Long Hand.

madder than a wet hen: Very angry.

marmalize: Cause great physical damage and pain.

midder: Colloquial medical term for midwifery, the art and science
of dealing with pregnancy and childbirth, now superseded medically by the term "obstetrics."

mitch: Either play truant or steal.

more power to your wheel: Words of encouragement akin to
"The very best of luck."

muirnín: *Irish*. Pronounced "moornyeen." Darling.

my/your/his shout: My/your/his turn to pay for the drinks.

neat: Of a drink of **spirits**, straight up.

no harm til you, but: I do not mean to cause you any offence—but
you are absolutely wrong.

no slouch: Very good at, a "slouch" being a useless person.

no sweat: Nothing to worry about.

not at him/herself: Unwell.

offside: Out of the line of fire or out of sight.

on the pour: Of a pint of Guinness. There is an art to building a
good pint of Guinness and it can take several minutes.

ould hand: Old friend.

oxter/oxtercog: Armpit/help walk by draping an individual's arm
over one's shoulder.

palaver: Useless talk.

peely-wally: Scots, but used in Ulster. Under the weather. Feeling
unwell.

petrol: Gasoline.

piece: Bread and spread, as in "jam piece."

power/powerful: Very strong/a lot.

pupil: In Ireland and Britain "student" was reserved for those attending university. Schoolchildren were referred to as "pupils," nor did graduation occur until after the granting of a university degree.

quare: Ulster and Dublin pronunciation of "queer," meaning "very" or "strange."

rag order: Dublin slang for untidily dressed and coiffed.

rapscallion: Mischief maker.

rear: Of a child. Bring up.

regius professor: Regius professorships were created by the British monarchs at the old universities of the United Kingdom. Queen Victoria granted the Trinity College professorship in surgery in 1868.

restful on the eye: Usually of a woman. Good-looking.

right enough?: Is that a fact?

rightly: Very well.

RMS: Royal Mail Ship.

ructions: Violent argument.

said a mouthful: Hit the nail on the head. Are absolutely right.

Sassenach: Gaelic term originally applied to Saxons, now used, usually in a bantering fashion, by the Scots and Irish to mean "English."

saving your presence: I am about to insult you, but please don't be offended.

scared skinny: Terrified.

scrip': Script, short for "prescription."

see him/her?: Emphatic way of drawing attention to the person in question even if they are not physically present.

shenanigans: Carryings-on.

shufti: Military slang, from the Arabic. Look-see.

sick line: Medical certificate of illness allowing a patient to collect sickness benefit.

skinful: One of the 2,660 synonyms or expressions for "drunk." (*Dickson's Word Treasury*, 1982)

skitters: Diahorrea.

skivers: Probably derived from "scurvy." No-good wastrels.

sláinte: *Irish.* Pronounced "slawntuh." Cheers, your health.

so I am/he is/it's not: An addition at the end of a sentence for emphasis.

spirits: Of drink, any distilled liquor.

spud: Potato. Also a nickname for anyone called Murphy.

sticking the pace: Showing no signs of ageing, fatigue, or decay.

sting: Hurt.

stocious: See **skinful.**

stone: All measurements in Ireland until decimalision were Imperial. One stone = fourteen pounds, 20 fluid ounces = one pint.

stoon: Sudden shooting pain.

sound/sound man: Good/good, trustworthy man.

surgery: Where a GP saw ambulatory patients. The equivalent of a North American "office." Specialists worked in "rooms."

swinging the lead: Malingering.

take the strunts: Become angry or sulk.

tanned: Spanked. As in "getting his arse tanned."

targe: Woman with a very sharp tongue, a scold.

terrace: Row housing, but not just for the working class. Some of the most expensive accomodation in Dublin is found in terraces in Merrion Square, akin to low rise rows of attached townhouses.

that there/them there: That/them with emphasis.

the day: Today.

the hat: Foreman, so called because his badge of office was a bowler (derby) hat.

the wee man: The devil.

thole: Put up with. A reader, Miss D. Williams, wrote to me to say it was etymologically from the Old English *tholian,* to suffer. She remarked that her first encounter with the word was in a fourteenth-century prayer.

thon/thonder: That/over there.

thran: Bloody-minded.

til: To.

'til: Until.

to beat Bannagher: Explanation unknown, but means exceptionally.

tongue's hanging out: Very thirsty.

tousling: Beating up, either verbally or physically.

townland: Mediaeval administrative district encompassing a village and the surrounding farms and wasteland.

wasters: No-good wastrels.

wean: Pronounced "wane." Little one.

wee turn: Sudden illness, usually not serious, or used euphemistically to pretend it wasn't serious.

wet the baby's head: Have a drink to celebrate a birth.

wheeker: Terrific.

wheen: An indeterminate but reasonably large number.

yellow man: A crunchy honeycomb toffee associated with Ballycastle, Northern Ireland.

yoke: Thing. Often used if the speaker is unsure of the exact nature of the object in question.

you know: Verbal punctuation often used when the person being addressed could not possibly be in possession of the information.

your man: Someone either whose name is not known, "Your man over there? Who is he?" or someone known to all, "Your man, Van Morrison."

youse: Plural of "you."

zizz: Forces slang. Nap.

Turn the page for a sneak peek at
the next novel in the Irish Country series

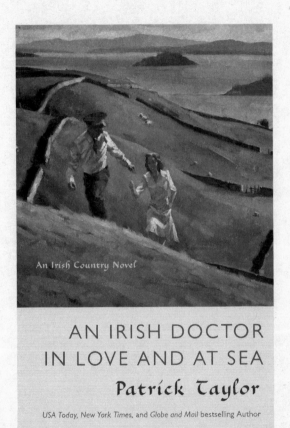

An Irish Country Novel

AN IRISH DOCTOR
IN LOVE AND AT SEA
Patrick Taylor

USA Today, New York Times, and Globe and Mail bestselling Author

Available October 2015

1

A Party in a Parlour

The Dublin coddle had been cooked to perfection and Doctor Fingal Flahertie O'Reilly had not been able to resist the sherry trifle for dessert.

"That was very good," he said, looking wistfully at the few smears of cream, custard, and strawberry jam on his otherwise empty plate. "I think I'll have a second . . ."

Kitty O'Reilly grinned. "Fingal, my love, you're already having a bit of difficulty getting into your gear. Don't forget, we have a formal black tie dinner tonight. You want to look your best for me, don't you?"

"Of course," he said. "For you? Anything." And while he seemed to say it in jest, one look into those amber-flecked grey eyes told him that inside he really meant it. He beckoned to the waitress in the familiar little restaurant on Dublin's Leeson Street, asked her for the bill, paid, then rose and helped Kitty to her feet. "How do you fancy a stroll, bit of a leg stretch? Work our lunches down? It's not too far back to the Shelbourne Hotel even if we go the long way round."

"Love it," she said, "for old times' sake." She took and squeezed his hand. "Remember I used to have a flat here on Leeson Street thirty years ago?"

"I do," he said, preferring not to recall too clearly that night, in 1936, when she'd told him that he'd put his work ahead of her once too often, and that as a couple they were finished. "And I remember," he said, "walking you from your hospital on Baggot Street to get to that very restaurant we've just been in."

They were turning onto Wilton Terrace, on the north bank of the Grand Canal, both relishing the walk in the crisp, late-September air, heading in the direction of Mount Street. The lawn that bordered the canal was dotted with widely spaced trees. He looked across the expanse of grass to the narrow waters and the reed-lined bank of the far shore. "It was a Sunday, I think," he said. "We were coming along the other side of the canal, and we stopped for a bit of *craic* with an old boy who was repairing the retaining wall. He and I smoked our pipes, as I recall, while he told us the history of An Canáil Mor."

"And then," she said, "you chatted with a bunch of stark-naked kids from the Liberties, swimming in the canal. Remember how hot it was?"

> . . . wherein the good old slushy mud seagulls did sport
> and play . . .

He sang a snatch from "Down by the Liffey Side," perhaps not entirely appropriate for the canal, but overhead real gulls soared and made harsh, high-pitched *gulla-gulla-gulla* screams on a breeze that brought the Dublin smells of traffic exhausts and mudflats of the nearby great river at low tide.

"One of the gurriers was a patient, and you gave him a bag of sweeties, and he called you 'the Big Fellah.' I could see how you were respected in the Liberties because you cared for your patients, and I loved you for it." She walked closer to him and he put his arm around her waist. "I've always loved you, Fingal," she said.

He hung his head. It was, he felt, superfluous to echo the sentiments like a moonstruck sixteen-year-old. He knew he did and she knew and that was what mattered. As they passed under the bridge carrying Baggot Street, he couldn't resist saying, "A lot of water has run under the bridge since then—"

"That," she said, "was a terrible pun, Fingal O'Reilly, or whatever—"

"It was a metaphor—"

"Right. A metaphor, a terrible metaphor, but a true one."

They were all alone under the bridge.

She grasped the lapels of his tweed jacket and kissed him. They parted and walked on, holding hands. "I love you and I love Dublin where we met," she said. "Strumpet City, Dirty Dublin, Baile Átha Cliath—the town at the ford at the hurdles."

O'Reilly smiled. "Me too."

He pointed to where a barge, brightly painted, engine putt-putting, diesel smoke belching from its funnel, butted blunt bows west heading for the midlands of Ireland. "Horses pulled most of them when we were youngsters here," he said, and thought, But you can't turn back the clock.

In its passing, the vessel chased a flock of mallard. The birds, sunlight shining from the drakes' emerald heads, flared, rose together, then circled, setting their wings, and pitching back into the canal with much ploughing of watery furrows, squabbling, and tail pecking.

"I've always loved ducks," he said. "Maybe it's time to put my gun away, but I'd miss Strangford Lough so much."

"And so would Arthur Guinness, the great lummox. He is a gun-dog, after all."

"You're right," he said, pulling her up the steps by the next bridge to Mount Street Lower. "Do you know I once assisted a gynaecologist in a private house here. He removed an ovarian cyst right in the woman's bedroom. My old boss, Phelim Corrigan, gave the anaesthetic."

"Such different times," she said. "Surgery's all done by specialists in hospitals now." She swung their hands in a wide arc. "Here we are. Merrion Square. Do you remember when we stopped to listen to a man haranguing a crowd of Blue Shirts about the Spanish Civil War?"

"I do. And I remember you insisting we stay to listen," and a few weeks later going off to Spain, my Kitty, he said to himself. My own fault, but it had hurt like hell. "And when you'd heard enough, we called for Bob Beresford, who had a flat here, and the three of us went to the horse races." O'Reilly's heart ached doubly for the lost years that might have been spent with Kitty, and for his long-dead friend. He said nothing for a while, remembering. Remembering.

Today, and indeed the rest of this weekend, was certainly a time for memories. In a few hours, he and Kitty would get into their best bibs and tuckers to attend the opening cocktail reception and welcoming dinner for the thirtieth reunion of their 1936 medical school class at

Trinity College. But those were fond memories, happy ones, and he recalled a snatch from an ancient English folk song he'd had to learn at school,

> Begone dull care, I prithee begone from me
> Begone dull care, thou and I shall never agree

"Right," he said, "time to get back to the Shelbourne. We'll cut across Merrion Square, nip along Merrion Street Upper, and take Merrion Row to Saint Stephen's Green. I'd like a nap before we have to start getting ready for tonight's festivities."

"Come on then," she said. "I do want you rested, and I'm really looking forward to seeing you in your naval uniform. I'll never forget the sight of you in it at one New Year's Eve formal dance when we were both students."

And Fingal O'Reilly, who hated formal dress, would for her sake struggle into his number one uniform in lieu of a dinner suit and black tie, ready to forge more memories of happy times together.

O'Reilly clapped as the applause grew for Sir Donald Cromie, plain "Cromie" to his closest friends, who had risen in his place at their table in a private dining room of Dublin's Shelbourne Hotel. He jangled a fork on an empty glass, and the high-pitched sound rose with the buzz of conversations and laughter, and the clink of cutlery on china, to the white-plastered ceiling, there to mingle with a cloud of pipe, cigar, and cigarette smoke.

O'Reilly winked at Kitty, who smiled back. God, but he loved that smile. He surveyed the other graduates from the Trinity College School of Physics, class of '36, and their spouses who had assembled for the opening cocktail party and banquet of their reunion. Sitting round linen-draped tables, most of the men wore sombre dinner suits, their satin lapels shiny, and the ladies added bright counterpoint in their evening gowns or cocktail dresses. The opposite, he thought, of dowdy ducks and flamboyant drakes like the mallard he and Kitty had seen earlier on the Grand Canal.

He looked back at Kitty. Her sleeveless empire-line dress of shot emerald green silk was punctuated by a corsage of deep pink moth orchid that his brother Lars had grown in his own greenhouse. She sported matching pink satin opera gloves, and her hair was cut in a pageboy style to frame her face. Kitty O'Reilly was, in his opinion, by far the most elegant and desirable woman here. And he wasn't the teeniest bit biased.

He grinned at the thought and tugged at the collar of his Royal Navy mess kit dress uniform jacket, with his medal ribbons on the left breast. He should have been wearing miniature medals, not just the ribbons, but for very personal reasons he hated his decorations, one in particular, but no one here would care that he was in breach of regulations, and it had been a long time since he had left the navy. He'd have been a damn sight more comfortable in tweed pants and a sports jacket, but the conventions must be observed. Kitty liked him to wear the damn monkey suit to formal occasions, and there was nothing O'Reilly would not do to please her. Two other people were similarly dressed. A fellow O'Reilly had barely known was in the full kit of an RAF squadron leader, medical. One of the women was in the dress mess kit of an officer in the Queen Alexandra's Royal Navy Nursing Service, with whose nursing sisters he had worked closely in Haslar hospital in 1940.

"Settle down, now, settle down," Cromie said, and the hum of conversation and clapping began to fade. "I know we've all got a lot of catching up to do, but first I must make a few announcements."

O'Reilly knew he should turn and start paying attention, but his gaze lingered over the little crowd. Thirty-five years ago the now middle-aged doctors had begun their medical studies as fresh-faced youths and a few lasses. As Donal Donnelly, Ballybucklebo's arch schemer and mangler of the English language, might have said today, "Back then the world had been everyone's lobster." O'Reilly shook his head. A lot had happened in those thirty-five years. He still had a full head of hair and wore his half-moon spectacles only for effect, but spectacles and thinning hair, if not bald pates, were the order of the day now. Charlie Greer, once a flaming redhead, now looked like a tonsured monk, with only a fringe of remaining hair. Used-to-be athletes had grown chubby, and he knew for a fact that he wasn't the only one wearing a cummerbund to hide the reality that the top button at his trousers' waistband was undone.

He thought about where their careers had led his classmates. Some were senior in their chosen fields here in Ireland. Others had made the pilgrimage back here from the United States or British Commonwealth countries. Fair play to them all. He hoped they were as contented as he, the principal of a general practice in the drowsy County Down village of Ballybucklebo, where season ran into season and little disturbed the harmony of life. He would be getting back to work on Monday, and as far as he knew, he'd not left anything that young Doctors Barry Laverty and Jennifer Bradley could not deal with.

He shook his head. Thirty years, the last twenty in Ballybucklebo— but his life had not been all peace and quiet since he had qualified as a doctor.

"Now wheest, the lot of you," Cromie said. "Wheest, and that includes you, Ronald Hercules Fitzpatrick."

The man in question, who, as had been his wont back in their student days, had barely uttered a peep all evening, at least managed a smile as laughter rang out. His gold-rimmed pince-nez shone and his large Adam's apple bobbed rapidly above a winged collar, one size too large, and a clip-on scarlet bow tie. His neck reminded O'Reilly of the grinning ostrich with a large lump halfway down its neck. The bird and its irate zookeeper, whose pint the animal had swallowed, glass and all, had been one of a number of classic posters advertising Guinness stout.

O'Reilly waited for the laughter to die.

Cromie said, "I hope you've all enjoyed your dinner as much as I have . . ."

O'Reilly patted his tummy. Gazpacho, sole almondine, iced champagne sorbet, beef Wellington, roast potatoes and seasonal vegetables, baked Alaska, and an assortment of cheeses and crackers had been complemented by chilled Pouilly Fumée, a Chateau Mouton Rothschild, and Taylor's port, 1941. He had declined the latter in favour of a glass of John Jameson's Irish whiskey. "Certainly was a nice snack," he whispered to Kitty, who made a mock frown and said, "Fingal, behave yourself."

". . . and so we've to thank the other members of the organising committee. Gentlemen, please rise: Charlie Greer and Fingal O'Reilly."

O'Reilly stood and smiled at his other male tablemate. Charlie, now a senior neurosurgeon at Belfast's Royal Victoria Hospital, was the man who had given O'Reilly his bent nose during a friendly boxing bout back in 1935. Together they had played rugby football for Ireland. Now Charlie had a comfortable potbelly and was an amateur, but internationally recognised, expert on the works of Mozart. His wife sat beside Cromie's. As girls, the two women had attended Cheltenham Ladies' College, a very exclusive school in England, an institution that aped the then-common boys' public schools' tradition of handing out nicknames. O'Reilly had known Mrs. Greer as "Pixie" and Mrs. Cromie as "Button" for so long he'd forgotten their real Christian names, if indeed he'd ever known them.

More cheers and a voice calling, "Looks like Tweedledum and Tweedledee to me."

O'Reilly caught a whiff of delicately scented tobacco from someone's cigar as he waited for quiet. Then he interrupted Cromie in a thick Northside Dublin accent. "Lord jasus, there's one in every crowd that wants to be the centre of attraction. If your man Edgar Redmond there was at a wake, he'd not be satisfied unless he was the feckin' corpse, would you, Edgar?"

More laughter.

O'Reilly nodded to himself. His old adage, *"Never, never let the patient get the upper hand,"* was equally applicable to heckling colleagues.

"Thank you, Fingal, for those few kind words," Cromie said, "and to quote Michael Collins, who, upon returning to the same hustings whence he'd been arrested while making a political speech and subsequently jailed, remarked, 'As I was saying when I was so rudely interrupted . . .'"

More laughter, and a voice saying, "Nice one, Sir Donald."

Cromie made a small bow. "Thank you, Sid. Now we of the self-appointed organising committee hope you enjoyed your meal. We are delighted that so many could attend. We'd particularly like to acknowledge Hilda Bronson, whom most of you will remember as Hilda

Manwell. Now please hold your applause or we'll be here all night. Please stand, Hilda."

A petite, middle-aged woman, completely grey-haired, but still as trim-figured as ever, wearing a short, floral-patterned, satin evening frock with a flared skirt, rose and smiled all round the room.

"Hilda and her husband have come all the way from Sydney, Australia, to be here, and it was a letter from her last year to Charlie Greer that got the ball rolling for this get-together. Thank you, Hilda, on both counts." Cromie, ignoring his own instructions about applause, began to clap, and everyone joined in as she, O'Reilly, and Charlie regained their seats.

"Now," Cromie said, "tonight is not the time for speechifying, but there are a few housekeeping chores I must attend to. I'll keep it short. The bar here will remain open until eleven tonight. Breakfast is informal tomorrow so take your pick of the dining rooms in the hotel, but we must convene in the lobby by nine thirty. It's no distance to the college where it all began thirty years ago. We will walk there and have a series of lectures."

Fingal did not need to pay attention. Hadn't he helped the lads plan the whole weekend of reception and a dinner tonight, talks tomorrow morning, so expenses could be defrayed against taxes, luncheon with your friends to be arranged individually, a free afternoon, a formal dinner tomorrow evening in the college, and a farewell breakfast in a private room in Bewley's on Grafton Street on Sunday morning?

He closed his eyes and in an instant could see himself all those years ago, sitting through dull, dry, droning dissertations on anatomy and physiology, hours spent in the formalin-reeking dissecting room, histology laboratories, the drudgery of the preclinical years. The excitement of walking the wards, seeing and treating patients, knowing at last that he'd been right, that medicine had always been his destiny. Years lightened by fun in pubs—Davy Byrnes or the Bailey, both on Duke Street; the Stag's Head; Neary's on Chatham Street—rugby matches, boxing, dances in a floating ballroom; movies like *The Thin Man* with William Powell and Myrna Loy, *Captain Blood*, *Top Hat*; meeting a grey-eyed student nurse—he smiled at Kitty—and losing her because of his own stupidity.

O'Reilly heard Cromie say, "And our guest faculty member at the dinner tomorrow will be the surgeon Mister Nigel Kinnear, who taught us, saw distinguished war service before returning to teaching, and who next year will be installed as Regius Professor of Surgery."

Prolonged applause.

Nigel Kinnear had supervised O'Reilly's trembling hands as he performed his first appendicectomy back then. And in those five years he'd laid the foundations to learning his trade and seen the growth of a lifelong friendship with Cromie and Charlie and—

"Mister Kinnear will give the first Bob Beresford Memorial Oration. Bob made the supreme sacrifice in 1943."

Bob Beresford, gentle gentleman, O'Reilly thought, and bowed his head.

What little subdued conversation there had been, died.

"I'd like us to rise and be silent for a minute in remembrance of Bob, Jean Winston, Archie O'Hare, and Phillip McNab, who sadly are no longer with us."

There was a scraping of chairs on the hardwood floor as everyone rose.

O'Reilly bowed his head. He'd known the other three, but Bob Beresford had been the fourth of the Four Musketeers. Dear Bob, probably the best friend Fingal had made in his life. He glanced at Kitty and saw how she was staring at him, concern in those grey-flecked-with-amber eyes. She'd known Bob, known him well, before the war, but it hadn't been until much later that both she and Fingal had learned of his death at the hands of the Japanese a year after the fall of Singapore where he had been serving in the Medical Corps in 1942. Bob had died looking after the sick and dying though mortally ill himself. "Greater love hath no man than this, that a man lay down his life for his friends." John 15:13. I miss you yet, Bob, O'Reilly thought, and felt a lump in his throat. He was grateful for Kitty's reassuring squeeze of his hand.

"Thank you," Cromie said, "and before you take your seats may I simply remark that I've finished the chores. I'd suggest that now the formal part of the evening is over, you all circulate and renew old acquaintances, but before that I'd like you all to raise your glasses and drink with me, 'To absent friends.' "

"Absent friends," came from the crowd as from one voice, none more heartfelt than Fingal Flahertie O'Reilly's.

Conversation and laughter began again slowly and then grew in volume. "I'll be damned. Sticky actually passed his speciality examinations?" he overheard someone say. "I don't believe you. Sticky . . . ?"

It was a nickname O'Reilly knew was often given to Maguires in Ireland, just as Murphys were always called Spud.

"He was so dense we didn't think he could pass wind when we were students. He just managed to struggle through medical school."

O'Reilly chuckled, as did the storyteller's audience.

"He didn't just pass. He took a gold medal, was having a stellar career when the poor divil had a stroke. He survived but . . ."

"Aaah, that's sad," a woman's voice said.

Indeed it was, O'Reilly thought. Sticky had always been a great class jester, a kind man. Fate could be very unkind. He was aware of someone at his shoulder and found himself towering over Hilda Bronson. "Hilda. Lovely to see you. Hilda Bronson, meet Mrs. Kitty O'Reilly."

"It's plain Kitty," Kitty said.

Hilda grinned. "We met at the graduation dance all those years ago," she said. "I thought then you seemed much too good for a great lummox like Fingal O'Reilly."

O'Reilly chuckled. "You always did call a spade a bloody shovel, Hilda."

"Us few women had to among all you men," she said. "Now meet my other half, Peter Bronson."

O'Reilly was offered a paw as big as his own, and damn nearly as powerful, by a tanned man who said, "G'dye, mate," in an Ocker Aussie accent as thick as Kinky's champ.

"Bonzer meeting you. Hilda says you played a bit of rugger."

"Don't let those two get started, Kitty," Hilda said. "When he's not running a law practice, my Pete eats and breathes rugby football. Now the Greers and Cromies have moved on, why don't we sit with you two for a minute? My feet are killing me in these damned stilettoes."

The gentlemen held the chairs for the ladies, then joined them.

"If memory serves, you were to play for the Wallabies on their '39 tour of the UK and Ireland, but the bloody war got in the way," O'Reilly said.

"Huh," said Peter Bronson. "I joined the Royal Australian Air Force, flew Beaufighters, even though my new wife," he smiled at Hilda, "wasn't too pleased."

"I'm sure Kitty wasn't either about you in the navy, Fingal," Hilda said, nodding at O'Reilly's uniform.

O'Reilly waited.

Kitty, always the soul of tact, said, her voice quite level, "I'm afraid I'd gone off to nurse orphans in Tenerife during the Spanish Civil War when Fingal was called up . . ."

He knew there had been more to it than just nursing. Tenerife had left Kitty with a ghost, and one that must soon be confronted. O'Reilly tried to make light of it. "Careless of me letting her go, I know."

"Fingal and I didn't get married until last year." Kitty smiled at him. "He's a slow learner."

"But slow and steady wins the race," O'Reilly said. "I'm a very lucky man." And to hell with convention, he bent and kissed Kitty while in his heart he knew his first wife, Deirdre, looked on, smiling.

"Good for you, O'Reilly," Hilda said, then her voice softened, became wistful. "Pete never talks about the war."

"Neither does Fingal," Kitty said.

"But I reckon you had an exciting one, cobber," Pete said. His voice was level.

O'Reilly frowned. "Oh?"

Peter pointed to a blue, white, and blue medal ribbon on O'Reilly's jacket to the extreme right of the ones for the Africa Star, the Atlantic Star, the 1939–45 Star, and the War Medal. "No need to talk about it, but the Pommies didn't hand out Distinguished Service Crosses for collecting cigarette cards or winning the egg-and-spoon races." His glance fell on O'Reilly's rank insignia, then Peter held out his big hand, which O'Reilly took. "I'm proud to meet you, Commander O'Reilly. Very proud."

O'Reilly lowered his head, and while he should have been flattered, he could only nod while in his mind whirled pictures of those still-vivid war years, some memories faded to pallid shadows, others indelible, his for life.

And for all of them he had this old uniform with its little pieces of coloured ribbon to indicate where his bronze stars and a silver cross should hang. And, when he let them surface, memories, a host of memories, memories of a journey that had begun on a British battleship in Alexandria Harbour in late 1940. But those were not for tonight. Tonight was for fun, but—O'Reilly took a deep breath—Kitty wasn't alone in having a ghost from those years. His, like hers, would always be there.

About the Author

Patrick Taylor, M.D., was born and raised in Bangor, County Down, in Northern Ireland. Doctor Taylor is a distinguished medical researcher, offshore sailor, model-boat builder, and father of two grown children. He now lives on Saltspring Island, British Columbia.

www.patricktaylor.ca
Facebook: Patrick Taylor's Irish Country Novels